# PHOENIX FIRE

To Becca)

Enjoy!

Tim O'Loughlin '06

# PHOENIX FIRE

## A NOVEL
## BY TIM O'LAUGHLIN

BodhiDharma Publishing
10849 Ambassador Drive • Rancho Cordova, CA 95670 • (916) 631-0258
www.bodhidharmapublishing.com

# Acknowledgments

I would like to thank the many readers of early drafts who offered helpful comments and encouragement, beginning with my wife and first reader, Edie. Others include author Donald Sydney Fryer, literary agent Georgia Hughes, my brother Michael O'Laughlin, Judy Morris, Doug Stein, John Hurst and Frieda Fergus. I would also like to thank Arnold Baker & Harry O'Laughlin for technical computer assistance and William Douglas Ackerman and Alice O'Laughlin for proofreading. Finally, I would like to thank David Boles for making publication of this novel a reality.

This is a work of fiction. Any similarities between the characters in this book and actual living people (or actual corporate entities) is purely coincidental. However, all book stores, music shops and restaurants mentioned in this novel exist, and are located where indicated in the text. The author recommends these establishments to any of his readers who find themselves on the Mendocino coast.

# Author's Note About Music

The music of two singer-songwriters, David Wilcox, and Emily Saliers of the Indigo Girls, provided inspiration that was essential to the writing of this novel. I am especially grateful, not only for their having allowed me to reproduce the lyrics to "Show the Way," and "The Wood Song," but also to Emily Saliers for creating the song that played in my head as I wrote this novel, as if it were the only selection available on some kind of internal cd player.

# PHOENIX FIRE

# PART ONE

I am not my name
I'm not defined by my possessions
I am not my occupation
Though I play that game
Poised above the unwritten page
The same actor on a different stage
I'm a new candle burning
With an ancient flame

# PRELUDE

ALDEG GROANED, HIS STIFF MUSCLES PROTESTING AS HE THREW off his blankets and raised himself from the straw-filled mattress. He reached back with one hand and massaged his painful lower back while steadying himself against the stone wall with the other. *What good is it to be a Mage when I suffer through the same aches and pains of old age as anyone else?* he wondered. He chuckled ruefully, reflecting that his powers, which could alter the shape of the universe, gave him no respite over the burning pain that seared down his leg and into his heel. He hobbled slowly through the corridor, pausing outside the room where his two apprentices slumbered. He shuddered. It might have been from the predawn cold, but more likely, it came from contemplating the choice that his destiny required he make all too soon. Next he passed the entrance to the vaulted chamber where he gave his apprentices instruction, then made his way up the stairs that spiraled up the inside tower wall to his private chamber at the top. From there, he had an unobstructed view, and he paused briefly to survey all that surrounded him. He was not limited to what he could see with his eyes, and he reached out with an unparalleled awareness that could detect any intruder, no matter how cleverly they might be concealed. He was as vulnerable as the next man to an artfully-thrown knife, or the bolt from a well-aimed crossbow, and attempts on his life had not been infrequent. The locals knew him to be a wizard, and believed that he was a necromancer whose black magic depended on human sacrifice. In their tales, he wandered the countryside under cover of darkness, killing with the merest wave of his hand, and taking his nourishment by consuming his victim's souls. He sighed inwardly. In a way, they weren't far from the mark about his abilities — although their foolish souls were safe from him. He *could* separate their life-force from their mortal flesh if he desired, leaving only an empty husk that would dwindle slowly until death took its inevitable toll. But their souls were immortal, just as he knew his own to be. And although he could send their spirits to a place from which return was impossible, the consequences of doing so would be unthinkable! Not that he wasn't tempted — how he would savor the experience! At times the thought of using that one specific power left him aching with need.

That particular spell was his most treasured secret. It was the heart of his power, but it had also presented him with his dilemma. He sighed as his thoughts returned to the choice that lay before him. To whom should he pass the knowledge? Which of his apprentices was most worthy to bear the burden and responsibility he had shouldered these many years?

The nature of the spell itself decreed that only one living person could possess it — and the power that came along with it. It was the knowledge of the spell that was the center of his power, for the spell could *never* actually be used. It was a trial to be sure, to have carried that secret. He had been filled with a desire to put the spell into action from the moment it had passed to him — a longing that was far stronger than he could have contemplated. Using the spell would be the peak experience of an exceptional lifetime. But the spell reopened a gateway — a portal that had been closed for centuries — and once that gateway was open, his powers would dwindle and diminish until they were a mere echo of what they had once been.

His apprentices knew that the spell could never be used. He had cautioned them repeatedly, as he taught both of them nearly all of it, determined to stitch the prohibition into the very fabric of their beings. He had saved only the final word for the time when he had made his decision. But which one should he choose? Which one could be trusted to keep the secret, and then pass it on unused?

FOR DECADES, ALDEG had despaired, fearing that he would never find a successor capable of taking up his burden. Then over the course of five years, he had found two. He corrected himself. *He* had found one. The other had found him. Word had come to him that a mere boy had been declared a sorcerer by local townsfolk fifty miles to the north and was to be burned at the stake. He raced through the night, nearly killing his horse in the process, but was rewarded handsomely when the boy's raw, untrained power blazed forth the instant he passed through the iron-bound door to his cell. He led the grateful lad past the hapless guards he had left sprawled outside, and brought him to his keep, and through the intervening years, Aldeg had shaped the boys power as he grew into manhood. Now, formidable in his own right, Aldeg judged him worthy and capable of taking up the burden. But three years after finding his first apprentice, Aldeg had been startled out of sleep by the awareness of yet another powerful presence. It was the same kind of raw, untrained ability he had encountered when he rescued Hayden — the name he had given his first apprentice. But this time, the power was a thousand times stronger, a roaring bonfire in contrast to Hayden's flickering candle — or even his own innate powers that had existed before he had possessed the spell that opened the gateway. He had traced the potent emanations and subdued the impetuous, untrained youth he found hiding behind a drapery in the great-room of his keep, and from that point on, two had vied for his favor.

They were opposites in many ways. Hayden was far more intellectual and trustworthy, but Rankin's greater power could not be ignored, though he was unpredictable, impetuous and possessed of a cruel nature that made Aldeg's own disdain for his fellow man seem like benevolence.

AS HE MADE his way down from his tower, Aldeg realized that he had made his choice. He could not allow himself to be seduced by Rankin's raw talent. After all, the secret was never to be used — it was knowledge to guard and pass on. And since the mere knowledge of the spell greatly enhanced the innate abilities of the one who possessed it, Hayden would be able to stand against anyone once he possessed it — even Rankin. He had intended to return to his sleeping chamber when he left his tower, but when he reached the entrance to the great-room where he had trained his apprentices, he abruptly changed direction, and to his surprise strode as purposefully through the doorway as his pain would allow, into the dim recesses beyond the portal. As he did, the merest flicker of movement in the corner of his eye caught his attention, but he did not have time to raise his defenses before he was throttled from behind. He gasped as a lightning bolt of pain lanced down his leg and into his heel, then screamed in agony as a razor-sharp dagger pierced his chest, sliding between his ribs before stopping a hairs breadth short of his wildly beating heart.

"The final word of the spell, my master," Rankin's voice hissed insistently. "Give it to me!"

*The choice has been made,* Aldeg realized through the red haze that was beginning to envelop him. *But in the end it was not mine after all.* He had no alternative — the torch had to be passed. He uttered the word, and a second later the blade completed its intended journey.


AS THE BODY of his master crumpled to the floor, Rankin jerked his dagger from the corpse, wiped it clean and rammed it home in the scabbard on his belt. For years, he had suffered Aldeg's slights while he bided his time. Now at last he had taken his revenge — with his master's death, and by slitting Hayden's throat a few minutes earlier. It had all been worth it! He had been willing to suffer these indignities in order to learn what the master could teach, but had long ago divined from the old man's mutterings that there was only the slimmest chance *he* would become the anointed successor. Aldeg claimed not to have made the choice, but the direction he was leaning had been clear. And since that direction was unacceptable, Rankin had known that he must take the matter into his own hands.

He surveyed the room and was struck by the fact that he had just now concealed himself behind the same drapery where he had hidden the first time he had entered this room, seven years previously. A smug, satisfied expression stole across his features as he made a mental adjustment. *He* was now the master of this keep. And from the moment he learned the final word to the spell he had felt his powers increasing. There was no one who could wrest from him what was now his — no one at all. He smiled darkly. There were other slights to avenge, and the day was young.

# 1

GAYLE DRAPER FIDGETED BEHIND THE COUNTER OF "THE ECLECTIC Attic," her small shop in the northern California coastal town of Fort Bragg. She tried not to glare at her only customer, a trim, sixtyish man with white hair and beard, who was browsing aimlessly after declining her offer of help. At the moment, he was fingering a colorful hand-woven shirt from Guatemala after having perused nearly all the other merchandise on the shelves. She tried to curb her impatience —it was only twenty minutes before closing time. But the urge for a cigarette was so strong that she doubted she could make it. She glanced longingly at the pack that was beckoning from it's ready spot in the top of her open purse and as usual, her resistance crumbled. She grabbed her lighter and the half-empty pack. "I'll be right outside," she called out. "I need a cigarette . . . give a holler if you need anything." The twinkle in her customer's bright blue eyes as he turned towards her surprised her, as did his response.

"Do you mind if I step outside with you?" he asked. "I'm more in the mood for conversation than shopping, anyway."

A strong sense of *deja vu* overtook her. "Do I know you from somewhere?" she asked as they stepped through the door together.

"I don't think so . . . it's only been a couple of weeks since I moved here from San Francisco, and this is the first time I've been in your store."

Gayle lit up and inhaled gratefully, feeling her body relax as the nicotine hunger subsided. She blew out a stream of smoke, carefully turning her head so she wouldn't get any in his face. "I just had the strongest impression that I'd met you before," she said, laughing. "But that's obviously impossible, isn't it." Taking another satisfying drag she asked, "Why did you move? Retirement?" She knew that an affirmative response would be likely. The Fort Bragg area was famous for its rugged beauty, and it boasted a large contingent of retirees among its inhabitants.

The man smiled wistfully in a way that spoke of a mixed blessing before responding. "I've been in the process of closing down my psychiatry practice for a couple of years. You can't just leave your patients hanging, and it took me a while to disengage . . . but yes, I'm finally retired."

Gayle took another long drag, followed by a short one, then stirred the sand in the ashtray standing adjacent to the door with the butt of her cigarette until the ember had been extinguished. "I'd give anything to be able to quit these damned things," she apologized, her words punctuated by small puffs of smoke. "I started when I was thirteen, and if I don't stop soon, they're gonna kill me." It was her turn to look wistful, as she stared at the half-full pack of cigarettes in her hand. Abruptly, she wadded it into a ball that she tossed into a trash bin that stood next to the ash tray. She grinned. "There . . . I quit . . . for as long as I can stand it, anyway." Her short laugh was almost a bark. "If I had a dollar for every time I've done that, I'd be able to retire too!"

"Are you *really* serious about wanting to quit?" he asked.

"Like I said, I'd give anything."

He reached out his hand. "My name is Larry Robinson. I think we need to be properly introduced before I say something that none of my colleagues would believe."

She tilted her head to one side and examined him warily as she shook his hand. "Gayle Draper," she offered somewhat reluctantly.

He smiled quickly, and her reticence was transformed immediately into an uncanny sense of comfortable familiarity. "Don't worry," he said. "I'm just going to offer you some help, and in my profession, we almost always wait for people to set an appointment a month in advance before we'll do that for anybody." His soft chuckle as Gayle returned to her place behind the counter was tinged with a hint of regret. "But like I said, I'm through with that part of my life," he continued, taking a seat on one of a number of chairs that had been arranged in a haphazard circle as if to accommodate a discussion group. "For the last fifteen years, my practice was devoted exclusively to hypnotherapy — have you ever considered that as an option?"

Gayle nodded and sighed. "That's one of the first things I tried . . . and I really gave it a good shot. I spent eight weeks driving a hundred miles each way to group sessions in Santa Rosa, but it didn't do a bit of good." She looked frustrated. "I'm a hopeless case, doctor. If I hadn't just wadded up that pack, I'd already have another one lit."

"Call me Larry," he said. "I gave up putting 'doctor' in front of my name some time ago — after a while, it just seemed too pretentious. But hear me out. I'm not referring to the usual kind of hypnosis." He gestured at the candles, crystals, statues of goddesses, tarot cards and books on metaphysics, meditation and the like in the New Age section of the shop. "You seem to have an open mind when it comes to non-traditional ideas."

Gayle's expression immediately brightened. "Metaphysics is one of my passions — I've been studying New Age ideas and philosophy for years. It's given me something of a reputation around here." Her engaging laugh rang out. "Trust me, you can't get away with much in a small town like Fort Bragg, and I've lived here all my life." She gestured towards the merchandise. "At different times, I've had a pyramid hanging over my bed, used homeopathic and Bach flower remedies and lead book-discussions on titles ranging from European mythology to Eastern religions. I've called the directions with pagans — even participated in Wiccan rituals with women who considered themselves to be witches."

He leaned forward. "Have you ever heard of past life regressions?"

"Of course," she said. "I can't say that I've ever done one — but reincarnation has seemed obvious to me for years. I'd be surprised if it *wasn't* possible to access past-life memories."

Larry stepped over to the counter and leaned against its glass surface. "I'm probably the most non-traditional psychiatrist you've ever met." he said. "I mentioned that my specialty was hypnosis. The rest of the story is that past-life regression therapy was the focus of my practice."

"How could a past-life regression help me quit smoking?" asked Gayle, looking puzzled.

"My clinical work has shown me that quite often present-day problems, whether emotional or physical, can originate in a past life. The deeply buried memory of the past-life trauma or experience is carried forward to the present life. Once the connection between the past-life event and the present-day problem is discovered, it can be broken."

Gayle found herself being drawn in irresistibly. "Are you saying that I can't quit smoking because of something that happened to me in a past life?"

"It's only a possibility," Larry replied, emphasizing his words with raised eyebrows. "But you'll never know unless you do a regression. And what I meant when I said that none of my colleagues would believe what I'm about to say is that I would like to do a regression for you . . . no charge."

"Why is that so odd?"

He smiled. "As a rule, psychiatrists try to lock their professional lives in their offices when they go home at night. They certainly don't go around offering their services to people they've just met." He looked slightly embarrassed, and directed his gaze past her shoulder to the view outside her plate-glass window before meeting her eyes once again. "You said that you felt like we'd met before — I have a similar feeling. My offer has to sound completely outlandish coming from a complete stranger." He shrugged. "You don't have to say yes . . . "

Gayle studied him for another moment more before she answered. The mere suggestion that she might refuse his offer made her feel anxious, while the idea of going along with his offer appealed strongly. She smiled and gestured towards a doorway at the rear of the store. "It's closing time anyway, and I've got a portable massage table in the back room that I can lie on. Just let me lock the front door and bring it out."

She rolled a brightly colored serape into a pillow and reclined on the padded massage table. "I go under pretty easily," she announced, gesturing towards the large windows that only partially obscured the sound of traffic passing outside. "I'm so used to being hypnotized from all those sessions in Santa Rosa that the noise and light won't bother me at all."

Larry took a seat in one of the circled chairs and directed her to relax completely, one body part at a time, starting with her right foot, and to concentrate on her breathing. "Imagine that you are walking on a path that leads downhill into a gathering mist," he said. "The further you go, the thicker the mist will become . . . You will find that the path rises before you . . . As you climb the hill, the mist will thin out until it finally disappears. When it does, you'll find yourself in a past life where you will find the reason you haven't been able to quit smoking."

A few moments later, Gayle spoke. "I'm walking next to a river along a dusty, dirt road that's bordered by oaks and cottonwood trees draped with wild grapevines. There are mountains in the distance, but they're a long way off."

Larry was pleased that she had accessed a past life so quickly. He moved on to questions that would help determine when and where the memory originated. "What are you wearing?"

"Simple black cotton clothing, a straw-hat and sandals," she answered. "My hands are tied together . . . I'm a prisoner."

"Are you a man or a woman?"

"I'm a woman."

"I'm going to tap you on the head three times, and you will come to your destination."

"I see a sign that says 'Courtland,'" she said immediately. "It's just a few dusty streets next to the river."

"Can you tell me what year it is?"

"1851," she replied, then her body stiffened. "They've brought me back to this terrible place . . . where *he* is." She shuddered and began to breathe rapidly as a tear made its way slowly down her cheek.

"What place is this? . . . Who is *he*?"

"It's a saloon with a room above it, where I've been forced to be a *hundred man's wife* — a prostitute. I was kidnaped in China and sold into slavery. *He* is the one who bought me. I hate him! He beat me until I hurt so badly that I would have done anything to get out of pain. He gave me opium — as much as I wanted at first. It took away more than just the physical pain . . . but now I can't stop using it." She paused momentarily, and then continued. "He thought my need for it would keep me here, but I left anyway. Now they have brought me back and he's going to beat me again!" Several more tears coursed down Gayle's cheeks, and Larry reached for the handkerchief he kept in his coat pocket.

"I want you to go to the next significant event in this lifetime," he said, reaching over to dry her tears. You won't experience any physical pain from whatever occurs, but you'll still be aware of what's happening."

Gayle began to breathe heavily, squirming on the table in spite of Larry's command.

"I'm in a small room and *he* is here. He's whipping me!" she moaned, raising her arm as if to ward off a blow, and then was suddenly much calmer. "I tried to get away from him and when I did, I fell against a window," she murmured. "It broke, and a piece of glass cut my throat so deeply that I died almost instantly. I'm floating above my body now. I can see myself slumped against the wall under the window. There's blood everywhere. *He* is swearing at my body and beating and kicking it." There was a pause. "Now I'm surrounded by twilight, and the mist I

- 20 -

walked through to get here."

"Walk through the mist and you will find the trail again," Larry prompted. "Then return to the place where you began your journey."

Gayle opened her eyes, blinking rapidly in the sunlit room.

"Is there a lesson here for you?" Larry asked gently.

Gayle looked at him thoughtfully. "It has to do with being in charge of my own destiny," she said, "and about owning the power to release myself from bondage. In that life, I tried to escape from slavery, but I failed." She winced. "But at least I *tried* to escape. I'm just as enslaved in this life as I was back then, but this time, *I* had a part in the enslavement — I'm my own victim." She slid off of the table, broke it down and returned it to the back room. When she returned, a look of calm resolve had settled over her features. "When it comes to smoking, I have the opportunity to choose whether or not to participate in my own enslavement," she continued. "In fact, it's entirely my choice." Her expression revealed her growing sense of revelation. "In that life, I died while trying to escape, but in this life, I'm going to die if I *don't* escape and break away from my addiction to cigarettes." She paused again for a moment, staring through the window of her store at the traffic on Main Street. When she looked back, she reached out to touch Larry's arm. "Thank you," she said. "Next to the birth of my children, I think that was the most powerful experience I've ever had!"

# 2

*I'M TOASTED. THAT'S AS MUCH AS I CAN DO THIS WEEK,* RYAN STRATTON admitted to himself, reaching over to flip on the switch to his answering machine and scanning his calendar one last time before leaving his law office for the weekend. He was already relishing two full days without having to concentrate on extricating his clients from their problems. He locked up quickly, and by the time he hit Highway One, just half a block from his office, his professional life could have been a million miles away. His aging Dodge Caravan made its way south through the heavy pre-weekend traffic down the coast highway towards the turn-off to his house on the ridge between Caspar and Doyle Creeks, half-way between Fort Bragg and Mendocino. The house sat at the top of a draw that funneled down to Doyle Creek below. It was nondescript and low to the ground, with rough-sawn redwood siding that had faded to silver from sun, rain and damp air, and a homey interior with rough-hewn beams and redwood flooring that opened out onto a broad deck flanked by large redwoods. The living-room was lined with bookshelves, stereo equipment, music stands and other paraphernalia. Stacked against the wall was his small army of instruments, including the six acoustic steel-string guitars that were his greatest extravagance.

He changed into comfortable clothes, grabbed a cold Dr. Pepper from the refrigerator, and picked up his well-worn '43 Martin D-18 before making his way outside where the late-afternoon sun filtered through the two redwoods that framed the view past his deck. After he settled into a chair and crossed his legs, he let his fingers idly caress the strings, allowing the music take him on an inward journey to a place where he could unwind from the week's tensions. Not long after he'd begun, his front door banged open to admit his friend, neighbor and frequent singing partner, Doug Ackerman, who joined him most Friday nights to play tunes and shoot the breeze. As Ryan strummed his guitar, he heard the refrigerator door open and close, and then Doug appeared carrying a bottle of beer and the Brazilian-rosewood Traugott guitar that was his pride and joy. An appreciation of handmade guitars was just one of their shared interests. Doug took a pull from his beer, and without a word launched into the introduction to "Teach Your Children," the old *Crosby, Stills, Nash & Young* song he and Ryan had been singing since the day they'd discovered their mutual taste in music. Ryan joined in, singing the melody while Doug's harmony soared above. When the final chorus was finished, Doug leaned back in his chair and gave him a speculative look. "I don't know how you're ever going to teach your children when you don't have any," he said. "And hanging around with me Friday nights, desperate and dateless, it's unlikely there's any change looming on your horizons."

"Well, if we can get some of these songs up to speed, maybe we can get ourselves a gig somewhere," Ryan shot back. "Then maybe I'll meet somebody who'll be swept off her feet by my music, and allow me to escort her home." He shrugged his shoulders. "At that point we could at least *practice* making children."

"You're pathetic," Doug scoffed, shaking his head. "The only gig we ever play is the jam session at the Eclectic Attic, and you've never had any luck there."

Ryan shrugged his shoulders again. Doug had a point, but he wasn't about to give him any satisfaction by admitting it. The conversation was one they'd had often, and though he knew Doug had nothing but the best intentions, the constant reminders that his love-life was at a low ebb didn't do him any good at all. It wasn't as if he were avoiding women! He just hadn't found the right one yet — if such a woman existed at all.

After a few more tunes, the evening mist began drifting in from the Pacific in earnest, and they moved inside. "I had an interesting conversation with Gayle today," said Doug when they were settled in Ryan's living room. "She said she quit smoking!"

"What, for five minutes?" asked Ryan sarcastically. "She's the most dedicated smoker I've ever met. I bet she goes through four packs a day."

"She said she had a session with a hypnotherapist, and ended up doing a past-life regression."

Ryan grinned. "What kind of crackpot has she gotten herself mixed up with this time?" Gayle's spiritual passions were a frequent source of amusement for both of them. "There's a slim possibility he's not cracked all the way," replied Doug, with a considering expression. "I've never heard of a bona-fide psychiatrist who did past-life therapy, but that's what she said he was. And it's been two weeks since she's had a cigarette."

"Are you sure? She's always buying a pack, smoking two or three and then crushing the rest of the pack so she won't fish them out of the garbage. Ten minutes later, she's running across the street to the liquor store for more."

"I talked with her for almost an hour, and she didn't light up once," Doug affirmed. "I can't remember her going that long before." He glanced at his watch and put his guitar back in its case. "Pam will be home any minute now — I'll leave you to ponder the mystery. I'll tell you, though, even if this hypnotist has credentials, I still think he's got to have some kind of an angle somewhere." He snagged the remainder of his six-pack from the refrigerator on his way out the door leaving Ryan to wonder how a past-life regression could cure an addiction to cigarettes.

The next morning, a light mist drifted down from the overcast sky, a common occurrence in the summer, especially when the weather was hot inland. *Five years on the coast, and I still love these damp, cold summer mornings,* Ryan mused, peering out his window and recalling the blast-furnace summers he'd endured growing up in Sacramento. He shrugged into riding shorts, tights and a long sleeve jersey and was soon spinning up Caspar-Little Lake Road on his mountain bike. Within a quarter-mile he was out of the redwoods and into a belt of pygmy forest, climbing at an easy pace, half-way between the high and the low range of his twenty-four gears. Two miles up the road the clouds began to thin out, and soon they punctuated the brilliant blue sky only occasionally. The pavement ended at the edge of Jackson State Forest, where the road turned to gravel and ducked under taller, older trees — redwoods, Douglas firs and coastal hemlocks. He veered onto a single-track trail that paralleled the road and wound through the trees, beginning to push the pace and to enjoy the challenges presented by the twists, turns, jumps and other obstacles of the trail. Years before, while still in his twenties, he had ridden motorcycles. Now, at age thirty-three, with a stronger sense of his own mortality, he found plenty of excitement on a mountain bike at much saner speeds. Not that sanity had much to do with the origins of the machines. Ryan sent a silent thanks to the visionaries from Marin County who had cobbled the original mountain bikes together out of 1930's Schwinn Excelsiors, touring-bike gears and powerful drum brakes. Their creations were the first that could be ridden down Mount Tamalpais's fire-roads at breakneck speeds, then peddled back to the top, and after twenty years of continuous evolution, the versatile machines now dominated the market.

Six-hundred feet above sea level at the crest of the ridge the single track rejoined the gravel road. He shifted into his big chainring for the descent to the Mendocino Woodlands Camp and Big River, a sleepy stream that met the ocean ten miles downstream at the picturesque town of Mendocino. Ryan had often wondered how the stream had gotten its name. Though it broadened out closer to the ocean, here, ten miles inland, Big River was a shallow stream that wound between gravel bars favored by sunbathers weary of the coastal fog. Even on the lower reaches of the river near its mouth it was seldom more than a few feet deep. Crossing the stream on a wooden bridge, he chose a trail that wound steeply up the side of the hill, and was soon down in his lowest "granny" gear — twenty-four teeth in the front and thirty-one in the rear. Gears this low seemed ridiculous the first time he tried them, but that was before he attempted a long off-road climb. His breath started coming in gasps as he wound up the narrow track. The trail zig-zagged up a switch-back trail, with the land falling off sharply, first to his right and then to his left. He was in deep shade the entire time with the second growth forest towering over his head, while the blackened stumps of the original trees lurked in the shadows.

By the time he got to "the big tree," he was ready to take a break. The tree was a true giant of the forest, the largest in the region. A sign erected by a lumber company indicated its age — over thirteen-hundred years. It rose 'only' one-hundred-dred-eighty feet into the air, far shorter than it would have been if its top hadn't been blown away by lightning strikes. The tree's bark was silvery-gray and covered with lichens, and it looked somewhat shabby compared to less venerable trees that hadn't endured periodic fires and storms beyond counting. The area around the tree was deserted, though this last local remnant of the primaeval forest was the frequent destination of hikers from the Woodlands Camp, as well as mountain-bikers and horseback riders. He lay on his back while he caught his breath, watching as puffy white clouds scudded past the top of the huge tree. On a visit to the Grand Canyon years before, he had spent a full day watching the changes in the quality of light on the limestone, awestruck by the graphic depiction of time etched into the canyon walls. Trees like the one he now contemplated evoked a similar response, but on a scale that he could grasp more easily. This thing was *alive!* It was ancient, but the scope of its tenure was something he could at least begin to understand. Somehow, he felt different when he was next to one of these trees, especially the really old ones, almost as if he could feel the echoes of the centuries it had taken for them to grow.

He chose a different route for the return trip — by way of an old logging road, rather than the singletrack. It was one thing to climb the narrow trail that clung to the hillside at three to four miles per hour, and quite another to try to descend it at speed. The logging road took a meandering route back to the bridge over Big River, where he found his tire tracks and followed them back the way he had come. Once he hit the pavement, it was a smooth glide all the way back to his driveway.

After a shower, he grabbed his D-18 and pointed his Caravan towards Fort Bragg for the weekly jam session at Gayle's store. The Eclectic Attic stocked a mixed bag of merchandise, as the name of the store suggested, with an inventory that changed from time to time, depending Gayle's passing interests. She restocked the best-selling items, and was always willing to special order something she didn't have. She and Ryan had been especially close friends virtually from the start, as if their first meeting was the renewal of an old friendship rather than the beginning of a new one. On one of his first visits to the store, Ryan brought his guitar and played a few songs. That led to a few impromptu concerts with Doug, and before long, they were dropping by regularly on Saturday afternoons to play and sing. When word got out that acoustic music was happening, other musicians began to show up, and an informal jam session was born. Three years after its unintended beginnings, it was even listed in "local events" newsletters put out for tourists and visitors. There was a small cadre of regulars, who played banjo, fiddle, guitar, bass, mandolin and harmonica, and some who showed up just to listen. Gayle bought a P.A. system and installed speakers outside so that the music could be heard on the sidewalk as well as throughout the store. Some Saturdays it seemed as though half the shoppers in town stopped by.

He arrived an hour before the jam session usually started. Gayle looked surprised to see him. "What brings you here so early?"

"Doug was spreading a rumor that was so wild I wanted to check it out," he answered. Gayle's face lit up as she came out from behind the counter to give him a hug. "You're talking to a person who hasn't had a cigarette in sixteen days! That's by far the longest I've ever gone since I was thirteen years old. I can't believe it's true, and I can't believe how easy it's been!"

"He told me that you did it with hypnosis — something about a past-life regression . . ."

"Isn't it a kick?" she said with a grin. "People have always laughed at me for the things I'm willing to do, but there's no arguing with this one! I'm even thinking about doing it again!"

"Why?" he asked teasingly. "Do you have any more bad habits you haven't told me about? I thought you shared *everything* with me." She punched him playfully on the arm. "It was just such a fascinating, liberating experience that I'd like to see where else it might take me — and who knows? Maybe there *is* more excess baggage I can cut loose."

"So tell me about it," Ryan urged as he deposited his guitar in the corner and sprawled on a small couch. "Who's the guy who did the hypnosis, and what was it like?"

"'The guy' is Larry Robinson, a psychiatrist from San Francisco who just retired," she said, turning a chair around and sitting down with her arms crossed over its back. "I really didn't spend much time with him, but I already know that I trust him completely. At first I thought I had met him before — he felt like an old friend — and he said he felt the same way about me. As far as what it's like . . . all I can say is that it was like a memory of something that had actually happened. It never felt like I was making things up as I went along." She grinned. "And look at the results!" She paused for a few moments recalling the experience, then snapped back to the present. "By the way, he asked me to an early dinner at his place out on Ocean View Drive tomorrow. He said to bring friends if I wanted. Are you interested?"

"Absolutely," replied Ryan. "How about inviting Doug and Pam too?"

"That would be great — I'll let him know." Gayle got up to help a woman who had been browsing while Ryan tuned his guitar and started arranging chairs and setting up microphone stands. A few minutes later, Gayle's customer left the shop with a brightly-colored serape from Guatemala and a broad smile.

"Tell me more about the past-life regression," he prompted.

"Hypnosis releases your inhibitions — makes you really open-minded and accepting of possibilities that you wouldn't ordinarily consider," she replied. "It's kind of like watching a science fiction movie — you don't get much out of it if you're always trying to figure out how they accomplished the special effects. Anyway, I started by walking along a mountain path into a mist. After the mist cleared, I was walking along a dusty dirt road next to a river. I was always the same person — the same woman I am now, except that after a while I was also someone else! It was strange, but it didn't feel unnatural at all. Larry asked me questions about what I could see, and where I was going — what year it was — things like that. As soon as he asked the question, I knew the answer. And every time I remembered something, I got a visual image."

She was silent for a moment, and Ryan saw that her eyes had lost their focus — almost as if she had been hypnotized again. Then she shook her head, as if to clear it. "So anyway, I walked into town, which was only a few streets next to the river. There was a sign that said 'Welcome to Courtland.' When Larry asked me the year,

I knew immediately that it was 1851."

"There *is* a little one-horse town that dates back to that time period, about twenty miles down-river from Sacramento," said Ryan, who had begun finger-picking a soft accompaniment to her story.

"Then I guess that's where I was. I was a Chinese woman — a prostitute who had been enslaved in China and brought over and kept in a little room above a saloon. It was the most desperate, hopeless life you could imagine. The man who owned me had gotten me hooked on opium to make sure I wouldn't try to escape." As she was speaking, her eyes brimmed over as she confronted the emotions raised by her experience. She wiped her eyes on the back of her hand. "Larry took me to the time of my death, and when he asked me if I had learned anything," she continued. "The answer was *right there*: I was re-living my addictions and slavery from that life, but *this time*, I was responsible for my own enslavement." She grinned at him quickly while wiping her hand off on her jeans before rising from her chair and launching into a cat-like stretch. "That's all there was to it. It's been just over two weeks and my emotional bond to the cigarettes has been gone ever since. I would feel as if I were giving short shrift to the courage it took to try to escape from slavery in that life if I picked them up again. I had the physical symptoms of withdrawal, but this time there was no question of giving in to the cravings. It was almost as if they were happening to someone else." She shrugged again. "For the most part, it's been painless."

Ryan put down his guitar as he stood up, gave her another hug and said, "I'm not going to argue with success — and Larry sounds like a real character. I'm looking forward to meeting him."

After the jam session, Ryan climbed back into his Caravan and headed back home. Evening was coming on and the fog that it brought called for a fire to take away the chill. As he stacked kindling and crumpled newspaper in the stove, he found himself thinking about Gayle's experience. When he lived in Sacramento, he'd ridden his bicycle to Courtland a number of times. While Gayle was describing the scene, he could visualize it all quite clearly, substituting dirt streets for the paved roads he'd ridden. *I can't believe how interested I am in this past-life thing,* he mused as he stretched out in front of the stove. His next thought caught him completely off guard. *I wonder if I should try it myself?*

# Interlude

IT HAD BEEN BAD ENOUGH WHEN ALDEG WAS THE ONLY WIZARD in the keep. The locals were so frightened of him that, except for the occasional foolhardy attempt on his life, they kept their distance. He was evil — of that there could be no doubt. And those who set themselves against him inevitably encountered their own demise rather than his. But, truth be told, when he was left alone Aldeg usually returned the favor. Nothing really changed when Aldeg took on his first apprentice, but that couldn't be said when Rankin, Sir Kay's former stable boy, arrived at the keep. Evil was no longer mere threat, as frequent, and seemingly random acts of violence and terror radiated out from the Wizard's keep. But even that was nothing compared to the living Hell that ensued after Aldeg and Hayden disappeared.

Sir Kay saw his duty. But when he mustered his vassals and led them into battle against Rankin, he refused to allow Eral, his eldest son, to accompany them, explaining that he would not leave the throne unattended. His prudence was warranted. No one returned from that ill-fated venture, save one whose mind had been completely destroyed, leaving him a gibbering cretin. After Sir Kay's ill-fated assault, Rankin declared himself lord — a pronouncement that galled Eral, Kay's reluctant but rightful heir. Eral had always known that one day he would have to leave his music and studies behind when his birthright called. He was "Sir Eral" now, though the title did him more harm than good — it was all that kept him from taking his young wife and fleeing from Rankin's reign of terror. Worse, as Kay's rightful heir, he was a hunted man, forced to disguise himself and his wife as peasants, and to live a life bordered on every edge by constant fear.

He leaned down and kissed his sleeping wife's forehead and then smoothed back her hair so that he could take in her face one last time before he set out to ask his own liege-lord for help against his murderous foe. She murmured in her sleep and his heart ached — with love, and also with fear and sorrow at the thought of leaving her undefended. But he saw no other choice than to make this journey. His obligation required it, and it was their only hope. Abruptly, he rose and strode outside, where his horse was already saddled and waiting. The responsibility was his alone and there was no time to waste.

# 3

LARRY'S HOUSE PERCHED ON THE EDGE OF A BLUFF OVERLOOKING
the Pacific, and the sound of the waves crashing on the rocks below proclaimed the
immediacy of the ocean's presence. Ryan, Pam and Doug arrived together to find
Gayle standing in the driveway next to a slightly built, athletic-looking man whose
friendly smile was wreathed by fine, silvery-white hair and a well-trimmed beard.

"Welcome! Come in, come in," he said, greeting them warmly. "Gayle's been
telling me about you . . . Thank you for coming!"

"Thank *you* for the invitation," Pam replied as they walked en masse through a
tiled entryway that led into a spacious living-room with floors of pegged oak covered with brilliantly-patterned oriental rugs. The entire wall facing the ocean emu-
lated a bay window two stories high.

"This place is beautiful," Pam exclaimed, moving to the window to take in the
view of the surf breaking over the jagged rocks below.

"I've been in love with it since the first time I walked through the door," Larry
agreed, joining her at the window. "It was built by a friend of mine who let me use
it whenever I could get up here. When I had the chance to buy it, my retirement
plans were set!" He gestured towards a kitchen and dining area that took full advantage of the view. "I took the liberty of asking Gayle what your preferences were
for drinks. Why don't we go into the kitchen and I'll get them for you."

Soon they each had a glass in hand, and had found places around the table,
where a lively conversation inevitably made its way to Gayle's triumph over nicotine. Doug's skepticism – honed by a career as a journalist, was immediately apparent – though under Pam's watchful eye he did his best to be polite.

"I'll concede that Gayle's success in quitting smoking after years of trying is
unexpected," he said, tilting back in his chair and peering out from under a raised
brow. "But can it really be chalked up to her past-life regression? And how did you
stray so far from the path your profession usually takes? It seems to me that your
training would have taken you in entirely different directions, even if you were on
the extreme fringe of Jungian psychology."

"It is quite a stretch," Larry conceded, not at all put off by Doug's rapid-fire
questions and inquisitorial tone. "Today, most people would categorize me as some
kind of dreamer, and in many respects they wouldn't be far from the mark. You're

also absolutely right about it being an unusual direction for a career such as mine to take. Truthfully, I was once even more skeptical than you. If something couldn't be proved through double-blind testing, I didn't give it any credence whatsoever. I considered myself an atheist, but I had a religion all the same — the religion of the scientific method — and it was as strict and unbending in its dogma as any fundamentalist faith." He took a sip of his sparkling water. "Initially, my emphasis was on psychopharmacology — the study of brain chemistry and the substances used to treat psychological disorders."

"That's the kind of left-brained approach I was talking about," Doug allowed. "How in the world did you get from there to past-life therapy?"

"During my internship I had the opportunity to work under a doctor who had made the study of hypnosis his life's work — I saw how it was used to treat a variety of psychological problems, and I found the subject fascinating. Still, it's a big leap from there to past-life regression therapy. Initially, I had no interest in anything of the sort. Early in my career I would have thought it inconceivable that there could be any valid use for such a technique in the clinical setting. As far as I was concerned, the couch and the prescription pad held all the answers." He rested his elbows on the table in front of him and leaned forward with his hands tented. "I was working with one particular patient when my entire life changed. It's been about fifteen years now, but I remember it as clearly as if it were yesterday. I had been seeing a young man named Keith for nearly eighteen months. It was an extremely difficult case, because of his multiple, overlapping anxiety disorders including fear of heights, fear of drowning, fear of crowds, fear of being alone — he never felt safe or comfortable, and he had become profoundly depressed. He couldn't take any standard medications because of his fear of gagging."

"Who wouldn't be depressed?" asked Ryan. "I think if I was in that kind of emotional turmoil, I might end up killing myself."

"He probably would have, except that his greatest fear was of death itself," Larry replied. "He imagined it would be like falling forever into an abyss while being slowly consumed by everything he had ever imagined torturing him, until he reached his own personal Hell."

"That poor man!" cried Pam. "Were you able to help him?"

"Not much at first," Larry admitted. "We made only scant progress using traditional psychoanalysis, so I decided to take a new approach — I wanted to see if hypno-therapy might help him. At first, we tried simple commands and instructions. While he was under, I would give him a post-hypnotic command not to let a particular anxiety bother him. It didn't help a bit. Then, I decided to try standard regression therapy. Sometimes the cause of an anxiety disorder can be the result of a childhood trauma. If the traumatic event that is the foundation of the anxiety is identified, it loses its power. Everything built on the 'foundation' will topple. I hadn't tried regression therapy on Keith before because he had *so many* different specific anxieties. I just couldn't imagine that all of those things could have been tied to childhood events. But I had exhausted my standard therapy tools."

"How did you get the idea to do a past-life regression?" asked Doug.

"I didn't. It just turned out that way. Keith was particularly susceptible to hypnosis, and as usual, he had achieved a deep trance very quickly. I asked him to go back to the time when his anxieties began. But rather than bringing up memories of childhood events, he went back into a life in ancient Egypt. At first, I didn't know what to make of it — I thought he might be fantasizing, or even joking with me. But I could tell from observing the movements of his eyes under his eyelids that he was in a genuine hypnotic state. I started asking him questions about what he could observe — generally using the techniques that I would have used during a childhood regression. We went forward in that life until the time of his death. The Nile had flooded, and he and his wife were trying to make their way to higher ground when the waters swept them apart — he drowned trying to save her. When we ended the session Keith was quite calm, which I found intriguing. He didn't ask any questions or make any comments — we just scheduled the next appointment and he went on his way. I, on the other hand, was about to burst with what had just happened. I had done childhood regressions many times, and nothing even remotely like this had ever occurred."

"Did you mention it to anybody?" Pam inquired.

"No," Larry replied. "Like I said, at first I thought it might just be some kind of fantasy, or perhaps a vivid dream. It was an anomaly — so I ended up doing nothing. A week later Keith came back. The first thing he told me was that he had completely lost his fear of drowning, and had gone swimming for the first time since childhood. His fear of water — and this had been one of the strongest and most disabling — was completely gone. His depression had lifted slightly too. I had to give up the idea that what had happened had been a dream or a fantasy — not after such a dramatic result."

"It was just like that for me with my smoking," Gayle interjected. "Once I had that past-life clue about addiction, suddenly I was in control of the situation."

Larry, looked at his watch and rose from his place at the table. "It's time I got started on dinner," he said as he made his way into the kitchen, located a broad counter's width away from the dining area, where he had arranged all of the ingredients for a stir-fry dinner in bowls next to a wok. "I'm never one to argue with success," he said as he began sauteeing onions in the wok. "The next session, we decided to focus on Keith's fear of heights. This time I commanded him to go back to the *past-life* when his fear of heights had begun. He went back to a lifetime in the mid-nineteenth century, when, at the age of twenty-three, he was a hand on a clipper ship based in New Haven, Connecticut. He was one of those seamen who had to climb way up into the rigging of the ship to haul in and let out the sails. He died when he lost his footing and fell to the deck of the ship."

"Did his fear of heights go away after experiencing his death in that life?" asked Gayle.

"It did indeed. By the next session, he reported that he had gone to the top of Coit tower in San Francisco to test himself — something he never could have done before the regression."

Doug's skepticism had not been overcome. "I take it that you were able to solve all of Keith's problems with past-life therapy?"

Larry refused to rise to the bait, answering reasonably, "Let's say that we got him to a place where he was comfortable enough with his life to discontinue therapy. It took several months, but by the time we were finished he was living a much more normal life." He smiled. "Keith had always been reclusive and shy of women and relationships, but he called me a few years ago to tell me that he'd gotten married, and that his oldest daughter was just about to start kindergarten."

"That must have been really satisfying," Pam observed.

"It was, but those hypnotherapy sessions by themselves weren't what changed my life completely, turned everything I believed in upside down, and started me on the path I've been following ever since," he said as he put water on the stove for tea and began to make coffee. "That happened a bit later. I believe it was during Keith's fifth past-life regression," he said, while scooping rich-smelling grounds into the coffee-maker's basket. "By then, I was tape-recording the sessions with Keith's permission. My scientific training, which made me want to record the results of experiments as accurately as possible, stood me in good stead. Sometimes Keith experienced more than one life per session. After experiencing a death, he went to what he described as 'the twilight in- between.' That's when, in the course of a few minutes, my life changed completely. I still have the tape of that session. I'll play it for you, but before I do, I should tell you that aside from the time he spent with me in session, Keith knew absolutely nothing about my private life. My office had nothing of a personal nature in it — therapists keep their distance as a rule, so that they are in effect a 'blank tablet' upon which the patient can project their own feelings and thoughts. I always made sure to keep that kind of distance in my professional relationships."

He moved to a cabinet filled with stereo equipment and turned on the power to the receiver and the tape deck. After he inserted a cassette and hit the play button, they heard a young man's voice alternating with Larry's, offering descriptions of things he was seeing, while Larry gave him guiding prompts. After describing a violent death — being crushed by a crowd of people trying to escape a fire in a sweatshop with too few entrances and exits — Keith described himself floating above his body surrounded by a glowing light. Then his voice, which had been fairly high-pitched, dropped significantly and became richer in timbre. "Your wife is here," he said, "and your brother, who is a small child. Your wife's name is Sarah, and your brother's name is Thomas. Sarah tells you not to worry. She wants you to know that she was asleep when the plane crashed, and she never felt any pain. She says to tell you that she is waiting for you — that you have shared many lives together and will be reunited after this lifetime. Thomas says to tell you that his life had a purpose, short as it was. He wants you to know that he loves you."

Then they heard Larry's voice, thick with emotion, "How . . . how do you know these things?"

"The advanced spirits are speaking through me," Keith continued in that strange, rich voice. "They tell me that I have lived twenty-seven lives."

Larry stood up and walked over to the tape recorder and switched it off, then turned to face them. The room was absolutely silent as each of them digested what they had heard. Doug spoke first. "My instincts tell me to look for a charlatan behind the curtain pulling levers, but I don't think I'm going to find one."

Larry chuckled softly. "Don't worry if you have trouble believing it — I could hardly believe it myself, and I was there when it was happening. My wife died in a plane crash ten years after we were married. It happened fifteen years before I ever met Keith. Thomas was my younger brother. He was born in the early thirties, with a birth defect — he didn't have any kidneys, and never left the hospital. There was no way that Keith could have heard of either one of them."

"What does it all mean?" asked Gayle.

"This experience, and my experience with hundreds of subjects since this recording was made, has convinced me that our powers of perception are quite limited on this plane of existence. But more significantly, it means that we don't have to fear death — our own, or the death of a loved one — those things are only temporary. We don't get off this merry-go-round, we just change horses." His bright blue eyes twinkled. "As for me, I found a compelling reason to become active in the ecological movement. It put a whole new spin on things knowing that I would have to live with the consequences of any ecological disasters we create."

*I'VE NEVER GIVEN eternity much thought,* Ryan mused after dropping Doug and Pam off. *Have we really been living life after life, coming back again and again?* Over dinner, Larry had described some of the things he had learned during the intervening years while taking hundreds of patients through past-life regressions. He said that coming to live on the physical plane of existence was like going to class — that we were here before, and are here now to learn lessons that bring spiritual growth, eventually allowing us to become "advanced spirits" ourselves. Two of the things Larry said really sent him spinning — first, that people *choose* the lives they lead in order to be presented with specific challenges and difficulties, and second, that we usually go through life after life surrounded by the same group of people. "Think about those who are important figures in your lives," he had suggested, "the ones you care for deeply — the ones who really make a difference, and on the other extreme, the ones you dislike immediately. There is a good possibility that your feelings for these people are based on the positive relationships or enmity that developed during past lives."

As he walked from his garage to his house, Ryan began to feel a familiar itch. For a number of years, beginning with a time when he was trying to cope with the painful end of a college romance, he had learned to process his emotions by writing songs. Some were sad, even gloomy. Others were funny and full of joy. A significant number were attempts to define his own spiritual journey. Ryan believed in spirituality, although he had only a vague idea of what he meant by that term. But when he contemplated the subject, he most frequently plumbed the depths of his own inner silences through music.

He picked up his custom cedar-top Olson guitar. It was especially suited for finger-picking, with a delicate tone that was warm, yet crisp at the same time —

entirely different from his Martins, which responded better to a heavier hand. Sometimes Ryan found songwriting difficult and frustrating as the words and melodies hovered just beyond his grasp. But his best efforts usually felt as if they were coming through, rather than from him. When a song came easily it was like magic. Tonight was one of those times — the muse was *very* strong. The ideas and concepts he'd heard from Larry and Gayle wove themselves quickly into a song. *I can see the direction I'm headed,* he thought after he was finished. He realized that he had developed a strong desire to experience a past-life regression first hand, and briefly wondered what had caused his surge of interest. Reincarnation was a concept he'd scarcely ever considered, but it now filled his thoughts, almost as if some outside force were compelling him. He looked at his watch and shrugged his shoulders — *why not?* It was still early. He picked up his phone and dialed the number Larry had given him.

"I wondered if you would be interested," said Larry when Ryan broached the subject of doing a past-life regression. "Is there anything in particular that you want to explore?"

"Is it better to look for something specific?"

"It's different for everyone. But in my experience, you're more likely to be successful if you're looking for something that matters to you — it tends to help bring past life events to the surface."

"I'll try to think of something, then. When should we do it?"

"What are you doing tomorrow evening after work?"

Ryan felt his heartbeat accelerate as the event leapt into focus just a day away. "Tomorrow would be fine, I guess," he gulped. "If I can stop hyperventilating by then."

Larry laughed. "Don't worry, no one has ever failed to come back from a past-life regression. You're completely in charge of everything you do. All you surrender are the blocks that keep you from accessing the experiences. Why don't you pick me up after work — it's often best to have the first session in your own home, in a room where you feel safe and comfortable."

*Whoa, you've really stuck your foot in it this time,* Ryan thought to himself as he put down the receiver. *All strapped in and ready for take off — but what will I find?*

# 4

IN A LUXURIOUSLY APPOINTED OFFICE ON THE THIRTY-SECOND floor of the Amalgamated Tower in the heart of San Francisco's financial district, Raymond Baker swiveled his wine-colored, leather-upholstered chair until he faced the credenza behind his scrupulously clean desk. He lit a cigarette, and then poured himself two ounces of single-malt Scotch whiskey from a crystal decanter. Reaching for a concealed latch, he opened a panel and retrieved a small mirror bearing a gold-plated razor blade and a large bindle of cocaine. He poured a measured portion onto the mirror's polished surface, chopped the crystals into fine powder, and divided it into two piles, then spread them into matching four-inch lines. *Alcohol, tobacco and cocaine,* he mused. *Most people can't handle them, or handle them badly. It brings their weaknesses straight to the surface, and with alcohol and tobacco, put them in public view.* Baker's own use of these highly-addictive substances was completely private — and governed absolutely by parameters he had set down years before. He never deviated from the limits he set for himself. That would be a sign of weakness, something that would never, *could* never happen.

He stared out at the lights on the Bay Bridge, with its series of spans arching over the water towards the East Bay. It was a million-dollar view, but it didn't register, let alone impress him. His thoughts were racing through the details of the corporate raid he was about to unleash on the Miller Lumber Company. He drew hard on his cigarette, and blew a cloud of acrid smoke toward the ceiling, where it was snatched away by the efficient air-conditioning system. Then he crushed the cigarette out, just as he was planning to crush Miller Lumber, with its ripe pension plan and huge reserves of old-growth timber. He inserted the end of a tightly rolled hundred-dollar bill into his nose and quickly snorted the cocaine. Two lines — just enough to balance the two ounces of whiskey. He leaned back in his chair and sighed contentedly. He'd done his homework well. Miller Lumber Company's pension plan had been conservatively managed, and was heavily invested in blue-chip stocks, bonds and diversified mutual funds. It was better than gold. As President, Chairman of the Board of Directors, and Chief Financial Officer for Amalgamated Insurance, Baker had absolute control over his company's acquisitions. For many months now he had been solidifying his position, and he was almost ready to snatch this poorly guarded plum. As soon as he was in charge, he would install himself as the new head of management, sell off the old investments, and replace them with bonds issued by Amalgamated. On paper it would be a fair trade. In fact, it would be the closest thing to theft that the Security and Exchange Commission and the Justice Department would allow. Baker had already honed the art of the corporate raid to a keen edge, ruthlessly acquiring thriving publicly traded companies and stripping them down as far as possible before selling off what was left. *Just a few more weeks and I'll have all of my ducks lined up* he thought, as he lit a fresh cigarette. *Just a few more weeks and the tree-huggers will be shitting fire!*

# 5

THE NEXT DAY AT WORK, RYAN FOUND IT HARD TO CONCENTRATE.
He spent the day in Ukiah, the Mendocino County seat, which was situated fifty
miles to the east on the far side of the Coast Range mountains. On this day, he was
representing plaintiffs in a personal injury case, and the purpose of the trip was
their depositions, which were proving to be an ordeal. One purpose of depositions
was to elicit information, but more often they were used to gauge the quality of
testimony. In Ryan's opinion, the way these depositions were being conducted was
a waste of everyone's time — the defense firm was just padding the bill. Liability
was so clear cut that witness credibility wasn't an issue — the defendant had plowed
into the rear of his clients' car while it was stopped for a red light, and was hard
enough to cause a chain-reaction accident involving all of the cars stopped for the
light. The last in line had been narrowly missed by a logging truck. But in spite of
clear liability, the insurance company had been particularly difficult, taking a belligerent posture from the outset. At first, the insurance adjuster actually disputed
liability, contending that the tail-lights in Ryan's client's vehicle, which was the
first to be hit, were not working properly. She refused to acknowledge the significance of the fact that Ryan's clients were third in line at a red light. After that, the
adjuster had taken the tack that the injuries suffered by his clients could not have
occurred as the result of this accident — there must be some other cause. Then, the
doctors and physical therapists were over-treating his clients — there was always
another reason why they wouldn't settle. What should have been a straightforward
case had turned into an endurance contest. Ryan had hoped that once he filed the
lawsuit and got the case into a lawyer's hands, he would have someone saner to
deal with. But the lawyer hired by the insurance company was cut from the same
cloth as the adjuster. Ryan had never had a case involving Amalgamated Insurance
before. He hoped he never had another.

The depositions lasted most of the day, and he only had time to return a few
phone calls before it was time to pick Larry up on his way home. When they
arrived, he led Larry into his music room. "I've got a surprise for you," he said. "I
took the things you and Gayle said and made a song out of it . . . I'd like to sing it for
you before we get started." He pulled his Olson out of its case and closed his eyes
so as to give himself the best opportunity to feel every nuance of emotion that had

flowed through him while he wrote the song.

> *Through the folds of time, surrender to the flow*
> *The link from now to then is one that doesn't show*
> *Through the misty glen of the twilight in between*
> *The Phoenix fire renews, fills the body, lets it breathe*
>
> *Oh breath of life, wandering soul*
> *Carry it on . . . let spirit grow*
>
> *The lesson's incomplete, journey's not yet done*
> *Death is not defeat but a passage to a new life begun*
> *We choose who we're to be, the path by which we go*
> *We work through pain and fear; they're the seeds of learning sown*
>
> *Oh, breath of life, immortal soul*
> *Carry me on . . . where spirits grow*
>
> *We must learn to love, judgment falls away*
> *Hate and anger only serve to bring us back to pain*
> *Memories from the past release us, let us choose*
> *The die's not firmly cast, the spirit's free to move*
>
> *Oh, breath of life, eternal soul*
> *Carry us on . . . let our spirits grow*

"I can tell that your interest has really been captivated," Larry observed after the last note died away. "What a wonderful way to process what you're going through! William Blake did the same thing with his poetry, but I think you've done him one better by weaving in a melody."

"Thanks," said Ryan, pleased, if slightly embarrassed by Larry's praise.

"Have you decided if you want to look for anything during your regression?" Larry asked.

"I have," Ryan answered. "I've been a musician my entire life, and even though I've always been better than average, there always seemed to be something holding me back — keeping me from being as good as my potential seemed to indicate I *could* be.

"You sounded fine to me," Larry objected.

"Don't get me wrong, I know I'm pretty good — it just feels as though there might be something preventing me from reaching my true potential. The first instrument I learned to play was the violin. Not long after I started, my teacher told me that I had the talent to be a professional. But after I got to a certain level I never improved — I couldn't seem to get past the plateau. My progress on guitar and mandolin was similar — rapid at first, then once I became fairly proficient I never improved, no matter how much I practiced. I was wondering if there's anything in a past life that might be holding me back."

"That sounds like an excellent subject," said Larry encouragingly. "It's obvious that you love music, and that should give you plenty of incentive."

Ryan chose the couch in his music room for the session, and was soon reclining with his head propped on a pillow. Larry began by directing him to relax one part of his body at a time. Then he suggested that Ryan visualize himself climbing a misty mountain path. Next, he said that he would count to twenty . . . that as he counted, the mist would become thicker at first, then thinner. When the mist dissipated entirely, Ryan would be in a past life.

The mist parted. Ryan found himself in a large, high-ceilinged room with hardwood floors, French windows and bookcases with glass doors built into one wall. There was a harpsichord in a position of prominence.

"Look at your hands and describe them to me," Larry suggested.

For a few moments Ryan was unable to speak, then the words tumbled out. "They're *girl hands*," he said, breathing more rapidly.

"It's very common to have been the opposite sex in a previous life," Larry reassured him.

Ryan breathed easier as he continued describing what he was seeing. "I'm wearing a long sleeved white dress with lots of petticoats that are very tight around the bodice . . . I'm seated at the harpsichord, having a music lesson . . . My teacher is a man, about forty years old. I'm younger than that, maybe sixteen or seventeen . . . My lesson isn't going very well."

"What is your music teacher wearing?"

"A blue velvet suit with knickers and grey stockings — like the people in the pictures of the signing of the Declaration of Independence — and he's wearing a white wig. I've been studying with him for three years."

"Do you know what year it is?"

"I have a feeling that the year is 1762."

"What is your teacher's name?"

Ryan waited for the information to come to him, paying only half of his attention to Larry's questions as he continued to experience the sensation of being in the room.

"I can't pick up his name, but he's calling me Felicity."

"Are you playing from sheet music?"

"Yes. It's a hand-written manuscript. It's Mozart."

"Is it hard to play?"

"Some of it is," Ryan replied. A small smile stole across his face. "Some of it is pretty easy."

He was silent for a while, observing the scene, then Larry asked him to go outside. Immediately, Ryan found himself observing the building where his harpsichord lesson had taken place.

"I'm standing on a pea-gravel driveway. The stones are white. The house is *very* large — light brown sandstone, two stories tall. It has a mansard roof ."

"Where does your music come from?"

"I could always play," Ryan answered simply before lapsing into silence. Larry waited patiently for a time, letting him drift. Then he shifted in his chair, and leaned forward. "I'm going to count to three, and when I'm done, I want you to go to the most significant event in that lifetime."

Felicity was back in the room with the harpsichord, this time playing the violin. She was giving a recital in front of perhaps forty people while her teacher accompanied her on the harpsichord. The men in the audience were dressed in fancy clothing and all of them wore powdered wigs. The women wore wigs also, and beautiful, ornate dresses made from velvet and satin. Ryan described the scene to Larry.

"Let the event unfold," Larry advised. "Experience it through to the end."

The emotions of excitement, pride and joy were as palpable to Ryan as if he was actually living out a lifelong dream. He was playing *extremely* well, captivating the audience with his performance.

"Where does this lead?" Larry asked eventually.

Sadness overcame him. "It doesn't lead anywhere," he said. "Only men are taken seriously as musicians."

"Go to the next significant event in this life," Larry prompted.

Ryan was standing outside the mansion, with the same vantage point as the last time. This time, it was late at night, and the mansion was being consumed by fire. He experienced intense feelings of grief and loss. Tears began to well out through the lids of his closed eyes. "The mansion is on fire," he moaned. "My patrons are trapped in there, my music teacher as well — they've got to be dead by now."

"Go to the next significant event."

"I'm living in the city now — I'm in my thirties, married, with two children, a boy and a girl. I clean houses for a living and I don't make enough money to buy another instrument, so the only place I can experience music is in church. I see a large, stone cathedral. The buildings in the city are all two or three stories tall and they're dark — from smoke, I think. It's very dreary." Ryan caught his breath, and swallowed a sob. "My children got sick and died," he said, tears once again coursing down his temples.

Larry waited a few moments, and then said: "Go to the time of your death."

Ryan found himself in a cold, dark room, lying on a narrow bed. He was burning with fever. Seated by the side of the bed was a red-haired woman. Somehow, he knew she was his sister. Then he felt himself separate from his body and float above it. He watched his sister wrap her arms around the limp body he had just departed, crying uncontrollably. Then he went to a place of grey nothingness and from there to the mist, where he found himself walking down the mountain path he had climbed to begin his journey. The mist thinned . . . the path disappeared . . . and he opened his eyes.

*     *     *

D'AURELIO'S WAS A small Italian family restaurant located in a tiny, out-of

-the-way strip-mall in Fort Bragg. Its paneled walls of knotty pine were barely able to contain the fragrant aromas of freshly-baked bread, spicy Italian food and the noisy conversation. After waiting for their turn, Ryan and Larry slid into an empty booth. After they placed their orders, Larry asked Ryan what he thought of his experience.

"I feel different," he said, "changed . . . it's hard to describe." He paused for a moment, trying to find the right words. "You've gone and shaken my foundations, you know. First, you cured Gayle's major-league addiction to tobacco, then you played that tape about the 'advanced spirits.' Now I'm not even the same person I've always been — I'm also a woman who's been dead for a couple of centuries."

Larry chuckled at Ryan's dry delivery. "Does it feel wrong or bad to you?" he asked.

"No — it's different than anything I've ever experienced, but at the same time, it feels *right*, like it's the most natural thing in the world. My outlook on things of a spiritual nature is definitely changing, although it's never been all that well defined. I think of it more as a journey than a particular set of beliefs. I've been trying to describe it in some of the songs I've written — I'll sing them for you some time if you'd like. *Phoenix Fire* is only the latest."

"Naturally, I've had longer to get used to the idea of reincarnation and the ability to access past-life memories," said Larry, "but in the beginning, I had to make a similar emotional and intellectual shift. Actually, when you think about it, belief in reincarnation is more common than the belief in an eternal after-life. Think of all the Hindus and Buddhists in the world. Even in our culture, 'karma' is a term most people understand, at least on a superficial level."

"Isn't that the truth," Ryan agreed. "How do the 'advanced spirits' fit in with that concept?"

"I had more conversations with them during Keith's therapy than what you heard on the tape," Larry said. "Ultimately there were eight sessions during which they communicated through him. Remember that the physical plane of existence is like going to school. We come here to learn, to experience life, love, pain, hate — even fear. The more times a person lives a life on this plane, the more opportunity they have to 'advance.' Some spirits get 'stuck,' though, and don't seem to advance at all. The 'advanced spirits' are those who have reached a high enough level that they no longer need to experience the physical plane of existence."

"I hadn't realized the power that the dominant religious beliefs in our culture have had over me," said Ryan, as he signaled to the waitress that he wanted a box for the unfinished portion of his pizza. "When I think about it, if you take the combined viewpoints of all humanity, those of us who grew up in this culture are a distinct minority."

"Let me give you a couple of quotes from the Buddhist tradition to think about in conjunction with your experience tonight," said Larry. "I find that for me, ideas from the religions of cultures where reincarnation is a common belief can be both enlightening and comforting. One of the basic concepts in Buddhism is that our ideas of ourselves as being 'separate' from others is an illusion. 'Buddha' means 'the awakened one,' meaning one who has *woken up* from the dream of being separate in a physical, material universe.  On the subject of *'enlightenment,'* Buddha is reputed to have said:  *'You are all Buddhas.  There is nothing that you need to achieve.  Just open your eyes.'*  Another of my favorite quotes is this one — *'It is proper to doubt.  Do not be led by holy scriptures, or by mere logic or inference, or by appearances, or by the authority of religious teachers.  But when you realize that something is unwholesome and bad for you, give it up.  And when you realize that something is wholesome and good for you, do it.'*  You may find yourself doubting what you experienced this evening.  There's nothing wrong with that — spirituality is by its very nature unknowable, and everyone has their doubts.  When that happens to me, I try to hold on to this quote that is also attributed to the Buddha: *'Be a lamp to yourself.  Be your own confidence.  Hold to the truth within yourself, as to the only truth.'"*

# 6

AUDREY PECKHAM PLACED THE RECEIVER BACK INTO ITS CRADLE after making the last call on her list. She had spent the majority of the evening soliciting donations for the Headwaters Organization for the Protection of the Environment, with relatively good results. The organization's base of operations was located in a converted house in Healdsburg, sixty miles north of San Francisco on the Highway 101 corridor, but their real work was done in courtrooms throughout Northern California and the Pacific Northwest. They were hardcore zealots, dedicated to saving old-growth forests by filing lawsuits against lumber companies that strayed too far from California Department of Forestry regulations, or whose activities threatened the habitats of endangered species. There hadn't been any old-growth forests near Audrey's childhood home in the Chicago area. But on a camping vacation from Southern California to Oregon she had developed a special affinity for the ancient stands. The contrast between the majestic virgin forests and the slashed, clear-cut hillsides had inspired her to try to find a way to save what was left of the old growth. Eventually, she and her friend Adam Gray had founded Project HOPE, as it was usually known, and had been among its most steadfast volunteers, putting in time almost every day after work, and most weekends, too. It was a relatively new passion for Audrey, and she still found it ironic that, at least as far as the lumber industry was concerned, it took volunteer organizations like hers to force the government to follow its own laws.

There was a map of the North Coast in the phone room depicting forested areas from the Santa Cruz mountains below San Francisco up to Southern Oregon. The last remaining stands of old growth forest — down to barely one-percent of what they had once been — were highlighted and color-coded. Most were managed by the U.S. Department of the Interior, or the California Department of Forestry, but a good portion was privately owned. The largest part of the funds raised by Project HOPE went for attorney's fees and court costs, and the rest went for the incidental expenses that arose as volunteers kept close track of endangered species whose habitat was found in the old-growth forests. The Endangered Species Act was Project HOPE's most potent weapon. They had obtained permanent injunctions against logging operations twice — a major accomplishment for an organization as small as theirs. These court victories made the organization extremely unpopular with a very vocal faction of the local population, and made the local conservative talk-show host practically foam at the mouth in apoplectic fits of rage. She bristled as she thought of Eddie Rapski, billed by KNZI in Ukiah as "the radical of the right." His show pandered to the lowest levels of society, with constant diatribes against gays, lesbians, lawyers, Democrats, anyone on welfare, "effete intellectual snobs" (Audrey wondered if Rapski or any of his listeners knew the meaning of the word effete), and his favorite target, environmentalists. Rapski was on a crusade to convince his lowbrow listening audience that *anyone* who did *anything* to try to protect the environment was not only a Communist, but was trying to put the entire region out of work. "Logging is the God-given right of the working man living in the Pacific Northwest," was the theme of a sermon he preached frequently. Audrey wondered if some lumber company had greased Rapski's palm. *Or maybe he really is just as short-sighted as he seems.*

Rapski was adored by his listening audience, most of whom wanted someone — anyone other than themselves — to blame for their problems. He carried on like he'd just gotten off the phone with God, with specific instructions on how to straighten out the mess liberals had made of the world. Audrey and Adam were convinced that some, if not all, of the occasional vandalism — mostly broken windows and graffiti — suffered by Project HOPE over the years had been instigated by Rapski's ranting and raving over the airwaves. Publicly, Audrey referred to him as "the ambassador of hate." Her words for him in private were much less kind. *Fortunately, I have the choice not to listen to him,* she thought with more than a little relief. Transcripts of Rapski's shows were available for a nominal fee, and were religiously purchased by Project HOPE. She and Adam both felt strongly that they should "know their enemy," but it literally made Audrey ill to listen to Rapski's poisonous ravings. She had discovered that reading transcripts of the shows wasn't nearly as painful as listening to them. Over time, prudence had dictated that they maintain a visible presence in the building and parking lots throughout the night following a Rapski diatribe against environmentalists. Almost inevitably, one or more pickup trucks full of angry young men would drive by, sometimes pulling into their parking lot to hurl insults. Since the all-night vigils had been instituted, their "visitors" had thus far driven away in frustration — squealing their tires and raising their hands with their middle fingers extended in a derisive salute.

Audrey was gathering her things together when Adam spoke from behind her. "Getting ready to take off?" he asked.

"I finally got through my list and I'm starving," she replied, surprised when she glanced at her watch at how late it had gotten. "I'm heading out for some Mexican food — do you want to join me?"

Adam's affirmative answer was a foregone conclusion — he was always ready to eat. They wandered over to "Taco Loco," a nearby Mexican restaurant with late-night hours. Audrey ordered a taco salad and a diet soda, while Adam ordered a huge plate of food and a Dos Equis beer. She glanced at his six-foot, one-hundred-fifty pound frame and wondered what kind of internal engine burned all the calories he consumed. Adam ate more than anyone she had ever known, and although he seldom exercised, he never gained an ounce.

After they ordered, Adam put on his sternest expression. "I heard from an unimpeachable source that you were thinking about cutting your vacation short, or maybe even skipping it entirely."

Audrey twisted in her chair uncomfortably, and took a bite of her taco salad before replying. "I know you think I'm a workaholic," she said finally. "Everybody has been after me to take a break, but there's so much to do!"

"And everything will still be here waiting for you when you get back," he shot back. "Look, we've been over this quite a few times. It's summer vacation, and most of the schools around here are off-session, so there won't be any consulting for you to do for another six weeks or more. Everyone has to take vacations. Your private-therapy clients will live through it and if they have a crisis, the other therapists at Peckham & Associates can help out. Besides, Tracey, Bill and Kristi are worried about you. Their collective *professional* opinion is that you *need* to take some time off."

"Have you been calling to check up on me?" Audrey asked heatedly.

"I haven't, actually," he replied calmly. "Bill and Tracey *both* called me yesterday. Neither of them knew the other had called. They said that in spite of the fact that you're completely worn out, you're waffling on taking your vacation, and that you really need one — something I've been telling you for over a year. You're being short with people and you're impatient more often than not — that's not the Audrey we know and love!" They ate in silence for several moments as the tension between them intensified.

Finally, Audrey sighed. "I don't know why I feel so driven. It just seems like there's never enough time to do the things that need to be done at Project HOPE — and my work with family-and-school partnerships is equally important."

"Yes," Adam responded, "and it would be a crying shame if someone who cares so much about both of these things worked herself into some kind of breakdown because she never took any time for herself. How long has it been since you left your work and Project HOPE behind completely and took more than a weekend for yourself?"

Audrey paused, trying to remember.

"Think back to before we started the project," Adam continued. "I know you haven't taken any time off since then."

"I remember now," she said. "It was the last summer that I was working at Napa Unified, before I started my private practice." She looked off into the distance. "I guess that would make it five years," she admitted reluctantly.

"Case closed," said Adam, hitting the table with an imaginary gavel. "I find the defendant guilty of severe self-neglect and sentence her to thirty days vacation on the Mendocino coast."

Audrey smiled weakly in spite of herself, feeling a bit chagrinned. "I guess I *have* been a little bit obsessed," she said.

"Trust me," said Adam dryly. "If your problem was drugs or alcohol, we'd have done an intervention on you long ago. As a matter of fact, if there was a twelve-step program for workaholism, we'd have driven you to meetings."

Audrey laughed, and the tension between them began to drift away.

"Actually, there has been a bit of an intervention," Adam continued after finishing off his burrito and downing the last of his Dos Equis. "You are officially on vacation as of *right now.*"

Audrey put down her fork, protesting, "But it's only Wednesday — I've got two more days before my vacation starts."

"All of your appointments have been canceled," Adam grinned, obviously enjoying himself. "If you show up at Peckham & Associates, they have orders to transport you to the coast by ambulance. Project Hope has its orders, and a group of volunteers will be in the parking lot to make sure that a certain stressed-out individual doesn't vandalize her soul any further." He stood up, leaned over and kissed her on the forehead. "You've been out-flanked, my dear, and there's nothing that you can do about it."

Audrey saw that any urge to cancel or cut short her vacation would be thwarted. And now that there seemed to be no option but to go, she actually felt a weight lifting off her shoulders. She visibly relaxed, and chuckled softly. "Okay, okay — I give in. It doesn't look as if I have any choice, so I might as well enjoy myself."

"No phone calls to the office or Project HOPE allowed," Adam admonished. "Don't even send us any postcards."

"Don't worry," she responded. "Now that this decision is on everybody else's head, I'm going to take full advantage. And you never can tell — I might enjoy the coast so much that I won't ever come back!"

# Interlude

ALTHEA RUBBED HER HAND OVER HER BELLY, SWOLLEN WITH Eral's child, and tears streaked her cheeks once again. She couldn't believe he was dead — that she would never feel his tender embrace again — that their child would never know its father. *All because of Rankin* she thought, and spat on the dirt floor of the hovel where she had been forced to seek refuge, hatred suffusing every fiber of her being. She had always hated him — from the days when he was Sir Kay's stable boy, always skulking around and leering boldly at her, even when he knew that she was aware of his lecherous gaze. She had been relieved when he disappeared, and then alarmed when it was reported that he was staying at the wizard's keep. But the times after he left were also the happiest of her life. Rankin was no longer lurking around every corner, hidden in the shadows like a draught of poisonous air. More importantly, she and Eral were finally old enough to declare their love for each other and to be married. She sobbed again as her loss stabbed through her even more intensely. Silently, she vowed that she would never rest until Rankin had drawn his final breath.

Suddenly, without warning, the door to the hovel burst asunder. The object of her hatred stood there, leaning casually on a staff of dark wood, carved with hideous figures. He was leering at her once again, with an expression that spoke of evil beyond anything she had ever imagined. "I wonder," he said languidly, and she felt herself chilled to the center of her being. "Will I impale your child when I take you, or will her death wait until afterwards when I carve you into pieces small enough for the buzzards to carry off . . .

# 7

THE NEXT SATURDAY MORNING, RYAN REPEATED HIS MOUNTAIN bike ride from the weekend before. At the "Big Tree," he lay on his back once again and stared up at the forest giant. This time, he had a new perspective. *Man, that's a lot of lifetimes,* he mused, pondering the span of years marked by the rings of the tree. He noted a significant shift in his thinking — reincarnation seemed so obvious now. He certainly didn't know too many people who were so advanced spiritually that they couldn't use another life or two — or even twenty or a hundred — for self-improvement. He laughed softly as the conversation of a couple of hikers coming up the trail broke his reverie — he couldn't remember ever having had a theological discussion with himself on a bike ride before. After greeting the hikers as they came up to the tree, he climbed into the saddle for the ride home.

*       *       *

AFTER A QUICK shower and a change of clothes, he grabbed his old Gibson mandolin and slot-head, twelve-fret Martin D28S and headed into Fort Bragg for the jam session. Again, he timed his arrival so that he could have a few words with Gayle before things got going. She had a shop full of customers when he arrived, so he busied himself tuning his instruments while he waited. He was still fiddling with the cranky tuning gears on his mandolin when Gayle walked up behind him and greeted him with a hug. Suddenly, he experienced a sudden explosive flash of recognition that made him gasp. When he turned around to face her, for an instant it seemed as if the features of the red-haired woman who had sat with him through Felicity's last illness had been superimposed over her familiar face. "You're my sister," he stammered, embracing her fiercely.

"Ryan, are you all right?" she asked, as soon as they broke apart, wearing a worried expression as she held him at arms-length. He took her hand and led her to a small couch that was just big enough for two. "I followed your lead and did a past-life regression last week," he said. "Wait until you hear what I have to tell you."

"I didn't know you were going to do a regression," said Gayle after he was finished. "Why did you wait so long to tell me about it?"

Ryan looked at the ceiling momentarily before answering. "Probably for the same reason you waited more than two weeks to tell me you quit smoking." He looked uncomfortable for a moment, then amended, "I haven't really thought about why I waited to tell you the truth. Maybe I needed some time to get used to the experience. I didn't tell anyone for a few days — not even Doug."

"You know, now that I think about it, that must have been a large part of why I waited to tell anybody about what happened to me, too," said Gayle. "I knew I'd quit smoking for good once I'd gone forty-eight hours. But what I really needed was an opportunity to process what had happened. Hey! What did you mean, calling me your sister?"

"You were there in my past life — the sister I told you about, the one with the red hair who sat with me when I died. That was you! The instant you touched me, I knew. It felt like a light switch had been flipped on in a corner of my mind. For a second, the image of my past-life sister was so strong, I thought I was seeing double."

"I wondered what was going on," said Gayle. "You looked as if you'd seen a ghost." She chuckled. " Come to think of it, in a way you had!" Her expression became thoughtful. "I wonder if that's why we've always been so close. Maybe we still have some residual 'sisterhood' going on in this life."

At that moment, the door to the shop opened as several regular jam session players arrived. Their conversation was left for another time as Ryan finished tuning his mandolin and then joined the others in a spirited medley of *Whiskey Before Breakfast* and *Over the Waterfall.* There were only four players when they started, but by the time everyone had taken a turn playing the lead, they had been joined by a number of others. As usual, the music began to draw people in from outside, and soon there was a small crowd standing or sitting close to the players while others wandered around the store checking out Gayle's merchandise. Just after they played *Si Bheag, Si Mhor,* the classic melody by O'Carolan, the seventeenth century Irish harper, Doug arrived. He and Ryan launched into some pop-music favorites from the seventies after which Ryan pulled Doug aside and motioned towards the door. They put their instruments in their cases and stepped outside. "I've got more news from the past-life regression front," Ryan reported as they strolled to a near-by liquor store for Dr. Pepper and micro-brewed beer.

"What now?" asked Doug, rolling his eyes.

"Seriously, I just recognized that Gayle was my past-life sister," Ryan replied. "She was the one I told you about who sat with me when I died in that past-life — I knew it as strongly as I know that you are you, and that I'm me — though come to think of it, that's not all that certain lately."

"You're buying this whole business hook, line and sinker, aren't you?" asked Doug, giving him a side long glance. "I always thought you were fairly well anchored."

Ryan shrugged. "If you had experienced what I did when Larry hypnotized me, you'd be buying into it, too."

"I guess it's just the idea of accessing past-life memories that makes me want to start looking in the nooks and crannies to try to find the hidden projector."

Ryan felt himself becoming irritated by Doug's steadfast skepticism. "I can understand your doubts about Larry — after all, you just met him. But do you really think that Gayle and I are just playing along? Do you think that Gayle *could* have quit smoking just to go along with someone's joke?"

"Don't get me wrong," Doug placated as they reached the liquor store and went inside. "I wasn't trying to imply that you were part of some kind of conspiracy — it's just that this stuff pushes my 'bullshit' button really hard. But I'll try to keep an open mind — that's the least an objective reporter can do. Can you live with that?"

Ryan's pique melted. "That's all I can ask for now. I might have reacted the same way myself before last week." He nudged Doug with his shoulder. "You really ought to try it though — then you'd have some firsthand experience to report on."

"No way," laughed Doug. "I'm going to remain an observer and keep my objectivity. Someone's got to stay in the here-and-now if only to reel the rest of you in."

As they strolled back to the Eclectic Attic, Ryan reflected that there was one area of his life that was entirely too 'reeled in." Suddenly, in a flash of intuition, he knew that he would be calling Larry in the very near future. There was something else he wanted to explore.

# 8

AUDREY'S PLEASANT BREAKFAST DID NOTHING TO IMPROVE HER mood.  As she returned to her room on the second floor of the Mendocino Hotel, she reflected that she had been on vacation for nearly a week, and had yet to derive any pleasure from the experience.  She felt unsettled and out of place, constantly trying to read, although she kept putting her book down in mid-paragraph, watching the surf from the headlands, driving to Fort Bragg to catch a movie — anything, as long as she was doing *something* — but nothing had helped her to unwind.  She had to work hard to restrain herself from calling Project HOPE to see if anything was going on.  Fortunately or not, the "conspiracy" had closed those doors.  And although she filled her days with long walks on the beach, watching sunsets, and wandering through the many shops near the hotel — all things she thought she'd been looking forward to — she still couldn't relax.  She was beginning to doubt that she would *ever* be able to wind down.  *What have I been doing to myself?* she wondered as she stood outside her hotel room door and hunted through her pockets for her key.  She finally located it and stepped into the beautifully appointed room that had begun to feel more and more like a prison cell with each day she failed to connect with the peace and serenity she'd expected to find.  She kicked off her shoes and curled up in the overstuffed chair where she had been attempting to read, and examined her options.  *Maybe if I fully commit to acting like a tourist, I'll start feeling less uptight.*  She resolved to explore Mendocino until she had discovered every nook and cranny.

After browsing through The Gallery Bookstore, a few doors down from the hotel, she crossed the street to visit the mobile pet-adoption clinic run by the Mendocino Humane Society.  Opening a small wire cage on the trailer that was used to transport the animals from the society headquarters in Fort Bragg, she picked up a small, wildly-purring black and white kitten, scratching it under its chin and between its ears, and stroking its silky fur.  She found herself smiling broadly for the first time in days, and then her face lit up with pleasure when a familiar voice behind her remarked, "It's too bad that these little guys aren't on the endangered species list.  Then we'd have an excuse to take them all home with us.  Later we could plant them in the redwood groves we wanted to protect."  She looked around to see the beaming face of  Larry Robinson, Project HOPE's most generous benefactor, holding out his hands for the kitten. Audrey handed the tiny creature over, and he cuddled it to the wool of his sweater-vest where it gazed hopefully up at him, purring loudly. She laughed with delight. "What's Project HOPE's most ardent supporter doing up here in Mendocino?" she asked. "You're supposed to be sequestered in your office seeing patient after patient so you can keep making those wonderful contributions!"

"I'm afraid that chapter in my life has come to an end, my dear," said Larry. "You are talking to a recently retired *former* resident of San Francisco. These days all I'm trying to do is convince myself that I'm not just here to enjoy the view anymore."

"That's marvelous," she said with a mischievous grin. "Everybody who retires tells me that after a few months, they're busier than ever, but if you've just taken the plunge, then you undoubtedly have *tons* of time available to volunteer at Project HOPE."

"Whoa, whoa, hold your horses," he chuckled. "There'll be some time for that later, but in the meantime, I have no intention of working as hard in retirement as I did when I was still seeing patients." He studied her for a moment. "Speaking of burning the candle at both ends, what are you doing here in Mendocino? I can't remember calling Project HOPE when you weren't there — at least on evenings and weekends. Who let you escape?"

Audrey blushed, and reached for the kitten that Larry had been stroking, cradling the blissed-out bundle of fur in the crook of her arm.

"They did an intervention on me at my office *and* at Project HOPE," she admitted. "I've been kicked out of both places with strict instructions to go 'be on vacation' for a month. It's the first time I've taken more than a long weekend for myself in five years."

"Good for you for taking time off, and good for them for making sure that you did!" exclaimed Larry. "How are things going anyway? It's been ages since we talked about anything other than saving the redwoods."

"That's a long and complicated story," she replied vaguely.

"You're on vacation, and I'm retired," he urged. "We've got all the time in the world. Why don't we put this little guy back in his cage and slip over to the Mendocino Cafe. It's a beautiful day, and I just love the view from their deck — I'll even spring for lunch."

"I can't turn down an offer like that," she smiled, placing the disappointed kitten back with its litter-mates. They strolled the short distance to the Mendocino Cafe, where they found a table outside. The restaurant was on a corner where two streets met, and the deck was protected from the wind on two sides by walls covered with flowering vines. As promised, the view of the ocean was spectacular. "What's good?" asked Audrey, surveying the menu and the "specials" board.

"The *California Nouveau* Mexican food is the big draw." Larry replied. "The last time I was here, the chicken Quesadillas were excellent. But today I think I'm going to try the Fettuccine Marsala. How about you?"

"I'm going to have the Huevos Rancheros," she said, and then, thinking of her friend Adam, smiled and said, "with a Dos Equis beer."

When the waiter came, they placed their orders and then sat quietly for a moment looking out at the ocean. A point of land extended out to sea a mile or two south of Mendocino, creating the small bay into which Big River flowed. In the distance, they could see the waves breaking on the rocks that guarded the far reach of the point, looking like a row of crooked, broken teeth from a dentist's worst nightmare.

"So . . . how does a vacation on the coast turn into a long, complicated story?" Larry asked.

"I've been here six days now, and I'm feeling increasingly anxious rather than becoming more relaxed," Audrey replied, unable to hide her dismay.

"You mentioned that you haven't taken more than a long weekend off in five years," said Larry. "How come it's been so long?"

"All this time, I've been telling myself that I was just too busy," she replied. "First, I was getting my private practice organized and running parenting classes on weekends, back when I was working part time for Napa Unified School District. Then, after I moved to Healdsburg and started Project HOPE, my free time was always committed. I've been trying to fix problems for families, or cause problems for lumber companies ever since." She reflected for a moment. "You know, if one of my clients were behaving this way I'd tell them they were structuring their lives to avoid dealing with their emotions." She twisted her mouth in frustration. "I was on the verge of canceling this vacation too, but my friends — especially Adam — literally forced me to go."

Talking about what was going on had brought Audrey's frustrations to the surface. Her voice sounded tight and her throat was becoming constricted. "Now I'm on this damn vacation, and all I'm doing is going through the motions," she continued. "I'm spending time 'contemplating' and walking the beach, and all of the other things I thought I'd been looking forward to. But all I feel is increasing anxiety. I watch a sunset, and say to myself: 'Okay, there's a sunset' . . . It doesn't matter if it's the most spectacular sunset I've ever seen, it just doesn't move me." She reined in the tumble of words that was pouring out of her as the waiter brought them their food and drinks. "I'm sorry," she apologized in a subdued voice after the waiter left. "I'm sounding a hell of a lot more like a client than a friend who just got invited to lunch — I didn't mean to vent all over you with my problems."

"Listening to problems is part and parcel of being a friend," said Larry sympathetically. "Clearly you've been filling your waking hours to the absolute limit, and I agree that it sounds as though you might be avoiding something. Was anything going particularly badly for you before you went into private practice?"

Audrey didn't answer right away, but stared out at the view, her brow furrowed in concentration. "I can't think of anything at all," she said at last. "Believe me, I've had this discussion with myself about a hundred times in the last six days. My life was going on in a normal fashion back when I lived in Napa. Then I got really involved in establishing Family-School Partnerships at Napa-Unified, and that gradually turned into my private practice." She looked stricken. "I *really* love what I do

— I've been able to design my own job and I feel like I've been making a difference in people's lives — doing something that *counted*. It's the same way with Project HOPE. You've been my most steady contributor for years — not to mention the time you've volunteered — *you* know how important that is! What have I been doing wrong?"

"It's not that you're doing anything wrong," said Larry calmly, taking a bite of his Fettuccine. "But the very 'rightness' of what you've been doing may have given you the perfect excuse to hide behind your activities — to immerse yourself so completely that you've been able to hide from what's really bothering you. I don't think that you'll have any reason to give up doing the things you love. You just need to find what's troubling you and face it down. Once you do, I'd be willing to bet that you'll be comfortable enough in your own skin so that you won't have to spend the next few years avoiding the person in the mirror."

Audrey didn't say anything for a while, appearing to devote her entire attention to her Huevos Rancheros. "Do you have any suggestions?" she asked finally. "I suppose I should get into therapy, but I keep thinking that I'd like to *enjoy* this vacation. I wish there were a way that I could find the answer more quickly."

"I do have a suggestion, actually," Larry replied. "Hypnosis was the mainstay of my practice. We could try to identify what it is that's bothering you. If we did, you might be able to get past this ennui."

"I've never been hypnotized," Audrey said thoughtfully. "What would we hope to accomplish?"

"Hypnosis is *focused concentration*," said Larry "When used in a therapeutic setting, it can allow the subject to circumvent the blocks that the subconscious has set up to isolate a person from a painful memory or emotion." He looked at his watch. "What are your plans for the rest of the day?"

"I had planned to act like a tourist until I felt like I was on vacation — but I wasn't having much success."

"Where are you staying?" he asked.

"Just up the street at the Mendocino Hotel.

"Why don't you show me your room," said Larry, signaling for the check. "While we're there, we can take a shot at finding what's bothering you."

As they walked to the hotel, Audrey reflected that although the idea of being hypnotized had never appealed to her before, she felt better that she had in days.

# 9

INSIDE AUDREY'S ROOM, LARRY DREW THE CURTAINS AND HAD her lay on her bed. Then he led her through a series of exercises to induce a progressively deeper state of relaxation. When she was fully under, he had her do some visualization, starting at the present and going back through the years, marking her progress by describing significant events. "I'm with Steve, my boyfriend," she said at one point. "It's the night that we broke up."

"Was there a reason for the break-up?"

"I wanted to have an exclusive relationship and most of the time he didn't," she murmured. "He was ten years older than I was — he'd been married before and had a couple of kids. He played music, and his favorite songs were the ones about being out on the road and not being tied down — but he never left the Napa Valley. He grew up there, and took over his dad's law practice. I think that's why he always thought he would find happiness somewhere else. We broke up after he moved to Los Angeles to go back to college and study music."

"Did you love him?"

"Yes."

Were you in love with him?

She hesitated. "I'm not so sure about that. I thought I was."

"Was he in love with you?"

"I know he loved me — that I was important to him, but he didn't want the same things that I wanted. I called him 'the elusive butterfly.' He didn't seem to be able to resist if a woman started flirting with him — he'd usually end up in bed with her, and then wake up with a hangover, feeling guilty. Then he'd come crawling back to me, and act like I was supposed to feel sorry for him because he'd succumbed to some woman's charms one more time."

"Did you always take him back?"

"Yes," she admitted — "but I always got even. I had a couple of men waiting in the wings I'd go out a few times and suddenly Steve would be in the mood for a more exclusive relationship."

"So you were dating other men as well?"

"Only as a reaction to his flings — I really wanted to get married and have kids. He seemed to fit the bill."

"How long ago was this last conversation — the one when you were breaking up?"

She paused for a few moments before answering. "It was five and a half years ago — just before I started my Family-School Partnership work with Napa Unified."

Larry led her back through another five years of "significant events," which included several traumatic episodes surrounding Steve's flings with other women. Going back further, she re-lived the joy and hope that she'd felt during the intense "honeymoon" of their initial courtship. When she could find no other significant events, he instructed Audrey to use the memories she had accessed in positive ways to overcome the problems that were causing her current emotional distress, and brought her out of her trance.

"I haven't thought of Steve in years," she said haltingly, blinking as her eyes adjusted to the light. "Do you think something about my relationship with him could be causing my problems now? We broke up over five years ago."

"The relationship ended just before you started devoting nearly all of your time to your work and Project HOPE," Larry observed.

"Are you saying that I've booked myself solid for the last five years so that I wouldn't have to look for a boyfriend? That's crazy — I've always dated a lot."

"Maybe you did before *and during* your relationship with Steve. But I bet you haven't been out on a *real* date in quite some time."

Her face colored as she thought about what he said. "You're right — that's another thing I hadn't even noticed. I *meant* it when I said that I dated all the time. But the truth is that I haven't been out on a date since . . . oh shit . . .since the last time I was trying to reel Steve back in."

"Take a look at the fact that you've been sitting around for six days trying to figure out what was bothering you, and yet you never once thought about your relationship with Steve as being a possible source of your feelings of anxiety. The fact that you haven't been out on a date since you broke up with him didn't even register on your consciousness. But when I had you go back through the "significant events" in your life, you spent more time on your relationship with Steve — especially the dysfunctional aspects of that relationship — than anything else." He crossed his arms and looked at her reflectively. "During the time you were going out with Steve, every event you identified as significant related to him."

"I can't believe how blind I've been!" Audrey exclaimed. "I learned about all of these behaviors in grad-school — I've identified them in other people — why couldn't I see what I was doing to myself?"

"That's one of the benefits that can occur with hypnosis. Focused concentration allows you to get around the blocks that prevent you from seeing what's going on in your subconscious. You shouldn't get down on yourself because you didn't recognize your own behavior. First of all, we can't be *completely* sure that what we discovered today is the cause of your problems. But hopefully it will be, and you'll feel increasingly better as you assimilate what you've learned. Secondly, this kind of self-examination is completely different from what you do on a day-to-day basis working with families. I'm sure you're aware that many of those who devote a significant portion of their practice to individual therapy spend at least some time on the couch themselves — all of us are constantly blind-sided by our own emotions. No, my dear, you can't realistically say that you should have seen it coming just because of your psychological training."

"I guess I just haven't done what I needed to do to figure out what was causing my problems. Hell, I didn't even know I *had* problems until I got over here and couldn't unwind."

"Speaking of unwinding," Larry said, standing up and looking at his watch, "Why don't we take a long walk, and then I know a fabulous spot for dinner. I noticed that you only picked at your food when we had lunch. I'm willing to bet that some exercise and then a really excellent meal will give you a good start towards enjoying the rest of your vacation!"

*     *     *

THE LITTLE RIVER Cafe was a tiny establishment, with six small tables shoe-horned into a ten-by-fourteen foot room. During their leisurely dinner, Audrey asked Larry about his transition into retirement.

"I've only been here a short time, but I've already struck up some friendships," he replied. "Gayle Draper has a wonderful shop in Fort Bragg called the Eclectic Attic. Ryan Stratton is a musician and poet who lives just inland from Caspar." He laughed. "But he doesn't make his living that way — he's a lawyer with his own law practice in Fort Bragg. You'd never guess he was an attorney unless he told you. There's a lyric in an old Kate Wolf song that describes him well, *'He had the eye of a painter, heart of a maker of songs.'* Doug and Pam Ackerman are Ryan's next-door neighbors. Doug is a retired newspaper reporter. He and Ryan play music and sing together. I haven't heard them yet, but I get the impression it's a special treat! Pam is a nurse, and I don't think I've ever met a more empathetic person in my life. Her patients have to be extremely lucky. I haven't had an opportunity to spend much time with any of them yet, but all of us clicked from the get-go." He paused for a moment and seemed to examine the food on his fork closely before going on. "Now that I think of it, there's a remarkable connection between us — a more substantial one than I would ever have expected, considering the short period of time we've spent together. But then again, I've led two of them through past-life regressions, and that tends to draw people closer together."

"Did you say *past-life regressions?*" Audrey asked, with her fork poised in mid-air.

"Yes, its actually quite similar to the kind of hypnosis that you went through today. The subject simply goes back to one or more past lives to find the experience that is causing their problem."

"You're putting me on, aren't you?"

"Not in the least — past-life regression therapy was the bulk of my practice for most of the last fifteen years."

It was Audrey's turn to be silent for several moments as she digested what Larry had said. "I don't know how to react to that," she said, finally. "I never thought I'd hear something like that from a legitimate source. It's almost as if you just told me that you believe in Santa Claus — I just don't know what to say."

"There's no need to *say* or *do* anything," Larry chuckled. "Our individual beliefs won't change the way things are — either reincarnation exists, or it doesn't. We can either access memories from past lives through hypnosis, or we can't. The saying and doing comes later, when we realize the significance of choices that we make in terms of how we live our lives. If we *do* come to believe in reincarnation, then certain things that we might have thought of as *very* important lose their urgency, while other things become quite important."

"Such as . . ."

"Take physical appearance for example. What's the *real* value of good looks in one lifetime? Good looks, especially the kind of 'good looks' that television and magazines tell us are so important, last for only a few short years. Compared to an eternity, what's the value of having unwrinkled skin for a few additional years?" He chuckled again, and then became more serious. "You and the others at Project HOPE, on the other hand, are working toward things that are really important. Personally, I believe that the people who devote their time or money to organizations like Project HOPE, or who are otherwise concerned about ecology and environmentalism have more advanced souls. On an unconscious level, they know that they'll be back, and will have to experience the consequences of what's going on in the here and now. *We will be our own descendants!* It just seems logical that those who would shortsightedly rape the environment for monetary gain most likely represent souls who are not very advanced."

Audrey laughed, enjoying the concept that she had a more advanced soul than fools such as Eddie Rapski. "I certainly can't fault your logic."

Larry glanced at his watch. "I have to be getting home," he said. "An old retired guy like me needs his beauty sleep."

"With all that you've given me to think about, I don't know if I'll be able to sleep at all," replied Audrey. "But I'm ready to give it a try."

Larry gave her his telephone number before he dropped her at the Mendocino Hotel, and asked her to give him a call to let him know how she was doing. As Audrey climbed the stairs to her room, she looked forward to enjoying some real peace of mind for the first time in ages.

# 10

RAYMOND BAKER KEPT HIS SLEEK, BLACK MERCEDES AT A STEADY
seventy miles per hour, eating up the miles between San Francisco and Cloverdale,
where the Miller Lumber Company's plant and corporate headquarters were located. He thought back to the phone call he had made the day before, savoring the
emotional agony and indignation of the soon-to-be demoted CEO. The man's pain
was almost palpable, even over the telephone, as Baker announced an emergency
meeting of the board of directors to deal with the issues raised by his recent acqui-
sition of a controlling interest in the company. *Weakling!* he thought contemptuously. *That sad piece of shit wore his feelings like a sandwich signboard.* No one
had ever seen Raymond Baker express emotion. No one ever would. His ice-cold
stare conveyed an indifference so profound it was indistinguishable from malice.
Few dared to look him in the eye. Fewer still dared to cross him, and of those,
none had walked away from the encounter unscathed.

The hostile takeover had been accomplished in just over two days. His agents,
who had been quietly purchasing the company's stock in small blocks over a period
of over a year, suddenly began putting their shares on the market at less than half of
their value. With the advent of Internet trading, the news of the prices at which the
stock was trading spread immediately. Brokers were contacted by nervous share-
holders, who assured them that the company was still fundamentally sound — in
fact, profits were up this year from last. There was no reason to panic — someone
was just short-selling the stock to try to make a quick profit. But the bull market of
the late 1990's had brought uncounted thousands of unsophisticated investors into
the market. Many of them had invested in Miller Lumber precisely because of its
stability. When the company seemed to be something other than the rock-solid
entity in which they had placed their trust, a great number of them put their shares
on the market, selling out for fifty, forty and finally twenty-eight cents on the dollar
before prices leveled out. Miller tried to buy as much stock as possible to stabilize
the price. But Baker had timed his move perfectly. It came at a point in time when
he knew the company would be cash-poor. He had his holding companies jump on
the stock that came available from the general public, then put it back on the market a few minutes later for a lower price than they had just paid, fueling the panic
even further. By the time the stock had been driven down to its lowest point, even

the most experienced investors were succumbing to the fears that Baker's tactics inspired. In the final tally, Baker was able to purchase a controlling interest at a third of the stock's real value. *Now on to phase two,* he thought as he sped through the warm summer evening.

He turned his radio to his "favorite" Ukiah radio station — KNZI. Amalgamated had acquired the station in another corporate raid, and now controlled it through a subsidiary. *Time to listen in on my little puppet, and see if his strings need adjustment,* he thought to himself. Eddie Rapski's voice, which at times was so oily it should have left a residue, rasped from the stereo speakers. He was lambasting a Methodist minister who had dared to preach a sermon about brotherly love that included equal treatment, and yes, love, for gays and lesbians. The minister made reference to the story about Jesus walking among the lepers and healing them, and had drawn the conclusion that gays who were afflicted with AIDS were the lepers of modern times. He urged his parishioners to reach out to their suffering brothers and sisters — to treat them with the same dignity and love as if the sufferer was Jesus himself, for after all, hadn't Jesus said, "that which you do for the least of my brothers you also do for me?" Rapski was relentless in his castigation of the minister for making such a comparison, daring to despoil the name of *Our Lord and Savior,* by speaking *His* name in the same breath as these vile sodomists and deviants. He shouted out from his bully-pulpit that Jesus would stand at the gates of heaven and drop-kick all of these *sinners* straight to Hell where they belonged! His hatred seared the air like tracer bullets. Baker leaned back into the soft leather upholstery and allowed the corners of his mouth to rise just a fraction of an inch. It was safe to allow this hint of emotion to cross his features here, where no one could see him. He decided that it was time to throw his pet a bone, while at the same time making sure that Rapski remained completely under his control.

# 11

RYAN CONTEMPLATED THE VIEW OF OAK STREET BEYOND HIS office's bay window. The building was a converted post-Victorian residence in Fort Bragg, and Ryan's personal office had once been the living room. The formal dining area adjacent to the front door, now served as a secretarial area, and a large bedroom lined with bookcases served as a library and conference room. A cozy kitchen in the back was the only part of the house that was completely original, providing a comfortable setting for lunches, or the occasional celebration.

He'd spent his day settling a divorce case. This had been one of the easy ones — no kids. Even so, wrapping up the details and getting the Marital Settlement Agreement finalized had taken the better part of the day. But at last it was time to attend to what had been at the back of his mind all day. He picked up the phone and dialed Larry's number. He was taken aback when Larry seemed to have anticipated that he would want to do another past-life regression. "Are you psychic as well as being a psychiatrist?" he asked, with a smile almost visible over the phone lines.

"Sometimes our training makes it seem that way," Larry chuckled, "but it's actually much simpler than that. The truth is that most people follow very similar patterns of behavior, while thinking they're having completely original experiences. You're far from being the first to be interested in a second session. In fact, in my practice it was so common that I scheduled a second session a week or two after the first one as often as not."

"Call me predictable then," Ryan allowed. "When can we arrange to do it?"

"If you're not busy, why don't you come over now?" Larry suggested. "Afterwards we can go get a bite to eat."

"I'll be over in a few minutes," said Ryan, and was soon on his way. He had been thinking of what, or actually *who*, he might be looking for since his conversation with Doug the previous Saturday. *Maybe, just maybe, I have a soul-mate,* he thought longingly once again. He'd had close relationships — even thought he'd found *her* one time — only to have his proposal of marriage rebuffed and the relationship broken off. His songwriting had its genesis during his "blue" period that followed. As he drove, Ryan softly sang a verse from a song he had written at the time.

*There's got to be somebody, who feels the way I do*
*But it's never quite that easy — one and one don't always make two*
*I know that I will find the someone waiting out there for me*
*The one who's thoughts are close to mine, she's waiting out there for me*
*She'll be the one I care about, and it will be so fine*
*The flow of life will turn about, and we will start the climb . . .*
*Life's a journey, never ending, always searching for the top*
*We fly so high and fall so low; the trip can't end, you just can't stop . . .*

This song, and several others with similar themes had been Ryan's introduction to the power of music as a tool to deal with emotional pain. He sang it so often — for himself at first and eventually for others — that he finally got sick of the song and tired of feeling sorry for himself. There had also been some side benefits in the form of several short-lived but healing relationships, with women who had heard the longing in the lyrics. But none of them had turned out to be that certain *somebody* he'd envisioned when he wrote the song. Ryan had never been particularly religious, but his silent prayer as he turned into Larry's driveway was, *please God, let it happen . . . just let it happen.*

After Ryan arrived, he described the discovery of his past-life connection with Gayle, and said: "I figure that's why we're such good friends now."

"My experience as a therapist supports your hypothesis," Larry agreed. "It's very common for people who have strong, loving relationships to have been involved with each other in past lives. Your current wife might have been your mother, brother, sister, or close friend. The defining element isn't the type, but the quality of the relationship. The advanced spirits told me that we choose the lives that we lead in order to live out a particular destiny. We're here to learn to help each other, to find the good, and the God in ourselves and those around us." He chuckled softly. "In a past life, you and Gayle might have even been linked romantically, although I don't think that's in cards in this life." He winked at Ryan. "But there could be someone who *is* your other half in the here and now."

He led Ryan to a reclining chair and turned the lights down low. After taking him into a deep trance as before, he instructed Ryan to picture himself in a large, many-sided room with a doorway in each wall. Tapping Ryan on the forehead, he said, "I'm going to count to five. One of the doorways will appeal to you, perhaps even summon you. You will open the door, and see a beautiful, peaceful light through the doorway. You will want to go there. As I count to five, you will start walking towards the light. On the count of five, you will step through the door and into a past-life. One, two, three, four, five . . ."

Ryan found himself crouched low behind a clump of willow bushes on the sandy bank of a clear, slowly moving stream. The peaceful feelings he had followed to this place had vanished. He was wearing fringed buckskin clothing and buffalo-hide moccasins. In one hand he held a bow, and in the other an arrow with owl-feather fletchings and a blue and red design on the shaft. He looked around him and saw that he was part of a war party. The realization came over him that he and the others were laying in ambush for a troop of blue-coated soldiers who would soon attempt to cross the river at this shallow ford. As he described the scene to Larry, he was suddenly in touch with a number of powerful emotions. "I feel very angry," he said. "I feel rage that burns with an ice-cold flame. I also ache with sorrow over my loss." He gulped back a sob. "But I cannot give in to my grief now. I must take my vengeance."

"What has happened to cause these feelings?"

As soon as Larry asked the question, Ryan knew the answer. "These blue-coated cowards attacked our camp while almost all of our braves were hunting buffalo. They killed everyone . . . all of the women, the elders . . . all of them." He winced as another memory surfaced. "They killed my wife . . . and my child, my newborn son. These cowards killed them all. They outnumber us and they are armed with guns and sabers. We have only our bows and arrows, but we will surprise them and kill as many as we can. It doesn't matter if I die . . . I want to die! They have taken my reason for living away from me!"

"Go back to a time when you were happy . . . before everyone was killed," Larry instructed.

Ryan shifted in the recliner. "It's evening. We have pitched our tepees in the cottonwood grove." His face lit up joyfully. "I'm with my wife — her belly is almost ready to burst with our first child. She is so beautiful, so sweet — I love her so much."

Larry paused for several minutes, allowing Ryan to savor the experience before they moved on. "Look at your wife's face, and concentrate," he instructed. "Do you recognize her? Is she anyone who you know from this life?"

"No — I've never seen her before."

"Look around you. Who is there?"

"My mother is here, and her sister — and my spirit-brother and his wife."

"Look closely at them — do you recognize any of them?"

"It's Gayle!" Ryan exclaimed. "My mother is Gayle — she's here in this life too."

"How about your spirit-brother and his wife. Do you recognize them?"

"It's Doug! And Pam!"

Larry directed Ryan to walk through the encampment and describe what he saw. "We have often made our camp here," Ryan began. "We follow the buffalo, as well as deer, antelope and elk. I'm very happy in this life. The greatest source of my happiness is my wife — I love her more than words can describe."

They continued their walk through the camp. "I am at the shaman's tepee," he said a moment later. "We are very close . . . he has been like a father to me."

"Do you recognize him?" asked Larry.

"It's you," Ryan replied wonderingly. "You were helping me in this life, too. We have been through many turnings of the wheel together. With each turn, we follow each other from one wheel to the next."

"Go back to the place where you are laying in ambush, and see what happens."

"I see them coming," whispered Ryan. "We can't shoot until we are sure that our arrows won't miss . . . Now they are here!" he spat suddenly. Then, "I shot *him* — the one with cruel blue eyes and blond hair — the one who gave the orders! My arrow pierced his stomach and he has fallen off of his horse. But the rest of them are shooting their guns at us!" He gasped, and his eyes fluttered wildly under closed lids. "I've been shot in the chest . . . I feel no pain, but I am dying . . . the hole is large enough to put my fist inside . . . I feel myself leaving this body."

Ryan's face was streaked with sweat and he was breathing hard, adrenaline coursing through his veins as he re-lived this battle from the distant past. But gradually his breathing came easier and he stopped sweating. "I'm floating above my body now," he murmured. "I'm with all of those who were killed. We are surrounded by a beautiful light, and you are beckoning to me, telling me that every-thing is all right — that I must cast off my anger. I am at peace here."

Larry let Ryan stay between lives for several minutes, then asked him to move on. "Go forward and see if you find another life," he instructed.

"I'm in a crowded room," said Ryan almost immediately. "It's an attic — ev-eryone is whispering, and very frightened . . . we're hiding from the Nazis."

"Do you know the year and where you are?"

"We are in the Warsaw ghetto. It is 1943. I've been living in the ghetto since I was thirteen years old — I'm seventeen now. Those of us who are left are all in hiding. The Nazis hunt us down like animals and kill us."

"Can you describe yourself?"

"My name is Marga — I'm a woman in this life — although almost everyone I live with still treats me like a little girl." Ryan's voice had become petulant as he remembered this slight. "I would be very pretty if I wasn't so skinny," he sighed. "There's never enough to eat — I've been hungry for as long as I can remember. If it weren't for Jurgen, I think I would kill myself."

"Who is Jurgen?" Larry asked.

"He is my boyfriend — my husband, although we have to be secret about that, because there was no rabbi to perform the ceremony. They say I am too young, but in God's eyes, we are married. We prayed together, and asked God to join our souls. I have loved him since I was a little girl. He is *so* kind to me. I would love to give him children! When I was younger he used to tease me, and tell me that he would marry me as soon as I was old enough. I didn't know then that he was serious, but I do now. We were meant for each other, and even though we have to live in this crowded attic, and hide from the Nazis, he makes my life worth living. If he dies before I do, I hope I die soon after, so that we will be reunited in para-dise."

"Is he in the room with you?"

"Yes, he just got back from his patrol." A note of pride crept into Ryan's voice. "He killed one of the Nazi scum tonight. The others are telling him he shouldn't have done it — they say it will only bring trouble." Ryan tossed his head as if to shake a lock of hair away from his face. "I don't care," he concluded. "At least we're doing *something*. We're never going to get out of this alive, anyway."

"Look at him closely. Do you recognize him?"

"Yes! He is my love! He was my wife in our life together when we were Oglala Sioux." Ryan's brow creased with worry, and he started breathing faster. "I must hurry. He is beckoning to me — he wants me to come to the hole in the wall that we use as a lookout. I can see through the hole now — we are above the second floor. A patrol of Nazis is coming toward us. Schwartz is leading them, the bastard!"

"Who is Schwartz?" asked Larry.

"He is one of the SS — an animal. Our spies have seen him torture our people to death as slowly and painfully as possible. I hate him more than the rest of them combined. *I recognize him!* He looks almost the same, and he's definitely the one I killed in the ambush in my other life! . . . Now they are stopping in front of our building — they are setting fire to the entire block!"

Ryan's breathing accelerated rapidly, and he began to sweat again. Larry took some tissues out of a box, and mopped the perspiration from Ryan's face. I'm going to count to three and tap you on the forehead," he said. "You will detach from this body and observe the scene without feeling any pain or discomfort."

"I'm floating above my body now," said Ryan a moment later, his voice still tense but not quite as agitated as before. "We are trying to get out using our secret escape route. We're on our hands and knees, crawling through a passage. But it is filling with smoke. I can see myself choking and coughing, and my eyes are water-ing . . . I can't go on . . ."

Ryan's voice became calmer. "This body has lost consciousness. I can see the flames starting to envelope the passageway."

"Is this the time when this life comes to an end?"

"Yes . . . I'm back in the light again. There are many spirits here — I recognize you. And Gayle's spirit, as well as the spirit of my son from the last life. Their love shines brilliantly!"

As Larry sat back in his chair to let him experience the time in-between lives, Ryan spoke again. His voice hadn't changed in pitch or timbre, but the inflections were different. "Your wife is here," he said. "She says to tell you that *The One without a Soul* will work a great evil unless we join together to prevent him from doing so."

"Whose wife?" asked Larry, his voice shaking slightly, instantly reminded of the times when the advanced spirits had spoken to him through his patient, Keith. Was it happening again? Could this be another communication from his beloved after so many years?

"It is *your* wife," said Ryan. "You know her as Sarah. She says to tell you that the love between you will endure, and that you *will* be re-united. She sends a warning: There is a great task before you — a task which you have attempted to perform many times before. The evil one from the two lives that you just led me through is at work again. You must stand fast against him, holding love close to your hearts through darkness and fear. You will be joined by companions, some of whom are known to you, and others who soon will be. All of you have been chosen. Every one of you has been a victim of *The One without a Soul* in past lives. The same thing will happen again unless you unite as living embodiments of the power of love. You must strive together against the fear that he in turn embodies. Should you fail, the world will suffer an irreparable loss — but if you succeed, an immense good will occur!"

"How will we know this *One without a Soul?*" asked Larry.

"His deeds from past lives will echo in your hearts — you will recoil from his evil. And his physical appearance is very similar in each lifetime as well. You must try to stop him, as you have tried so many times before. You and your companions will be led to remember struggles from past lives, but only you and one other will know the true significance of what is taking place. The knowledge the others are allowed to possess is limited. They will be unaware that your struggle is symbolic of a much larger conflict — that it will have repercussions and effects far beyond their present lives. Although they will have an awareness that the things happening to them are special and unusual, they are not allowed to know the tremendous significance of the conflict in which you are engaged. When he awakens, the soul through whom I speak will not remember my words. Godspeed, my love. I will be waiting for you."

Larry had goose bumps over his entire body. He felt the pain of the loss he had suffered a half-century before blossom anew. But now, as he wiped away a stray tear, his heart flooded with joy over the assurance that they would be reunited. He looked at the clear, unlined face of the young man reclining before him, joyously basking in the glow of a love he had yet to experience — at least in *this* life. He was one of the companions, obviously, but who were the others? Gayle? That seemed likely. Pam and Doug? They had been present in the Oglala Sioux lifetime that Ryan had described. As he brought Ryan back to the present, he felt as if he would burst with curiosity, but forced himself to act normally. "How are you feeling," he asked after Ryan opened his eyes.

"I'm vacillating between profound joy and unbearable impatience — I never knew what *real* love felt like before, and for the first time, I'm sure she's out there somewhere!" Frustration was stamped on his features as he continued. "I can't decide if I should put on my walking shoes and go knocking door to door, or just wait and assume that she'll come along at the appropriate time." He sighed audibly. "Until tonight I was starting to think I might never find someone who was just right for me. Now, having had just a taste of that kind of love, I don't know how I can endure waiting a moment longer."

"I would bet that you'll find her at a time that's exactly right for both of you," Larry surmised.

"You're probably right," Ryan sighed and shook his head. "I should have realized what would happen to me if I found a love in a past-life. Now I won't be able to think about anything else."

"I hate to use a cliche, but anticipation will only make the moment sweeter when you find her. Besides, I can't imagine that fate would toss you this bone too far in advance."

# 12

ALMOST NO ONE MADE EDDIE RAPSKI NERVOUS, BUT WHEN HE looked at his hands, they were shaking visibly, and he knew that dark stains had begun to spread under his armpits. He stared at the phone-message that had thrown him into a panic, and thought back to the one-and-only time he had seen Raymond Baker in person, three years before. His circumstances had changed radically since then. At the time, he had been a pharmaceutical salesman, ranging across northern California, visiting doctor's offices and hospitals to peddle his company's products and hand out free samples. The money was decent. He always paid his rent and owned the pink slip on his well-traveled Mustang. He even kept up with the outrageous alimony payments to his ex-wife. Mostly, he paid his bills on time. But there was precious little left over after the bloodsucking government got their share. At the end of the month, he barely had enough to pay his tab down at the lodge. It was a shitty life, but the lack of money wasn't the worst of it.

Eddie Rapski had been born with a silver tongue — a gift of persuasiveness that made a career in sales a snap. But what he truly loved, his real interest, his *passion,* was to comment on the sad state of society. The country could use a dose of *his* kind of politics: real, God-fearing, right-minded, conservative politics — the kind he had learned hanging around his father's barber shop. Eddie smiled fondly. The old man had dispensed a good measure of his opinion with every haircut. There was nothing complex about his politics — or about Eddie's. They were something a man could sink his teeth into. Right was right and wrong was wrong — how could there be any argument? People called him a bigot, but he didn't give a fuck. They were just a bunch of pussies whose feeble liberal minds couldn't grasp plain common sense. Even at the lodge there were only a few people willing to listen to him long enough for it to do them any good. In the long run, he hadn't been able to convince all those idiots much of anything. And in his opinion, the lodge had gone straight downhill the day that they were forced to let the niggers and the spics in. Not that any niggers or spics had actually joined. There had been one application, but the nigger withdrew it after he found a burning cross on his front lawn. Still, when Eddie and two of his "brothers" did their work, it had been without lodge sanction. The lodge had even denounced the cross burning! *The bastards should have given us a fucking medal for keeping the riffraff out!* he muttered when he thought about it. Instead, people in the lodge had begun to shun *him,* as if they were better than he was! And someone had made an anonymous phone call to his employer and ratted him out. Eddie had been called on the carpet and had to lie like hell just to keep his stinking job as a *commissioned* salesman! After that, he had been afraid to speak his mind at the lodge — and where the hell else was he supposed to exercise his constitutionally guaranteed right of free speech? He had been burning with resentment and aching for a chance to quit his sales job and find something new when Raymond Baker offered him the opportunity of a lifetime.

Eddie had come out of the lodge on a moonless, misty night, half in the bag, and was stumbling out to his car when the big, black Mercedes glided up next to him. Baker was behind the wheel, and when he told Eddie to get into the car to discuss a business proposition, Eddie was torn. Part of him just wanted to get the hell away from this spooky asshole and find a place to take a leak. But his curiosity and frustration — face it, his greed — won out, and he got into the car. They drove around aimlessly on rural roads while Baker told Eddie what he wanted — as if Eddie had a choice. The moment he climbed into that gleaming black Mercedes, the deal had been sealed. He had sold his soul — what little there was to sell. Baker didn't say that he wanted anything special in return — not then, and not since. He just said he wanted Eddie to host a conservative talk-show on his radio station, something Eddie had dreamed about for years! There were no catches, no holds barred. He would be given the freedom to talk about whatever he wanted — forget about being politically correct. Somehow, Baker had become aware of Eddie's views, and he *wanted* to promote them. Deep down though, Eddie knew that there would be a day of reckoning, and he told himself that he was willing to pay the price. If he heard them at all, he ignored the shrieks of fear and regret as his soul plunged into a tortured wasteland.

His salary as a talk-show host was ten times what he had made as a salesman. Of course, that meant that his bitch ex-wife could apply for more alimony — except that her car went over a cliff in a freak accident just three weeks after the Eddie Rapski show went on the air. No alimony, no ex-wife — Eddie felt as light as a feather. Soon he was living in a thirty-six-hundred square foot home with a swimming pool and a huge rec-room complete with pool-table and a full bar on a hill overlooking Ukiah. His high-mileage Mustang made way for a new Corvette, and the most expensive restaurants in the region became his haunts. Those were the perks, but more importantly, he had a soapbox from which to expound his views. And best yet, he had an audience!

Eddie was absolutely convinced of the inherent truth of his message. He had given no real thought to why he was right — why his views *should be implemented to rejuvenate and cleanse society.* The *real* truth, that he was a mean-spirited, small-minded bigot — a buffoon whose ideas, if they were put into effect, would produce a society very much like Nazi Germany — never occurred to him. What endeared Eddie to his loyal listeners, spurred them to action, and struck fear into the hearts of saner souls, was his naive sincerity. His message had tremendous appeal to a growing and very fervent portion of society — skinheads, white supremacists, racists, misogynists — name a prejudice and Rapski twisted it into moral superiority. During his first two years on the air, his market share steadily expanded. Growth went exponential when the show was syndicated, and his message began to spread like a cancerous tumor. All the time, he tried not to think about the unspoken debt he owed Raymond Baker.

It had been easy until tonight — other than the occasional phone call, Baker hadn't made direct contact since that first meeting. Eddie stared down at the phone message again. It was simple enough. All it said was that Baker would be calling him at home to let him know where to meet him, nothing else. Eddie's mind raced through every worst-case scenario he could imagine. He absolutely depended on being in Baker's good graces — one word from *him*, and Eddie would be back on the road, mired in a mundane, meaningless existence. He knew that his radio program had been successful beyond all expectations, but in spite of that, he was scared shitless. *Why would he want to meet with me now? Could he possibly know about my secret? There's no way — I've been too careful. It would be impossible — unthinkable!*

How long had it been since he had indulged himself? Two weeks? Three? It always started with a combination of bewilderment, disgust, anxiety, and overriding everything else, an unimaginably powerful craving. Eddie hated fags and niggers. Hated, hated, hated them, with a passion that ignited some of his most fiery rhetoric. But that didn't mean he could stay away from them . . . especially when the fags *were* niggers. Could anyone have seen him? He sifted through the details — from the moment he had pulled the Corvette across two parking spaces in the parking garage in Sausalito on the north side of the Golden Gate bridge — how else to keep assholes from banging their doors into the sides of his well-polished ride — to the time he returned to his car. He had already used his cell-phone to summon a taxi, and it was waiting out on the street. When he gave the driver the name of a street in the area in San Francisco where the male prostitutes cruised, he had to restrain himself from smacking the asshole when his eyes twitched to his rear-view mirror to check Eddie out. *Fuck him. He doesn't know who I am and I'll never see him again.* He never used the same cab company two times in a row, and so far he hadn't had any repeat drivers — God knew there were thousands of them. He was glad that he was only a radio personality, and that there hadn't been any photo-advertising campaigns blasting his image all over creation. His heart had begun to hammer in his chest with excitement and anticipation as they reached the end of the Golden Gate bridge, and he had a full hard-on by the time they were cruising for one of his "pieces of dark meat."

When he had left the shabby hotel room, he had sworn it would never happen again. But that was a promise he'd never been able to keep. Only his narcissism kept him from hating *himself* for his own hypocrisy. He didn't succumb to his desires that often — five, maybe six times a year. And so far the chameleon-like abilities he had developed during his years as a salesman had allowed him to blend in and kept him safe. *Could Baker know? Could this be the reason why he wants to meet with me?* A nagging thought sprang into Eddie's mind, not for the first time. He had never discovered how Raymond Baker had known to contact him in the first place. Baker had simply appeared like an avenging angel through Eddie's drunken haze. *I can't deny what he's done for me,* he thought, *but he sure doesn't feel much like an angel now.*

When the phone rang he nearly fell out of the chair where he had been fidgeting. His heart seemed to stop when Baker told him to be at the Tripletree Lodge in Santa Rosa at eight o'clock sharp. Eddie looked at his watch. It was six forty-five. He could make it if he left immediately. He hurried outside to his Corvette, threw it into gear, and raced off at a pace that nearly matched his heart-rate.

*    *    *

THE HOTEL SPRAWLED across the slope of a hill that overlooked Highway 101. When Eddie roared up, his stomach was tied in knots. He quickly found the room that Baker had indicated, and when he looked at his watch, saw that he had made it with only a minute and a half to spare. He gave himself every available second to catch his breath, then knocked on the door. Baker's muffled voice, bidding him to enter, made him shudder involuntarily. When he tried to grasp the handle of the door, his hand was so slick with sweat that it slipped and he had to squeeze with all his might to get the knob to turn. The doorway opened into the first room of a suite, set up as a parlor or living room, complete with a wet bar. Raymond Baker sat in shadow at the far end of the room in a wingback chair that faced the door, his face as impassive as stone. Eddie made no attempt to shake Baker's hand or engage in any other pretense that they were anything other than master and servant. "You wanted to see me?" he asked obsequiously.

Baker didn't beat around the bush. "This meeting has several purposes," he said. "First, I want you to know that I recognize that you've done well with your show. So far, you haven't made any serious mistakes."

"Thank you," Eddie said slowly. He was so uncomfortable in Baker's presence that he was just barely able to get the words out past the lump in his throat. He wondered what mistakes he'd made that weren't *serious*.

"Second, I want you to step up your campaign against the environmentalists. Concentrate on the ones that oppose logging."

"No problem," Eddie responded.

"Third, there is the matter of your compensation. You will be receiving a bonus of twenty-five thousand dollars, plus a fifty-percent raise starting immediately."

"Thank you," Eddie responded woodenly, feeling no happiness over his added good fortune. Ever since he had gotten into Baker's car that misty night three years ago, he seemed to have lost the ability to really *enjoy* anything. Even with all of his success, there was little sense of fulfillment. He still hated all of the sick pukes he railed against, but the rest of the time he was numb — except on his trips to San Francisco when a potent cocktail of exhilaration, self-loathing and fear made life interesting.

"Lastly, I have a warning for you," Baker said, rising from his chair and glaring at Eddie ominously. "I don't want you to jeopardize your effectiveness with your listeners by making any more of your forays into San Francisco."

Eddie thought he was going to throw up. He felt like he had been sucker-punched, and he could hardly breathe. *He knew! Baker knew!! What was the purpose of the compliments and the raise when he knew?*

"You're wondering why I have been so generous when I knew what you were up to," said Baker, appearing to read Eddie's mind. "I don't care what you do or who you fuck, or how you *really* feel about what you say on the air — just make sure that you do as I say. You think you've been discreet, but you've just been lucky. From now on, you *will* be discreet." He handed Eddie a piece of paper. "Memorize this phone number, then burn it. Never write the number down! When you're in the mood for one of your little trysts, call the number and leave a message. The next night, come to *this* suite at precisely eight o'clock. Two of your favorite sources of indulgence will be here waiting." He gestured towards the door to the suite's bedroom. "In fact, two are here right now."

This time, Eddie didn't know what to say at all.

"Don't fuck this up, Eddie," Baker said, walking to the door and then turning back to face him once more. "If you do, I can promise you that you'll wish you'd never been born." Abruptly, he turned and left the room, leaving Eddie feeling nauseated. He walked to the wet bar, ripped the plastic off the hotel-cup, poured it full of whiskey and tossed it down neat, thankful for the way it burned his throat — the pain reassured him that he was still alive. But the empty feeling that echoed within him was even more profound than before. He didn't even feel relieved over not having to worry about Baker catching him fucking black queers.

It wasn't until much later that he opened the bedroom door to see what was waiting for him.

# 13

OUT ON HIS SMALL DECK THAT OVERLOOKED THE OCEAN, LARRY had just placed a thermos of hot tea and his new Charles de Lint novel on a small, glass-topped table tucked behind a plexiglass windscreen. He was about to draw up a chair when his phone began to ring. When he answered, Audrey blurted, "Larry, it's been three days since I remembered all those things about my relationship with Steve. Am I supposed to feel better yet?"

"You seemed to be well on your way when we went to dinner," he responded. "Have things taken a turn for the worse?"

"I felt okay the day you did the hypnosis," she allowed. "What you said about forgetting my troubles with Steve and then losing myself in my work to avoid new relationships seemed so obvious. But by the next day I was back to where I was before, and now I'm ... I don't know, maybe two ... three ... I can't tell you how many times more anxious than I was before! I've got this intense feeling that I should be *doing* something, that time is running out. But I have no idea what to do! I went on this vacation *now* because it's slower at Peckham & Associates and Project HOPE than at any other time of the year. Intellectually I know that everything is under control, but emotionally I'm coming unglued. If this is what taking a vacation does to me, I'm going to work straight-through for the rest of my life!"

Larry smiled at Audrey's unintended humor, glad that she couldn't see his face. "It doesn't take much diagnostic ability to say that we didn't hit the mark like we thought," he said. "You certainly wouldn't be getting worse if we had."

"I've been thinking a lot about what you told me about past-life regressions. Could doing one help my anxiety?"

"It can help if a past-life trauma is the cause," Larry affirmed. "Are you considering it?"

"If anyone had told me a week ago that I would be willing to do something so bizarre, I would have told them that they were a lunatic," she said. "But I'd try almost anything to stop feeling the way I do. Besides, ever since you told me about it, its been on my mind, like some kind of weird obsession. I hate to beg, Larry, but could I do one ... soon?"

"I'm not sure that I would call what you're doing 'begging,'" Larry objected.

"Trust me. What you just heard is the closest I ever get to getting down on my knees and groveling — at least when it comes to asking for help with my own personal problems."

"When would you like to get together? I'm available just about any time."

"Are you busy now? This feeling that I need to *do* something is so strong that I'm just going to be pacing around until I take action.

After a fleeting but longing glance at his new de Lint novel, Larry said, "Now is a good time, to tell the truth." He gave her directions to his house, and she arrived twenty minutes later, looking quite distressed, but hopeful, nonetheless. They sat and talked for a few minutes, and when it seemed to Larry that she had relaxed sufficiently to begin, he had her recline in the same chair Ryan had used just a few days before. Her recent experience with hypnosis helped her to achieve a deep trance relatively quickly.

This time, he had her walk through a beautiful, pristine valley, and come to a clear, shallow river with a firm, sandy bottom. "Walk across the river as I count to ten," he instructed. "When you come to the other side, you'll be in a past-life." He waited a few moments. "Where are you, what do you look like, and what are you wearing?" he asked.

"I'm in some kind of tent — a tepee, I think. I'm nursing my baby. He's a beautiful little boy." Audrey's voice had lost all suggestion of the anxiety that had been consuming her, and was filled with awe as she experienced the joy of mother-hood for the first time — without the usual preparation of pregnancy. "My baby has black hair and dark skin. I have dark skin and black hair too. It's very long, and it's plaited into two braids that hang past my shoulders. I'm naked, except that I'm covered with a buffalo robe. I see clothing made of buckskin folded and ready for me to wear. I am Oglala Sioux."

Larry was startled by the similarity between Audrey's regression and the one Ryan had experienced just days before. He couldn't remember a time when two subjects in a row had regressed to such comparable lifetimes.

"Is there anyone there with you,?" he asked.

"My husband's mother is here. She is a mother to me, too. She raised me after my own mother died. Her son — my husband — is several years older than I am. I have always loved him, and he has always loved me. As soon as I was old enough, we were married. The shaman, his wife and his daughter are here also. They have taken care of me through my pregnancy."

"Do you recognize either of them as being anyone you know in this life?" Larry asked.

"I can visualize my husband's face, but I don't recognize him or the shaman's daughter . . . or the one who is my mother-in-law," she replied. "But my baby is Adam, Adam Gray from Project HOPE . . . and the shaman is . . . you!"

Larry suddenly knew with complete certainty that the life to which Audrey had regressed would end horribly when a regiment of U.S. Army soldiers wiped out all of the inhabitants of the encampment. He was almost tempted to stop the session, but knew that if there were lessons for Audrey to learn, she had to experience the painful, devastating losses that were about to occur — in her life as a plains Indian and perhaps in another life in the Warsaw ghetto to follow. With resignation, he continued his questioning.

"Where is your husband?"

"He is with the others — they have gone to hunt buffalo. The herd is only one day from here. They've been gone for three days now. They should be back very soon." She began to speak happily and excitedly. "He left before our baby was born. I can't wait to see the look on his face when he sees that I have brought him a son! He will be so pleased."

Larry gritted his teeth, and asked her to go to the next significant event. She described the sudden thunder of horses' hooves, and her terror at the sound of gunfire. Then she was running, still naked, with her baby clutched to her breast after her tepee had been set on fire. She died horribly, as a yellow-haired soldier rode her down and ran her through with a saber. The baby was immediately trampled to death under the steel-shod hooves of her killer's mount. Afterwards, she and the soul that would become Adam Gray floated above their bodies as Audrey described the familiar spiritual light encountered by nearly all of his patients. Then, as Ryan had before her, she entered a life in Nazi-occupied Poland — this time, as a man living in the Warsaw ghetto — a soldier with a very young lover who would have been his wife if there had been a rabbi to perform the ceremony — a life where she died of smoke inhalation just before the body she occupied in that lifetime was consumed by fire. When she reached the twilight in-between once more, Audrey described herself as being surrounded by the spirits of those who loved her. "They are talking to me," she said. "They say that we must fight hate and fear with love. Only love is real, all else is illusion. We are never separated by death. Those who have died either join us in other bodies, or watch over us like angels. When we encounter the one who embodies pure evil, we must not lower ourselves to his level. We must approach him with love in our hearts. The power of hate ultimately turns against the one who wields it. Those who succumb to fear and hatred must return lifetime after lifetime. People can only grow when they allow themselves to be guided by love in everything they do."

Larry would have been astounded by what she was saying just a short while ago. Now, it only confirmed that she must be one of the companions the advanced spirits told him would join him in conflict with *The One without a Soul*.

Afterwards, they sat in front of Larry's woodstove sipping chamomile tea while Audrey, visibly calmer now, pondered her past-life experiences. The flames visible through the glass doors of the stove flowed in a strange, liquid dance that illuminated their faces with a soft orange light in the dimly lit room. "Those lives were filled with terrible horror and ultimate joy at the same time," she mused. "I've never experienced the kind of happiness that I felt with my newborn child. It was different than the love I had for my husband." She looked at Larry with a mischievous grin. "Adam was much, much cuter then than he turned out to be in this life!"

Larry chuckled, pleased that Audrey had regained her sense of humor. Adam Gray was one of the kindest, most generous and reasonable souls either of them had ever known. But his tall lanky body and over-sized features could never be described as handsome. He wasn't *quite* ugly, but he came awfully close.

"Now that I've experienced my soul-mate's essence, I can see why things never worked out with Steve, or anyone else." she said thoughtfully. "I'm feeling much better now, too — I can feel my anxiety melting away more and more each minute! This past-life therapy must be what I was supposed to do." A look of determination settled across her features. "Now, I've just got to find him."

As soon as Audrey had finished speaking, she had a flash of intuition. She acted on it immediately, speaking brusquely, "Spill the beans, Larry. Where have you got Mr. Wonderful stashed?"

"Wha . . wha.. what are you talking about?" Larry stammered, blushing furiously, completely flustered by her sudden, stern accusatory tone, not to mention the fact that he had been trying to think of a way to introduce the two of them without violating his professional ethics.

"You're not the only one with psychological training around here," she said. "We're both in the detective business, and we both do our detecting in other people's heads. *You* were in one of those lives, and you've probably been back to them yourself — or maybe you took somebody else. And you've been unusually quiet — like the cat who swallowed the canary. I bet you've got a secret that you're just dying to tell. So spill the beans — just when were you planning to give me and Mr. Wonderful the chance to meet each other?"

Sometimes Larry forgot how direct Audrey could be. He briefly struggled with the ethics of the situation and decided that if both Audrey and Ryan agreed, he could introduce them. "Assuming that you're correct in your analysis, I would have to get his permission," he said carefully.

"Does Mr. Wonderful know that he has a soul-mate?" she pumped.

"Audrey, I can't even tell you if such a person exists, let alone tell you something like that!"

She rose from her chair and crossed her arms. "I'm going to go outside to look at the ocean," she said. "Perhaps you could make a phone call or two and find out if Mr. Wonderful exists, and if so, whether or not he wants to talk to me . . . no, don't say a word, I know what the ethical rules require. I'll be there until you come for me. I won't see you phone, if that's what you intend to do, okay?"

Without waiting for a reply, she went outside, across the deck and down the three steps to the path that led to the edge of the bluffs, where she stood with her arms clasped across her chest while the cold breeze coming in off the ocean tousled her hair. She listened to the crash of the waves against the rocks below for less than a minute before she heard footsteps behind her. She turned find Larry holding out his portable phone with the mouthpiece covered. "His name is Ryan Stratton," he said. "I mentioned him to you the other day. He's one of the friends I've made here in the last couple of weeks. He's at home, just five miles from here. He regressed to the same two lives that you just did three nights ago, and he's *very* anxious to meet you."

He handed the phone to Audrey, who took a big breath, and then slowly let it out before speaking. "Hello, Ryan," she said, as a tear ran down her cheek. "My name is Audrey Peckham. We've never met, at least not recently — but the last time we were with each other, my name was Jurgen, and yours was Marga . . ."

# 14

RYAN'S HEART WAS BEATING SO HARD HE THOUGHT IT MIGHT jump out of his chest. He had been telling Doug about having found a soul-mate in a past-life, and that Doug and Pam had been there and seemed to be soul-mates too.

"I could have told you that," Doug had replied, "even though I'm still not buying into reincarnation like you are." Then he added, "It's becoming harder to hold on to my skepticism with all that's been going on lately. But I *do* believe in soul-mates. Pam and I clicked from the moment we met."

Then the phone had rung, and within a minute, incredibly, impossibly, he was talking to his soul-mate for the first time — at least in this life. He gave her directions to his house and slowly put the phone back into its cradle, feeling suddenly shy and apprehensive.

"What in the world was that about?" asked Doug. "You're as nervous as a drop of water on a hot griddle."

"You wouldn't believe me if I told you," Ryan replied. "I don't even believe it."

"After all of the crazy things that have been happening around here the last few weeks, almost nothing would surprise me. Somebody is obviously on their way over — who is it?"

"She said her name was Audrey," said Ryan. "She's a friend of Larry's, and I think we're probably going to get married."

"What? Okay, I take it back . . . I deserved that one. Seriously, who was it?"

Ryan's expression was dreamy as he was momentarily taken back to the love he had experienced during his past-life regression. Then he snapped back to the present, where he found Doug waiting for an answer with a look of consternation that abruptly turned into one of enlightenment. "You're not talking about the one from when you were hypnotized?" His eyes opened a bit wider as Ryan nodded mutely. "And she's on her way over, right now?" Again, Ryan nodded without saying a word. Doug hooted, jumped up from his chair, and grabbed Ryan in a bear hug. "When will she be here?" he demanded.

"Just a few minutes," Ryan answered. "She was at Larry's — she said she'd be right over."

"Then I'm out of here, pal. The last thing you need is to have your old buddy Doug hanging around when you meet the love of your life." He opened the door and took one last look back, shaking his head. "I can't wait for Pam to get home. She's going to go wild over this!"

Before Ryan could say another word, Doug was gone. Just a few minutes later, he heard an engine and the crunch of gravel under a car's tires. The summer evening was still young, and it would be an hour or more before the sun went down. He opened his front door to find an attractive thirty-ish woman whose hair fell to her shoulders in soft, brown curls, climbing out of a red Volvo. They walked towards each other slowly, with tentative smiles on their faces. When Audrey stepped shyly up to him, he gently embraced her. After a few moments they broke apart, continuing to face each other and hold each others hands. Ryan was the first to speak. "I'm torn between saying how nice it is to meet you, asking you how you've been since we were in that crawl-space in Warsaw, or trying to describe the incredible love I've felt ever since I found out about you."

"I don't know how to act, either," said Audrey. "My rational mind is screaming at me, telling me that this is foolishness and fantasy. How could there be *anything* between us, let alone love? We're meeting *right now* for the very first time! I never knew until an hour ago that you even existed . . . but now that we're here, it seems as if I've been waiting for you my entire life." She smiled quickly. "I can think of worse dilemmas."

"That's exactly how I feel," said Ryan. "Except that I've always hoped that someone special was waiting for me. I even wrote a song about it — I'll sing it for you some time if you like."

"I think I *would* like that," she replied. "Larry described you as a poet and musician who happens to practice law for a living."

He smiled. "I can't really find much wrong with that description. I spend more time practicing law, but music is what sustains me."

Ryan suddenly realized that they hadn't moved an inch since their first embrace. "I'm not being much of a host," he said. "Would you like to come inside? Maybe we could start getting to know each other by comparing what we remember from our past lives. We can see how similar our memories are."

"That sounds fine to me," she replied, letting go of one of his hands as he led her into the house.

"This place is charming!" she exclaimed, as they entered the living room with its view of the deck outside and the redwoods, pines and hemlocks in the draw. A quick tour of the house took only a few minutes, and then Ryan put water on the stove for tea before leading her out to the deck. As their conversation ebbed and flowed, they grew more comfortable, and before long, were laughing and talking animatedly, thoroughly enjoying each other's company. Audrey gave Ryan a brief history of her past few years — her private therapy practice, and her consulting work with school districts. When she described Project HOPE and how important saving the old-growth forests had become, it seemed to Ryan that the glow of her personality burned most brightly. He, in turn, told her about growing up in Sacramento, going to school and working there before moving to the coast. When the fog drifted in, they moved inside and sat in front of a fire that Ryan built in his woodstove. As they told stories, talked of goals and aspirations and simply reminisced, they laughed often. Before long they punctuated what they were saying with gestures that ended with a touch, then a caress, and finally, with a kiss. Together for the first time, they were also swept away by a deep, abiding love that had blossomed and flourished over the course of many, many lifetimes, adding depth and richness to every nuance of expression. Kisses and caresses quickly fueled a passion that was far beyond anything either one of them had ever experienced, as love took over completely. Not long afterwards, their clothes lay in a tangled pile on the floor as they made tender love that seemed to be the physical expression of the binding of their souls.

Later, they went upstairs to Ryan's bedroom, where he found Audrey a long sleeve flannel shirt to wear. Ryan threw on a pair of shorts and a sweatshirt and when they came downstairs, he put more wood in the stove. They sat on the couch, watching the amber glow of the fire through the stove's glass door, their arms and legs entwined, while the music from a David Wilcox CD poured softly from the Celestion speakers. Audrey reached up and stroked the hollow of Ryan's cheek with the back of her index finger. "What are you thinking?" she asked.

"Right now, I was thinking that I've always wanted to get married and raise a bunch of kids," he said. "I don't know squat about the 'raising kids' part, but I do know that I want to grow old with someone I love."

Audrey snuggled up under his arm. "Is that a proposal?" she asked, her smile an invitation.

He pulled her closer to him and kissed her tenderly. "If I think about it, it seems like it's way too soon. But being with you feels so *right!*" He brought her fingers to his lips and kissed them lightly. "I can't imagine *not* spending the rest of my life with you." He rose from the couch and took a step towards the wall where his guitar cases were lined up in a row. "I know this isn't the traditional way to propose, but I do have something that's been waiting for you," he said as he started to reach for his Olson guitar. Then looked back. "At least, now I know that you're the one it's been waiting for." He sat down next to her and began to fingerpick some introductory notes. "It's a song I wrote that I've never sung to anyone else — I hoped that some day I'd have a chance to sing it for someone — the *one* I was waiting for. That person is *you*, Audrey." He leaned over and kissed her again. "I can hardly believe this is happening. Nothing could have prepared me for the way I'm feeling right now. I love you so much, it almost hurts." He felt like he was diving into a bottomless pool as he looked into her eyes and sang the words that had sprung from his heart's desire.

> *The wonder of it all, it seems*
> *Comes floating down life's endless streams*
> *Of possibilities that ripple through*
> *The melody of me and you*
> *And while we walk on golden paths*
> *Delighting in everything we pass*

*All the while, we'll listen to*
*The melody of me and you*

*Me and you, how good it sounds*
*Me and you, love, how good it feels*
*You're the person I care about*
*I know your love is real*

*Now the time has come along*
*The two of us shall be as one*
*A harmony will be written to*
*The melody of me and you*
*We take good heed of all we pass*
*This love of ours is going to last*
*We'll sing together our whole lives through*
*The melody of me and you*

*Me and you, it's a growing thing*
*Me and you love, what will the future bring?*
*Whatever songs we sing, whatever we do*
*You know that I love you*

*And that's something I'll always do*
*Through any crisis we pass through*
*You know that I'll be listening to*
*The melody of me and you*
*There's nothing can tear us apart*
*No hesitation in our hearts*
*The melody is in a symphony*
*And as it unfolds, we can plainly see*
*Ever growing it will always be*

He put his guitar down, took her in his arms, and even though he knew it was impossible, tried to express everything he felt in one kiss. "I'm yours, if you'll have me," he said when it finally ended.

"Our souls were made for each other," she replied, "The answer is yes, and there's *no* hesitation in my heart."

Later that night they lay snuggled together. Her back was to him and they fit like spoons, his arm wrapped around her, holding one of her hands. He buried his nose in the tumble of hair that cascaded down the back of her neck and breathed in her delicious scent. His heart was full, and he was filled with wonder as he thought of the words of his song that he'd sung to himself a few days before, which now appeared to have miraculously come true.

*I know that I will find the someone waiting out there for me*
*The one whose thoughts are close to mine, she's waiting out there for me*
*She'll be the one I care about and it will be so fine*
*The flow of life will turn about, and we will start the climb . . .*


He still knew so little about her. They had talked for hours, but had only scratched the surface. Yet during their lovemaking he had experienced a depth of feeling and emotion that had left him breathless — a bonding that resonated through every fiber of his body. Audrey had drifted into an easy slumber just after one in the morning, but although the bright red digits of his clock showed that it was past two, Ryan was still awake. Eventually, he slept, but before he did, a thought seemed to come from out of nowhere. *Things in life usually tend to balance themselves out . . . but it would take a huge disaster to offset the happiness I'm feeling right now.*

# 15

THE NEXT MORNING, AUDREY WAS THE FIRST TO WAKE. SHE slipped out of bed without disturbing Ryan, wrapped herself in a terry-cloth robe she found hanging on a hook, and tiptoed softly down to the kitchen, where coffee had been made the night before, with a timer set to brew in the morning. She poured herself a cup and wandered into the living room, noting the stacks of instruments in their cases. She had taken piano lessons as a child, and when she was dating Steve, he had shown her enough chords on the guitar to play a few songs. But since Steve's flings with other women invariably started while he was playing a gig, she had developed an indifference to all things musical. *Time to exorcize that demon*, she thought to herself. *Things didn't work out with Steve because I was meant to be with Ryan.* She was suddenly stunned by some of the superficial similarities between the two men. They were both lawyers in private practice. Both were musicians, who played guitar and sang. *I wonder if Ryan is into bicycles the way Steve was?* Opening the sliding glass door, she stepped outside and sat on a bench that overlooked the draw. Breathing deeply of the fresh, crisp air, she watched the morning light filtering through the trees. It was quiet enough that she could hear the faint roar of the surf two miles distant. A short while later, Ryan joined her, his own cup of coffee in hand. He stood behind her and gently stroked the side of her face. She reached back and brought his hand to her lips, kissing his fingers, then tilted her head so that he cupped the side of her face in the palm of his hand. Neither of them said anything for a few moments, watching as a Stellar's jay landed on a nearby branch and scolded them thoroughly before flitting off through the trees.

"It's real, isn't it," said Ryan after a bit. "When you weren't in bed, I thought it all might have been a dream. But then I saw your clothes on the chair, and was able to reassure myself."

"It had better be real," Audrey smiled up at him. "I've been sitting here wondering how we're going to work out the details of putting two separate lives in two separate towns together."

Ryan put his hands on her shoulders, gently kneading them.

"I'm finding it really hard to think about practical things like that right now," he said and then leaned down to kiss her. "This deck is still a virgin," he went on, undoing the sashes on their robes. "I've got a very comfortable futon and a blanket just inside the door." A few moments later, she said, "I don't think this deck is going to stay a virgin much longer."

As they lay entwined, savoring the afterglow of their lovemaking, knowing that the "I" and the "thou" had become "we," the phone rang. Doug was on the other end of the line when Ryan went inside to answer it. "You better get yourself ready to come over or you're going to have some visitors," he said. "I sneaked over and made sure her car was still there — what was her name again?"

"Audrey," replied Ryan.

"Right — Audrey — got it. Anyway, I sneaked over to make sure that Audrey's car was still there. It is, of course, and frankly, I can't restrain Pam any longer! I told her that you found this past-life love, and that just as you were telling me about her, she called you on the phone and wanted to come over. Help me out, Ryan — I practically had to tie her up to keep her from calling you before now."

Ryan laughed at Doug's theatrics. Pam's sense of decorum made most of what he said highly unlikely. "I'll tell you what," he offered. Just give us a little time to make ourselves presentable, and then we'll be right over, okay?"

On the deck, Audrey had risen from the futon and put her robe back on. She looked at him questioningly as he joined her.

"That was my best friend and neighbor, Doug. He was here when you called, but beat it out of here in a flash to give us the chance to be alone when we met. He and his wife Pam are dying to meet you." He looked concerned. "I promised we'd be over in half an hour — I should have asked. Do you want to go?"

"Of course I do," she replied. "And if we both take a shower at the same time, we can take twice as long and be just as efficient."

Half an hour later, they walked the short distance to Doug and Pam's house. It was girdled by a large sun-drenched deck that faced a fenced clearing where a garden had been planted in raised beds. On the deck, a table was arrayed with a tray of cut fruit, muffins, coffee and orange juice. Pam and Doug rose from their chairs as Audrey and Ryan walked towards them, hand in hand. Pam came down the steps and greeted Audrey with a sisterly embrace. Audrey hugged her closely, then studied her at arm's length. "It's so good to see you . . . again." she faltered, sounding as awkward as she felt. "I recognize you from yesterday's session with Larry. You were so kind to me in that lifetime."

Pam's blank expression spoke volumes.

Audrey turned to Doug. "I thought Ryan said he told you about the lives we all lived together — that both of you were there with us."

"He did, he did," said Doug. "I just got so excited by your phone call that I completely forgot to tell Pam that *we* were there, too. You have to forgive me — this is all a bit over my head. It's hard to look at it as more than just a fantasy."

"Believe me, I was there yesterday, myself," Audrey laughed. "I've known Larry for years, but I only found out that most of his professional practice had to do with hypnosis and past-life regressions a few days ago." She looked up at Ryan and gave him a smile before continuing. "Ryan and I compared notes on our past-life experiences. We had virtually the same memories, albeit from two different points of view. In one life, we were Oglala Sioux. My father was killed when I was small, and my mother died a short time later. I was taken in by Ryan's mother." She looked at Pam. "Larry was a Shaman, and you were his daughter. I have a specific memory of the two of you together. You were a medicine woman."

"That might explain the way I feel about him," said Pam. "We've only met once, but there was an instant bond. It felt like I'd known him forever."

Audrey turned to Doug. "I recognize you, as well. You and Pam were husband and wife in that life, too. If you have the same kind of relationship with Pam that I've discovered with Ryan, you're a very lucky man!"

Pam put her hands on her hips, and glared at Doug in mock anger. "If Ryan told you that we were married in a past life and you didn't tell me, you're in big trouble!"

"Ah, but you'll forgive him when you hear what he said," interrupted Ryan. "When I told him that the two of you had been married in that life, and were probably soul-mates, he said that he could have told me that the two of you had been together before — that your connection was far too strong to have been forged in just one lifetime." Ryan grinned at Pam. "That's a pretty strong statement from a guy who doesn't even believe in reincarnation."

"In that case, I guess I can forgive him, then." Pam said, and then reached for Doug's hand. Half seriously, she leaned close to him and said, "We're really missing the boat here, honey. Everybody else is finding all these amazing connections, and we're completely in the dark. Why don't we do it too."

Doug glanced away, and the moment grew awkward. "I don't really know why I'm so reluctant," he finally replied. "I know that Gayle, Ryan and now Audrey all seem to have had beneficial experiences. But that doesn't make me chomp at the bit." He gave her a sidelong glance. "Even if we had the same experience that they did, I'd probably think that we were either experiencing mass hysteria, or that we were all suffering from the same mental defect." Pam immediately punched him in the arm and in a stage whisper muttered that he should behave himself when they had company.

The four of them made their way to the table where the brunch Doug and Pam had prepared was spread, complete with white table-cloth. After they filled their plates, Pam reached over and took Audrey's hand. "Doug tells me that congratulations are in order. But are you sure about this? I mean, I know about the past-life connection and all, but isn't getting engaged the day you meet still a little hasty?"

Audrey glanced at Ryan, looking perplexed. "When did you have the chance to tell them? I heard your conversation on the phone with Doug this morning — you didn't tell him then, and we've been together the rest of the time."

"I think I can clear this little mystery up," Doug chuckled. "When Audrey called last night, I asked him who it was. His answer blew me away, and so I told Pam. I quote: 'She said her name is Audrey. She's a friend of Larry's, and I think we're probably going to get married.'"

"This was even more impetuous than I realized," said Pam. She turned to Ryan. "You obviously *did* ask her — and she's accepted . . . and you knew that you wanted to marry her before you even met her? When you'd never even seen her — only talked to her long enough to give her directions to your house? I can't *believe* what I'm hearing."

"If you had experienced what I did when I was hypnotized, you'd understand," replied Ryan, taking Audrey's hand. "The love I felt was more powerful than anything I had ever experienced." He laughed. "But the lawyer in me will remind you that I only said I would *probably* marry her. I didn't actually propose until I'd known her for *at least* three hours!"

"I know it sounds completely crazy," Audrey joined in, "and if it was happening to anyone else, I'd be giving them an earful of advice about 'waiting to get to know each other,' and 'not jumping in too deep, too fast.' But I don't have any doubts at all." She squeezed Ryan's hand. "I know we're going to have to spend some time apart. My work is in Healdsburg, and it's too far for commuting to be practical. But I'm sure we'll work things out." She gave Ryan another smile. "We'll find a way for both of us to do the things that we love, and still be together."

"I hadn't even started to think about all the driving," said Ryan, looking stricken. "I don't think my old Caravan is going to like spending that much time on highway 128 at all. Maybe I'll have to get something that handles the curves a little better."

Pam laughed. "I've never met a guy who wasn't looking for an excuse to get a sports car," she said. "Just remember, you've still got to be able to carry your guitars and your bike." She turned back to Audrey. "Tell us a little bit about yourself — we know more about who you used to be than who you are now."


"I TAKE BACK everything I said," Pam laughed after Audrey had given them a brief history. "After hearing just the little you've told us, I can see that you and Ryan are a perfect fit. The past-life connection is just icing on the cake. Now, if you can put up with the kind of music that he and Doug play, and if your idea of a good time is a mountain bike ride . . . "

Audrey chuckled. "I haven't done too much cycling, but I'm willing to try it." She squeezed Ryan's hand. "And I *really* liked the one song I've heard so far. I'll find out more at this jam session I keep hearing about. I'm really looking forward to meeting Gayle, by the way. Ryan told me that he recognized her as being his mother in our lives as Oglala Sioux, which would make her my stepmother in that lifetime."

"Speaking of Gayle, did either of you think of giving her, or for that matter, Larry, a call to let them know what's been happening with our two lovebirds here?" asked Doug. When Ryan and Audrey shook their heads negatively, he went inside and came back with a cordless phone. Ryan called Larry first, and told him about the instant romance.

"He said he feels like Yente the Matchmaker from *Fiddler on the Roof*," Ryan reported after he rang off. "And he said that he'd meet us at the jam session." He dialed Gayle next. She answered on the third ring. Ryan told her he had a surprise for her. "It's a long story," he said, "but in a nutshell, I've discovered that you're my mom as well as my sister. And things have been proceeding at a rapid pace around here — I've fallen madly in love with your step-daughter — we're going to be married. We thought we'd come over to get your blessing." He grinned, knowing how ridiculous he sounded.

"Ryan, you're not making any sense at all," Gayle scolded. Then she paused, and said "Oh my God. You found your love from a past-life! I bet you fell head over heels with each other the moment you met."

Ryan was dumfounded. "How could you have known?" he asked.

"I didn't until just now — but Ryan, you know how I've always been a little bit psychic?"

"Sure."

"It's getting stronger — for the past two or three days, half the time I've known what people were going to say before they started talking — it's really weird. But that's getting off the subject, Buster. How long have I been out of the loop this time?"

Ryan laughed. "Relax 'Sis,' or 'Mom,' or whoever you are. We met last night at eight o'clock. All we've done this morning is have brunch with Pam and Doug. This is honestly the first chance I've had to tell you . . . well, we did call Larry first. But we're all coming over to your store just as soon as we can get organized, and you'll be able to meet her."

Ryan looked over at Audrey. "I hope I'm not rushing things for you — I'm just so proud and excited, I can't wait to introduce you."

"Are you kidding?" she replied. "Don't forget, I already know her soul from when we were Oglala Sioux. I can't wait to see her again! I've been having a terrible time for two weeks, walking around with this anxious feeling that something was supposed to be happening. Now it's happening — I'm in love and meeting old friends for the first time. I feel like celebrating!"

While they finished their brunch, they shared bits of their histories with each other for a while longer, then Audrey and Ryan walked back to his place to load some instruments into the car. Ryan carefully stowed his old Martin D-18 and a binder full of his favorite songs into the trunk of Audrey's Volvo. He couldn't help staring at her as they drove down Road 409 to Highway One. Audrey glanced over at him, and then back at the road.    "I still can't get over it either," she said, glancing at the clock in the dashboard of her Volvo. "Yesterday at this time I was wrestling with myself about whether or not to call Larry and tell him how bad I was still feeling. It hasn't even been a *day* and my entire life has changed! I'm so happy I can hardly stand it. I just hope these good feelings last for a while — they're certainly overdue!"

*     *     *

LARRY SMILED AS he put down the phone. Even though he told himself that fate would have brought these two together sooner rather than later, he was still tickled by the role he'd played. Nonetheless, his pleasure was tinged with apprehension.

Difficult times were coming, and he wondered, *How long before things turn nasty?*

An hour later, he pointed his Subaru Legacy towards Highway One, and turned north and crossed the bridge over Noyo Harbor where the local fishing fleet rode at anchor. Fort Bragg had once been a major fishing town, but the catch was way down from what it had been in the past. Commercial fishing was yet another casualty of ecologically unsound forestry practices that had gone unchecked for generations. At first, no one had known the effect that the highly erosive logging practices would have on local fisheries — that the salmon and steelhead population in the Pacific would be decimated, as streams and rivers became warmer from their exposure to the sun, and silt covered their spawning beds. The problem had resulted from the massive amount of earth-moving and excavation, not to mention the denuded hillsides the loggers left behind. In the early days of logging, berms of soft earth had been mounded up to provide a soft landing for the huge redwoods, to keep the brittle wood from splintering when they fell. Even after scientists discovered the connection between logging and the decline of the salmon population, politicians had been horrendously slow to act. Perhaps the timber industry had a stronger lobby than the fishing industry. Or maybe the legislature just couldn't fathom what to do when a band-aid solution wouldn't work. *The environment is far more sensitive than people realize — the web of all creation is affected when a single strand is pulled,* Larry mused, as he pulled into a parking space near the Eclectic Attic. *But we can only perceive the strand we're pulling at the time. Usually we don't listen when someone halfway across the web starts complaining about the effects of our actions — we don't believe that what they're complaining about is even possible until it's too late.*

The others had arrived before him, and were engaged in a lively conversation in the area where the jam sessions took place. He noted that Audrey and Gayle had found each other, and had their heads together. Doug, who had seen Larry come in, intercepted him and gestured to the two women. "They're 'renewing' their relationship," he said conspiratorially, "You would have thought that Gayle had already experienced this 'Plains Indian' life everybody keeps referring to. She takes to everybody who comes into her store like a long-lost relative anyway, but the way she and Audrey have hit it off is uncanny. Maybe they really *were* together in a past life."

"Probably a lot more than just one," Larry replied. "We're talking about eternity here, Doug. We go through many, many lives before we reach the level of the advanced spirits. In the meantime, here we are, together, time and time again."

Just then Ryan noticed Larry, and beckoned to him. Gayle and Audrey both rose from the couch as he walked their way. Audrey was the first to greet him, saying, "Larry, I don't know if I can thank you enough." She and Gayle took turns giving him a hug, before she continued. "Ryan and I are just as much in love as we were in those past lives, and now that I've found Gayle, I feel — how can I explain it — *complete*, for the first time since . . . well, maybe for the first time *ever*."

"You and Ryan had no choice but to find each other," he objected. "It may seem like I'm the one who made things happen. But I'm only a tool that fate used to bring you together.

A strange expression crossed Gayle's face. She said, "You know, I've been getting a feeling that this is all leading to something big, and its going to happen soon. It's not just all of the odd things that have been happening lately — there's more. There's something that's just beyond the edge of what I can perceive. But I can sure feel it — Hell, I can almost see and touch it! She looked around at all of them. "I don't want to cast a pall over things, but these feelings are coming with a strong sense of foreboding."

Ryan walked over to Audrey and put his arms around her. "The past-lives we experienced might give us a clue," he said. "I'd bet money that the bastard I put an arrow through — the same one who ended up torching us in Warsaw — is the source of the cloud you feel on your horizon. If he was there in our two consecutive lives, he could be in this one too. Is something going to happen right away?"

Gayle closed her eyes and concentrated.

*It's beginning,* thought Larry. *Audrey, Ryan, Pam and even our skeptic Doug are all casually accepting this psychic phenomenon as if it were commonplace! It's just as the advanced spirits said it would be!*

"No — whatever is out there isn't focused yet — it's still forming," said Gayle after she opened her eyes. "So let's concentrate on the wonderful things that are happening right now!" Then she shook her finger at Ryan and Doug. "And speaking of wonderful things, I haven't heard a note of music from either one of you since you arrived. Let's hear something before I have you arrested for loitering."


Ryan and Audrey left the jam session early, saying that they needed to continue getting to know each other, and it wasn't too much later that the rest of the musicians and spectators had packed up their things and drifted off, leaving Gayle and Larry alone in the store. "We've got a lot of catching up to do, Larry," Gayle said after the last one had departed. "My friend Linda works for me here part time, and she'll be over in a few minutes to start her shift. Do you have some time? I've been getting a strong feeling all day that we need to talk . . . are you up for a walk on the beach?"

"Nothing would suit me better," Larry replied. "Do you have a place in mind?"

"Why don't we drive up to Cleone and walk down to MacKerricher Beach State Park and back? That should give us plenty of time to talk, and we can check out the seal colony. I haven't been out on the point to watch them for quite some time."

They were soon on the beach, which stretched more than a mile back to the park. They strolled along on the firm sand as the ice-cold Pacific Ocean surged in and out next to them. Larry was momentarily lost in thought, mesmerized by the action of the surf. *The waves crashing on the beach form an almost perfect metaphor for reincarnation,* he reflected as he watched the breakers rush up onto the beach and slide out again. *The advanced spirits say that we are all one — just as the ocean is one body of water. The individual waves are distinct, yet they're all a part of the same body of water. Each wave is filled with its own energy, yet subject to the influence of all the other waves. When a wave reaches the shore the energy is dissipated, and the water rushes back, where it is filled with new energy, time and time again.* He came out of his reverie, when he realized that Gayle had asked him a question. "I'm sorry, I drifted off there for a moment," he apologized. "What did you say?"

"I had the strangest experience when Audrey was telling me about the past lives she and Ryan experienced," Gayle repeated. She stopped for a moment and stared out as a huge wave broke against a jagged rock, sending a great flume of spray arching through the air. The rock completely disappeared as the crest of the wave surged over it, and then emerged through the rushing water as it sluiced down in a three-hundred-sixty degree waterfall. "When she was describing things, I *knew* exactly where they had been — as if I had been there too." She turned back to Larry. "I've always found it fascinating to study the ways that people express their spirituality. But even when I felt the *most* connected, those rituals were simply that — the *expressions* of the people who were doing the rituals. Now, there's something happening to me that's never happened before. I believe that I'm finally, actually, on the receiving end of *real* input from the spiritual plane." Her expression became more earnest. "To quote Wayne Dyer, I've always considered myself to be *a spiritual being having a human experience*, but to have my spirituality become such an actual, concrete part of my daily experience . . . I don't know if I'm ready."

"I don't think you're going to have much choice in the matter, nor will I," Larry responded. "You and I have both been preparing for what is happening to us for a very long time — not just during our present lifetimes, but over the course of many lifetimes."

As they reached the park and climbed a stairway leading from the beach to a parking lot, they walked in companionable silence, each with their own thoughts. A raised wooden walkway which had been built to protect sensitive native grasses lead out to the point. At the end of the walkway, a platform facilitated the viewing of the colony of harbor seals that congregated there, sunning themselves on the rocks and swimming through the tide-pools. As they approached the platform, Larry came to the sudden realization that he had to reel in his analytical side and completely abandon the role of therapist. He had to stop being the one who asked the questions and then listened passively while others confided their deepest feelings, supplying them with the answers to their problems as if he was an all-knowing font of knowledge. Gayle was clearly the *other* besides himself who would be privy to the true nature of the conflict. If the two of them were going to work as closely together as he thought they were, it had to be as equals. He had to be as upfront with her as it was clear she was being with him. That meant changing long-entrenched habits, breaking down barriers that had been painstakingly constructed as he trained for his profession. Fortunately, as his practice had gravitated to one devoted almost exclusively to past-life therapy, his own spiritual connection had been enhanced and strengthened. Every time he was presented with additional evidence of the immortality of the soul, his outlook on life had been subtly changed. On a personal level, he had become more at peace with himself, willing to allow himself to simply *be human,* not the God-like icon that society demanded medical doctors to be. Still, the processes necessary to *be the therapist* remained firmly in place. He had slipped naturally back into the role of the therapist with Gayle when he led her through her past-life regression, but now he had to jettison his unconscious one-upmanship completely.

They reached the platform at the end of the raised wooden walkway, and climbed down to the rocks below. Gayle pointed out a spot that was sheltered from the rising wind. As they watched the swirling action of the water in the tide-pools where seals swam, looking like whiskered old men, Larry ventured, "I think I can help you understand some of the things you've been experiencing." *Look at what I just said — I automatically put myself in a position of dominance just by the way I structured my sentence.* Silently, he took a moment to ask the universe for help. He had no idea who or what God, or god or goddess or however people wanted to describe the divine was, but he did know with absolute certainty that there was *something* out there. And he knew that a part of that *something* could be found in himself. He called on that *something* to help him be who and what he needed to be in order to make the changes that he knew would be necessary. "Let me tell you about what has been happening to me this week," he said after a moment. "I've had some communications which are similar to the ones I had during my patient Keith's regressions — I was told that there will be an immense struggle, and that only two of us will be aware of what is going on . . . "

Gayle reached out suddenly, taking one of his hands in hers, her eyes wide. "We need both hands," she said, reaching for his other hand, then, more urgently, "Close your eyes." As soon as he did, Larry was filled with an awareness of what he and Gayle had been to each other over time, as if memories hidden behind a series of veils were successively revealed. Larry had been a powerful presence in each life — a mage, a priest, a shaman. Gayle had been his female counterpart, yin to his yang in the struggle with *The One without a Soul* — never a lover, but a spiritual soul-mate nonetheless. Separate, they were perfectly ordinary people. In each lifetime, when they had become aware that they were joined in opposition to *The One without a Soul*, a metamorphosis occurred, and they became a conduit for spiritual energy from another plane of existence. The identities of the others who were aligned against their ancient enemy were also revealed. Of primary importance were Ryan and Audrey, soul-mates across eternity, whose destinies had intertwined to bring the possibility of a new hope that would be both a shining beacon and a harbinger of change — although what that change might be was not revealed.

When they opened their eyes, blinking at the brightness of the light reflecting off of the surface of the ocean, they shared a new understanding. The questions that had haunted Gayle's eyes had been replaced by a *knowing.* She smiled in a way that communicated her understanding of the tremendous sense of responsibility he had borne since the first time he had been contacted by the advanced spirits. She squeezed his hands, still clasped in hers, and said, "This burden belongs to both of us, friend." Larry felt a huge weight lift off his shoulders, and as they walked back along the beach, he reveled in the simple, joyful power of love.

# 16

ON THE SHORT TRIP FROM THE ECLECTIC ATTIC BACK TO HIS
house, Ryan was struck once again by how quickly things were happening. It
hadn't been twenty-four hours since the first time he heard Audrey's voice, and
here he was, madly in love — *engaged! I've never done anything remotely like this
before,* he thought. *No, that's not quite true,* he amended, recalling a number of
'snap' decisions he had made concerning relatively momentous issues. Buying his
property was probably the most significant. He hadn't hesitated for a second after
hiking around with the Realtor, even though the decision meant quitting his job in
Sacramento, moving to a town where he knew practically no one and starting his
own practice. And everything stemming from that 'snap' decision had worked out
wonderfully.

He glanced at Audrey's feet to see what kind of shoes she was wearing as they
pulled up in front of his house. They were fine for what he had in mind. "I'd like to
show you something special," he said, leading her down the hillside towards the
creek that flowed at the bottom of the draw. Soon, the sound of falling water could
be heard, as the ground fell away steeply in front of them. The last fifty feet before
they came to the creek were so close to vertical that Ryan had built a stairway into
the side of the hillside that ended at a bridge he had constructed just upstream from
a twenty-foot high waterfall. Doyle Creek was a sleepy little stream this time of
year, with just enough water flowing over the waterfall to be audible. On the far
side of the creek, a second stair led down from the bridge to the base of the falls. It
was dim and cool in the grotto formed by the sides of the canyon, with hummocks
of ferns dotting the gravel stream-bed, and logs scattered about like giant, moss-
covered pick-up sticks. The branches of the trees that clung tenaciously to the steep
banks arched overhead, forming a leafy ceiling high above.

"Ryan, this is absolutely gorgeous!" exclaimed Audrey, as she took in the var-
iegated patterns of light that sifted through the sun-dappled leaves and the liquid
rope of the waterfall flowing over the mossy face of the cliff.

"I thought you'd like it," Ryan grinned, putting his arm around her. "It was a lot
harder to get down here the first time I came — we had to make our own path, and
it was *much* harder to get back up the hill before I put the stairway in. But I
practically raced back up to make an offer on the property after I'd seen this waterfall. I was living in Sacramento at the time, and just like that, I quit my job and

moved here."

She reached for him and kissed him. "Look at all of the choices we made that eventually brought us together. When I think about how hard I fought coming on this vacation, and how many times I almost went home, it almost makes me ill! You and I might never have found each other if I hadn't come."

"I don't know," Ryan grinned. "From what Larry tells me about soul-mates, it seems like we're destined to be drawn into situations where we'll meet. Come to think of it, I was planning to go to the Healdsburg Guitar Festival in August. It's an international festival where Luthiers bring a few of their instruments for people to try out. I bet that if I went to Healdsburg for the guitar festival, I would choose your favorite restaurant to eat lunch. You would be there, of course, and while we were waiting to be seated, we would have gotten into a conversation, decided to share a table, and before we were done with the salad I would have proposed!"

Audrey laughed, and took up the tale where Ryan left off. "Being the cautious type, I would have put you off until the main course, or maybe even desert before accepting. After all, it's a woman's prerogative — even her duty — to keep the man in her life guessing about what she's thinking."

"I just love *being* with you," said Ryan, reaching for her hand and kissing it before leading her back up the hill, where they spent the rest of the day in quiet conversation and finished it the same way as the night before, falling into exhausted slumber afterwards. This time, Ryan was the first to drift off, leaving Audrey to lay awake while she contemplated the man who slept beside her, snoring lightly. She was strangely calm about a situation that would require one or both of them to make major sacrifices in terms of career and lifestyle when they got married. *I don't understand why I'm not worried,* she thought as she was drifting off. *Maybe it's all of this talk about fate and destiny.* She snuggled closer to Ryan. *Whatever happens, I'm sure we'll work things out.*

# 17

THE MILLER LUMBER COMPANY WAS A RELIC LEFT OVER FROM the early days of coastal lumbering, with a few notable differences. Miller had been one of the first to start re-planting, and to abandon the highly erosive practice of building earthen berms to catch the giant trees when they fell. A family-owned organization for many years, the company had kept nearly ten thousand acres of old-growth Redwood, Sitka spruce and Douglas fir forest, now generally referred to as "The Miller Tract," in its virgin state, at the direction of James H. Miller, son of the founder, who held the reins of power for over fifty years. He was a fiscal conservative, but was unafraid of innovation. On his extensive travels, both in the United States and Europe, he often visited lumber-producing areas, looking for ways to help his company attain higher profits, both in the short term, and over the long haul. By the time he took charge of the company, the long-term effects of over-cutting, clear-cutting, and other standard practices of the day were becoming increasingly obvious. He instituted changes based on long range planning — which ultimately won the company the reputation of being on the cutting edge of environmentally sound logging practices. When the company went public after his death, the conservative policies he instituted had proven so successful that they were carried over religiously by succeeding boards of directors.

Miller Lumber's pension plan had been managed just as responsibly as their forests, and it was a monument to sound, diversified investment. But it was vulnerable. No one had ever thought that there might be a need to protect the pension plan from the management of the company itself. Management had *always* been ethical — there had been no reason to believe that it would ever change. This attitude was the company's soft underbelly, just waiting for a predator like Raymond Baker to happen along.

He took control of the company like a firestorm. The blue-chip stocks in the pension plan were sold off, and replaced with bonds issued by Amalgamated Insurance — not the highly rated stock of the company itself, which by anyone's standards was financially sound, but with the kind of questionable securities known as junk bonds that had brought the Savings & Loan industry to its knees in the 1980's. Baker found this takeover particularly sweet. Harvesting the old-growth forest presented a new and interesting challenge. It wouldn't be easy to jump through all of the hoops set up by the California Legislature and Congress, but if anyone was up to the daunting task, he was the one. His financial resources were vast, and he was completely unencumbered by any ethical sensibilities. It didn't matter what rules were broken. He just had to make sure that the game was played in such a way that when *he* broke them, he would never be caught.

Late the first night after taking over, Baker was back in his office in San Francisco. His nostrils still burned from the cocaine he had snorted moments before as he took a sip of his single-malt Scotch. Contemplating his plans for the coming months, he felt a delicious sense of anticipation. For a man who thrived on the pain and discomfort of others, destroying a virgin forest might prove to be the ultimate tonic! He expected protests and lawsuits. He would feed on all of it, devouring the conflict and the anguish of the "little people" as they watched *their* precious trees fall. He sipped his whiskey and lit a cigarette, imagining the havoc that would be created when the trees came crashing to the ground. Earlier that day, while he was still at the Miller Lumber Company offices, he had called a meeting with the bureaucrats who took care of the day-to-day business of the company. They regarded him in the same way they would a rattlesnake they found sharing their bed — but he was the one who held *their* heads in a noose at the end of a stick! When Baker announced his plans for Miller's pension plan, their dismay was almost enough by itself to bring him to contentment. He put the icing on the cake when he issued orders to begin harvesting as much of the old growth as possible — as quickly as possible. No-one had spoken out. Baker loved nothing better than kicking people who were already down and out, with the possible exception of taking them down when they thought they were invulnerable. He'd experienced it all today. First, he took their company, then he took their financial security and finally, when no one dared to raise their voices against his rash orders, their pride.

He put the tightly rolled hundred-dollar bill to his nose and abruptly snorted the second line of cocaine, drew hard on his cigarette and took a sip of his Glenfiddich. He truly enjoyed this combination. Cigarettes — for most, an invitation to a painful death, but only if a person let them rule their lives. Alcohol — perfectly legal, but more devastating than half of the substances that society banned. Finally cocaine, which served to focus the pleasure he derived from the other two. Yet the pleasure of using them hardly compared to the sense of power he felt when he contemplated his absolute mastery over these substances. He would never relinquish that. *Control,* he said to himself. *Control is the key!*

# 18

SUNDAY MORNING DAWNED BRIGHT AND CLEAR ON THE RIDGE between Caspar and Doyle Creeks. The unusually fine weather that had been favoring the Mendocino coast continued to hold, with an almost unprecedented number of consecutive sunny days. Usually, the legendary dry summer heat of the Sacramento Valley to the east pulled a blanket of clouds up against the ramparts of the coast range in a foggy attempt at osmosis that left the north coast shrouded in mist for weeks at a time. Typically, this resulted in cold, damp mornings that only reluctantly resolved into clear weather. Doug spent the early hours of this fine summer day cutting a Bishop pine into firewood for the winter. It wasn't the best firewood — its ready combustibility required frequent trips to the woodpile to replenish the stove. But it was free, and the trees grew like weeds. Let others pay a premium for cords of oak trucked from further inland. He'd push a few more wheelbarrows up the hill, and save money while keeping his muscles toned.

After muscling the last wheelbarrow-full up the hill and stacking it in his wood rack, he ambled towards his house, mopping perspiration from his forehead as he went. Pam was lounging in the sun on the deck, enjoying a morning cup of coffee when he came up the driveway with his work gloves clasped in one hand. She had thoughtfully brought an insulated carafe and an extra cup outside with her. He poured himself a cup of coffee and grabbed a muffin from the plate next to the carafe before collapsing into the chair next to hers.

"I can't believe this weather we've been having," she remarked as she stretched lazily and reached for a bite of Doug's muffin. "Mmmn . . . this is good. I love it when the strawberries are in season. I think strawberry muffins are probably my favorite kind."

"Whatever kind of muffin I'm eating when you want a bite is your favorite kind," Doug teased.

"Can you guess what I've been thinking about while I've been sitting on this deck all morning?" Pam asked, ignoring his barb.

"It wouldn't have anything to do with past-lives, would it?" asked Doug feigning alarm and surprise.

She swatted him lovingly before answering. "Seeing Ryan and Audrey so entranced with each other has certainly brought back a bunch of memories. We have the best marriage of anyone I know, but I have to admit that twenty-seven years and three kids has allowed *some* of the romance to fade. I guess I'm a little jealous — I can't help thinking that it would be nice to re-experience some of that with you. I've been thinking that a regression to a past-life version of our relationship might add a little spark." She smiled fetchingly. "Who knows? Maybe we could fall in love all over again — it was so much fun the first time!"

"I knew this was coming," said Doug, sounding exasperated. "What's wrong with what we have already? It suits me just fine."

Pam sat up in her chair. "Don't tell me that my plucky reporter has found something he's afraid of!" she exclaimed. "I think that's it! You're afraid, aren't you?"

He looked at her sheepishly. "I know it doesn't make any sense — I just dread the idea somehow. Maybe it's because I've always felt that this life is all you get — that an afterlife, or reincarnation, are just fantasies dreamed up by desperate people who can't bear the concept that their precious selves could ever cease to exist." He adopted the lighthearted tone of voice he always used when he knew he was being unreasonable, but was unwilling to concede the fact directly, and said, "The experiences Gayle and Ryan described — Audrey too, not to mention Larry — just don't fit with the philosophy of skepticism and agnosticism it's taken me a lifetime to develop."

"That still doesn't answer why you're afraid to try it."

Doug thought for a few moments. "I don't even like to think about dying. Do you remember how long you had to hound me before I went to Ryan's office to make out my will? Being a skeptical agnostic allows me to avoid the subject entirely — if I don't believe in an afterlife, then I don't have to worry about trying to attain some kind of perfection to make sure I get the right result. Now that I think about it, my agnosticism probably got its start when I went to a 'fire and brimstone' church with a friend of mine when I was twelve or thirteen. I certainly knew then that I wasn't going to be hanging out with those folks, or living the kind of life they said was necessary to avoid roasting in the fires of hell. That stuff may be okay for some, but I came to the conclusion that it was all a bunch of happy horseshit. And up 'till the last couple of weeks I've successfully avoided the subject." He looked at her thoughtfully while he took a sip of his coffee. "Maybe I haven't wanted to go back to a past-life because I haven't wanted to experience dying," he continued, "even if it was just as a memory carried forward."

"That has the ring of truth to it," Pam allowed. "You know, it's strange, but I never would have guessed what your beliefs were — I wonder why we've never had conversations like this before."

"Probably because the whole subject of life after death hasn't seemed relevant until a few days ago. Neither of us were raised in church-going families — when would it ever have come up?"

"I guess you're right," Pam said. Then she cleared her throat as if she was about to say something.

He looked at her questioningly. "You've got something up your sleeve, haven't you?"

"I knew that I wanted to try hypnosis after the conversations we had yesterday, so I invited Larry over," she admitted. "You can do what you want, but I'm going to see what everybody else is talking about."

Doug groaned. "I can't let it get around that I was unwilling to check out a source — even if I am retired."

"That's the Doug Ackerman I thought I'd married," Pam said as she rose from her chair. She took a quick glance at her watch. "He'll be here in forty five minutes — you have time to take a shower." She laughed. "You don't want to be all sweaty when you meet me in a past-life, do you?"


"HOW WOULD THE two of you like to try something a little different?" Larry asked with a grin as they were getting ready.

"You're not going to physically transport us back to the other lives or anything, are you?" Doug asked with a laugh.

"No — no — nothing like that," chuckled Larry. "It's just that we already know you were once Oglala Sioux because both Ryan and Audrey remember you from that lifetime. What I had in mind was to try to take you back to that particular past-life, rather than something more random."

"I'd go for that," Doug agreed. "When I played cowboys and Indians as a kid, I always wanted to be the Indian."

"It's settled then," said Larry. "Who's first?"

"I might as well get it over with," Doug groaned dramatically, making himself comfortable on a couch in the living room. Pam brought Larry a straight-backed chair from the kitchen table and then curled up in a comfortable armchair behind and off to one side.

Larry gave Doug the same sorts of commands he had given the others, directing him to relax his body sequentially and progressively, and before long he was in a trance.

"I want you to walk through a pristine valley that will open onto a grassy plain," Larry directed. "You will come to a shallow river filled with clear running water. As I count to ten, you will wade across that river. When I reach ten, you will step onto dry land, into a past-life where you are an Oglala Sioux — a life where I am a shaman and Pam is my daughter." He counted slowly to ten, observing that Doug's eyes had rolled far back under his eyelids — a sign that he was deeply under. A moment later, Doug said, "I'm on the far side of the river."

"Look at your clothing and tell me what you're wearing," said Larry. He was quite surprised when Pam began to speak from behind him, describing her clothing at the same time that Doug was describing his. Larry turned around to see that she had been inadvertently hypnotized while he was giving his commands to Doug. This had never happened during Larry's private practice — he had always worked one-on-one. He thought for a moment, and then instructed them that they should take turns answering his questions. When he asked Doug to describe his surroundings, Doug described a semi-permanent camp, with several lodges built of saplings and sod in addition to the tepees that Ryan and Audrey had described during their regressions. He also mentioned that he could see Pam — although she was in a different body.

"What is she doing?" asked Larry.

"She's standing with me, waiting for her turn to describe what she's seeing," said Doug.

Larry was astounded. This was completely out of the realm of what he would have considered possible. When Pam took her turn, she described the same scene that Doug had, filling in a few details that he hadn't mentioned. Larry asked Doug if he could see the things that Pam had just described, and Doug replied in the affirmative. *Now I really have to play it by ear,* thought Larry, his mind racing. He instructed them to go to the most significant event in that lifetime. They took turns describing a council meeting during which Larry's own past-life self debated with the other elders in the tribe about whether to allow Pam to become a shaman. "Go to the most important part of this event, and repeat what everyone there says," he requested. As Doug began to speak, Larry felt a chill, as he realized that the first words Doug said had issued from his own lips in that long-ago lifetime.

"My tribesmen," Doug began. "I ask for the blessing of the elders as well as the spirits as my daughter begins her training as a shaman."

"Except for one other, that path has only been taken by men," Pam said, giving voice to an objection that had been made many years before. "Perhaps the spirits will be offended if another follows her."

"Were the spirits offended when *Walks unseen* took the path of the shaman? I remind you that those of us who sit at this council do not determine this matter. The spirits make that choice. Is it right to go against their desires? Who are we to sit in judgment when the spirits have seen fit to lead *anyone* to this path? Can one among us say that ill has come to the people because *Walks unseen* has become a shaman?"

"There is a new evil in this land. These new ones, the destroyers with their blue-coated soldiers came after *Walks unseen* took the shaman's path."

"And she has led us away from danger time after time, giving us warning when the blue-coats were coming. She was a gift from the spirits in our time of need, not some evil omen! My daughter is the most talented healer I have ever encountered. She has already learned all of the herb-lore that I can teach, and she finds new uses for old remedies. She too is a gift from the spirits in our time of need. Who says we shouldn't use this gift?" There was a long pause. "Then let it be so."

Larry had an intuitive flash, perhaps ignited by a distant memory of his own, as the council meeting unfolded. When Doug and Pam stopped speaking he asked if *Walks unseen* was at the council meeting. They said that she was not. "Walk through the camp, and see if you can find her," he instructed, and waited as they went to look for her.

"We are at her tepee — her body is here, but she is spirit walking," said Pam.

"Do you recognize her as someone you know from your present life?"

"It's Gayle," Doug answered. "She looks very different, but her spirit shines brightly."

"Go to the time when she returns from her spirit walk," Larry instructed.

"She is speaking," said Pam almost immediately. "She says she has a message for you — that now is the time to wake her future self to the knowledge of the power and skills she possessed when she was called *Walks unseen*."

Every hair on Larry's body stood on end as he realized that in her life as an Oglala Sioux, Gayle had sent a message forward in time.

"She is speaking again," said Pam. "She says that you must never forget that love is the answer."

After these breathtaking revelations, it was difficult for Larry to contain himself as the regression ran its course. Pam and Doug experienced event after event with each other — only a few of which had been reported by Ryan or Audrey. They had been virtually inseparable in this lifetime, with Doug playing a supportive role while Pam exercised her strong gifts as a healer. One of the last events she recounted was assisting in the birth of Audrey and Ryan's child just before the entire camp was massacred. As the end of the lifetime approached, Larry instructed both of them to separate themselves from their bodies and become observers. They died together, as they had ever been in that life, ridden down from behind and shot in the back as they tried in vain to escape. Afterwards they were surrounded by the often-described spiritual light filled with loving presences. Larry waited to see if they would enter the lifetime in Nazi-occupied Poland as Ryan and Audrey had done. When neither of them did, he brought them back to the present. Doug lay still for a few moments looking over at Pam, who returned his gaze. They didn't speak, but just sat, drinking in each other's presence. Larry rose quietly and stepped outside, aware that perhaps for the first time following a past-life regression, his input was completely unnecessary.

They came outside fifteen minutes later, holding hands. Pam came to Larry and put her arms around him, saying nothing for a very long moment. "This has been the most healing experience in my entire life," she said finally in a voice that cracked with emotion. "My relationship with Doug has been the tempered-steel center of my existence. Being able to experience our love in a different setting, where his main purpose was to support me in what I was doing, adds a depth and dimension that I could never have known otherwise. But the greatest gift this experience has given me is having a father. My own dad died in the second world war." She was crying now, the tears streaming down her face. "Now that I know what you and I were to each other, I'm not going to give that part of it up." Doug stepped up and embraced the two of them. They stood in silence, and as they did, Larry was filled with love for this wonderful woman and her soul-mate. Pam wasn't the only one who had been given a tremendous gift. During the session, he had almost been able to see, feel and touch everything that either one of them described. He had felt the depth of his relationship with Pam as he defended her in the council meeting. The emotions Pam had just described echoed in his own breast. *I know we're in for terrible times in the very near future,* he thought, hugging Pam back fiercely. *But love has already made it all worthwhile.*

# 19

THE HAMBURGER RANCH & PASTA FARM SAT ON THE NORTH END of Cloverdale, guarding the junction of old Highway 101 and Highway 128 — the winding strip of asphalt that meandered through oak and vineyard studded hills and then through the redwood groves along the Navarro River to the coast. Adam Gray perched on a stool at the counter, and ordered a Dos Equis beer and one of the award-winning hamburgers that made the restaurant a local landmark. He wondered if any of the men who had arrived before him might be the one who had called Project HOPE and given him a set of instructions out of a spy-novel. He had begun his trip by driving aimlessly around in Healdsburg to make sure that he wasn't being followed. The town was small enough that Adam knew a good percentage of the people who lived and worked there. The third time he drove past Clark's Music, he wondered if anyone he knew would notice, and think he'd lost his mind. After making sure no one was following him, he turned his aging Honda north on Highway 101 towards Cloverdale. When he got to Highway 128, he made the turn and continued for a mile or so before making a U-turn and returning to the Hamburger Ranch. All this activity was supposed to give him the opportunity to detect to detect a tail if there was one, but it merely made Adam feel silly.

The caller had asked if he was familiar with the restaurant.

"Sure, I know the place."

"Sit at the counter — do you know what you're going to order?"

"I'll get the Italian fungi burger and a Dos Equis."

"Don't change your mind," the caller admonished. "When the waitress asks you how you like your food, tell her that it's the best burger you've had since you ate at The Dog House in Bodega Bay — or something like that — anything, as long as you mention the Dog House, okay?"

Adam repeated the entire list of instructions back, and the caller seemed reluctantly satisfied. Once again, he stressed that if Adam thought there was a *possibility* that he'd been followed, he was to abort the trip. *I'm probably dealing with some kind of nutcase who thinks he's a character in an episode of Mission Impossible,* Adam thought. But in spite of the man's spy-novel sensibilities, when he said he had information vital to Project HOPE's cause, Adam figured the trip was worth it.

When his order arrived, he chewed slowly, relishing the high-calorie meal as it disappeared into his skinny frame as if it was being sucked into a black hole. He came close to uttering a reflexive "fine," when the waitress asked him how he liked his hamburger, catching himself just in time. Feeling foolish again, he reeled off a short tale about a burger that was "to die for" at The Dog House — but that the one he was eating was even better. For the next twenty minutes he waited apprehensively for someone to engage him in conversation. He was surprised however, when the owner of the restaurant, whom he recognized from a photograph accompanying a favorable restaurant review, came out from the kitchen wiping grease-stained hands on a cook's apron. "Adam," he said, reaching out to shake hands. "Why didn't you tell me you were here? I'd have put a few extra mushrooms on your burger."

Adam glanced at his plate where a pile of mushrooms still swam in the juice from his hamburger, and then back at the owner. He realized that this man had to be another player in the little drama his mysterious caller had orchestrated. "Why don't you come back to the kitchen as soon as you finish," the owner continued. "I'll buy you another beer, if you'll keep me company for a while."

Adam devoured one last spoonful of mushrooms, casting a longing glance at the few that remained before draining the remainder of his Dos Equis. "I'm ready now," he reported, wiping his mouth on a napkin that was already drenched with the residue from his meal. None of the small audience of diners in the restaurant were paying them the least bit of attention. "Get me that beer and let's go."

The owner selected another Dos Equis from the cold-case and led Adam through the door to the kitchen, and on to a storage room in the back. He didn't say anything else, and quickly lost his friendly expression in favor of a look of apprehensiveness. He handed the beer to Adam when he reached the door to the storage room. Ducking his head through the doorway, he said, "He's here. Everything looks normal out front — I recognize two of the locals, and the rest of them have kids — they can't be anything but tourists."

"Let him in then," said a voice from inside the storeroom.

Adam walked inside where he found a man in his early forties, dressed in blue jeans and a plaid shirt, open at the neck. Adam bit back the flip remark that had been on the tip of his tongue. He could see from the man's expression that whatever game he was playing, it was deadly serious. "What can I do for you," he asked in a neutral voice.

"Is there *any* possibility that you might have been followed?"

"I followed your instructions to the letter," Adam replied. "I'm sure I would have noticed if anyone followed me. What's this all about anyway?"

The man gestured to two folding chairs that had been set up in the middle of the room facing each other and sat in one of them. Adam took the other. "I'm the computer engineer over at Miller Lumber," he began. "I maintain the computers in the offices — set up the networks, install programs and trouble-shoot. Any problem with the desk-top computers starts and ends with me. I even wrote the program that took care of the Y2-K problem in the IBM mainframes that control the machinery in the mill." He shifted nervously in his chair. "My job requires me to go virtually anywhere, at any hour. There are computers in every part of the mill, and someone always needs my help."

Adam nodded, wondering where the conversation was going.

"We've just been the victims of a hostile takeover by Amalgamated Insurance," said the man, looking at Adam expectantly.

"I heard about that," he acknowledged.

"As a result of the takeover, we've got a new president of the board, and he's an environmentalist's worst nightmare."

Some of the man's anxiety was beginning to rub off on Adam. He took a large swallow of beer and asked, "What do you mean?"

"You're familiar with the Miller Tract?"

"It's the largest privately owned stand of old-growth redwoods in Mendocino County . . . Of course I'm familiar with it."

"This new president of the board seems to have something personal against old-growth forest — redwoods in particular. He's the scariest fucker I've ever seen in my life, if you'll excuse my profanity. I'm sorry — I don't usually swear, but this asshole is really bad news." The man was obviously in acute distress. His face looked drawn and his eyes were bloodshot, as if he hadn't slept much recently. "He's got us making preparations to harvest the tract — all of it, or as much as we can get away with. He wants to get as close to a clear cut as we can. He pulled the guys who do the wildlife studies off the job they were doing and told them to get their data together and start preparing an environmental impact report and a timber harvest plan." The man couldn't sit still any longer. He got up out of his chair and began to pace in the small room. "They're not saying much, but I think he's been trying to get them to bend the Department of Forestry regulations, or even ignore them entirely. He demands absolute obedience, and has management walking around in a daze like a herd of cattle — I've never seen anything like it. Speed is his highest priority — he doesn't care how much it costs."

"What's the rush?"

"I have no idea why he wants it done so quickly — it's not like the trees are going anywhere. But he's acting like he's on some sort of timetable — you'd think that there was a war on or something. As far as why he wants to do it at all?" The man paused, trying to put his thoughts into words. "This sounds crazy, but I honestly think that he just wants to piss-off as many people as possible."

"Why would anyone want that?" Adam thought out loud.

"He's evil," the man said in a low voice, sitting back down in his chair. "As pure an evil as I've ever encountered. I haven't talked to him personally — computer engineers are glorified mechanics as far as management is concerned, and frankly, I couldn't be happier that I'm part of the background, and more or less invisible. The last thing I want is to be noticed! But I was walking past a room today and heard him talking to some of the upper management guys. He was spouting this series of incredibly irresponsible orders, and no one said a word. Those are all career men. They've helped this company hold its place, and even prosper in a highly competitive market. If it was anybody else they'd be telling him that he was nuts, and refusing to do what he said. But this guy is so ice-cold, I think he could probably stop your heart just by looking at you." The man's eyes looked haunted, and his Adam's apple moved up and down in his throat as he swallowed. "I'm not sure he's completely human."

Adam felt his armpits beginning to drip and his mouth felt dry. "What's his name?" he asked.

"Baker," the man replied. "His name is Raymond Baker, and I honestly believe that if he knew I was here talking to you, I wouldn't stand a snowball's chance in hell of making it home."

"Why did you arrange the meeting then?"

"I work for a lumber company because it gives me an opportunity to work with all kinds of computers — I love the creative aspects of the work. Up to the time that Baker took control of Miller Lumber it was a great job. But now I've been presented with a dilemma." He looked down at his shoes, embarrassed. "I'm a religious man, Mr. Gray, and I like to consider myself a good man." He looked uncomfortable, as he struggled to find the right words. "There's something sacred about that forest. I feel closer to God when I'm out there than I do when I'm sitting in church. If I had my way, that tract would never be logged — it's always been my hope that some government agency or private conservancy would buy it." He lowered himself into his chair and leaned forward, resting his elbows on his knees and staring at his hands. "What Raymond Baker is trying to do is a sin in my book, plain and simple . . . there's no way it could be for a legitimate purpose! The bad publicity alone could bring about the end of the company, and at the very least it would cause serious damage." He lifted his head. "There'll probably be boycotts on all of the lumber we produce, and deservedly so. It's just plain bad business." He looked up at Adam. "And I have some loyalty to the company — it's been good to me. I figure that the only chance Miller has to survive in the long run is if you environmentalists are able to stop this madman from accomplishing what he's setting out to do."

He stood up, and Adam saw that their liaison was nearly over. The man's expression was haunted, but he spoke with a firm resolve. "You can call me John Smith for now. Maybe some day I'll feel safe enough to tell you my real name." He opened the door and ushered Adam through. As Adam made his way back through the restaurant and back out to his car, the man's final words were etched indelibly into his memory, "I may be signing my own death warrant, but I'm Project HOPE's man on the inside."

# 20

LARRY AND GAYLE SAT TOGETHER IN HIS KITCHEN DRINKING hot chocolate and staring out at the steel-colored ocean under the low overcast sky after Larry described Pam and Doug's unintended joint hypnosis. For the moment they were both silent, sipping their chocolate reflectively. "So it looks like it's my turn in the barrel again," Gayle said finally.

"That's the message you sent to your future self," Larry agreed. "My interpretation is that you need to go back to that life to learn how to spirit-walk — and whatever else you were able to do. Pam and Doug had no doubt that you were really spirit-walking . . . they called you *Walks unseen*. All indications are that you actually *could* leave your body while you were meditating. And there's the message you sent, clearly meant for me: I'm to wake you to the abilities you possessed at that time. The only way I can see to do that is to lead you back to that life."

"I think I'm right on the edge of being able to go spirit-walking already," Gayle said thoughtfully. "Do you remember when I did that channeling, or whatever it was, at the store yesterday? When I said that I could sense danger, but that it was far off?"

"How did you do that, anyway?"

"I closed my eyes, and simple as it sounds, I just reached out . . . with some sixth sense, or maybe with the other five all put together. I could feel danger in the distance, not physically, but out in the future." She cocked her head slightly to one side and stared at Larry, then asked, "Have you ever done any past-life regressions yourself, or are you just a voyeur?"

Larry looked a bit sheepish at her last comment. "I attempted to do one about ten years ago," he replied. "A colleague of mine came to me for training, and I agreed to be one of his subjects. I don't know why, but it didn't work for me — there's a fairly large percentage of people who don't seem to be able to access past-life memories through hypnosis. I've been hypnotized before and since, so that's not the problem. I always assumed that I was one of those who, for whatever reason, just couldn't access past-life memories." He looked chagrined. "I guess you could say I am just a voyeur."

"Maybe it just wasn't time yet," said Gayle.

"What do you mean?"

"Maybe this is one of those things that had to wait until the appropriate time . . . Perhaps you never considered doing it again because you weren't *supposed* to do it until now."

"Are you proposing that you hypnotize me?" he asked.

"That might be one way to do it, but it isn't what was on my mind. Call it a hunch, or maybe it's more of this prescience I seem be developing, but I think we're supposed to do the next regression together."

"What?"

"I think that's part of the 'message' from Pam and Doug's regression — that we have the ability to go back into these past-lives *together* if we try."

Larry sat back in his chair and scratched his head. "I'm trying to figure out how to be the hypnotist and the subject at the same time — I'm not sure how I'd go about doing that."

"Didn't you tell me that we hypnotize ourselves all the time? Like when we drive somewhere while we think about something else entirely?" Gayle asked. "Is there some way we can do that intentionally?"

Larry took both of their cups to the sink, rinsed them and placed them in a rack to dry. "This is really beyond my training or experience," he said. "I'm drawing a blank."

"Let me concentrate on the question, and see if anything comes to me," said Gayle. She closed her eyes again for a few moments, and then laughed as she opened them again. "The answer's as obvious as the noses on our faces," she said. "I don't think I even used any psychic ability to figure it out — the way you get to be the hypnotist and the therapist at the same time is to use a tape-recorder."

Larry was taken aback by the simplicity of her answer. "You're absolutely right! All I have to do is tape the session — if a joint hypnosis is in the cards for us, it could work."

"What are you standing there for, Doctor?" Gayle asked, doing a fair imitation of Peter Lorre. "It's time for you to build the time machine!".

At first Larry found his own recorded voice distracting as he listened to the series of commands, prompts and suggestions he had recorded, but after a few moments he was able to focus his concentration and follow along. Once past that small hurdle, he found that he had little trouble surrendering to the process. He had chosen the familiar theme of a walk through a picturesque valley, and the crossing of a broad, shallow river to take them back across the intervening years. His disembodied voice counted to ten as he focused on all of the details, allowing himself to feel the pull of the current and the suction of the muddy silt under his bare feet. The "observer" within his consciousness knew that he was fully engaged in the experience when three-quarters of the way across his foot slipped on a rounded stone and he almost lost his balance. After he stepped out of the water on the far bank, he saw a woman making her way up the bank just downstream. Gayle looked more than a decade older than he had visualized her when the others described her during their sessions, but there was no mistaking her. He looked down at his own hands. His skin was dark and weathered, with prominent veins and dark age-spots on his forearms and the backs of his hands. His gray-streaked white hair hung past his shoulders in braids that were bound with deerskin thongs. Both he and Gayle were wearing buckskin clothing. "We seem to have made it across together," said Gayle as she took both of his hands in hers. "You are called *Spirit guide*," she continued, and then pointed to a path which led away from the river. "This is the way to our encampment. The advanced spirits spoke to me on the way here — we need to go to my lodge. Once there, I will remember the skills I need to take back from this life."

As they walked, the twists and turns of the path seemed familiar. Before long they veered towards a copse of cottonwood trees where a number of tepees stood, wreathed in campfire smoke. There were people walking about the camp, but they paid Larry and Gayle no particular attention. When they came to two tepees that stood slightly apart from the others, Gayle strode purposefully to one of them. Inside, she wasted no time, but knelt and began a ceremony of purification, setting fire to a bundle of sweetgrass with a coal from the banked fire in the center of the tepee. As she completed the ritual, the form of a raven gradually superimposed itself over her features. By the time she was finished, Larry could see her totem as clearly as her human shape. She looked at him expectantly. Larry knelt, and performed the ritual, duplicating every word and gesture. When he was finished he experienced another lifting of the veil — similar to what he had experienced at Seal Point — as memories that had been obscured by his death were restored to him. While Gayle could send her spirit outward in the form of a large raven, Larry's totem padded silently through the spirit world wearing the shape of a large puma. When he encountered souls who needed guidance from one wheel of life to another, he could help them find the way.

*Walks unseen* allowed her spirit to separate from her human form. She cawed once, then spread her wings and flew out through the open flap of the tepee. Larry experienced a slight sense of dislocation as the spectral form of a puma detached from his own body, taking the greater part of his consciousness with it. He padded outside, where he could see the raven perched on a branch of a cottonwood tree, watching him with eyes that glinted like agates. She took to the air, and he watched her soar into the sky on broad wing-strokes. While he was waiting for her to return, he noticed a tiny woman walking through the encampment, closely followed by a very large man. Both of them carried bundles of twigs, leaves and flowers. He would have recognized Pam and Doug, even if he had not recently taken them back to this lifetime.

*Spirit guide* searched the sky, but *Walks unseen* was no longer in sight. He turned and padded back to the tepee where their two human forms sat, eyes closed, facing each other while their spirits wandered. He merged with the body that his spirit had occupied during this lifetime. When he closed his eyes and opened himself to whatever might come, he was rewarded with a series of insights that taught him different ways to travel between lifetimes — knowledge that provided an alternative to hypnosis. A short while later, *Walks unseen* flew back through the open flap of the tepee — although her use of the doorway in her spectral shape was completely unnecessary. When their spirits "walked," physical barriers meant nothing. The raven merged with the form of the woman, and *Walks unseen* opened her eyes.

"I have learned what I needed from this lifetime," she said, rising from the buffalo robe. He too rose and reached for her hand. Once it was firmly grasped in his, Larry, who was also *Spirit guide* , led them back across time and into his living room.


"ARE YOU OKAY?" Gayle asked a moment later as she sat up from the couch where she had been reclining.

"I'm fine — I only have one question," said Larry. "Can a raven *really* feel safe when she's that close to a puma?"

Gayle's engaging laugh made it impossible for Larry to keep his serious expression intact. Their eyes met, and he knew that they had reached a new stage in their mystical partnership.

"This is starting to get really spooky, Larry," she said. "It feels more like an episode of The Twilight Zone or The X-Files than an overcast day in Fort Bragg. Do you think we'll be able to handle it?"

"Even the advanced spirits don't have that answer," he replied. "This conflict has spanned uncounted lifetimes, and it's obvious that things haven't gone well at all in the past. But I get the feeling that there's at least the possibility that things might go in a different direction than they ever have before."

"I keep having to pinch myself to be sure that I'm awake," Gayle murmered, her voice tinged with awe. "I'm just a shopkeeper in a resort town — my spiritual beliefs have kept half the town amused for years! What am I doing involved in something like this?"

"Everyone who became embroiled in the most momentous conflicts in human history was still just a person," he replied. "But when the divinity within us is unleashed, amazing things happen. Did Mohammed ask to be the prophet of the Muslim faith? Did Jesus choose his fate?" He raised his cup of chocolate in salute. "I don't think we're in that league, and we're obviously getting our instructions piecemeal, but I *can* say with absolute conviction that I would rather be in our shoes, knowing that some great good may come from our efforts, than to be simple foot-soldiers without a clue."

# 21

RYAN ARRIVED AT HIS OFFICE LATER THAN USUAL MONDAY morning — fortunately he had no court appearances and his first appointment of the day was in the afternoon. Sally was there before him, and the smell of French Roast coffee wafted through the air. They worked well together — Sally was more friend than employee — a very good thing in an office as small as his. Their relationship had started on a professional basis — Ryan had handled her divorce a few years before, and had just finished her case when his previous secretary quit on short notice. He asked Sally to fill in on a temporary basis, and before long, stopped looking for a replacement.

He had been looking forward to surprising her with his news. Sally was a relentless matchmaker, and she had done her best to find someone for him among her friends and acquaintances, with no success.

"How was your weekend?" she asked after he'd poured a cup of coffee.

"Pretty good, actually," he answered, keeping his expression as neutral as possible. "I met the love of my life Friday night. We haven't set a date yet, but we're engaged to be married."

Sally looked up quickly, trying to determine the nature of Ryan's prank. "Right," she responded. "And pigs are flying in and landing at San Francisco International Airport. Okay — I'll play along, but I know what you do on Friday nights. How did you manage to meet the love of your life while you were sitting at home playing music with Doug?"

Ryan tried to keep a serious expression, and for the most part succeeded. "She called me on the phone, told me she knew me from a past-life and asked if she could come over." He grinned widely. "Her name is Audrey . . . she'll be by a little bit later."

Sally looked at him expectantly, waiting for him to explain his strange joke. Ryan said nothing, but just stood there beaming. "My God!" she exclaimed after a moment. "I think you're serious!"

"As improbable as it sounds, every word is true."

"More like impossible," she said. "Okay, give me some details. You can't just come in here and drop something like that in my lap without telling me the whole story — not that I'll believe a word of it until I actually see her walk through the door."

"You know the past-life regression I told you about? Last week I did another one to see if I could find a past-life connection to a lover." He looked a little sheepish. "I didn't mention it before-hand, because it seemed like such a desperate move. But I found myself in two succeeding lifetimes, madly in love with the same person. Larry told me that this meant that we were soul-mates — that we'd probably been going through life after life in relationships where we had close emotional ties to each other."

"But that doesn't explain how she called you . . . "

"Audrey has known Larry for years. She's been taking a vacation in Mendocino. Friday she did a regression with Larry too. When she went back to the same lifetimes I did, they put two and two together. Larry called me to ask if I wanted to talk to the woman from my past lives, and before I knew it, I was giving her directions to my house. Until I left for work this morning, we spent every possible minute with each other."

Sally shook her head in disbelief. "I can't believe it," she said. "It sounds like something out of a fairy tale. You were kidding when you said you were getting married, weren't you? I just can't imagine you jumping into something so permanent this early in a relationship."

"We haven't set a date yet, but both of us are completely sure that we want to spend the rest of our lives together. It's finally happened, Sally! I've finally found the woman of my dreams!"

Sally shook her head. "After all the effort I put into trying to find someone for you, I *should* be upset that you've gone and done it all by yourself." She turned to go back to her desk, then looked back. "I may forgive you, but I still won't believe it's actually true until I see her."

Ryan stepped into his office, flipped through his calendar and began to organize his week's work. He had trained himself to be disciplined in his practice — a trait that had not come to him naturally. But being efficient and well organized was the point where he drew the line when it came to trying to define who he was when he was practicing law. He had never tried to create a gulf between himself and his clients, firmly believing that most of the bad reputation lawyers had was caused by fear on the part of clients and arrogance on the part of the members of his profession. Clients were almost always fearful about how their case would turn out — rolling the dice in the legal system made them feel helpless and out of control. And although he couldn't always make things go the way they wanted, he could at least ease their fear of the unknown. The last thing he wanted was to pretend to be in an all-knowing position of power. That kind of approach, which depended on the lawyer's exclusive knowledge and the client's ignorance, could do nothing other than create resentment. He did his best to be the same human being while practicing law as he was the rest of the time. At his office, unless he had a court appearance, he dressed for comfort — jeans and flannel shirts if the weather was cool, which was most of the time. His clients seemed to appreciate his casual approach to office attire, and they definitely appreciated his efforts to educate them regarding the legal process.

He spent the morning fielding phone calls, reviewing his cases, and making a list of priorities for both he and Sally to attend to. Shortly before noon, he caught a glimpse of Audrey's arrival through the window and heard Sally's muffled greeting. After that, the murmurings of conversation came through the door. He smiled to himself, deciding to let them make their own introductions. A minute later, Sally buzzed him on the intercom.

"Okay Ryan, I concede — I have to admit that the completely incredible story you told me this morning was true. Audrey wants to know where you're taking her to lunch."

Ryan opened the door to his office and stepped into the secretarial/reception area that had formerly been a dining room. An intercom wasn't really necessary — the only reason that he had installed it was for the privacy of his clients. When the door was open, he and Sally could engage in a conversation from their respective work areas just by raising their voices. "Why don't I grab some sandwiches," he said as he walked up behind Audrey, put his arms around her, and kissed her on the neck behind her ear. "We'll eat in the kitchen and the two of you can get acquainted."

He stepped around the corner to Down Home Foods, a little health-food store that sold sandwiches to go. When he returned, he found Audrey and Sally chatting away like old friends.

"Don't worry boss, I'm not giving away the worst of your secrets," said Sally with a mischievous grin. "By the way, how much did you say my raise was going to be?"

"I'm beyond blackmail," Ryan said in a deliberately smug tone. "If she were going to get rid of me, she would have done it lifetimes ago." Then, *soto voce,* "Just don't tell her about that one quirk of mine — you know the one I'm talking about."

Audrey laughed. "I'm sure that we both have things in our lives that we regret, but I seriously doubt that there's anything that could make me change my mind. Like Ryan said, this relationship has been going on for a *very* long time. This is the third lifetime that we *know* about, but there could even be more."

Sally was taken aback by the matter-of-fact way that Audrey spoke about their past lives. "You two are completely serious about this, aren't you?" she asked slowly, not wishing to offend, but with a scarcely veiled doubt lurking behind each word.

Audrey reached out and touched Sally's arm. "I never would have believed it myself as recently as Friday afternoon. I know it sounds like both of us have gone off the deep end," she took Ryan's hand and smiled, "but if this is what it's like to be out of my mind, then I'm willing to be crazy for the rest of my life."

"I didn't tell Sally much about you," Ryan put in, "only that we know that we were lovers in past lives. Why don't you tell her about Project HOPE?"

After hearing about Audrey's efforts to save the old-growth, Sally asked if she had given any thought to hiring Ryan. Before Audrey could answer, Ryan said, "Not a chance! That's a specialty area of the law — I wouldn't know which door of the courtroom to use, let alone know what to do once I got inside. The firms that the lumber companies hire have virtually unlimited budgets, and they've got some of the best lawyers in the business. Most of them started specializing before they graduated from law school — I'd be hopelessly outclassed."

"We've actually got an extremely competent attorney who has handled all of our suits so far," said Audrey. His name is Michael Holland — like Ryan said, he's a specialist in environmental law, and he's an absolute genius! He's been able to blow the silk socks right off the lumber companies' corporate lawyers. We consider him Project HOPE's secret weapon. I don't believe that we would have been half as successful if he hadn't been handling the litigation."

"Where did you find him," asked Sally.

"Actually, he found us," Audrey replied. "He's a real character — he used to work for a firm that represented some big lumber companies over on the other side of the state. When he moved to Ukiah, he decided that he wanted to do work that made him feel good about himself. He's a practitioner of 'deep ecology,' meaning that he believes that the best chance the ecology movement has is to concentrate on taking action at the personal and grass roots level rather than through legislation. Michael lives very simply, and tries to be as self-sufficient as possible. There's no Mercedes or BMW in his driveway — just a small truck that's been modified to run on solar power. He has a beautiful garden, and he made his own house out of hay bales, stucco and salvaged lumber. You should see it — it's covered with solar panels, and there's even a windmill out by the garden." She looked sheepish. "He rides his bicycle practically everywhere, even to court — I always feel like some kind of hedonistic sinner whenever we both leave his office at the same time. He takes off on his bike or whizzes away in that electric truck, while I roar off in my own hydrocarbon haze."

Ryan leaned back in his chair and looked at his watch. "I hate to break up the party, but I've got to get ready for my client this afternoon, and I've got some research I need to do first." He looked at Audrey. "Got plans for the afternoon?"

"I thought I'd take a walk around Fort Bragg," she said. "I've never spent any time here. When I get tired of that I'll drop by the Eclectic Attic and visit with Gayle."

After she kissed him goodbye and departed, Sally turned to Ryan. "That woman is an absolute jewel! If you do anything to screw this up you'll have to answer to me!"

Ryan grinned. "Isn't she wonderful! I just can't get over how lucky I am."

"You're both lucky," said Sally. "I haven't been trying to fix you up with everyone I know just out of boredom. You're a real catch — you should see some of the press releases I used to put out about you — you'd die from embarrassment. And you should see the way you look at her. Well, that's easy enough — just pay attention to the way she looks at you. If it wasn't so sweet, it would be sickening."

"Thanks for the vote of confidence," he said. "And I'm glad you like her — she's going to be around for a while." He grinned broadly. "Maybe an eternity!"

## 22

WHILE SHOPS IN MENDOCINO CATERED ALMOST EXCLUSIVELY to tourists, the ones in Fort Bragg were just as often geared towards the more pedestrian needs of the local residents. Still, there was no lack of interesting nooks and crannies to peer into, the Eclectic Attic being only one of them. Audrey wandered the sidewalks for several hours, ducking into a shop here and there — finally enjoying her vacation in one of the ways she had anticipated. When she had her fill of window-shopping, she made her way to the Eclectic Attic where she found Gayle sitting behind the register in her canvass-slung director's chair, talking on the phone. Gayle finished her telephone conversation quickly. "How's my adopted daughter?" she asked.

Audrey laughed. "I'm fine — I couldn't be any better. How's my favorite medicine woman?"

"Much more in tune to that lifetime than I was the last time we were together," Gayle replied cryptically.

"Did Larry take you back too?" asked Audrey, excited to have another confirmation.

"More than that! In the morning he did a regression for both Pam and Doug, and then in the afternoon it was my turn — we *all* went back to that lifetime!" Other than her conversations with Larry, Gayle had not spoken with any of the other companions since her communications from the advanced spirits. She and Larry had not been given any explanation as to why only they would be privy to the big picture. She decided to see what would happen if she told Audrey everything that had taken place. "Some interesting things happened during the regressions," she remarked. "Larry set out to hypnotize Doug while Pam sat in the same room. She got hypnotized too, and when they both went back to the same lifetime, they were able to see, touch, talk and otherwise interact with each other *in the past-life* as if they had actually traveled back in time! Larry said that as far as he knew, this was an entirely new phenomenon." She studied Audrey's expression for a moment, but Audrey made no sign that anything untoward had been described. "That's pretty exciting by itself," she continued, "but they're not the only ones who have had a 'dual' regression experience. Larry and I figured out a way for him to hypnotize both of us, and we were able to do the same thing."

"That's nice," said Audrey distractedly, her eyes flitting about the room at the various displays and merchandise as her attention began to drift. "Larry said this doesn't happen often?" she asked vaguely.

"That's what he said. Group hypnosis is pretty common — that's what they do during those hypnosis shows in comedy clubs. But according to Larry, what happened today is entirely new."

"What happened during your regression?" Audrey asked, although she had picked up an article of Guatemalan clothing, and was giving it much more attention than she was to their conversation.

*I wonder if she'll really react the way the advanced spirits said she would,* thought Gayle. *I'm about to say some things that would normally make me sound like I was ready for the asylum.* "Larry and I went back for a specific purpose. He had received a message during Doug and Pam's regression — from *me* in that lifetime. I was a shaman, and had certain powers in that lifetime that I need to have in the present. The message said that Larry needed to send me back so that I could remember and retrieve those powers. When we went back, I learned how to assume the shape of a raven, and to venture out in that form, both in the spirit world and the physical world. It's called spirit-walking. I can do it here in this life, or during a past-life regression. Larry learned how to do similar things."

Audrey's facial expression didn't change at all. Instead, she asked, "Does this relate to those 'spooky' feelings you were describing on Saturday — the ones where you sensed some kind of danger coming?"

"You're right on the money," Gayle answered, thinking, *Audrey is accepting these things as if I told her that I went to the store for a carton of milk!* She smiled. "But that's enough of past lives for now, okay? You and I haven't had a decent opportunity to talk. This might be our only chance for who knows how long. I have the sneaking suspicion that Ryan is going to try to monopolize your time as much as possible."

They spent the next few hours telling each other about their lives — the relationships they had been involved in, what their families had been like and other personal experiences. As they talked, the past-life connection reinforced the instant rapport they had experienced when they first met. Feelings of camaraderie and closeness continued to blossom, and by the time Audrey was ready to leave to go meet Ryan, their friendship was in full bloom. They felt like sisters, like mother and daughter, father and son, brothers, or lifelong friends, and it was likely they had been all of these things to each other. Then, while they embraced as Audrey was about to leave, Gayle was almost bowled over by the power of the revelation she received the instant she and Audrey made physical contact. It was completely different from what she had experienced out on the point with Larry two days before. That had been like a series of curtains lifting. This was more like being struck by lightning. She was jolted to her core as she received a vision of the future that could be — the future that would come to pass if they were able to succeed in their confrontation with *The One without a Soul.* She gasped, and held on to Audrey for support. The vision passed as quickly as it had come, but its power and significance left her feeling weak, and completely awestricken.

"Gayle, are you okay?" Audrey asked, holding her at arms-length, and looking concerned. "You're as white as a ghost . . . "

"I'm okay," Gayle replied slowly. "I'll be fine in a minute — sometimes the psychic flashes I get take a little something out of me, and I just had a powerful one." She leaned on the top of the counter, and made her way to her director's chair. Audrey stood next to her, uncertain as to what to do. Gayle reached out and took Audrey's hand. "I have a question for you," she said gravely, but with a twinkle in her eye. "Have you and Ryan picked a date yet?"

"To get married? We haven't discussed a date," said Audrey, confused by the rapid change of subject. "Does this have anything to do with the psychic flash you said you had?"

"It has everything to do with it," Gayle replied with a big smile. "I think you better plan on a wedding pretty soon, sweetheart. You don't want to *show* too much in your wedding dress . . . even in these times, people tend to talk . . ."

"What! . . . are you saying that I'm . . ."

Gayle beamed, and kissed Audrey on the cheek while she squeezed her hand. "You've got some big news for that fiancé of yours. I don't know if you're even far enough along for a test to show it, but you're going to be a mother in just about nine months — and it's going to be a girl!"

Audrey couldn't speak for several moments. Her eyes opened wide, and she reached down and placed her hand on her abdomen.

"Are you sure? How do I tell Ryan about this? We just met — I don't know if he's going to be ready for a baby yet."

Gayle laughed. "I can tell that I still know Ryan better than you do, at least when it comes to this. He's wanted to get married and have kids for as long as I've known him. This is the best news you could possibly bring him — although I'll admit it's coming a lot sooner than you would have planned. But trust me, Ryan will be thrilled!"

Audrey departed, bursting with her news, leaving Gayle to ponder the balance of the revelation she had been given. She picked up the phone and punched in Larry's number. "I just got a big piece of the puzzle," she said when he answered. "Maybe the biggest one of all. I don't want to tell you over the phone, but we need to talk right away."

"You close at six, don't you?" he asked. "Why don't we grab an early dinner as soon as you can leave? I could meet you at *The Restaurant* — that's as good a place as any for a quiet conversation, and it's right across the street from your store."

"That's perfect," she shot back. "Meet me here and we can go over together."

During the next hour she had only two more customers, and had just finished tallying her cash receipts when Larry appeared at her door. "I can't believe how glad I am to see you," she said, taking him by the arm and leading him back outside, turning to lock the door behind her. When a break in traffic came, they walked across Main Street to *The Restaurant*. Gayle asked for a glass of Chardonay before they had even been seated.

After the waiter had shown them to a table, Larry said, "You can hardly sit still! This must *really* be important!" Just then the waiter brought Gayle her wine and a glass of water for Larry. Gayle's hand shook slightly as she picked up her glass. She drained a good portion in several quick swallows, took a deep breath, and said, "To start off with, Audrey is pregnant — she's going to have a girl."

"That sure didn't take long . . . the way you're acting, the baby must have something to do with the piece of the puzzle you mentioned."

"You're right." said Gayle. "We knew that Audrey and Ryan will bring us a talisman if we are successful. *This little girl is going to be the talisman — the harbinger of change.*" She took another swallow of her wine, and leaned closer to Larry. "If we succeed, this child will be something that this world hasn't seen in a long, long time, maybe never before! Let me run a few names past you, Buddha, Zoroaster, Mohammed, Jesus — what do they all have in common?"

"Obviously, they are the prophets, saints and semi-divine or divine humans around which whole religions were established," Larry replied.

"There's one more thing," said Gayle. "They're all men."

Larry sat dumbstruck, as the implications of what Gayle was telling him began to dawn on him. "Are you saying that Audrey's little girl is going to be some kind of Christ or Buddha?" he asked.

"It's bigger than that, Larry. When we engage *The One without a Soul*, our conflict will have the potential to create a shift in the dominant energy that has controlled everything that has happened on this planet — including the way people have related to each other for thousands of years!" She paused for a moment, and took another sip of wine. "Have you seen the bumper sticker that says 'It will be a great day when our schools have all the money they need, and the air force has to hold a bake sale to buy a bomber?'"

"Sure, I've seen that one," Larry affirmed.

"How often have you seen that bumper sticker on a man's car?" she asked.

"My God!" . . . Larry's eyes grew wide as he followed Gayle's train of thought.

"Things run in cycles, Larry. The tide goes in, the tide goes out — the pendulum swings. Masculine energy has been dominant for God only knows how long. *The One without a Soul is* the worst extreme of what that masculine energy has to offer. *He* is representative of 'man-the-destroyer,' the paradigm that has been invoked consciously or unconsciously every time men are sent against men or nation against nation. It's that kind of energy that corrupted the most brilliant scientific minds of the twentieth century into building weapons of mass destruction that could destroy all life!" Gayle stopped for a minute, her eyes glistening with emotion. "Larry, if we succeed, we're going to see a shift to a feminine perspective — a perspective that cherishes life rather than trying to control and often destroy it. We were made in God's image, but only one half of that image has had much influence for millennia. I believe that God is a duality — God and Goddess all in one. If we succeed, the Goddess energy will become dominant. It will start from a spiritual perspective, but will eventually affect the flow of energy on a worldwide basis. Can you imagine what that would mean?"

"How many mothers ever willingly sent their sons, and more recently, their daughters off to die?" asked Larry, mostly to himself. "It could mean the end of war, the end of poverty, the end of the exploitation of children — the end of laws designed to perpetuate the social status of women as second-class citizens, and that's just a short list." They were both quiet for a few moments. Then Larry asked, "What happens if we're not successful?"

"Everything keeps going in the same direction it's going now."

"And all of this depends on what we do?"

"That's the message." she replied. "We're like pieces on a cosmic chess board. We don't even know how the conflict will be played out. But if we can let love flow through us to counteract the hate and fear that *The One without a Soul* unleashes, it will happen." There was a new strength in her demeanor as she elaborated. "We can't let hate and fear control our emotions or our actions. Only by using love against evil can this shift come about. There's no Old Testament Jehovah girding up the loins of His champion to smite the evil-doer. This is about the divinity looking to its feminine side. And when God is also Goddess, Audrey's baby will be *Her* first interface with all of humanity. This could be a new beginning for the world, and the end of the world as we know it!"

# 23

"THE SPOTTED OWL," INTONED EDDIE RAPSKI, "HAS BEEN GIVEN more rights by liberal judges than the God-fearing working-class people of our community. Do these birds pay taxes? No! Do these birds contribute to the larder of the unemployed lumberman so that he can feed his children? Not on your life! Have you, or anyone you've ever met even *seen* one of these 'precious' birds? I doubt it! Now, ask yourself. How many times this week have you stopped and said to yourself, 'Gee, things would sure be a lot better right now if I could just see a Spotted Owl.' How many times has this happened, my friends? *Never!* And why is this? Because, except for when an honest businessman cuts down the trees on his own land — trees that will grow back as thick as the hair on a dog's back in a few short years — we never hear about the damned Spotted Owl! And I'll tell you something else, my friends. Perhaps this isn't very Christian of me, but some of God's creatures just aren't as important as *people!* As far as I'm concerned it doesn't matter if they continue to exist! I don't care about giant cave roaches from Trinidad. I don't care about . . ."

Adam Gray hit the power button on his car radio, cutting off the irritating sound of Rapski's voice in mid-sentence. Unless he was mistaken, the radio pundit's stance had of late become even more stridently anti-environmentalist than ever before. It seemed that every time Adam chose to "monitor the enemy airwaves," he tuned into another Rapski diatribe about the struggles of the saintly lumberman. Or sometimes the topic was liberal judges, or the corrupt Congress, or the spineless Secretary of the Interior. Rapski had become the lumber industry's biggest cheerleader. He glanced down and checked his odometer, making sure that he followed the directions exactly. He was on his way to another meeting with "John Smith," their inside source at Miller Lumber. *God, I wish Audrey was back,* he thought for perhaps the hundredth time. But he wasn't going to do anything that might cut her vacation short — not when they had all gone to so much trouble to make sure she took an entire month off in the first place. She would be back in a couple of weeks, and at the present time there was really nothing they could do anyway. Although "John Smith" had advised them that the Miller Lumber employees were working around the clock to prepare the environmental impact report for a major Timber Harvest Plan, Project HOPE's aerial surveillance, which consisted of a flyover of the Miller Tract in a rented Cessna every few days, hadn't revealed any new activity.

Today's meeting was in Hopland, fifteen Miles north of Cloverdale on Highway 101. Adam's diversionary tactics included taking a tour of Fetzer Winery — he would be contacted afterwards during the wine-tasting and given further instructions. *If things weren't so serious, all of this cloak-and-dagger stuff might even be fun,* he thought as he turned down the driveway that lead to the Fetzer parking area.

While he was tasting a Pinot Noir, a young woman wearing a Fetzer Winery nametag walked up to him. "Sir, are you the owner of a grey Honda Accord parked in the lot outside?"

"Is there some problem?" Adam asked, holding back a smile. He truly enjoyed the improvised dialogue these clandestine meetings generated.

"I'm afraid there is," she said seriously. "We seem to have made a mistake. There was a grey Honda Accord parked in the same area of our parking lot for over a week. We accidentally assigned two different people to the job of towing it to a storage lot. The first person towed the correct vehicle, but the second person towed yours. If it's not too much trouble, could I give you a lift to where it is now?"

"No trouble at all," Adam replied. This third meeting had the most elaborate scheme yet — the second had been in another restaurant's back-room further up Highway 101 in Ukiah. The pleasant young woman led him to a late-model Ford van. She stayed completely in character — if she even knew she was playing a role — making small talk about the winery while repeatedly apologizing for the inconvenience they had caused. They drove behind a large barn-like building, out of sight of the areas where the general public was allowed. Adam spotted his car, and to his surprise, parked next to it was a second Honda the same color and model as his. *This is getting too weird,* he thought. Then he considered how nervous Smith had been both times they had met. The man was clearly afraid for his life, and was obviously taking every precaution he could. Adam got out of the van and bid the pleasant young woman goodbye. She drove off immediately, and after standing there for a moment, he began to amble towards his car. Just then, a door to the large barn-like structure opened, and a burly man he had never seen before beckoned from within. He changed directions and stepped through the doorway into a dimly lit area filled with gigantic stainless steel vats and the heady aroma of fermenting grapes. "This way," said the man, inclining his head. Adam followed him down a corridor formed by the exterior wall of the building and a row of tanks. They arrived at a small office built against the wall in a corner of the building with windows facing the interior of the building that were blocked by Venetian blinds. The man opened the door and inclined his head again, indicating that Adam should step inside. When he entered the office, the man he knew only as John Smith shut and locked the door behind him, saying, "You must think I'm off my gourd to be so cautious."

Adam took in Smith's tired-looking eyes and his gaunt, care-worn face. "I thought you might be some kind of nutcase the first time you called me," he admitted. "But I knew better as soon as we talked. The lengths you go to conceal our meetings seem awfully extreme, but if it makes you feel safer . . . "

"You've never met Raymond Baker," Smith countered. "I avoid him as much as possible, and still haven't had any direct contact yet. Believe me, I intend to keep it that way." Abruptly, he looked remorseful. "Six months ago I had an opportunity to get a job taking care of the computers in a manufacturing facility down in the Bay Area. I didn't take it, even though it would have meant a substantial increase in pay because I wasn't willing to move back to the city." He sat down in a chair, and looked up at Adam. "There isn't a day that goes by that I don't think about that decision, and wish it had gone the other way. That bastard has turned my life into a nightmare." He looked stricken. "It makes me want to kill him, and that might be the worst thing of all."

Adam surmised that Smith had little or no chance to give voice to his true feelings about Baker with anyone else. He was cautious to a fault, and probably didn't even talk things over with his wife — if he had one.

"But I didn't call you and ask for you to come up here just so I could complain about Raymond Baker," Smith continued. "I wanted to warn you that the environmental impact report is nearly finished. I've never seen one produced so quickly before."

"Does it have any weak points?" asked Adam.

"Not on the face of things," Smith replied. "But the field studies of the habitats require at least two full years to complete. If Miller had any plans to log the Miller Tract, they were way off in the future until Baker took personal control of the company." He peered at Adam through his tired, bloodshot eyes. "I haven't looked at the computer files where the data was stored, but I know that the wildlife biologists whose names appear on the environmental impact report have been working on other projects most of the past two years." His worried look became more pronounced. "I haven't been able to talk to them about it — I haven't seen them since shortly after Baker took over. But the reports indicate that the plan to harvest the Miller tract has been in the works for years. That simply isn't true."

"Baker's got to know that the shit is going to hit the fan when he files his Timber Harvest Plan," said Adam. "What does he think the wildlife biologists are going to say when they find out that their reports have been doctored?"

"My guess is that he plans to pay them off at that point, if he hasn't already. And if they won't take the money, he'll find a permanent way to keep their mouths shut."

"Are you serious?" asked Adam, a thrill of fear running down his spine.

"There's no doubt in my mind whatsoever," Smith responded. "There's already been a death, and though I can't prove it, I'd bet my life-savings that Baker is connected with it."

"What happened — an on-the-job accident?"

"He's much more subtle than that," Smith responded. "Most of the top management have rolled over and done whatever Baker tells them to do — I told you the first time we met that they were acting like a bunch of sheep. Well, there was a black sheep in the bunch. His name was Loren Rosso, and he was the only one who had the guts to stand up to Baker."

"What happened to him?"

Smith sighed. "He wasn't in the best of health. The truth is that he drank too much, and didn't quit smoking soon enough — but I'd bet anything that Baker had something to do with the heart attack they say killed him. It's just too much to believe that the one person in the whole company who stood up to Baker — and threatened to go to the newspapers — ended up dead the next day."

"He threatened to go to the newspapers?"

"That's what he said he was going to do. He went into Baker's office the day before he died. You could hear him yelling, although if Baker said anything, you couldn't hear it — like I told you before, he's a fucking ice cube. Loren came slamming out of Baker's office all red in the face and he yelled back over his shoulder that he wasn't going to let Baker ruin the company he'd worked for all of his life . . . that the story would be on the front page if he had anything to do with it. I heard later that he had an appointment with a reporter the next morning, but he never made it. He had his 'heart attack' while he was eating breakfast, and was DOA at the hospital." Smith reached out and put his hand on Adam's arm. "We can't be too careful," he urged. "I told you the first time I talked to you that I didn't think he was completely human. He may be flesh and blood, but I'm even more spooked than I was then. That's why I've been going to such lengths when it comes to meeting you." He let go of Adam's arm leaving a sweaty handprint on the sleeve of his shirt. "I only hope I've been cautious enough. If not, I'm sure to join Rosso, and you're in danger too."

Adam had to struggle not to react to Smith's last remark. "Do you have any idea how we can prove that those reports were faked?" he asked, trying to appear calmer than he felt.

"I have an idea, but I don't want to say what it is right now. Let me work on it . . . I'll get back to you if I come up with anything."

After his meeting with Smith, Adam drove his Honda slowly off the grounds of the winery. The meeting had been very disturbing. Up to this point in time, Smith's description of Raymond Baker, while frightening, had seemed somewhat overblown. Even now, his conjectures about the cause of Loren Rosso's death might just be paranoid ramblings. But Adam's gut had confirmed the truth of everything Smith said, and the warmth of the day did nothing to take away the chill he felt as the result of that knowledge. Project HOPE had gone up against some of the largest lumber companies on the West coast. The rules of the game had always been straightforward — raise the money, do the research, and if there were grounds to seek a temporary restraining order or a preliminary injunction, then Michael Holland filed suit and they went to court. They had won a time or two — more often they had lost — but neither side had ever taken the law into their own hands. Now there was evidence that someone had entered the picture who was playing by an entirely different set of rules. Adam made a decision as he was driving back to Healdsburg. He couldn't leave Audrey out of the loop any longer. He hated to do it, but he knew he had to track her down and let her know what was going on.

# 24

RYAN SAT AT HIS COMPUTER, PROOF-READING AND PUTTING THE finishing touches on a demand-letter to a recalcitrant insurance adjuster. Sending the letter was probably futile — it was getting more and more difficult to settle cases as insurance companies took an increasingly hard line. It never ceased to baffle Ryan why an insurance company would pay a defense attorney twice as much to avoid paying a legitimate claim than it would take to settle the case. He glanced at the clock. Sally had been gone since five, and he was just putting in time until Audrey arrived. His practice was large enough to keep him as busy as he wanted, but unlike many attorneys, he seldom worked late into the evening — practicing law was a way to make a living, but it was far from being the center of his existence. A few minutes later he saw Audrey hurrying down the sidewalk towards his office. He flipped the switches on his computer and printer, and was just about to switch off the lights when she burst through the front door, her eyes flashing brilliantly. "Ryan, I've got such wonderful news to tell you!" she bubbled. Then her face clouded, and she looked inexplicably nervous and uncomfortable. ". . . At least I hope you think it's as wonderful as I do," she said falteringly.

"What's got you so excited?" he asked as he put his arms around her. She replied cryptically. "The song you sang to me the night we met, The Melody of Me and You . . . " She took one of his hands and slowly placed it on her stomach below her navel, then looked up at him hopefully. "We wrote the harmony," she said, biting her lip. "Ryan, we just met, and this is *way* too early for this kind of thing . . ."

"Wait a minute, hold on," he cut in. "Are you saying you're going to have a baby? How do you know? Don't you have to wait for your period not to come or something?"

"Gayle told me — she had one of those flashes of intuition like the other day. She says we're going to have a baby girl!"

Ryan couldn't speak. He drew Audrey towards him, gently rocking her back and forth as he held her. Finally, he said, "If I say anything, I'll start to cry," and then true to his prediction began to shudder as tears welled out of his eyes. That started Audrey off too, and for most of a minute they rocked back and forth with their arms wrapped around each other and tears streaming down their faces. When he was able to speak, Ryan said, "I thought you had already made me the happiest man alive, but now you've taken me to a whole new level!"

"I hope things start slowing down," Audrey said, laughing through her tears. "I don't know how many more changes I can deal with in such a short time."

"I hope they do too, love," Ryan replied. Then his practical side took over. "Don't you want to make an appointment with a doctor, or get a home pregnancy test to confirm Gayle's intuition?"

"We can do that if it would make you happy," she said. "But didn't you say she's a genuine psychic?" She looked stricken. "Do you think she could be wrong?"

"I know that Gayle wouldn't have told you that you were going to have a baby unless she was completely sure. But I'm going to go crazy unless I get some scientific verification. We could stop at the pharmacy on the way home, and get one of those tests."

Audrey laughed and kissed him. "It's so wonderful to be with a man who's asking me to make sure that I'm pregnant because he *wants* a baby." She looked up at him, and reached up with her index finger, to touch the tip of his nose before snuggling up to him in a tight embrace. "You're not the only one here who thinks that they're the luckiest person in the world," she whispered.

Later, as they sat in Ryan's living-room, talking about the things they had liked and disliked about weddings they had attended, Audrey got a peculiar look on her face. "I'm having the strangest feeling," she said. "It's really more of a compulsion."

"Does this have anything to do with just finding out that you're pregnant?" he asked jokingly. "You're not craving pickles and ice cream, are you?"

"No, it's nothing like that. I just have the feeling that I want . . . no, that I *need* the others . . . Pam, Doug, Gayle and Larry to be with us . . . I can't explain it."

"Maybe being pregnant has brought out some latent psychic abilities," chuckled Ryan, lightly brushing her hair from her forehead. "I don't care who spends the evening with us as long as I'm with you." He picked up the phone and dialed Doug and Pam's house. Pam answered, and Ryan invited them over, saying that they had a little surprise for them. He called Gayle next, and then Larry. Setting the phone in its cradle, he said, "They'll all be here soon," noting how relieved Audrey appeared to be by his announcement.

Doug opened the bottle of wine he had brought with him soon after he and Pam arrived. Audrey politely refused a glass, smiling as she thought about the reason for her refusal. Soon thereafter, Gayle and Larry arrived together. "What's this surprise you've got for us, Ryan?" asked Pam when they had all gotten comfortable.

"Why don't you tell, Gayle," said Audrey. "You're the one who discovered it in the first place."

"Audrey came to visit me this afternoon," said Gayle, "and we had a really nice visit. Then when she was about to leave, I was hit with a flash of intuition that was so powerful, it almost knocked me off my feet." She glanced at Audrey and smiled. "I think I would have fallen down, but Audrey was giving me a hug goodbye, and I was able to lean on her." She took a sip of the wine Doug had poured for her. "The flash of intuition told me two things." She looked at Audrey again. "I'm sorry I didn't fill you in on the whole story, honey, but I thought that the part I told you was quite enough for you to handle just then." She looked back at the others. "The first thing I learned is that Audrey and Ryan are going to be the proud parents of a baby girl in just about nine months."

There was a sharp gasp from Pam. She rose from her chair and came over to give Audrey a sisterly embrace. Doug leapt up and grabbed Ryan in a bear hug, slapping him on the back. Both of them sported ridiculously huge grins.

"Are you sure?" asked Pam after a moment, looking first at Gayle, and then at Audrey. "It's more than a bit early to tell."

"I'm as sure of this as I am of the fact that we're all sitting here right now." Gayle replied.

"I've never known her to be wrong when she's this certain about something like this," Ryan added. "But just for my own peace of mind, Audrey and I got a home pregnancy test on the way home. We should be able to get a verification tomorrow morning."

"What's the other part of your flash of intuition?" asked Audrey. "The part you didn't tell me about this afternoon."

"That's less concrete," said Gayle. "You remember the insights I had Saturday afternoon — the ones about something big on the horizon that was going to be dangerous?"

They all nodded.

"The second part of the insight I got, is that whatever is coming is going to happen *really* soon."

As if in response to her announcement, the telephone rang, startling them all. Ryan picked up the phone and spoke briefly for a moment and then wrote down a telephone number. He held out the phone number to Audrey. "That was the clerk at the Mendocino Hotel. I mentioned that you'd be staying with me when we checked you out. Someone named Adam Gray is trying to get in touch with you — isn't he your friend at Project HOPE?"

"It is," she answered, glancing at the number before dialing it. "I hope nothing's wrong." Her look of concern deepened as she spoke to Adam. Finally, she said goodbye, and slowly put the phone back in its cradle.

"You were right, Gayle," she announced. "The shit has begun to hit the fan." Then she told them what she had just learned about the hostile takeover of the Miller Lumber Company, and its new president's plans for the Miller Tract.

- 125 -

# Part Two

No way construction of this tricky plan
was built by other than a greater hand
But with a love that passes all our understanding,
Watching closely over the journey

Yeah, but what it takes to cross the great divide
Seems more than all the courage I can muster up inside
But we get to have some answers when we reach the other side
The prize is always worth the rocky ride

But the wood is tired, and the wood is old
And we'll make it fine, if the weather holds
But if the weather holds, we'll have missed the point
That's where I need to go.

    from     "The Wood Song"
              By Emily Saliers

# 1

MICHAEL HOLLAND OPENED HIS EYES AND SCANNED THE GLOW-
ing numerals on his alarm-clock, observing that it was only nine-thirty in the morning. His telephone, which had jolted him out of a deep slumber, continued to ring
insistently. Grumpily, he threw off his covers, muttering under his breath that whoever had the gall to call him this early had better be prepared for the consequences.
Michael had always been a night-person, and his internal clock seldom allowed
sleep to overtake him before two or three in the morning. He made sure that everybody who was likely to call knew his time-table, and his standing rule that he was
*not* to be called before ten. The last thing he *usually* did before going to bed was to
turn on his answering machine and disable the bell on his phone. Last night he had
forgotten, and now he was paying the price. He walked down the hallway to his
office and picked up the receiver, answering with, "This better be good." When he
heard Audrey Peckham apologizing for calling so early, his irritation eased considerably — Audrey was one of his favorite people, and he was willing to cut her some
slack. Within a minute, all irritation over lost sleep was forgotten. The corporate
machine he had once served so ably was on the move again, giving him another
opportunity to atone for his past.

He stepped into his bathroom for one of the long showers he used to ease
himself into wakefulness. It was a luxury he had paid for in advance by installing
three solar collectors to heat the water for his house, allowing him to take a guilt-
free hot shower until his entire body resembled a prune.

He made the trip from Ukiah to Healdsburg in the solar-powered truck he used
when distance or weather made cycling impractical. As he pulled into the parking
area at Project HOPE's headquarters, he saw that Audrey's Volvo and Adam's
Honda were parked in their usual places. He pulled around to the side of the
building, where signs warned that the parking space was reserved for electric vehicles. Part of Michael's arrangements with Project HOPE included this solar-
powered refueling station made up of a solar panel on the roof and a set of large
batteries that filled a former utility closet. After plugging the truck into the re-
charging system, Michael entered through the back door. When Audrey saw him,
her face lit up with a brilliant smile. As she walked towards him, he felt a slight
sense of disorientation. She seemed so different that it was almost as if he was

seeing a different person — although he couldn't quite put his finger on exactly what it was about her that had changed, other than a radiance he'd never seen in her before. Every step was marked by a new energy, and even her skin seemed to glow. He couldn't remember seeing *anyone* look so vibrantly alive.

"Michael, it's so good to see you," she said, and when he reached out to shake her hand, he was surprised when she brushed it aside and offered him a hug. Audrey had never been exactly *cold* with him — and he considered her a good friend — but even this small intimacy crossed a line that had always been there before.

"Audrey, what's happened to you?" he asked. "You're positively glowing! If this is what taking a few weeks off does for you, then you need to take a break more often." He was surprised when Audrey blushed crimson. "What's going on?" he asked, looking first at Audrey, and then at Adam who was lounging on a beat-up couch against one wall, grinning wickedly. "I have the distinct impression that everyone in the room is privy to something that I'm not."

"So much has happened since I've seen you, I don't even know where to start," Audrey began.

"What she *really* means, is that she doesn't know what to tell you first — that she's engaged, or that she's going to have a baby!" Adam interjected, looking smug at having been the first to break Audrey's news. Michael, as Adam had anticipated, was stunned by the announcement. The look on his face was so comical that Audrey and Adam both burst out laughing.

"What is this, some kind of joke?"

His question made them laugh even harder, and soon they were both gasping for breath with tears brimming from their eyes. Finally, Audrey was able to get a few words out between paroxysms of laughter. "It really isn't funny . . . I don't know why we're laughing so hard . . . I guess we're just blowing off steam." She took a few deep breaths, as the last few shuddering giggles escaped. "It sounds crazy, but it's true . . . I'm in love, I'm going to get married . . . *and* I'm going to have a baby!"

Michael kept his face deadpan for several moments before responding in the dry fashion they had come to know so well. "I was *hoping* you would have a good time on your vacation," he said, sending Audrey and Adam into further fits of laughter.

*I've laughed more in the last week than in the past five* years, thought Audrey after they settled down. She realized that her new, or actually re-discovered, love, not to mention the renewed friendships from past lives, changed her whole outlook on life. It was as if she had stepped off some dismal treadmill after years of placing one foot in front of the other in an endless imitation of Sisyphus. Briefly, she thought back to the weeks of angst she had gone through on her vacation before she had found Ryan, and breathed a sigh of relief that she had persevered. Upon reflection, she realized that she might not appreciate how happy she was feeling now if she hadn't gone through that experience.

She spent the next half hour bringing Michael up to date on the high points of her vacation, expecting disbelief when she described the past-life connections she and her new friends shared, but Michael didn't blink an eye. Adam, who was watching Michael's reaction closely, was nonplussed by Michael's calm acceptance. "You don't even seem surprised," he remarked wonderingly. "It took me half an hour to scrape my jaw off the floor when I heard the part about the past lives."

Michael studied Adam for a moment and then lifted one eyebrow. "Apparently, some of us here are more parochial than others," he observed. "There's nothing strange about hypnosis — it's been used in psychotherapy for many years to recover lost memories. For a few years until the appellate courts decided otherwise, testimony about memories that had been retrieved under hypnosis was even considered reliable enough to be allowed as evidence in court. As for reincarnation — half the world believes in it. I don't find it strange that Audrey had an experience that would tend to validate a belief held by that many people."

Adam looked at Audrey, and asked, "What does he mean by parochial? I thought that referred to a Catholic elementary school."

Audrey smiled. It was a joy to slip back into the easy comradeship and the well-defined roles they played at Project HOPE in times of stress. Michael's humor became as dry as a bone, while Adam inevitably played the buffoon.

"The word 'parochial' derives from parish," admonished Michael, looking over his half-glasses at Adam. "Referring to one who is provincial — whose knowledge is limited in breadth and scope to that which can be gleaned from the area immediately surrounding the parish church. It's the opposite of cosmopolitan." He turned back to Audrey. "I simply don't know how we're going to save the old-growth forests from the forces of evil if this young man doesn't do *something* to improve his vocabulary    and speaking of saving old-growth forests, I want a full briefing on the new developments at Miller Lumber." He pulled a chair up to the table that dominated the room, dug a legal pad out of his briefcase, and gestured for the others to join him. "Adam," he said. "Why don't you tell me what you know, starting from the beginning." Adam took Michael's cue and left the joking behind. He began with the first phone call from "John Smith" that led to their clandestine meeting at the Hamburger Ranch, and told his tale. He had near-photographic recall enabling him to repeat his conversations with Smith virtually verbatim. When he was finished, he and Audrey waited expectantly. Michael leaned on his elbows with his hands tented in front of him, supporting his chin. After several very long moments he leaned back, and clasped his hands behind his head. "We're not on familiar ground anymore, my friends," he said. "From a business standpoint, Raymond Baker is insane. The primary goal of every business is to make money. On the face of things, the redwoods in the Miller Tract look like gold nuggets scattered on the ground just waiting to be picked up and turned into cash. But if he files a Timber Harvest Plan to cut a maximum amount of old-growth forest, he's going to ignite a firestorm of protest and negative publicity. And if he's actually intending to file an environmental impact report based on falsified data . . . it just doesn't make sense." He stood up and walked over to a water cooler that stood against the wall and filled a glass with water. After taking a drink, he turned back to face them. "He's like an unschooled chess player whose opening gambit sacrifices the queen instead of a pawn. I don't trust what I've just heard — it feels false — it's too easy, perhaps even a trap of some kind." He looked at Audrey. "You said that this man might be one-and-the-same as the one who victimized you and your friends during your past lives?"

Audrey nodded. "That's what Ryan thinks."

"We need to tread very carefully here," said Michael. "This situation could become very, very dangerous indeed."

# 2

AFTER ALMOST A FULL DAY AT THE OFFICE THAT WAS, FOR THE most part, spent staring out the window and thinking about Audrey, Ryan finally accepted the fact that he wasn't going to get anything done and quit early. He decided it wasn't all that strange that he couldn't concentrate on his work. After all, in less than a week, practically everything in his life had been rearranged — *not that I'm complaining,* he thought with a grin. On his way home, he visualized and re-lived the startlingly-few hours he had spent with his beloved. He had always known that he wanted to get married and have a family, but the script his imagination had created required a re-write now that he knew who had been cast in the opposite role — or roles, to be completely accurate. "What am I going to do with a daughter?" he had asked Audrey. "I've got no experience — all I ever had were brothers!" His idle daydreams about having a family of his own hadn't even contemplated the fifty-percent possibility that one or more of his children might be female. Audrey laughed. "I'll be there to help you," she said, and reminded him that her professional specialty was child discipline and family dynamics. Her reassurances brought him some comfort, but he still worried. He thought of some of the horror stories he had heard while practicing family-law, especially with teenagers. Who knew what could happen?

He hadn't been home long when Larry called, and said, "I was just wondering if you might like to have some company tonight. But then again, you've been through quite a lot in the past week. Maybe you'd rather be alone so that you can sort things out."

"That's all I've been doing all day," Ryan observed drily, recalling his lost day at the office, which had produced the grand total of three letters. "I think I've had all of the solitary introspection I can take — come on over, I need to get out of my own head."

Fifteen minutes later, Larry pulled his Subaru into Ryan's driveway. When they had gotten settled in Ryan's living room, Larry said, "The last time you and I had a chance to sit down and talk, you were chomping at the bit to try to find your past-life love. "It's been what . . . a week? And now you're engaged, with a baby on the way." He smiled wryly. "You know, I always find it gratifying when someone takes what they've learned while under hypnosis, and integrates the experience into their present lives . . . but this really takes the cake!"

Ryan laughed, but then his expression became more serious. "The other thing

I have to integrate into my life is the conflict that Gayle foresaw. My guess is that it will happen when Project HOPE files suit against Miller Lumber over their plans to log the old growth — assuming we're correct, and Raymond Baker is our past-life enemy. Gayle keeps saying that we need to hold love in our hearts when it happens — I don't get it."

"You're going to have to look to your philosophical side if you want to understand," said Larry. "In the end, it boils down to a conflict between love and fear. Fear breeds distrust, hatred, envy — everything that leads to human conflict. I believe to the core of my being that God, or whatever you choose to call the Divine, is love — a more pure form of love than we can possibly imagine. And the opposite of love — Divine love, or any other permutation — is not hate, but fear."

"That reminds me of something that you said the other day that I've been meaning to ask you about."

"What's that?"

"Just before my second regression, you said you had learned from the advanced spirits that our purpose on this plane of existence was to 'find the good and the God in ourselves and everyone around us.'"

Larry nodded.

"It was as if you were repeating my own beliefs back to me — that God isn't something 'out there,' but is a part of all of us."

"You might be surprised at how common that belief is. It's fundamental to most Eastern thought, not to mention the Lakota Sioux tribes, including the Oglala Sioux." He winked. "See how it all works together?"

Ryan nodded. "I tend to process my thoughts about spirituality by writing songs about them," he said. "Would you like to hear my own stab at the concept?"

"I'd love to," said Larry. "I really enjoyed your 'Phoenix Fire' song the other day, I've been wondering when I would get to hear some of the others."

Ryan picked up his old Martin D-18 to accompany himself on what was one of his most introspective songs. "I call it my 'song to the inner spirit,'" he said, and began to fingerpick softly before adding his voice to the music.

*Shapes the wind, Sings the hymn*
*Stirs the cauldron of creation*
*Sits within, glimpsed through doorways dim*
*Shines with love, sings in adoration*

*When I feel the force, the power, and the light shines bright*
*It seems I'm on the brink of a great insight*
*But then the moment passes, There's a curtain across the door*
*I haven't found an epiphany that will last forevermore*

*I can't know the unknowable, I can't see what can't be seen*
*I cannot grasp what seems to me to be within a dream*
*But when I search deep down within my soul*

*I feel the echoes of the answers that my heart longs to know*

*Search my heart, And from the start,*
*I find peace in deep reflection*
*God in me, Oh great mystery,*
*Let me find my true connection*

*The journey to the source follows an intimate trail*
*Yet when I draw close, it slips behind a veil*
*To live my life with love provides the only key*
*It gives texture to the shroud that cloaks the mystery*

*I can't know the unknowable, I can't see what can't be seen*
*I cannot grasp what seems to me to be within a dream*
*But when I search deep down within my soul*
*I feel the echoes of the answers that my heart longs to know*

*Slow the pace, Live the faith*
*Interweave a new compassion*
*Feel the dream, In all its extremes*
*Let love find its new horizons*

*When I feel the force, the power and the light shines bright*
*It seems I'm on the brink of a great insight*
*I see with crystal vision, the door is opened wide*
*I listen to that still, small voice that calls from deep inside*

*I can't know the unknowable, I can't see what can't be seen*
*I cannot grasp what seems to me to be within a dream*
*But when I search deep down within my soul*
*I feel the echoes of the answers that my heart longs to know . . .*


Larry had closed his eyes in order to better concentrate. When he opened them he said, "That kind of poetry springs directly from your soul, Ryan. How many more of these are there?"

"More than twenty. My songs are where I try to define my spiritual questions. I certainly don't claim to have any answers. In fact, you could say that questions are the common theme that runs through my songs. I'm always amazed at the gall of people who not only claim to have concrete answers about the unknowable, but who try to shove those 'answers' down other people's throats. But we've gotten side-tracked from my question. Assuming that Raymond Baker is the one we remember from our past-life regressions, how do we treat a bastard like him in a loving way while we're trying to kick his ass across the courtroom?"

"Baker himself must not become our focal point," said Larry. "We need to try to fill our hearts with love — for the forest, for the endangered species whose nesting habitat would be destroyed — for the part of the earth we are trying to save." He looked at Ryan. "But the most difficult part conceptually, is that we must try to accept and acknowledge that there is a piece of God in Raymond Baker, too. For as surely as God is a part of each one of us, God is a part of Baker, no matter how shrunken and twisted his soul has become. Your song said it very well. Even Raymond Baker could hear the echoes of the answers, if only his heart longed to know what those answers were."

# 3

RAYMOND BAKER STOOD AT THE WINDOW OF HIS OFFICE IN San Francisco, looking out at the bay, where unnoticed by him, sailboats scudded across the waves while tankers and freighters plied their way along the shipping lanes. His mind was completely absorbed by the events of the past few weeks, and his plans for the future. He had not enjoyed himself this much in a long, long time. The management at Miller Lumber were dancing like marionettes on strings that he, the puppet-master, held and pulled at his whim. It was going to take much more effort to get the logging of the old-growth in the Miller tract jump-started than he had originally thought. But the process that would circumvent the environmental laws, and bamboozle the bureaucracies created to implement them was underway. He was determined to do whatever it took to accomplish the task. According to California Department of Forestry regulations, a tract of land had to be studied for at least two years before logging could take place, so as to ensure that none of the animals on the endangered species list would be adversely affected. Baker hadn't anticipated that Miller would be asleep at the wheel when it came to their most valuable asset. The tract had been divided into observation zones years before, but the stations in the zones had only been manned for a little over a year — and then only sporadically. The data they had collected barely knocked on the door of what was needed. Fortunately, only a few people at Miller had been privy to that particular bit of information. For the most part, he had cowed them into submission — every time he walked into a room, he half expected to see brown stains appear on their pants. Only one of them had given him any trouble. Taking care of that piece of shit had been a slick operation. Baker allowed a smile to crease the ordinarily frozen mask of his face while he savored that triumph. His research through the health records of the management-level employees had revealed Rosso's bad habits and questionable health. *The perfect ruse.* He thought back to his rapid response to Rosso's threat to go public with what he knew. But Baker had anticipated that Rosso would try to create trouble for him — no one with any brains could have missed the fool's glowering stares and mutterings during the briefings he'd given. Rosso was as predictable as they came — he even ate at the same greasy spoon every morning. It had been child's play for Baker's trusted assassin to slip the rapidly-disappearing chemical into his coffee, and then leave the restaurant before Rosso collapsed at his table, his face imbedded in the biscuits and gravy that had brought his heart to the brink of disaster in the first place.

The others in management suspected foul play, of course, just as Baker intended. They needed the yoke of fear to keep them on the right path — *his* path. The autopsy had shown a heart attack as Baker had known it would. Rosso's health was terrible — that was common knowledge. There was no way to call his death homicide, let alone pin the blame for it on him. He had immediately felt his hold over the rest of the management team tighten. Rosso's death showed them what their fate would be if they crossed him. And with everyone who knew about the wildlife study data under his thumb or out of the way, it had been child's play to re-create and modify the field-data so that it appeared that the studies had been properly carried out for the requisite time period. That was one of the most beautiful aspects of his takeover. Miller Lumber had been considered so socially responsible by the eco-freaks, that they hadn't been monitoring the company's old-growth for endangered species as they did with every other lumber company. There was no one who could dispute the manufactured data upon which his Timber Harvest Plan relied.

Later, after he had achieved his precisely measured altered-state of consciousness, Baker reviewed the time-table he had established for the project. Things were right on schedule. He wondered how much the environmentalists knew, or thought they knew. There had been reports of almost daily flyovers by small aircraft — activity that was highly unlikely out in the middle of nowhere, unless someone was trying to monitor activity on the ground. He allowed a brief smile to flit across his features. For some reason, the upcoming fight with the environmentalists intrigued him. As a rule, he considered environmentalists to be such utterly useless pieces of shit, that he found it odd he even cared. But from the beginning of this project, the thought of enraging them had been particularly appealing. It would still take some time before he cut a swath through their world. But the sense of anticipation that was building while he was waiting would only make things that much sweeter when the day of reckoning came.

# 4

GAYLE SAT CROSS-LEGGED IN FRONT OF THE ALTAR SHE HAD BUILT on the living-room floor of the small house off Pudding Creek Road that she rented just north of Fort Bragg. The house was close to town, yet far enough from the constant stream of traffic that flowed in starts and stops down Highway One, that she could retreat there and envelop herself in silence any time of the day. The altar's shape and contents had changed over the years, depending on the current direction of her spiritual meanderings. The most recent addition was the portrait of a raven as the centerpiece. She had taken the bird in as a broken-winged foundling a few years before — completely unaware that the raven was her totem animal. That discovery explained the unusual connection she had always felt with the bird while she was nursing it back to health. It had finally disappeared from its perch one blustery winter day, never to return, but it had gone through several molts before winging off to find a new home. The altar contained a bundle of feathers she had gathered during those times, as well as several of the crystals that helped her focus her energy. The most recent addition to the altar was a two-foot long redwood splinter taken from an old-growth stump behind her house.

Although she was reasonably certain that the impending conflict and the identity of their adversary had been defined, Gayle intended to put all doubt behind her. She lit a bundle of sweetgrass, and performed the ritual gestures she had learned during her regression to the Oglala Sioux lifetime. Then with her fingertips lightly touching the bundle of feathers and the redwood splinter, she closed her eyes, held the image of a raven in her mind and shifted the greater part of her awareness into her totem as she sent it forth.

She soared through the ceiling and roof of her house and out into the misty air above, and with wingbeats that had no correlation to the distance traveled, she set out over the mountains towards Cloverdale. When she arrived at the Miller Lumber complex, she circled over the vast piles of uncut logs, the huge buildings and massive kilns. Following the sharp reek of raw fear that escaped from the largest office building like a tendril of smoke, she drifted through the walls and was immediately buffeted by the miasma of angst and despair left behind by those who worked here. She had purposely waited until after normal office hours to make this journey — although she knew that the rest of the mill would still be operating. The emotional residue that haunted the room became increasingly dense as she approached one particular inner office. If she had been in her human form, she would have held her breath, and even in her spectral shape, her heartbeat accelerated as she drifted through the wall. *He* wasn't there, and she mentally heaved a sigh of relief. But she had her confirmation all the same. *The One without a Soul* had lingered here. He didn't so much leave a psychic stink behind him, as the sensation that all vitality had been sucked away, leaving behind nothing but utter hopelessness. There was no longer any room for doubt. This room had become the lair of their ancient enemy.

The return journey was accomplished by allowing her physical self to become aware of how far her soul had strayed. The life-force that connected body and spirit did the rest, and within seconds she opened her eyes to find the painted eyes of the raven staring back at her with what she would have sworn was approval.

She rose, and stretched the stiff muscles that had held her motionless while her spirit wandered, then phoned Larry, leaving a message on his machine when he didn't answer. She had taken to calling each member of their small band on a daily basis, ostensibly to verify that all was well. The act of phoning was a comfortable ritual more than anything else — if *The One without a Soul* harmed any of them, she was sure she would know it instantly. She dialed another number, and spent a few minutes in conversation with Pam. Ryan was next. When Larry answered Ryan's phone and told her that he was enjoying a private concert of some of Ryan's original compositions, she discovered why he hadn't been available to answer his own phone. She smiled as she heard the music in the background. Ryan had been a prolific composer over the years, and Larry was in for a full night if they got through even half of his repertoire. She told Larry about her spirit-walking journey, and that her after-hours trip to the Miller Lumber Company office had confirmed that Raymond Baker was indeed *The One without a Soul.*

"Did you really have any doubts?" he asked.

"As much as anything, I wanted to test out what I learned during our regression at a non-critical time," she admitted. She described the residue of fear she had found painted on the air, and the strange vacuum-scoured *lack* of any aura that *The One without a Soul* left in his wake. As she did, she shuddered. Now that she had returned to her body, the memory of the experience made her feel nauseous, the mere echo of *The One without a Soul's* presence causing a visceral reaction.

Her last call was to Project HOPE, where she suspected she would find Audrey, who had a reputation as a tireless campaigner, willing to work at every possible job that the organization had to offer, from president of the executive board on down. A person whose voice Gayle didn't recognize answered the phone, and she waited while Audrey was summoned.

"God, it's good to hear a friendly voice," Audrey said when she picked up the phone. "I don't know whether the service that prepares our phone-lead lists got us mixed up with the National Gun Association, or if that asshole Rapski is actually having success turning people against us, but I can't remember talking to more jerks in one night since we got started."

"Who is 'that asshole Rapski?'" Gayle asked.

"He's a radio talk-show host whose show is broadcast out of Ukiah. He's so far to the right politically that if he went an inch further he'd have to change his name to Adolf. He's been raving against environmentalists for years, and he's always had it in for Project HOPE — probably because our headquarters are just a few miles away from the radio station. For the past few weeks we seem to have been his only target."

"I can see now why you refer to him as an asshole," said Gayle. "He sounds like a real loser."

"He's got quite a following of loser wannabees too," Audrey confirmed. "They tend to take their cue from the things Rapski says between the lines. We've had to keep a twenty-four hour watch to make sure that vandals don't get any opportunities to make their hero happy — even though nothing in particular is happening on the legal front. I wonder what it will it be like after Miller Lumber files its Timber Harvest Plan and we file a lawsuit to try to block it."

"Has anybody ever looked into the ownership of the radio station where Rapski's show originates?" asked Gayle.

"You know, I don't think anyone has — we've never even thought of looking beyond Rapski himself."

"I think I'll ask Doug to check it out," said Gayle. "I understand that he used to unearth all sorts of deeply buried relationships between politicians and their supporters when he worked for the Times, and something like this would be right down his alley. If there's a tie between Rapski and Baker, we need to know about it. But hey — there's more to life than dealing with people like Baker and Rapski. How are you coping with being away from your sweetheart? I know what new love is like — you're in physical pain if you're away from the other person too long."

Audrey sighed. "I'm holding up okay, I guess. We've been talking several times a day — I shudder to think about our phone bills. It would probably be cheaper for one of us to quit working than to live in different towns and pay the long-distance charges! But Ryan has arranged his schedule so that he can take the next few Fridays off. As soon as things calm down around here, I'm going to try to do the same. Right now, there's absolutely no way — you wouldn't believe how stacked up things got at Peckham & Associates while I was gone. The way things look, the first time I'll be able to take any time off will be for a maternity leave."

"Just remember this, daughter," said Gayle putting as much authority as she could into her voice. "I know it's a cliché, but nobody *ever* lay on their death-bed and lamented the fact that they hadn't spent enough time at the office! You're going to have to learn how to juggle your work *and* Project HOPE *and* your family, but *right now* is the *only* time that you and Ryan will have just to yourselves — except for the occasional weekend — for the next twenty years or more. Take it from one who's been through it, honey, you need to spend as much time with your man as possible. Don't let a single opportunity slip away!"

After she hung up the phone, Audrey stared at it thoughtfully. Gayle was absolutely right. She could let the world drag her around like a rat being worried by a terrier, or she could take charge of her own life, and make time for the things that were *really* important. How many times had she told her own counselees that the most important things in life were relationships, not money? How often had she admonished them to "carve out time" for the people they cared for? As difficult as it was going to be, she had to turn over a new leaf and take her own good advice. She picked up the phone again and punched in Ryan's number. It would be a while before they worked out how to spend more time with each other, and she intended to do some of the "carving" on her end of things. In the meantime, she decided that she may as well be resigned to being the phone company's best customer.

# 5

THE TWO-HOUR DRIVE FROM CASPAR TO HEALDSBURG SEEMED endless. Ryan tried to keep his impatience in check as he followed a lumbering motorhome through the twists and turns of Highway 128. The driver seemed oblivious to the long line of cars stacked up behind him, ignoring every turnout. Ryan reminded himself that there were several long straight stretches where he would be able to pass just a few miles down the road. After Cloverdale, he would be on Highway 101 and his velocity would be limited only by his willingness to risk a speeding ticket. The four days since he had seen Audrey were the longest he could ever remember enduring. In order to cope with his frustration over the pace he was being forced to travel, he visualized her beautiful face and practiced what he was going to say to her. It felt as if he had slipped into some kind of emotional timewarp and resulting teenage crush. Even though they talked frequently on the phone, he still felt as if he had been transformed into a love-struck adolescent trying to get up the nerve to hold a girl's hand for the first time. It was totally irrational. They were engaged — she was carrying their child — but he couldn't help feeling nervous. At last, he came to the straight stretch he had been anticipating, blew past the offending motorhome, and pushed his Caravan up to speeds that would have seemed excessive to most, but still left him feeling as if he were mired in molasses.

As he came to the southern end of Cloverdale on Highway 101, Miller Lumber loomed on his right. There were acres of redwood logs stacked and tagged, waiting to be processed, and a smaller area where finished lumber was waiting for shipment. Miller wasn't a huge conglomerate like Georgia Pacific or Louisiana Pacific, but it was considerably larger than the Redwood Empire mill on the north end of town. Ryan shuddered involuntarily. He felt as if he was skirting the lair of a dragon without knowing whether it was slumbering or about to burst forth belching flame on its way to wreak havoc and destruction.

An hour later he was on the outskirts of Healdsburg, following the directions Audrey had given him to the converted house on the south end of town that Project HOPE called home. It looked very much like he had imagined it, complete with the hand-painted sign out front and solar collectors on the roof. His schoolboy fears evaporated the moment he stepped out of his car. Audrey had been watching for him, and was already hurrying toward him, with a radiant smile that drilled a hole directly through his heart. Their relationship was so new that although they had only been apart for a few days, she felt slightly smaller than he remembered when they embraced. He couldn't remember anything feeling better than just holding her close — until she kissed him. As they walked inside, all activity ceased, and they — mostly *he* — became the center of attention. Adam Gray was the first to walk up to Ryan with his hand extended. Before he could introduce himself, Ryan said, "You must be Adam — I've wanted to thank you for making Audrey take her vacation. If it hadn't been for you, I might never have found her."

"How did you know which one I was?" Adam began. "No, wait — let me guess. Audrey told you that I was the tall skinny one, right?"

"She described you right down to your Birkenstock sandals," Ryan said with a grin. Audrey introduced him to the others who had gathered, leaving Michael Holland until the end. When she introduced him, Michael reached out to shake hands, and said, "I don't know whether to welcome you as a fellow attorney, or curse you for dashing any faint hope that Audrey might ever cast her eye in my direction," winking at Ryan and chuckling over Audrey's startled glance. "I'm just kidding, of course — I'm almost old enough to be her father. Welcome to Project HOPE, Ryan."

"I've heard so much about you and Adam, it seems as if I already know both of you," Ryan replied. "Audrey told me about your work for Project HOPE — I'm impressed. Any solo attorney who takes on big business has my deepest admiration. With all of the resources the big firms have, every victory must have been an uphill battle."

"It wasn't exactly a walk in the park, I'll admit that. But remember it's been my area of specialty for years — I was there when they wrote the book! I don't know if Audrey told you, but for the first twenty years of my career, I represented lumber companies. I know all the moves — every trick they can pull because I used to pull them myself. I'll tell you some war-stories some time."

"I'd really like that," Adam replied. "I've been a general practitioner ever since I hung up my shingle in Fort Bragg. Even when I worked for a firm in Sacramento, the partners specialized, and I ended up with the odds and ends." He chuckled. "At the time, I thought that I was missing out, but in retrospect, it was the best possible preparation I could have had for a solo law practice in a small town."

"All right, guys — that's enough shoptalk," Audrey cut in. "I'm sure you'll have a lot of opportunities to talk about the law tomorrow morning."

"Tomorrow morning?" Ryan queried.

Audrey blushed slightly. "I guess this is part of my personality that you haven't seen yet — I'm known around here as the 'schedule-queen.' I knew that you wanted to go for a mountain bike ride while you were here, and I wanted you and Michael to have a chance to get to know each other. Since I have to work tomorrow morning, I thought that the two of you might enjoy going on a ride together." She looked hopefully at Ryan.

"It's a great idea." he replied reassuringly, then turned to Michael. "I've heard that there's some great riding around here."

"It's not quite as spectacular as what you have on the coast, but it has its own charm," he replied. "We've got a number of options depending on what you're up for."

Audrey snuck a peek at her watch. "My boyfriend here doesn't know it yet, but I've been making even more plans. He and I have dinner reservations this evening, and I think he may want to change clothes before we go." She leaned over to kiss Ryan quickly. "It's my treat tonight, sweetheart."

"You better watch out, Ryan," said Adam with an evil grin. "If your calendar is clear now, you might consider putting a padlock on it — otherwise Audrey will get you so booked up that you'll have grey hair before you get your next opportunity for spontaneity."

Audrey tilted her nose into the air before responding in a tone of voice designed to convey the image that she was royalty, and Adam a lowly knave. "This man is in love with me, you oaf. There's nothing you could possibly say to turn him against me." Imperiously, she turned to Michael. "Any chance that I could slap a restraining order on this thoroughly repugnant personage before I leave, Counselor?"

Michael glanced at his watch and shook his head. "I'm afraid all of the courts are closed."

"Nothing lost — in any event, the time has come for us to take our leave," said Audrey in her "queenly voice," and then, unable to keep up the pretense any longer, she burst out laughing. The way they related to each other reminded Ryan of his law-school years. A unique camaraderie often developed among people who went through adversity together. Clearly the relationships at Project HOPE had been forged into friendships that were *very* special.

*   *   *

AUDREY'S HOUSE WAS a small, two-bedroom affair built in the 1930's, when it was not uncommon for houses of its size to incorporate a number of hand-crafted features. The living room had a fireplace and its walls blended into the ceiling in uninterrupted curves. There were hardwood floors throughout and built-in cabinets with leaded glass doors in the dining room. She had converted the smaller bedroom into a combination office/entertainment center, with a television, stereo, and a work area where a personal computer commanded a position of prominence.

A wonderful smell was emanating from the kitchen, and the dining room table had been set for two. "I thought you said we had dinner reservations," said Ryan, taking in the plum colored table cloth, fancy silverware and candles that waited only for a flame to complete a most romantic atmosphere.

Audrey answered from the smaller bedroom, where she was putting a CD on the stereo. The music she selected completed the mood perfectly, and the look on her face indicated that she had been planning this moment for some time. "We do have reservations — a table for two at the only restaurant I can think of where I can be just as romantic with my man as I want." She drew him close and kissed him in a way that was very different from the one she had given him at Project HOPE, then led him to the bedroom wearing a bewitching smile, and soon nothing else. "Our reservation is in half an hour," she breathed into his ear, "but I don't think the cook will mind if we're a few minutes late."

Much later, after they had finished their pasta shells stuffed with ricotta cheese and mushrooms, spinach salad with mandarin oranges, and chocolate-pumpkin cheesecake, they sat at the table basking in the warm afterglow of their lovemaking and the simple but elegant meal. Ryan studied his love's face, doing his best to memorize the details of every curve, line and shadow — every nuance of expression that crossed her face as the flickering candle-light made it into a changing canvas upon which her features danced delightfully. Their hands touched across the table, fingers caressing fingertips. He decided that there would never be a better time for his own surprise. Without releasing their tentative contact, he rose, and stood in front of her.

"Ryan, what are you . . ." Audrey began, but he simply put his finger to her lips. Then he knelt slowly on one knee and kissed her hand.

"I have a romantic streak of my own," he whispered, feeling a tremendous up-welling of emotion, as he reached into his pocket for the small velvet-covered case he had been fingering all evening. "I wished that I had a ring to give you the night we met . . . but it's really better this way. If I had gotten one before, it would have been out of either false hope or desperation. As it was, my heart was full of nothing but love for you, and happiness for us when I picked it out."

Audrey opened the box and slid the engagement ring she found there onto the fourth finger of her left hand. When she reached her hand out to admire it, the diamond caught the glow from the candles, and reflected it back at them as if it were catching the flame of the love that filled their eyes. "Ryan, it's lovely . . . You didn't have to do this!"

"I know," he responded. "But this ring is important, and not just as a symbol of our love and commitment." His eyes twinkled. "Men might not notice, but I don't want every woman you tell about our engagement to take a look at your left hand and think I'm some sort of cheapskate."

They both rose, Ryan from his knee and Audrey from her chair, kissed briefly and then simply held each other, moving slightly to the music coming from the stereo. "You seem to know just what to do to make me feel special," she said after a few moments. "I really *did* want an engagement ring! Ever since I was a little girl, I wanted to be proposed to in a romantic setting." She extended her hand, watching it as the ring caught the candle-light once more. Then she returned her gaze to Ryan. "It's really perfect, you know. First you sang me the song you wrote before you even knew who I was, and I just got the ring and the romantic, candle-lit setting I've always imagined. Even if I didn't know about our soul-mate connection, I would know that we were meant for each other."

Ryan chuckled softly, caressing and kissing her hair. "You're not going to get any argument from me. By the time I had spent as much time with anyone else as I've spent with you, I was already making adjustments and figuring out how to cope with all of the rough spots and sharp edges." He led her to the couch in the living room. A fire had been laid in the fireplace, and though it was warm, he lit a match and held it to the crumpled newspaper under the kindling. "I don't feel any of that with you," he continued. "Everything is so incredibly easy — so right! I can't imagine anything better." He moved his hand down to her stomach, and she placed hers on top of his. "How are you feeling?" he asked hesitantly, not knowing exactly how to phrase the question.

"Wonderful . . . Complete . . . Happy . . . I've never felt better in my life. I think I feel different, but that's probably just because I *know* I'm pregnant." She reached up and stroked the hollow of his cheek, a gesture that somehow warmed him as much or even more than a kiss. After that, there wasn't much conversation, or need for it as they savored the rest of the evening and the love that made their cups overflow.

# 6

THE MUSCLES IN RYAN'S LEGS BURNED AND HIS BREATH CAME
in great ragged gulps as he struggled up the steep hill in pursuit of the two riders
ahead of him. His jersey was soaked through with sweat and the bandana he had
rolled and tied around his forehead as a sweatband was completely saturated. He
tried to keep his mind off the pain in his thighs and calves by calculating how far he
could ride until a new bead of sweat fell from his nose and splashed against the top-
tube of his bicycle frame. The etiquette of "group" mountain-bike riding dictated
that there was really no *group* at all — unless two or more rider's abilities were
evenly matched or a consensus was reached that everyone should ride at the slowest rider's pace. The "together" part of going on a group ride came during rest
periods, usually at the top of a climb. To his chagrin, Ryan found that he was
unable to match the pace set by Michael and the friend he'd brought along. His
frequent solitary rides kept him in excellent shape — he knew only a few people his
age who could keep up with him. But the two men who had disappeared up the trail
ahead of him were on another level entirely, and the fact that both of them were at
least fifteen years older than he was added salt to the wound.

The densely-forested mountains near the coast where Ryan usually rode were
every bit as steep as the rolling, oak-studded hills east of Healdsburg. But there
was a major difference. Almost every road or trail that Ryan traversed in his rides
around Fort Bragg had been built with the idea of transporting huge sections of
redwood logs to the mills, and they were graded accordingly. In contrast, the steep
goat-track he was following now seemed to have been designed with the sole purpose of giving him a heart attack. He could ride most of it, but there were several
times he had to dismount and push. On those occasions he especially appreciated
the light weight of his Ibis mountain-bike, with its titanium frame and top-end
components. He reached for his water bottle, and took a long pull, relieved that he
had thought to put an extra one in his jersey pocket, then continued to grind up the
hill in his lowest gear.

Eventually, the trail crested and he found his riding companions lounging on a
sunlit patch of dry grass. In order to avoid the heat, they had started from Audrey's
house at six-thirty in the morning, but the air was already beginning to warm up
despite the early hour.

"Have you been here long?" Ryan gasped, as he got off of his bike, flopped down, and began to massage his calves to see if he could work some life back into them.

"Not too long — just five or ten minutes, Michael replied, with a twinkle in his eye. It was acceptable in the strange etiquette of the mountain-biking community to comment about, and even enjoy the suffering of a fellow mountain biker while making light of one's own exertions. Everyone suffered when the terrain tended toward the vertical — they just suffered at differing rates of speed. "This trail is quite a bit steeper than the logging roads you're used to," he observed "How're you holding up?"

"I'm fine, now that I'm getting a chance to catch my breath," said Ryan, taking a pull from his water bottle and unwrapping an energy bar. As he spoke, he realized that it was true. Now that his heart-rate had slowed, he felt great. His endorphins, the brain-chemicals that produced the physical euphoria commonly known as the "runner's high," had kicked in.

Their route had meandered up the side of the mountain, through stands of oak and laurel, as well as the occasional redwood. They were now several miles from the closest paved road and had gained nearly a thousand feet in altitude. The vista before them looked like a patchwork quilt comprised of vineyards and stands of trees on a background of dry, brown grass. Ben Meyers, Michael's friend, looked relaxed and rested — and apparently ready to climb back on the bike at any time. Ryan intended to stretch this break out as long as he could. He asked Ben what he did for a living, hoping that the answer would be a long one.

"I'm a wildlife biologist," Ben replied. "My specialty is ornithology — that's the study of birds — in my case, seabirds. That's how I met Michael — I was one of his expert witnesses in Project HOPE's last trial up in Humboldt County. The proposed logging would have resulted in what is called a 'taking' of the Marbled Murrelet, which is a rare seabird we're trying to bring back from the edge of extinction."

"What do redwoods and Douglas firs have to do with seabirds?" Ryan asked, actually becoming interested instead of just buying time out of the saddle.

Ben took a swig from his water bottle before answering. "The Marbled Murrelet spends most of its time on the ocean feeding on fish. But the reason we needed to stop the logging is because they nest in trees — specifically, trees in old-growth forests three feet in diameter or more, with large limbs that they use as a nest platform." Ben had been looking out at the panoramic view below them. He turned back towards Ryan. "They don't actually build nests — they just lay their eggs on branches that are at least a hundred-fifty feet above the forest floor. Cut down the trees, and the birds won't lay eggs. No eggs, no baby Murrelets — they're about ready to die out. They've been protected by the Endangered Species Act since 1992 — that's when the Wildlife Service appointed a group of us to review what it would take to ensure their survival as a species. We're trying to help bring them back, and if possible to get them off the endangered list." He picked up his water bottle and the peel from a banana he'd wolfed down earlier. "We've reached the conclusion that the species is in such desperate shape that *all* nesting habitat is critical, so we've been keeping watch on all of their known nesting areas."

"Is the Miller tract one of those?" Ryan asked.

Ben shook his head. "We don't know for sure, but probably not — it's a few miles further inland than they've ever been observed to nest — but as far as we know, nobody's been out there to check, either."

Ben and Michael rose and put their helmets and gloves back on. Ryan took their cue and donned his own, groaning silently. Ben had warmed to his subject, and continued as they picked up their bikes and prepared to take off on the next part of the ride. "If a forest is a nesting area for a protected species, *and* a whole lot of other conditions are met, then a lumber company can be prevented from logging, even on their own land. The Endangered Species Act states that it is a 'taking' of the species when an activity destroys a nesting habitat — it's considered "harassing" the birds because it prevents them from nesting, and harassing the birds is prohibited by the act."

"I get the picture," said Ryan. "It sounds like it must have been awfully complex litigation."

"There were expert witnesses popping out from everywhere during the trial," Michael laughed. "Six testified for us, and then there were the "whores" who testified for the lumber company. They tried to sell a bunch of false science to the judge. He could tell that it was just money talking, but it still makes me hot every time I think about it." He threw his leg over the top-tube of his bike and started off. His parting words drifted back "But I feel worse when I remember that I used to hire bastards just like them when I worked for the other side."

At the next rest stop, Ryan was twenty minutes behind the other two. Michael had sprawled on the ground to wait, while Ben was some distance off, taking in the view. Their superior fitness and conditioning had allowed them to keep going at the same pace as when they had first left the pavement behind. *At least there's not much chance I'll ever fall in love, get engaged and learn that I'm going to be a father in the same two-week period again. It cuts too severely into my conditioning program* Ryan consoled himself sarcastically as he took off his helmet and his gloves. His face lit up as he thought of his love. She, and the amazing changes that had so recently taken place in his life were never far from his thoughts.

"Snap out of it, Ryan," drawled Michael, jolting him back to the present. "I caught you dreaming about Audrey again, didn't I?"

"Mea culpa" said Ryan, using up a large portion of the Latin vocabulary he'd picked up in law school. "What gave me away?"

"I knew that 'deer-in-the-headlights' look in your eyes didn't come from that last climb — not with the shit-eating grin that went along with it."

Ryan laughed at Michael's good-natured ribbing, but he felt his ears turn red nonetheless. Rather lamely, he said, "It's been such a big change and it's happened so suddenly . . . "

Michael held up his hand, then rose from where he had sprawled and put a brotherly arm around Ryan. "All kidding aside, I can't tell you how happy I am for the two of you. I've watched Audrey work as if she were possessed for as long as

I've known her." He shook his head. "At least I thought I knew her. Since she came back from the coast, she's a new woman. The Audrey that I knew and loved was a hollow shell compared to the woman I've seen ever since you came into her life."

Ryan felt embarrassed and proud at the same time. "I never knew how 'incomplete' I felt before I knew her. Did she tell you about our soul-mate connection?"

"Are you kidding?" Michael exclaimed. "I had her on 'direct' for nearly an hour, and the cross-examination took twice as long, even though I had to conduct it myself!"

Ryan laughed, and took a sparing sip from his water bottle. He was down to his last one, and only half remained. "I should have known that you'd have ferreted out the whole story straight off," he conceded. "You seem to be very open to the concept — I think I would have been more skeptical."

"I've had a run-in of my own with the supernatural," Michael confided. "I'm a recovering alcoholic. Eight years ago, I was in the process of drinking myself to death when I experienced my own personal miracle. Late one night I was laying on the couch in my living room on the edge of unconsciousness." He stared off into the distance for a moment and then went on. "I was just drifting off, when without warning, my head was filled with a bright white light. My emotions had been dulled by my constant drinking, but they returned in a rush, and I was filled with an incredible sense of awe. Emanating from the light was the purest, most overwhelming love I've ever experienced. I heard a voice — a command, really. It was short and to the point: '*you must quit drinking.*'" He looked back at Ryan. "I've never forgotten the way I felt at that moment — and I haven't found it necessary to have a drink since that night." His smile was warm and genuine. "After what happened to me, I certainly can't find fault with anyone else's experiences that might be considered . . . shall we say on the spiritual side?"

Just then, Ben strolled over and said, "It's really starting to heat up! We should get a move on or we're going to get cooked." He saw Ryan's worried glance at his near-empty water bottle and grinned. "Don't worry about the rest of the ride. We call this spot 'recovery ridge' — it's all downhill from here."

They donned helmets and gloves, and set off down the hill. Ben took the lead, followed by Michael and then Ryan. Soon they were re-tracing their tire-tracks on the first stretch of trail they'd taken after leaving the pavement, riding together now in consideration of Ryan's relative state of fitness. At Audrey's house, they all went inside to get a cold drink. Ryan had just cracked open a Dr. Pepper and poured a couple of glasses of ice-water for his friends when the telephone rang. It was Audrey, sounding more agitated than he'd ever heard her before. "It's for you, Michael," he said, handing the phone over. "Miller Lumber filed their Timber Harvest Plan and the California Department of Forestry has already approved it. It looks as if all hell is about to break loose."

# 7

RAYMOND BAKER TOOK HIS PLACE AT THE HEAD OF THE TABLE
in the conference room at Miller Lumber, and began issuing orders to the management team. The meeting more closely resembled a military briefing than anything
else. And from Baker's perspective, that's exactly what it was. The enemies were
well defined — governmental agencies with their laws and regulations, the environmental groups, and finally the individual protestors that he expected to flock to
the Miller Tract. Logistics played heavily in Baker's favor. The Miller Tract was
perhaps the most remote and inaccessible area in Mendocino County. The old-
growth itself was completely surrounded by second-growth forest that ranged from
fifty to one-hundred-fifty years old. The entire tract was draped over steep, mountainous terrain that stretched to the boundaries of the Jackson State Forest, where
only a few old logging roads were maintained. From the site where the logging was
to commence, the closest of the State-maintained roads in Jackson forest was nine
miles distant. The old logging roads that crisscrossed the second-growth forest in
the Miller Tract were impassable, choked with deadfalls and washouts. Not even a
four-wheel drive vehicle could get through. While planning his assault on the old-
growth redwoods, Baker had dismissed the advice of his more experienced staff,
who had strongly recommended re-opening a number of old roads to create alter-
nate routes in and out of the tract. Re-building old roads would not have been a
huge problem — it was much less difficult to re-build old roads than to engineer
and build new ones. But Baker wanted to keep the area as inaccessible to vehicular
traffic as possible, guaranteeing that there would be only one easily-guarded portal. Two days before, he had issued orders to expand an old staging area near the
site where logging operations would commence. Since then, work had gone on
around the clock, and the clearing was now large enough to accommodate the necessary equipment. Much of it was already there — they had been moving equipment to the clearing non-stop for days in anticipation that the road might soon be
blocked by a living wall of protestors.

Baker concluded the meeting and sent his lackeys packing. It was time-con-
suming to micro-manage a staff who dared not breathe unless he commanded it,
but in this operation, it was absolutely necessary. After the management team was
gone, he closed his eyes and tried to concentrate. There was something nagging at
the edges of his consciousness, just beyond his reach. The feeling had been there

for over a week, and it was getting stronger. Something needed to be attended to —
of that he was sure. But no matter how many times he reviewed his well laid plans,
he couldn't find a chink or a crack anywhere. He concentrated harder. Nothing
came, although he knew it would eventually. He never missed an important detail.
He never had, and never would.

# 8

WHEN MILLER LUMBER FILED THEIR TIMBER HARVEST PLAN WITH
the California Department of Forestry, and it was approved with unprecedented
speed, word spread like wildfire. Project HOPE, and every other organization
dedicated to the preservation of old-growth forests, sprang into action. At Project
HOPE, the emergency phone tree was put into use immediately. There was old-
growth to save, and nothing else had a higher priority. Ryan and Michael arrived
within an hour of Audrey's phone call, and Ryan was introduced to yet another
aspect of his intended, as the previous day's glowing happiness was replaced by an
air of cool efficiency. Even Adam's jesting was left behind as everyone present
focused on the needs of their star-player. Michael Holland was the calmest person
in the building. No stranger to working under pressure, he was in his element. A
natural athlete, he had quarter-backed his high-school football team to three winning seasons, and also competed in baseball and track. In college he had focused
his competitive energy on academics, graduating Magna Cum Laude. In the legal
arena, his twenty-five years of experience had removed every bit of mystery from
the task ahead of them. He knew every move and every possible counter-move,
and like a master chess player, planned his strategy far in advance.

He looked at his watch before he spoke. "There's no way we can get a petition
for a temporary restraining order on file today. We'll have the whole weekend to
prepare the petition." He directed his attention to Ryan. "Do you have any experience in Federal Court, or with temporary restraining orders?"

"No federal court experience whatsoever, and I'm afraid I'm clueless when it
comes to environmental law, but I have to apply for TRO's all the time in my
Family Law cases."

Michael put a hand on his shoulder and smiled. "The procedures are essentially the same. I'm going to need all the help I can get here, and if you can lend a
hand, I'd really appreciate it. Two heads are always better than one, especially
when we get short on sleep." He tilted his head to one side, and appeared to size
Ryan up. "How fast can you type?"

Ryan grinned. The same manual dexterity that allowed him to breeze through
a difficult musical passage on guitar, mandolin or fiddle translated straight across
to the computer keyboard. "I can type almost as fast as you can talk. Consider me
voice-recognition software with a law degree."

Michael returned the grin. "Excellent." He turned to Audrey and Adam. "I've got my laptop with me, and all of the relevant case-law on compact disc, but we're going to need at least two laser printers, and a couple more computers, all loaded with the same word-processing program."

"We have a computer here if we need it — although that's where we store our database containing all of the names and phone numbers that Project HOPE should be contacting over the weekend," said Adam.

"I've got a computer and printer over at Peckham & Associates that we can use this weekend, and my home computer is also available," said Audrey.

"Okay then," Michael said. "Why don't the two of you round up the computers and printers." He returned his attention to Ryan. "I'm going to set you up in a corner with my laptop and a list of cases to read. If you're going to be able to help me think things through, you'll need to read the major cases." He smiled encouragingly. "If I have anything to say about it, by the time we're through here, there's going to be another expert in this area of the law."

Adam and Audrey left together while Michael and Ryan began organizing the conference room at the back of the building into a law office. Soon Ryan was seated at a hastily-erected folding table, scrolling through the pages of the first case on his list while Michael poured over Miller's Timber Harvest Plan, making notes and occasionally staring off into space. Adam and Audrey returned a few minutes later, and set up two computer workstations. All of them were focused on their immediate tasks, but in the forefront of each of their minds was the question of what was going on out at the Miller tract. How much damage would Baker do before they could stop him? Michael tried not to let his emotions show as he read the wildlife studies and environmental impact report with increasing dismay. Thanks to the information leaked by John Smith, he already knew that the studies had been fabricated, and was hoping for some obvious flaw that he could exploit. But the plan itself and all of the supporting studies were completely consistent with each other, and appeared completely in order. Michael didn't let it show as he finished reading, but he was very worried. This was going to be the most difficult test of his abilities yet.

After four hours, the screen on Michael's laptop computer had become an unbearable tyrant. Ryan's eyes burned, and when his stomach growled, he realized he was famished. When he tried to remember what he had eaten for lunch, he realized that the last thing he had eaten was an energy bar out on the trail. His back and neck ached after the hours of leaning over the small computer — sitting in this hunched-over position was the last thing he needed after a long, difficult mountain-bike ride. And although he had gleaned a thumbnail sketch of environmental law in the area, he was relieved that his role was limited to being a sounding board and spear carrier for Michael rather that the "go-to guy."

On the other side of the table, Michael had been going over Miller's plan and reviewing portions of court decisions trying to find grounds for the court to issue a temporary restraining order. To obtain relief under the Endangered Species Act, he would have to show that there was a likelihood that an illegal "take" of a species protected by the Act was about to occur. The most logical species was the Spotted Owl, a species that nested exclusively in old-growth forests, and had a very broad range. The Miller tract should have been an ideal habitat for the birds, but according to the wildlife studies, there had been *no* Spotted Owl sightings at all. Three Project HOPE volunteers were trying to find the wildlife biologists who had signed off on the report, but so far they had come up empty. Michael wasn't surprised — it would be hard to track almost anyone down this late on a Friday afternoon. Noise had begun to drift in from outside of their makeshift "law office." Michael stood up and stretched, realizing as Ryan had a few moments earlier, that he was painfully hungry. "Time to break for dinner, Ryan," he said. "In all of the excitement, we forgot to eat lunch."

"I'm starving too," Ryan agreed, rubbing the back of his neck and arching his back to try to get the kinks out as they emerged from the back room into the main office. The news about Miller Lumber's logging plan had created a groundswell of activity. The telephones were all in use, and everywhere Ryan looked there were people walking purposefully about. He wandered from room to room trying to find Audrey, and eventually found her in a room that was dominated by a photographic mural of redwoods and rhododendrons covering two entire walls. She and Adam were sitting at large table surrounded by mis-matched chairs, reviewing a computer printout. They looked up when Ryan and Michael entered the room. Adam gestured to the printout that was spread over the table. "We just got the transcript from Eddie Rapski's morning show," he said. "I think he may have stepped too far over the line this time."

"What are you talking about?" asked Ryan, picking up a few pages of the transcript and glancing at them.

"Eddie Rapski is the talk-show host down in Ukiah I was telling you about," said Audrey, "the one who thinks he's best friends with God."

Adam tilted back in his chair. "His show is a fairly accurate gauge of what the reactionary element of society is thinking — more or less because he tells them what they're supposed to think. So we obtain transcripts of every broadcast — they're available to the public. We started getting them when we noticed that there was a correlation between vandalism here at Project HOPE and what Rapski had to say on his show." He made a face. "None of us can stand to listen to the broadcasts — I don't know why, but it's not quite as bad when it's in print."

"What is our dear friend up to now?" asked Michael.

"Just listen to this," said Adam, shuffling through the pages of the transcript until he found what he wanted, and read aloud, "'There is no doubt about it! Things have got to change! These vermin, these scum who flock to our community are all outsiders! Who are they to try to tell us what we can and can't do in our own back yard? Let them foul their own nests with their crazy leftist ideas! Here, in the heartland of California, *we will control our own destiny*! And what should we do when these outsiders come among us and try to tell us how to mind our own business? Why, my friends, we should show them the door! Yes, sir! I'm talking about the bum's rush! And if they resist? Well, I'm not one to stoop to violence, but it seems to me that if a man finds a stray dog in his own back yard, he has a right to boot it out. And if we want to show some deviant the way out of our neighborhood, then there's no better way to do it than a boot in the backside!'"

"Jesus Christ!" exclaimed Ryan after Adam stopped reading. "Where did this Neanderthal come from? He's clearly advocating violence against demonstrators! No one has any right to run someone out of their community just because they disagree with their views."

"That's what I meant when I said I thought he had crossed over the line," Adam replied. "Sheriff Fields has been reluctant to do anything about Rapski so far, even though it's been obvious for some time that attempts at vandalism here at Project HOPE *only* occur after Rapski has laid into us on his show. These people aren't exactly what I'd call discriminating."

"I don't think what he said goes quite far enough to get him in trouble," said Michael. "Though I have to admit it's awfully close." He turned to Ryan. "What do you think?"

"There might be a slim chance for a conviction if someone actually went out and did what Rapski said," Ryan responded. "But nasty as it is, it's probably still constitutionally protected." He shrugged his shoulders. "It's been a long time since I thought about those kinds of issues. But there *is* an issue that Michael and I came to talk to you about. Food! Our stomachs were finally able to override our brains, and we realized that we were starving."

Audrey looked surprised. "Ryan, I'm sorry — we were supposed to go out for lunch, and with everything that's been going on, I forgot."

Ryan reached for her hand and smiled warmly. "Don't worry about it — it's not as if I didn't forget, too. Is there a good place nearby?"

"During times of crisis, Taco Loco becomes a second home for us," Adam said, unconsciously licking his lips. "I was thinking that we should head over there for something to eat even before you brought it up."

Audrey laughed and swatted Adam playfully. "Tell me if there has ever been a time when you weren't the first one to think about eating!" She glanced at Ryan. "Adam is known as 'the bottomless pit.' He eats twice as much as anyone else, and never gains an ounce." She grinned mischievously. "We're sure that his stomach is a black hole in disguise — he doesn't move around enough to have a fast metabolism."

It was Adam's turn to take a swat at Audrey, and within seconds, they were chasing each other around the room, acting much more like elementary school children at recess than adults. As Ryan watched them blow off some of the tension they were all feeling, he was reminded that Adam had been their son in the Oglala Sioux lifetime — if only for a few days. *I only met this guy yesterday,* he mused, *but it does seem like I've known him forever.* After Audrey and Adam declared a truce, the four of them walked the short distance to Taco Loco. As predicted, Adam ate twice as much as anyone else. They kept the conversation light, only occasionally drifting back to the problem that lurked in the backs of their minds. All too soon the meal was over, and they were back at Project HOPE, immersed once more in their individual tasks.

Three hours later, Ryan turned off Michael's laptop. He couldn't focus his eyes anymore, and he had a headache from the tension in his neck. Just as he was going to tell Michael that he was cooked, Audrey burst into the room. "John Smith is on the phone!" she said. "Adam is talking with him right now. He wants to set up another meeting, and this time he wants him to bring our lawyer!"

# 9

IT TOOK SEVERAL HOURS, FOR DOUG TO COMPLETE HIS RESEARCH at the public counter of the corporate division of the Secretary of State's Office in Sacramento. He had chosen to do his research the old-fashioned way, rather than trying to puzzle his way through an Internet search. The photocopied documents in the file sitting on the seat next to him contained the results — a paper trail that led directly from Raymond Baker to Radio Station KHAT — home of "Eddie Rapski, the radical of the right." The broadcasts originated in Ukiah, but the content was undoubtedly dictated by Baker. Doug had to admit it, Gayle's intuition had proven correct once again. By this time, he was no longer surprised — when it came to hunches, she was batting a thousand. Briefly he wished he'd had a source like her back when he was a reporter, although if truth were told, in those days he would have been too skeptical to follow up on anything she said. As he drove, he glanced repeatedly at the file. He was amazed by the extent of Baker's long-range planning. Eddie Rapski had been on the air for three years, railing away at environmentalists and championing big business, while Raymond Baker had only staged the takeover of Miller Lumber six weeks previously. He wondered what other obstacles lay in their path, placed there by Baker far in advance, like land-mines buried in what appeared to be neutral ground.

It was almost dark when he reached Project HOPE. The parking lot was nearly filled by a variety of cars, including a group of motorhomes and campers circled like wagons. Doug pulled his blue Toyota pickup into a slot next to an ancient Dodge Power Wagon with a two-story shingled structure built directly onto its frame that looked as if it dated back to the late sixties or early seventies, and headed inside. He found a hubbub of activity, with small clumps of people speaking earnestly between themselves while others bustled about. Doug asked a young man wearing baggy shorts and a tie-died rainbow-colored t-shirt if he knew where Audrey was, and was directed to the rear of the building. Doug entered a room filled with tables that were laden with computers, printers, and the canary-yellow pads that those in the legal profession seemed to require. Audrey and Ryan were sitting together, looking tired, but excited. "Welcome to 'protest-central,'" Ryan quipped when he saw Doug. "This place has been hopping since we found out that Miller's Timber Harvest Plan had been approved. You heard about that, didn't you?"

"Pam told me when I called from Sacramento," Doug affirmed. He gestured at the jumble of paper, machines and other paraphernalia strewn on the tables. "I can see that you've already gotten started on the legal end of things. How is it coming?"

"Michael Holland is our mastermind in that department," Ryan replied. "But I couldn't tell you what he's thinking. He's mostly been staring off into space and looking concerned."

"Where is he, anyway?" asked Doug. "I've been looking forward to meeting him."

"He's off with Adam Gray. Our informant from Miller Lumber called to ask for another meeting, and told Adam to bring Michael with him this time."

"That's a change, isn't it? It's a bit hard to keep the people that I haven't met straight, but if memory serves me right, Adam is the only one who's had any contact with the mysterious Mr. Smith."

"You're right, it is a change," said Audrey. "And there's another change. The meeting is at the Hamburger Ranch again — all of the other meetings were at a new location. Our guess is that Smith got short on time — we're hoping he has something for Michael that will bring a smile to his face."

"That brings me to the results of my research in Sacramento," said Doug holding out his folder. "I don't know if we're going to be able to use it one way or the other, but I've been able to trace a solid connection between Eddie Rapski and Raymond Baker."

"Those bastards!" exclaimed Audrey, her face flushing with anger. "No wonder Rapski's been all over our case ever since he came on the air." As she went on to describe some of her deepest and most strongly held feelings for Rapski and the man behind him, Ryan and Doug were startled, not so much by her vehemence, as by her creative choice of words and phrases. But they shared her feelings completely — their common regression experience as Oglala Sioux had acquainted them with the spirit that now animated Raymond Baker. *This is a side to Audrey I haven't seen before,* thought Ryan, chuckling to himself over some suggestions she had for Rapski about what to do with certain parts of his anatomy. Nonetheless, her intensity concerned him. "I was having a conversation with Larry just the other day," he said in a roundabout manner when she came up for air. "He reminded me of what he and Gayle have both been saying all along — that the message from the advanced spirits is that we have to approach this conflict with love in our hearts, or we have no chance of success." Audrey colored slightly as he spoke. "I'm not pointing any fingers," Ryan went on, winking at his fiancé. "I don't have quite your flair for description, but I feel the same about Baker as you — and if there's a connection to Rapski, then those feelings extend to him." His brow wrinkled in frustration. "But I'll be damned if I can tell you how we're supposed to *love* these bastards into submission! Larry tried to explain his ideas on the subject to me in general terms, but when it came to specific examples, the things he said went right over my head."

Just then, there was a commotion in the entryway of the headquarters. They hurried to the door and saw that Adam and Michael had returned. Michael was carrying a sheaf of documents, and he didn't have to say a word to make everyone breathe easier — the look on his face said it all.

"I'm afraid some of John Smith's paranoia is well grounded," Michael remarked after they had reached the sanctuary of their temporary law office and he had been introduced to Doug. "There are a number of people here at Project HOPE with whom we're not personally familiar, and prudence dictates that we take some special precautions." He looked around the room gravely. "Everything I say in this room needs to stay here — at least until Monday. Our conversation with Mr. Smith was very interesting. It seems that when he was working on the Y2-K problem in the mainframe computers, he installed a set of programs designed to capture data that had been accidentally deleted." Michael pulled out a yellow legal pad and the rest of them leaned close. "All of the desk-top computers at Miller were already linked together in a network," he said, drawing a series of small boxes connected by lines. "That's quite common in an organization of this size — it allows for e-mail between workers, and for people to access information stored in one computer from a terminal somewhere else. But here's where it gets interesting." He drew a larger box and then drew a line that intercepted one of the lines linking the smaller boxes. "Smith linked the two IBM mainframes that control the actual milling process into the desktop network, then wrote a program that would capture anything deleted from the desk-top computers — a *secondary* backup deletion-recovery system to the one he'd already installed within the network of desk-top computers. He never mentioned the back-up program in the mainframes to anyone. That's the reason no one ever knew about it — whenever anyone inadvertently deleted something from their computer, the primary data-retrieval program caught it."

"He's taking forever to get to the best part," Adam interjected. "We got the details on what Smith was telling me the last time we met. Right after Baker took over and started issuing orders about getting a Timber Harvest Plan prepared for the Miller tract, Smith reviewed the field-data for the wildlife studies. He got suspicious when Baker insisted that the field-data be put in protected files. Smith set up the files, but left a back-door into the system. He went back in to check things out, and saw that the wildlife studies that support the Timber Harvest Plan didn't match up with what he remembered from his conversations with the biologists."

"We already knew that Smith has a special fondness for old-growth groves," said Michael, taking up the story again. He turned to Adam. "I think you said he described them as being sacred, didn't you, Adam?" Adam nodded and he continued. "Before Baker took over the company, Smith got to be friends with the wildlife biologists who were doing the wildlife studies out in the old-growth. Of course, they're always doing a study somewhere — all Timber Harvest Plans require wildlife studies, whether they're cutting virgin forest or not. Smith didn't think that the wildllife biologists had been out in the old-growth often enough to have completed a proper study, though, so he checked the retrieval program in the IBM mainframe. That's part of what he turned over to us tonight — the *actual* wildlife studies. And along with the original studies, are a number of documents that are essentially 'forgeries in progress.' Whoever faked the studies that were submitted to the government dumped these documents from the data-retrieval program in the desktop-network, but they didn't know about the other one."

"So we caught Baker red-handed?" asked Audrey excitedly.

"Let's put it this way," said Michael. "I think that the documents will be enough to get us a temporary restraining order — along with Smith's sworn affidavit. We're going to need his testimony for the actual trial though, and he's been reluctant to reveal himself — he was afraid that Baker would kill him just for talking to us, let alone testifying against him in court. Now that he's turned over the documents, he's decided that things have gotten too hot for him to stay at Miller a moment longer. Seeing us was the last thing he did before leaving Cloverdale. He had us memorize a phone number where we can leave a message for him — it's somewhere in the Bay Area, but that's all we know." Michael took in the drawn, tired faces that surrounded him. "We've all put in an extremely long day, and we've got an even longer weekend ahead of us. I suggest we call it a day and get as much rest tonight as we can." He winked at Ryan before turning to Audrey and shaking his finger at her. "That means that you have to let my right-hand man get some sleep tonight." Audrey blushed slightly before she stepped back into her role as 'imperious queen' and haughtily replied that she didn't have the foggiest idea what he was talking about. Then in a stage-whisper told Ryan that he'd be lucky if he got *any* sleep at all. They left in high spirits. Audrey had every confidence in Michael's abilities — as long as he was smiling, she could relax.

Later, after Ryan had drifted off, Audrey lay next to him unable to sleep. The memories of dying at the hand of Raymond Baker as an Oglala Sioux, and again in the Warsaw Ghetto, kept intruding into her thoughts no matter how hard she tried to concentrate on things that were more pleasant, such as the new life growing inside her womb. The euphoria she had felt when Michael told them about Smith's evidence had dissipated, leaving her feeling anxious and apprehensive. She thought of Ryan's gentle reproach when she had exploded upon learning of the link between Rapski and Baker. *How in God's name are we supposed to deal with love in our hearts with the likes of these two?* she wondered. *I'm filled with fear just knowing that they're out there . . . no doubt plotting the same kinds of death and destruction as before.* Eventually, an uneasy sleep took her, although the question of how to hold love in her heart still troubled her almost as much as the proximity of their ancient enemy himself.

# 10

A STRANGE AND INTENSE SENSE OF URGENCY WOKE GAYLE EARLY the next morning. She lay in her bed for a few moments, trying to determine whether she had heard something to cause her to wake so abruptly. The bright red glow of the display on her digital alarm clock read six-thirty — fully an hour before her alarm had been set to wake her. Rising from her bed as silently as possible, she crept through her house, but found nothing amiss. She shrugged her shoulders, and decided that she might as well get an early start on her day. There was no question of getting back to sleep — her overpowering feeling of urgency was just as strong as the moment she had opened her eyes. Returning to her bedroom, she dressed quickly, then she made herself a pot of coffee. Half way through her first cup, she felt a feathery touch that seemed like the wings of an angel brushing against the edge of her consciousness. She placed her half-full cup of coffee on the table and closed her eyes, trying to stay calm, though her heart had begun to beat just a bit faster. Once again, it seemed as though a veil or curtain was lifting, exposing yet another layer of awareness that had been concealed until that moment. The room around her seemed to disappear as the feathery touch resolved into a more direct contact, and with it, the knowledge that she was in the presence of a soul of such shining purity that it made her ache with joy. Tentatively, with a great sense of awe, she opened herself to whatever might come.

She felt as if she were coming home to a place she had never been before — as if a lens that had always skewed her perception had at last been removed. She understood immediately that she was in the presence of *she* who would bring a new kind of grace to the world — if love could conquer fear. An inaudible voice re-sounded inside of her.

*The conflict begins in earnest today, daughter. Your part is a large and im-portant one — the guidance you provide will be essential to help the others attain the necessary state of mind. They have much to learn before they will be able to rise above their pain and grief, and it will be your task to help them attain that knowledge and understanding.*

Even while basking in the spirit's loving, comforting presence, Gayle felt her heart sink. "How can I teach what I don't know myself?" she asked wordlessly.

*You know far more than you are willing to admit. Your spiritual journey — in this life and the others that preceded it — had a purpose. It has brought you to a place where you can understand and accept what has been happening — to be able to comprehend that what you are experiencing here with me is not illusion. Seldom does one who is given access to ultimate truths feel worthy of bearing the burden that comes with such knowledge.*

There was humor and tenderness as the spirit "spoke." For an instant, Gayle's thoughts drifted back to a church-camp she had attended the summer she turned twelve. She had gone off to the two-week long camp with one of her friends from school — a Bible camp run by a fundamentalist church with a very different approach to salvation than had been preached from the pulpit of her own small church. Gayle was excited to go, happily expecting to hear more about her savior. She had already come to love Jesus as a close friend, just as her Sunday school teachers said would happen if she opened her heart. But at the camp's opening worship service, instead of hearing about Christ's love, she heard a long graphic description of the suffering He endured on the cross. Then she was told that it was highly doubtful that her faith could ever be enough to justify such a sacrifice. Gayle couldn't believe what she was hearing. Her parents had taught her about love, faith and charity — she had never been exposed to sermons about Hellfire and brimstone, or told that she must bear the guilt for acts she had never committed. She made a critical error in judgment when she told her friend that she didn't believe a word of what the camp director said — that *she* was going to Heaven because she *loved* Jesus, not because she was *afraid* of him. Her friend was sure that Gayle had doomed herself to roast in Hell forever. With the best of intentions, she repeated what Gayle had said to the camp director — including Gayle's statement that she didn't believe Jesus was mean enough to send people to Hell. The camp director saw his duty. He made Gayle's salvation his highest priority.

It was child-abuse, though it never would have been seen for what it was in those days. The camp director might have been recognized as misguided, but no one would have labeled his activities the psychological torture they actually were. He himself would have been shocked to know that many would consider him a sadist as he projected his twisted theology, drawn from his own self-loathing and fear, on innocent children. Gayle was given individual Bible instruction that concentrated on the most brutal and barbaric passages in the Old Testament. The director wanted to be sure that Gayle understood what would happen to her if she did not repent. He prayed over her — just the two of them, and then with groups of campers. The evening sermons specifically mentioned "the one among us who has not been saved." She held out most of a week, then succumbed to the pressure she felt from every side. She confessed her "sins," and was re-baptized in a full immersion ceremony at the camp reservoir. Her "conversion" bought her a few days peace, but the humiliation of the experience — all done in Jesus's name, forever changed her relationship with Christianity. The foundation of her simple faith cracked, and all that had been built on it came tumbling down. After her return to Fort Bragg, she suffered from anxiety attacks and presented severe behavioral problems every time she was forced to attend church. Even after counseling sessions with their minister during which she told about what had happened to her at camp, and was reassured that God loved her unconditionally, she refused to go back to Sunday school.

As Gayle thought of that bitter experience, she found she could no longer hold on to this oldest and most cherished resentment. It melted away, to be replaced by compassion for those who had been so misled. And as her thoughts snapped back to the present moment, she saw that the momentary straying of her attention — as well as the healing that had accompanied it had been no accident. She detected a feeling of approval as the spirit began to communicate again, picking up their wordless dialogue from the point where Gayle's thoughts had drifted.

*No one ever volunteered to be a prophet. Prophets are rejected more often than not. It is in the nature of humankind to strive after ultimate truth, but then to cast it away when it is revealed as if it were dross.*

Gayle was alarmed by the intimation that she would be a prophet, but the spirit was quick to soothe her.

*Do not fear, daughter. The prophethood of which I speak is limited, at least for the present. You will be a conduit of knowledge and support from this plane to yours, but the message you carry will be limited to those who are in conflict with The One without a Soul. They are already aware of your many spiritual gifts and insights, and have learned to trust them. Those who are most closely aligned with the conflict are already beginning to grapple with the question of how to hold love close to their hearts when those same hearts are torn asunder by the events that transpire. They need to be shown that love is the only thing that is real — that everything else, including the physical world in which you find yourselves, is illusion.*

"I've heard that the physical universe is an illusion," Gayle "said," "but I've never understood how that could be true. "I'm sitting here in a chair in my livingroom — I just drank a cup of coffee — neither of those things are illusions." Gayle smiled in response to the spirit's unmistakable and very infectious mirth. There was a quality of lighthearted happiness and utter joy woven into every aspect of *Her* being.

*The illusion is very convincing, to be sure. Let me explain — surely you have seen diagrams of atoms that show the nucleus and the electron? An atom is built on the same scale as a solar system, it is made up almost entirely of the space in-between the nucleus and the electron. At the subatomic level, there are huge gaps between the component parts of an atom. But even the component parts of the atom which at first appear to be solid, are themselves made up of even smaller particles. And when those components are broken down, it turns out that they have no mass — they're pure energy. What this means, is that everything you consider to be solid and immovable is actually constructed of something that has no more physical substance than a shadow. This is why you are able to pass through what appears to be solid matter when you spirit-walk in the shape of your totem. Most people would call the journeys you take in spirit-form to be mere fantasy or hallucination. The opposite is true — it is the solidity of the physical universe, not the spirit realm, that is the illusion.*

"How does this help us to hold love in our hearts while we are being confronted by evil?"

*The other illusion is our apparent separateness from one another and from the divine. We are all a part of the Divinity, and at the same time, the Divinity is undivided — we are all one.*

"How can it be both ways at once?"

*Imagine that the Divinity decided to play a game — that it decided to divide itself into an uncountable number of parts. The object of the game is for all of the parts to come back together. But to make things more interesting, none of the Divinity's component parts would remember their true nature.*

"I'm beginning to see where this is leading."

*What I have described is exactly what has happened. We are all a part of the Divinity, that, in its essential nature is a unified whole. Each of us is separate, but the divine can be found in all of us. We are following the rules of the game that I have described. We are trying to find our way back home — to rediscover our essential unity with the other souls that make up humanity, and with the Divinity. The thing that binds us, that guides us and shows us the way, is love. Love is the glue that binds this universe and all of the other universes — all of what in our present state of being we call infinity — together. The pure energy that physicists have discovered to be the essence of physical matter is Love. Even The One without a Soul is a part of the divine. He has exercised his free will — that power which is humankind's most precious gift. In the process, he has gone far astray — much like the fallen angels in the scriptures with which you are familiar — but he is still a part of the grand design. For in this game, many obstacles were placed on the path upon which we tread when we return home. The physical plane of existence was created so that the Divinity could experience all that it is not — including everything that comes from becoming so focused on individuality that the idea of our essential unity is incomprehensible. That is why much of life is filled with struggle as we try to overcome adversity — the Divinity didn't want the game to be too easy.*

Once again, Gayle felt the unmistakable sensation that the spirit was laughing joyfully, able to embrace the totality of human experience without trying to argue with it.

*You and your companions will have a chance to bring me to your plane of existence — if all of you can remember that love is the only thing that is real. Everything that happens is part of the game the Divinity set into motion. Discomfort and pain are ultimately illusions, and are very, very temporary — yet absolutely necessary. Tell them, daughter! The Divinity itself wants you to succeed — there is a cyclical element to the game that is currently out of balance. Fear has caused that imbalance. Help them to understand that fear is the absence of love — the casting off of the glue that binds us all together, and that fear is the ultimate expression of the illusion of the separateness of self and the primacy of the individual. The One without a Soul is the physical embodiment of the illusion that we are separate and distinct from one another — that we are in control of our own destinies.*

"Are you saying that we are not in control of what we do? I thought that we had free will."

*There are always choices. The Divinity could no more cast off its own free will by separating itself into many parts than it could change its essence. But when the game commenced, the Divinity decreed that at some point in the distant future, when it had learned all that it could in its divided, unknowing state, the illusion of separateness would evaporate and the awareness of our divine nature would be restored to what are now component parts. The idea that we control our own destiny is a concept that is born of the extremely limited perception of reality that we are allowed to experience. Our choices lie in the immediate, physical world, which, as I have explained, is an illusion. Our ultimate destiny finds its expression in the world of spirit. For certain individuals, it also finds its expression in the physical world. I am one of those individuals, daughter — as, to a certain degree, are you and your companions.*

"Then it is our destiny to succeed?" Gayle asked hopefully.

There was compassion in the spirit's answer. *Whether or not you will be successful is hidden — even from me. You are powerful spiritual beings. The rules of the game insist that there be adversity. Conflict is necessary, for without it there would be no spiritual growth — no advancement of the spirit. Even The One without a Soul is a necessity. He is a part of the grand design. Without him, the conflict that is necessary could not take place — though what formed his particular destiny is a mystery, even to me.*

Gayle felt the contact begin to fade.

*Only love is real, daughter. You know it in your heart — help the others to come to this same knowing . . .*

Gayle opened her eyes to view a world that would never look the same. Steam still rose from her coffee cup — the communication had taken place within a single instant in time. She felt incredibly light and buoyant as the happiness that had emanated from the spirit continued to fill her to suffusion. For the first time in her life, she *knew* that love was the answer to every question she had ever asked.

# 11

AT PROJECT HOPE, EDDIE RAPSKI'S OBNOXIOUS VOICE FILLED the air. Leisurely reviews of transcripts were a luxury they could no longer afford. *"There is a plague coming to our community this weekend,"* the 'Radical of the Right' rasped. *"They will descend upon us like the locusts from the Bible! And who am I referring to? For it is a 'who,' and not a 'what!'— Tree Huggers! Protestors! They are the spawn of Satan himself! They'll be easy to recognize, especially the younger ones with their faces pierced with metal, their tattoos and their day-glow hair. It makes me sick just to think about this scum surging up the highways from Berkeley and Marin County — those bastions of Liberalism! And what are they here to do? My friends, out in the middle of nowhere there are some trees that Miller Lumber Company has owned for over a hundred years. They have decided to cut some of these trees, providing needed jobs for the hard-working members of our community. They have all the proper permits! They've jumped through the government's ridiculously restrictive hoops, and yet these outsiders are on their way to try to stop the logging. What does that make these protestors? It makes them criminals! They are here to trespass! They are here to engage in vandalism and destroy logging equipment! They are here to spike trees so that God-fearing, hard-working lumbermen will be injured! They are here to cause riots in the streets of our communities! And what will the police do about it? Nothing! They will call these assaults on our community freedom of assembly! But let me tell you this, my friends: freedom of assembly, constitutional right though it is, doesn't allow the spawn of Satan to break the law!*

*What are we going to do about it? What are we going to do when these lawbreakers invade our community and cause trouble? When our own police won't even protect our community? I say we form a posse! I say we form a militia! That is our constitutionally guaranteed right! When we see these protestors breaking the law, we need to make some citizen's arrests! And if we have to break some heads to make those arrests, then so be it!"*

"I have a very bad feeling about this," said Adam. "People are going to be pouring in from all over. Yesterday, Rapski was talking about escorting people out of the community — by which he obviously meant that his radio audience should try to intimidate people into leaving. Now he's talking about 'citizen's arrests' — but what he's actually calling for, is for some of his yahoo followers to attack demonstrators." He shook his head in disbelief. "What could he possibly hope to accomplish? And if Baker is behind this, what could his motive possibly be? If he thinks that a violent conflict between environmental activists and a bunch of redneck morons is going to drum up public support for Miller Lumber, he's crazy — that's exactly the opposite of what would happen."

"Then maybe his motive isn't to try to shift public opinion in his favor," said Michael quietly.

Ryan had come to appreciate and respect Michael's intuitive understanding of psychology. "What do you think he's up to?" he asked.

"We've been assuming that all of Rapski's actions are taken at Baker's behest," Michael postulated.

"Agreed." said Ryan.

"*We* all know that this conflict has been carried out over the course of many lifetimes — but let me ask this question, is *Baker* also aware of how long this has been going on?"

The question stopped all of them in their tracks, and the silence that followed was charged with mental activity as Doug, Ryan and Audrey grappled with the question.

"I have no basis for my answer," said Doug finally. "Call it the hunch of an old investigative reporter — but I don't believe he does."

"I feel the same way," said Audrey." She looked up at Ryan. "What do you think?"

Ryan's brow was furrowed, and he stared off into the distance. He thought for a few more moments before answering "He's probably not aware of his own motives. Look at all of the apparent coincidences it took to bring all of us together. Many of those were set in motion *years* ago, and none of us knew what was going on. We've only known about the conflict and been aware of Baker's existence for a few weeks. I'm thinking that if Baker knew who we were at this point in time, he would already be seeking us out and trying to eliminate us. But to the best of our knowledge, there haven't been any attempts on our lives. I would bet that he doesn't even know we exist." He looked around the room at each of them. "Once we confront him directly, *then* he'll focus on us. In the meantime, whatever force has caused this conflict to continue in life after life will undoubtedly lead him to engage in activities that will draw us out."

"It's time to get ready for the ride, folks," said Michael. "Baker has dealt his cards so that we are absolutely *compelled* to respond. As soon as we file our lawsuit Monday morning, we're going to blow our anonymity all to hell!"

# 12

IT WAS ELEVEN-THIRTY IN THE MORNING — TIME FOR EDDIE
Rapski's show, and as usual when the "radical of the right" was on the air, Brad
Sharkey had his ear glued to his radio. He poured the last of his third beer of the
morning down his throat, and belched enthusiastically. "Fucking tree huggers," he
muttered, echoing Rapski's sentiment as he listened to his hero. After a lifetime
during which very few official voices ever said anything that made sense, Brad was
grateful that *someone* in authority was finally saying things he could agree with.
Of course, the fact that the "authority" Rapski claimed was a figment of his own
imagination went completely over Brad's head. He was as fully invested in Rapski's
delusion of self-importance as was Rapski himself. For Brad, *Authority* belonged
to those who were on radio or television — or those who had the power to make
*him* be silent — such as the police, his probation officer or the judges who periodically threw him in jail. He was in awe when he listened to Rapski. It seemed as
though there might actually be some hope that this screwed-up world could be set
straight — if Rapski could only get the liberals to shut the fuck up and get the God-
damn government to do what he told them.

When Brad was half-way through his fourth beer, he got a strong craving — a
not-uncommon occurrence this far into a six-pack. He glanced at his watch. Good.
It wasn't too early in the day to call his connection. A few minutes later, a rooster
tail of dust streamed back from his beat-up Ford pickup as he made his way up the
hill to Fred Witkowski's place. Fred wasn't the best company in the world, being
pissed off most of the time. But he cooked up the most potent crank in the region.
Before he left, Brad remembered to toss the rest of the case of beer he was working
on into his truck. Sometimes Fred would lay out enough lines for both of them to
get completely wired if Brad supplied the beer.

He pulled into Fred's trash-strewn yard where the remains of three or four
partially-dismantled cars were positioned like sentinels in the jumbled weeds on
the edges of the clearing and waited while the dust clouds swirled around the cab
before dissipating. Fred came out of the rust-streaked mobile home and kicked his
wildly barking Pit Bull into submission. The dog guarded Fred's little enclave well
— Brad still had deep, puckered scars on his calf from the time he forgot about the
damn thing. He had only remembered when the animal came racing around the
corner of the trailer at full speed and latched its powerful jaws around his leg.

Fred's booted kicks had finally convinced the beast to let go, but not before it had bitten cleanly through Brad's jeans and deep into the flesh of his leg. He never made *that* mistake again, no matter how fucked-up he got — not after a trip to the emergency room and fifteen stitches! Fred took his time chaining up the dog, but eventually it was safe to leave the cab. Brad grabbed the three six-packs and followed him inside, where an emaciated woman wearing a blue nightgown sat at the dinette next to the tiny kitchen, smoking a cigarette while she painted her fingernails. Brad couldn't remember her name — she was the forth or fifth to share Fred's trailer in the past two years. For the life of him, Brad couldn't figure out how Fred always managed to get a woman to live with him — his temperament was only slightly better than his dog's. When she saw Brad come through the door, the woman gave him a contemptuous look, rose from her chair, then collected her bottle of nail-polish and sauntered down the short hallway to the back of the trailer without saying a word. *Uppity bitch,* Brad thought, then shrugged his shoulders — if she wasn't there, and Fred shared his stash, there would be more for both of them.

Brad asked if he could turn on the radio so that they could listen to Eddie Rapski while Fred weighed out the crank. Fred grunted his assent — he was aother loyal listener — and soon Rapski's voice filled the confined space of the mobile home's kitchen and dining area. *'There is a plague coming to our community this weekend,* "Rapski spat. *'They will descend upon us like the locusts from the Bible! And who am I referring to? For it is a 'who,' and not a 'what!' — Tree Huggers! Protestors! They are the spawn of Satan himself! They'll be easy to recognize, especially the younger ones with their faces pierced with metal, their tattoos and their day-glow hair. It makes me sick just to think about this scum surging up Highway 101 from Berkeley and Marin County — those bastions of Liberalism!* "

"Fucking Liberals!" said Brad, trying to imitate the tone of voice that Rapski used, and coming fairly close.

*"And what are they here to do? My friends, out in the middle of nowhere there are trees that Miller Lumber Company has owned for over a hundred years. They have decided to cut some of these trees, providing needed jobs for the hard-working members of our community. They have all the proper permits! They've jumped through the government's ridiculously restrictive hoops, and yet these outsiders are on their way to try to stop the logging. What does that make these protestors? It makes them criminals! They are here to trespass! They are here to engage in vandalism and destroy logging equipment! They are here to spike trees so that God-fearing, hard-working lumbermen will be injured!"*

"God-damn queers." Fred muttered, as he tried to concentrate on weighing out the methamphetamine.

"You're fuckin' right!" agreed Brad enthusiastically, bringing his fist down on the table for emphasis. Unfortunately, this wreaked havoc with Fred's efforts to weigh the drugs, as the flimsy surface shuddered under his blow, scattering the rough grains and crystals. "Watch it, man." warned Fred, with a dark glance that conveyed pure malice. Brad was immediately conciliatory. He knew that Fred's hair-trigger temper could be directed at him as easily as it was towards his Pit Bull or his girlfriend. "Sorry, man — I fucked up." he said quickly. "I'll be more careful." The quick admission of wrongdoing mollified Fred, and the two of them turned their attention back to the broadcast.

*"They are here to cause riots in the streets of our communities! And what will the police do about it? Nothing! They will call these assaults on our community freedom of assembly! But let me tell you this, my friends: freedom of assembly, constitutional right though it is, does not allow the spawn of Satan to break the law!*

*What are we going to do about it? What are we going to do when these law-breakers invade our community and cause trouble? When our own police won't even protect our community? I say we form a posse!"*

"Right on!" Brad shouted at the radio.

*"I say we form a militia! That is our constitutionally guaranteed right!"*

"Fuckin' 'A,'" Fred chimed in, his attention riveted to the broadcast now that the crank had been weighed out.

*"When we see these protestors breaking the law, we need to make some citizen's arrests! And if we have to break some heads to make those arrests, then so be it!"*

"Goddamn right." Brad shouted again, popping open two of the beers, and silently exulting when Fred pulled out a mirror and poured out a large pile of his own stash, shoving it over to Brad so that he could chop the large crystals into lines of fine powder. Brad warmed to his task, and the two of them spent the rest of the morning working on the beer and the drugs. Fred was generous that day, and as the drugs and alcohol built up in their systems, Rapski's exhortations to violence made more and more sense. Two hours after Brad arrived, he and Fred were in his truck, with Fred's illegally modified semi-automatic rifle concealed behind the seat-back, hauling-ass down the hill. Brad intended to do right by Rapski — to make him proud. As he stopped by the local market to pick up another case of beer, he wondered if they would get to be on the radio show with Rapski if they kicked enough liberal ass. *Only one way to find out,* he thought to himself as he climbed back into the pickup. *Time to go make some fuckin' citizen's arrests!*

# 13

THERE WAS A LARGE, RELATIVELY FLAT, CLEARED AREA ON STATE Forest property where the two-lane track that lead into the Miller Tract intersected the county-maintained gravel road. Over two hundred people had gathered in the clearing, and the intensity of the crowd made the air feel as if it were charged with electricity. The demonstrators were protesting loudly, often chanting in unison and beating drums for emphasis. Banners with slogans such as SAVE THE OLD GROWTH, A THOUSAND YEARS TO GROW — A THOUSAND MINUTES TO DESTROY, and many others were stretched between trees or from poles driven into the ground. The local news media were there in force, from the single volunteer reporter sent by the public radio station in Philo to television crews from Ukiah, Santa Rosa and San Francisco.

Facing them, blocking the road leading to the old-growth, was a phalanx of Miller Lumber Company employees and a small contingent of counter-demonstrators, who had shown up at Eddie Rapski's urging. The counter- demonstrators were crowded together off to the side of the Miller Employees. They had come with vague ideas of "taking things into our own hands," and "doing what is right for the citizens of our community," concepts that had sounded simple enough when Rapski talked about them on the radio. But now that they were here, they found that they hadn't the faintest idea what to do. The demonstrators out-numbered them by more than five to one, and in spite of what Rapski had said would happen, the Sheriff, who was personally present, along with a number of his deputies, seemed to have things under control. For the most part, the Rapski contingent stood silently with their arms crossed or with their hands on their hips, trying to look righteous and tough whenever a television camera was pointed in their direction.

Raymond Baker was enjoying himself tremendously. The anger over what he had set in motion fed him like an invigorating tonic. Even the vague, perplexed unease of the counter-demonstrators added to his pleasure. He never felt better than when he was able to disturb and vex the types of human excrement that surrounded him today. His initial plans had not included his own personal presence at any demonstrations, though he presumed they would occur, but when he had risen that morning, he found that he had changed his mind. He wasn't going to make any statements — indeed he had instructed his employees that no one was to reveal his identity — but something had told him that he should be there.

A group of experienced demonstrators, whose skills had been honed during demonstrations against the Pacific Lumber Company in Humboldt County, were negotiating with the Sheriff over the best way to orchestrate symbolic acts of trespass. Sheriff Fields wanted no part of the headaches and paperwork that the arrests would create, but he also understood that he was going to have to lock a few of them up. He was well aware that arresting a few non-violent demonstrators for symbolic trespasses would be much easier to deal with than uncontrolled attempts to gain access to the area where the logging was taking place.

It was while these negotiations were under way that a beat-up pickup with rusted-out quarter panels came roaring up the main road towards the crowd of demonstrators. The truck had no muffler, and the cacophony created by the racing engine covered the sound of the automatic weapon fire that began to erupt from the passenger window. It was only when people started dropping and the screaming began, that Sheriff Fields realized he had a massacre on his hands. The truck made only one pass — nearly losing control as it came to the far end of the straight section of road that skirted the clearing, but the gunfire was devastatingly effective — it seemed that every bullet had found a mark among the tightly massed crowd. Sheriff Fields quickly dispatched two squad cars to chase the gunmen, and then ran to his radio to summon every possible deputy, ambulance and life-flight helicopter in the area. Then he ran to the back of his cruiser, grabbed a first-aid kit from the trunk, and went to try to save as many lives as he could.

When Brad came around the bend and saw the crowds, he let out a whoop that he could barely hear over the sound of the now-unmuffled exhaust. The rusted out muffler and tailpipe had been threatening to take leave of their tenuous grasp to the truck's undercarriage for months, and when Brad high-centered the truck while trying to make it through a deeply rutted section of road, the pipe and muffler were both history.

By the time they arrived at the Miller Tract, Brad had completely forgotten about making "citizen's arrests." When he saw the crowds, he followed his first impulse, which was to race his truck up the gravel road and get the rear-end loose so that he could spray the protestors with gravel before beating it out of there. He scarcely paid attention to Fred, who by this time was cradling his illegally-modified, fully automatic rifle. Fred always kept his rifle by his side, and Brad had seen it so often that it no longer registered on his consciousness. Fred had retrieved the rifle from behind the seat-back while the truck had been high-centered, and had been holding it loosely on his lap ever since. It wasn't until they were bearing down on the crowds of people that Brad noticed that Fred had pointed the gun out the rolled-down window of the truck, and had his finger on the trigger. Panic surged through him as he realized what Fred was doing. *Shit! This crazy motherfucker's gonna try to kill everybody!* There was no time to say anything, and even if he had, it wouldn't have been heard over the roar of the truck's engine. He kept his foot on the floor, hoping that if they passed the crowd quickly, Fred might miss. Half of his concentration was on the rapidly approaching bend in the road. The other half was directed behind him, as he checked to see what damage Fred had done. The third time he checked his rear-view mirror, he saw that Fred's spray of bullets had been as effective as a scythe in a wheat field. Fred never uttered a word, just kept his trigger-finger squeezed tight until the bullets in the clip ran out. By that time, they were nearly to the end of the straight stretch of road that skirted the cleared-out area. Brad jammed on his brakes, and the truck slid sideways. "Motherfuck!" he screamed as the truck fish-tailed wildly before luck and instinct allowed him to bring it back under control. Fred remained silent, taking a new clip of ammunition from where it lay on the seat next to him, and ramming it home.

"You crazy asshole! What in the fuck did you do that for?" screamed Brad over the din from the unmuffled engine.

Fred turned in his seat, and trained both his automatic rifle and his emotionless gaze on Brad — a gaze that Brad belatedly realized was completely insane. "Shut up and drive, motherfucker, or I'll take you out too," he replied evenly.

Brad had absolutely no doubt that Fred would do exactly what he said , and bit back his reply. In spite of near-toxic levels of alcohol and methamphetamine in his system, the events of the last ninety seconds seemed to have cleared his head. He glued his attention to the steep, narrow, gravel road as it wound its way deeper into the forest, and wondered what advice Eddie Rapski would give him now.

*     *     *

AT PROJECT HOPE, everyone had been taking a break from other activities, and were gathered around a television set, watching the news coverage of the protest. It started with a brief description of the Miller tract, and the recent takeover of Miller Lumber by Amalgamated Insurance. Taped footage including aerial photography of the Miller tract was shown, along with maps showing where the tract was located. The scene cut to interviews with some of the protesters, with the sound of drumming and chanting in the background. The camera panned across the much smaller group of counter-protestors, who stood together like a flock of lost sheep, glowering alternately at the protestors and the cameras. Finally, the cameras focused on the contingent from Miller Lumber, standing in front of two large bulldozers that were angled so that their huge blades came together to block the road to the old growth. Among the Miller contingent was a tall, athletic-looking man with angular features and striking blond hair. Audrey reacted violently as soon as she saw him, her sharp intake of breath punctuating the air. She turned to Ryan, who was already reaching for her protectively, as if there was an immediate threat to their safety. "My God! It's *him*!" she moaned, burying her face against his shoulder. Ryan was overcome with a combination of panic and anger the instant the blond-haired man's visage appeared on the screen. Even after the scene shifted back to a close-up of the television reporter, he was still in a full-blown flight-fight reaction, barely able to control the urge to bolt and run.

"He looks exactly the same," Audrey continued, choking out the words. "I never thought about it before, but he looked the same in the other lives too." Her voice trembled as she asked, "How come he looks exactly the same while we're in completely different bodies?"

"He looks very similar, but not exactly the same," said Ryan grimly. "I must have gotten a better look at him before — at least during the Oglala Sioux lifetime. But he does look *almost* the same. And even on television, he *feels* the same. There's no doubt in my mind — we've just caught our first glimpse of Raymond Baker."

Michael observed Ryan's and Audrey's reactions appraisingly. Any lingering doubts he might have harbored about the validity of their past-life experiences vanished as he watched how they reacted. "If this is what happens when you catch a glimpse of Baker on television, you'll need to steel yourselves for when you're actually in the same room with him," he said. "There's no doubt that will happen at some point in the legal proceedings."

Their attention was drawn back to the television screen as the sound of a roaring engine came over the speaker. Then they watched in horror while the live-feed from the television camera caught the stark, surreal images as the massacre unfolded. The live-feed continued until someone at the station came to their senses and switched back to the news anchor. Those gathered around the television at Project HOPE stared at the television in shock, unwilling to believe what they had just seen.

*   *   *

GAYLE WAS LOUNGING in her director's chair behind the counter at the Eclectic Attic talking to Larry on the phone when the shooting started. A wave of nausea hit her and she doubled up and collapsed across the top of the display case. She knew from the visitation that morning that the dreadful thing she felt was taking place out at the Miller tract. Instantaneously, with an ability she hadn't known she possessed, she sent her totem out to the site where the carnage was taking place. In her raven form, she could see pain and terror painted on the air much more vividly than the residue of fear she had seen in the Miller Lumber offices. A beat-up pickup was still strafing the crowd, and she was filled with grief and horror as she watched people being hit and crumpling to the ground. She could sense their anguish as they lay suffering, and in some cases, dying. Shifting her consciousness back to her physical body, she brought the phone close to her lips. "You're needed at the Miller tract," she uttered in a hoarse whisper. "Larry, send your totem *now*!

Larry had been sitting at his kitchen, taking in the view of the ocean while he conversed with Gayle, when suddenly he too was hit by a wave of nausea. He reached down with his free hand to clutch at his stomach, and then after a few moments heard Gayle's urgent command. A veil lifted, and he suddenly knew what was required to make such a journey without the usual preparations. While his physical body remained seated in the dining area of his home, his consciousness divided, and the spectral figure of a puma streaked across the landscape. *Spirit guide* had been summoned.

*   *   *

THE DEPUTIES IN hot pursuit of the murderers were in a vehicle that was far more powerful and endowed with much better handling than the old pickup truck they were chasing, and as the road zig-zagged down the face of the mountainside, they steadily made up ground. Soon they were at the edge of the thick dust clouds stirred up by the pick-up's churning tires. The deputy in the passenger seat of the lead car was less than excited about the prospect of taking on a crazed fool with an automatic weapon and nothing to lose. He glanced down at his service revolver and the shotgun clipped to the dashboard and shook his head, fervently hoping that the assholes in the truck would lose control and run off the road. He didn't care if they went over a drop-off, or into a tree. They could take their choice.

In the speeding truck ahead, Brad was trying to figure out what to do. He was in a pinch like he'd never been before, and the drugs and alcohol in his system didn't improve his thinking — which had never been one of his strengths in the first place. He didn't know if Fred had snapped before they started this ill-fated trip, or at some point along the way. It really didn't matter now — the man beside him had just taken out God-only-knows how many people. Brad had always considered himself a bad-ass. He was tall and strong, and more often than not relied on his fists to get himself out of trouble — though if the truth were told, it was usually his fists and his attitude that got him into hot water in the first place. He sneaked a quick look at Fred, with his expressionless eyes and the automatic rifle he caressed with negligent assurance. Brad knew that in this situation, his fists were completely useless.

As he braked sharply for a switchback, he glanced in his shuddering rear-view mirror and saw the front end of a police car come into view just as he entered the turn. "They're gaining on us," he yelled at Fred. By this time, they were around the turn, and Fred could see the police car through the cloud of dust that blossomed out behind the truck.

"Next switchback, slow down — I'll take the motherfuckers out." Fred yelled back. He turned around backwards in the seat, looped the seatbelt through the belt that held up his pants, and then leaned out through the passenger window with his rifle pointed behind them. Brad slowed down as Fred had directed, but then had a flash of inspiration. There was a large redwood just ahead, right beside the road on the passenger side. He made a quick decision, and guided the truck as far to the side of the road as possible, and then veered sharply into the tree. The wet-sounding thud of Fred's body being crushed against the tree mixed with the screech of metal against wood, and Brad almost lost control of the truck as it rebounded, causing what was left of Fred to bounce back into the cab, spraying him with gore. When the truck came to a stop in the middle of the road, he put his hands on top of his head, hoping to Christ that when the deputies got to him, they didn't shoot first and ask questions later.

\*     \*     \*

WHEN THE PICKUP truck raced by and started shooting at the demonstrators, Raymond Baker could scarcely conceal his delight. The waves of panic and fear that emanated from the crowd, especially the wounded, gave him a better rush than cocaine ever had. It made him feel absolutely invigorated! Years of careful planning had created a result that was everything he could have hoped for. *This must be the reason why I needed to be here*, he thought as he watched the pickup truck roar down the road and nearly lose control before it skidded around the corner and out of sight. Then a flash of movement caught his eye, and he focused his attention on a raven that was flying low over the crowd. Instantly, he was filled with rage more powerful than any emotion he had ever experienced, and an inexplicable desire to kill the bird. His hands balled into fists, and he began running towards the spot where the raven circled. Then suddenly, he became aware that there was a mountain lion roaming about among the fallen, licking the faces of several who were apparently dead. Baker stopped in his tracks, nonplussed. His rage had increased geometrically the moment he saw the puma. But what was a puma doing in the middle of a crowd of people? And why weren't the people close-by reacting to its presence? Then, as suddenly as they had arrived on the scene, the raven and the puma vanished. Almost as quickly, Baker's rage disappeared, leaving him feeling strangely empty and disconcerted. He shook his head as if to clear it. Had he been hallucinating? Could such a thing even happen to him? He watched as the Sheriff leapt into action, dispatching two police cars to chase down the killers, and then using his radio to summon help. When the Sheriff rushed with his first aid kit to attend to the wounded, Baker shrugged his shoulders. Except for the sudden appearance and disappearance of the raven and the puma, everything was proceeding wonderfully. With a carefully manufactured look of concern, he hurried over to where Sheriff Fields was attending to the wounds of one of the fallen to offer his assistance.

# 14

ALL ACTIVITY AT PROJECT HOPE CEASED AS THE GRISLY DETAILS were announced and updated. Although the television coverage made everyone sick to their stomachs, none of them could stay away. Four had died, and six of the eleven wounded were in critical condition. Sheriff Field's prompt action was credited with saving the lives of three who had been transported by life-flight helicopter, and who nearly bled to death as it was. Soon, the identities of the "alleged" murderers were being broadcast, and rather incredibly, the sole survivor of the duo gave an interview. Those at Project HOPE watched with a mixture of revulsion, anger, and strangely enough, pity, as the reporter questioned the lanky, blood spattered man, identified in a caption at the bottom of the screen as Brad Sharkey. The reporter asked Sharkey if he was aware that he was under arrest, and that he was entitled to talk to a lawyer before he said anything to the police. "I don't need no lawyer to tell you that I'm innocent," Sharkey scoffed. "We were just gonna do what Eddie Rapski said and make some citizen's arrests when the cops didn't do their jobs right!" The man's slurred words were delivered emphatically, and his overconfident demeanor showed him to be completely out of his depth. He was obviously enjoying the attention he was getting, though, and spoke directly to the camera. "I had no idea that Fred was gonna shoot anybody," he added as the camera went for a close-up of the reporter's expression of disbelief.

"Did you know that Mr. Witkowski had an automatic weapon with him in your pickup truck?"

"Well, of course, I knew it," said Sharkey, looking at the reporter as if he were witless. "But that doesn't mean nothin. He's had that rifle with him practically every time I seen him for the entire three years I knowed him, but he never shot nobody before. Like I said, I figured he brought his gun so that we could make citizen's arrests." His tone turned belligerent. "These protesters can't get away with taking away our jobs. They're a bunch of communists!"

"So you're a Miller Lumber Company employee, Mr. Sharkey?" the reporter asked, egging the man on.

For the first time, Brad Sharkey looked away from the camera. "I'm between jobs right now, but that's beside the point," he muttered. Then he raised his head, sputtering, "Eddie Rapski says we got to run these riff-raffs out of town," while gesturing at the protesters with hands that were cuffed together at the wrists.

"And were you going to run this riff-raff out of town by shooting at them, or just brandishing your automatic weapon?" asked the reporter.

"I already told you." said Sharkey, sounding exasperated, as he seemed unable to get his point across to the reporter. "We just came here to break some heads and arrest people."

"Whose heads did you come here to break, Mr. Sharkey?"

Brad Sharkey opened his mouth, but nothing came out as he heard the words he had just said repeated back to him. He looked confused for a moment, and then his bravado fled as some latent survival instinct told him that being on television might not have been such a good idea after all. "I changed my mind," he said. "I don't want to talk no more — get me that lawyer you were talking about."

The camera panned to the reporter speaking into his microphone. "There you have it. A KRXQ exclusive interview with Brad Sharkey, who has admitted that he and his companion came to this site at the suggestion of radio talk-show host Eddie Rapski, with the intention of breaking some heads . . ."

Ryan switched off the sound on the television abruptly. "That moron hasn't got a clue about what is really going on. He's going to be in prison for years, maybe the rest of his life, and he'll never know why. He sure as Hell won't ever know that he was Raymond Baker's foot-soldier."

Just then, Ryan heard Audrey's sharp intake of breath, and felt her shudder. He looked back to the television screen where Audrey's attention was fixed. The sound was still off, but he too flinched and a his heart beat faster when he saw Baker's chiseled face filling the screen. Adam reached over and turned the volume back up.

". . . no reason for this senseless violence. On behalf of Miller Lumber, I will be contacting the management at KNZI, and will personally demand that Eddie Rapski be fired for his part in this senseless tragedy! Miller Lumber deplores the irresponsible broadcasts that obviously played a part in what has transpired today. We intend to see that the perpetrator of this terrible crime, as well as Eddie Rapski — the man who called for this kind of activity in repeated broadcasts — be brought to justice! Miller Lumber has nothing but sympathy for the victims of this sense-less, savage criminal act. We intend to establish a trust fund for the victims and make a substantial contribution."

The camera returned to the reporter, who took his cue, asking, "Where can our viewing public send their donations?"

Baker appeared to give the matter some thought before answering. "This should really be handled by an independent organization — would your television station be able to set this up?"

"Absolutely!" The reporter beamed. "Send your contributions in care of this station to the 'Miller Victims Fund.' The address will appear on your screen in just a moment, so get your pens and pencils ready."

Audrey was nearly apoplectic. "That bastard!" she spat. "He set this all up to take the heat off of himself and shift it to Rapski!" She was as enraged as anyone Ryan had seen, even during the most acrimonious divorce he'd handled. He too was struggling with his anger, but Gayle's and Larry's admonishments helped him to temper his reaction. He reached for Audrey's hand, saying, "If we succumb to fear and anger, we play right into his hands."

"What am I supposed to do about my feelings," she fumed, "just stuff them? I can't *do* that! That bastard made this whole thing happen, and now he's trying to act like some kind of *savior!* And he's probably going to get away with it." There was a wild look in her eyes that alarmed Ryan almost as much as the massacre itself. I can't just 'not feel' what I'm feeling!"

As she was speaking, the door from the parking lot swung open to admit Larry and Gayle. Gayle took in the scene and rushed over to Audrey, putting her arms around her in a motherly embrace. Ryan experienced a strong sensation of *deja vu* and wondered how many times he had seen a tableau like this one.

"Grief is appropriate, but not rage," said Gayle, her voice filled with a new authority. "Your anger only feeds the one who has committed these atrocities. It is far easier to become angry, rather than to allow yourself to experience your pain."

As Gayle spoke, Audrey's face, which had been rigid with anger, softened. Her eyes overflowed as Gayle's exhortations gave her permission to experience her pent-up grief. She buried her face in Gayle's shoulder, and began to shudder silently.

"The souls of those who were killed are at peace," Gayle said matter-of-factly while she stroked Audrey's heavy brown hair. "They knew how these particular lives would end before they ever entered these bodies. Each of their deaths led to spiritual development — perhaps serving as atonement for transgressions against others in past-lives. The same is true for those who have been wounded — it was their choice, freely made, before they were ever born, with full knowledge of the consequences."

Audrey said nothing for several minutes, but just held Gayle tightly. When she finally spoke, her voice was hoarse. "I'm so scared! I can't stop thinking that Baker's going to do the same things to us, and that we'll be as helpless as the demonstrators who got shot." She reached for Ryan's hand. "I don't think I could stand losing what I've just found."

"Let's hope you don't have to worry about that," said Ryan, squeezing her hand. He raised his eyes to Gayle, then looked over at Larry. "I see you know about what happened out at the Miller tract today."

Gayle and Larry exchanged a glance. They had left Fort Bragg for Healdsburg as soon as possible after returning to their bodies. On the way, they had discussed their new "instantaneous" spirit-walking abilities, and how frustrating it was that they would not be able to share what they were able to do with the others. The advanced spirits had informed them from the beginning that the two of them would be the only ones who would be aware of the higher levels of the complicated scheme in which they were embroiled.

"We came as soon as we heard about it," Larry replied. "It seemed like we should all be together — to lend each other support, if nothing else."

"We need to bring you up to date on a number of things we've discovered,"

Ryan said. He described the documentation Doug had uncovered that linked Baker and Rapski together, and their speculations as to whether Baker knew about the continuing nature of their conflict, or their individual identities. As he spoke, Larry and Gayle exchanged knowing glances. In their totem forms, they had both been able to feel the presence of *The One without a Soul*, and although they couldn't read his thoughts, his emotions had been broadcast as if from a hundred-thousand-watt transmitter. They had felt his rage, but also his confusion when he saw their spectral forms — confusion that tended to confirm the others's speculations. Doug winked at Gayle and said, "I don't think it serves much purpose to go to the effort of verifying your premonitions and hunches any longer. I'll admit to being the most skeptical person here, and I'm convinced."

Finally, Audrey told them about the newscast during which Baker had placed the blame for the massacre squarely on Rapski. "That's what sent my anger off the scale," she said. "Seeing that sanctimonious bastard pretending to be some kind of benefactor, when he was the one who made it happen in the first place, really made me burn!"

"Audrey, you have to listen to me," said Gayle, taking her arm and leading her to a beat-up couch that stood against the wall. "When you let anger take over like that, you are succumbing to fear — and fear is the opposite of love." She looked at the ceiling, trying to find the right words. "Anger breeds fear, which then breeds anger again in an endless cycle. The reason that we have to hold love in our hearts, *no matter what happens,* is to break the cycle! We won't be able to defeat Baker unless we can learn how to do exactly that. And unless we defeat him, this struggle will just go on and on, again and again in life after life. We have a unique opportunity here — we've been given a chance to get off the merry-go-round."

"All of us have been talking about *the struggle* and *the conflict*, but I've never really heard anyone define it," said Audrey. "I've always assumed it meant stopping Baker and Miller Lumber from logging the old growth in the Miller tract."

"That's part of it," said Gayle. "The rest of our task is to outlive him."

"What?"

"In every previous incarnation, he has been able to do away with one or more of us — usually all of us — before he died. We must not raise our hands against him to bring about his death, because that would be the ultimate denial of *love*. *Nonetheless*, we must survive him. And throughout the conflict we must hold love in our hearts without allowing ourselves to be consumed by fear."

"That's a tall order," Adam observed dryly.

"It's a very tall order," Gayle agreed. "That's the biggest reason we've never succeeded in the past."

"How do you know these things?" Michael asked. As Gayle turned to him, he held out his hand. "My name is Michael Holland, by the way — we seem to have skipped introductions." He looked around the room. "You're Gayle, obviously. I've heard a lot about you — I think you know everyone here except for me and perhaps Adam."

A smile crinkled Gayle's face as she paid close attention to Adam for the first time. "The last time I was with this young man, I had just assisted in his birth in another lifetime." She said with a grin. "You really were a cute baby, you know."

"Too bad that quality couldn't have shown up in this life, too," Adam replied with a wry expression. "I understand I got bumped off just after I was born back then. What a bum deal! I could have been handsome for seventy or eighty years. This time around I look like a modern-day version of Ichabod Crane!"

Gayle turned back to Michael with a smile still etched on her face after her short interaction with Adam. "Let's just say that up to this point, the advanced spirits have chosen to communicate through Larry and me. Then we pass on what we learn to the others." A speculative look crossed her face and she wondered how Michael would react to the kinds of information that flew right over the heads of their companions. *Plenty of time to check that out later,* she thought to herself. "Even Larry and I don't have the whole picture yet," she went on. "We keep getting more information all the time. So far, whenever it's come it's just in the nick of time!"

"I'm glad to hear that." said Michael with an earnestness that Gayle found endearing, if surprising. "If spiritual entities are going to be lending assistance, then I would prefer them to be on our side." He walked over to Ryan and put his arm around his shoulder, "I hate to be rude, folks," he said as he led Ryan into their impromptu law office. "But my associate and I have to get to work." He winked at Gayle. "I don't think that Ryan and I will be able to count on any celestial assistance when it comes to the legal end of things."

# 15

EDDIE RAPSKI THREW HIS REMOTE AT HIS TELEVISION SCREEN as hard as he could, then chuckled mirthlessly when it bounced off harmlessly. The futility of the act seemed symbolic, somehow. He had just turned the TV off after watching Raymond Baker throw him to the wolves. And although it was the third time the clip had aired, he still couldn't believe it was actually happening.

*"I will personally demand that Eddie Rapski be brought to task for his part in what has taken place today . . . "*

Eddie shook his head incredulously. *Baker* was the one who made him issue a call to action — practically told him what to say! Why was *he* pointing the finger at Eddie, and calling him a criminal? *I guess he's going to call himself up on the phone and urge himself to fire me,* Eddie thought sarcastically when Baker spoke about contacting the management at KNZI. He surveyed the large recreation room, with its fully stocked bar, custom pool table and state-of-the-art home theater system. There was no way he could hang on to the house without a job — not that it had ever given him any real pleasure anyway. With the exception of when he was on the air, he couldn't remember the last time he'd really enjoyed himself. For three years now he had been living out his dreams, but none of it had ever really touched him. Success brought him this house, to be sure, but he had never shown it off — he had no friends. He had never returned to the lodge after the night Baker gave him his job at the radio station, not that those jerks had ever been *real* friends. No one except his listeners gave him any respect. At least he still had that — the respect of his listeners. *They* wouldn't blame him for something that someone else had done. His ratings were strong enough that he shouldn't have trouble getting another job after all of this had blown over. He corrected himself. He could get a job if the truth about Baker came out. *I wonder if I would have the courage to call him a liar in public?* Strangely, after hearing Baker denounce him on television, there seemed to be a new clarity to his thinking, almost as if he had woken from a bad dream. Maybe he could tell the truth! But the memory of the terror he had felt during his last encounter with Baker was still fresh in his mind. If he crossed Baker, he'd probably end up dead. Then again, if he didn't cross him his life probably wouldn't be worth living. "Jesus!" he exclaimed, as he leaned over and put his head in his hands. *Damned if I do — damned if I don't.*

# 16

"THERE REALLY ISN'T ANY MAGIC TO THESE LAWSUITS, BUT THEY do have some rather substantial proof requirements," said Michael rather drily as he organized the documents that John Smith had given them. "At first blush, the task is fairly daunting. To get the court to issue a temporary restraining order, we have to present the judge with enough facts to show that a property owner should be prevented from doing something on his own land that is completely legal — even exalted. Every judge grew up with stories about Paul Bunyan and Babe the Blue Ox." He studied Ryan over the top of his reading glasses. "In this case, the operation even has the approval of the governmental agency that regulates the activity." He flipped through a few pages before continuing. "Many people have a perception that the federal government seizes every possible opportunity to micromanage their lives, but the fact is, when it comes to the federal judiciary, they're extremely reluctant to intrude into the lawful affairs of private citizens. If there's a national conspiracy, then the entire nation is involved, because Congress tells the courts exactly what they can and cannot do." He chuckled. "Near as I can remember, I've had the opportunity to vote for representatives to both houses, not to mention the president, on a regular basis."

Ryan smiled at Michael's mild sarcasm. It was becoming clear that he was a gifted teacher who started with the basics and built on that foundation step-by-step. Mastery of this kind of teaching was essential to the practice of law — a huge part of every lawyer's job was to educate *someone*, whether it was their own client, a judge, or a jury. "You're making it sound next to impossible," he observed.

"That's only the first step." Michael said even more dryly. "Underlying everything is the judge's awareness that huge amounts of money are at stake. In this case, Miller Lumber has committed itself to a *very* aggressive Timber Harvest Plan. There's been a huge amount of money spent deploying personnel and equipment already. The judge knows what it will cost Miller Lumber if he issues the injunction."

"What are our odds then?" asked Ryan.

"Thanks to these documents, they're actually pretty good," Michael replied, breathing a sigh of obvious relief. "If the environmental studies had been properly done, we wouldn't stand a chance — that's why I was so worried. I can see why the Department of Forestry approved these plans so quickly. On the face of things, the area Miller proposes to log appears devoid of all life-forms, let alone animals protected by the Endangered Species Act. Thankfully, these documents demonstrate that the reports are fraudulent." Michael peered over his half-glasses again. "And you know how irritated judges can be when they catch people lying."

"How were the wildlife studies altered?" asked Ryan, leaning over the table where Michael had spread out a number of documents.

"The studies were created in-house," Michael replied. "Apparently Miller provided secretarial services to the wildlife biologists. That gave Baker the opportunity to create entirely new documents — all they had to do was make the text and the page numbers match up to the final signed page of the preliminary study, and everything appeared to be valid."

"What about the wildlife biologists who prepared the studies in the first place? A plan to cut this much old-growth was bound to create controversy, and the massacre made it national news. Where are they? They must have known that the studies they did were just preliminary, and never could have been adequate to support a Timber Harvest Plan."

"That's right, and to top it off the field work was all done under circumstances that were highly unlikely to produce any sightings of Spotted owls or Marbled Murrelets — those are the endangered species whose habitats were most likely to be disturbed." Michael took off his glasses and polished their lenses with the tail of his shirt, before putting them back on and peering at the documents again. "It's been several weeks since anyone has seen or heard from the biologists," he continued. The private investigator we hired has come up empty handed, but we *do* know that someone paid their rent and utilities for the next six months in advance. That alone seems unusual. Frankly, I suspect foul play. The way I see it, if these biologists were part of the conspiracy, it wouldn't have been necessary to alter their reports." He handed one of the documents to Ryan. "This is the original report. You can see that it has eighty-seven pages of text, followed by exhibits — summaries of field study data that support the conclusions in the report. In the original document, the pages containing the exhibits are also numbered." He took back the first document, and handed Ryan a second one. "Now, take a look at this. They started by modifying the exhibits. The first thing they did was to delete the numbering from the exhibits — that way they didn't have to worry about getting those page numbers to match." Michael flipped back to one of the field-data summaries. "See how in this document the field studies start more than two years earlier than they did in the original documents? The original notes taken out in the field probably went through a shredder as soon as Baker gave the orders to start falsifying documents."

Ryan studied the original for a few minutes. "Either I'm reading this wrong, or there weren't any sightings of Marbled Murrelets or Spotted Owls even when preliminary data was being collected."

"Think about it, Ryan — Miller Lumber was in the business of cutting down trees, even before Baker acquired the company, and finding an endangered species that would force them to cancel or modify long-range plans wouldn't have been a high priority. This is a situation where slipshod work would have been preferable. These particular wildlife biologists weren't as bad as some — there are some real toadies out there. But even though their work wasn't as thorough as it could have been, they leaned towards the industry whenever they could. All in all these two were fairly well respected. If they had been dishonest, Baker could have bought them off as soon as he showed up on the scene. As it is, I'm inclined to give them the benefit of the doubt. There are two possibilities as to how they got these results — either there are no endangered species out there, or they used poor or incomplete methodology. These birds are hard to find, even if you're motivated." He leaned back in his chair. "Take the Marbled Murrelet for example. When I found out about their nesting habits, I could see why they've become endangered — it's amazing they survive at all. The only places they nest are in old-growth redwoods or Douglas firs within thirty miles of the ocean — although to call it 'nesting' is a bit of a stretch. The female lays an egg in a depression on a large branch a hundred-fifty feet or more off the ground. And that branch has to be a fair distance below the crown of the tree, so that the egg will be concealed from above, because the eggs and young chicks are especially susceptible to crows, jays and other predatory birds. Add to this the fact that adult birds mate for life, and don't nest every year, and the odds for survival seem almost insurmountable. The only way these birds have kept going as a species is because they're extremely secretive. Even the experts almost never actually see them in their nesting habitats. Most 'sightings' — somewhere around ninety-five percent — are from having *heard* them."

"I didn't read anything in the original report about attempting to *hear* the birds," said Ryan — what do they listen for anyway?"

"The cry of the Marbled Murrelet is very distinctive — it's described as a *keer*. They also make what they call a *jet* sound when they're in a steep dive. The sound of their wings as they fly through the air is also unique. The birds are so secretive that it only takes *one* sighting over a two year period in order to designate a stand of trees as nesting habitat. There are a number of parameters within which the observer has to operate, too — time of day, weather conditions — the absence of other noise sources such as the sound of a creek that's running high." He flipped past several pages. "Check this out — they were searching for Marbled Murrelets in March and April — the birds wouldn't be nesting until April at the earliest. June through September are the times when there would be the greatest possibility of a sighting."

"There weren't any observations at all during those months!"

"Exactly. But remember that everything they were doing was just preliminary — Miller Lumber had no immediate plans to log the old-growth until Raymond Baker came along. Putting wildlife observers out in the Miller tract would have been a low priority." Michael put the documents Smith had given them aside, and picked up a copy of the Timber Harvest Plan Miller had filed. "Now, if you were to read through these exhibits," he said, handing it to Ryan, "you'd find that all of the accepted methods of trying to locate Spotted Owls and every single aspect of the *Pacific Seabird Protocol* for sighting Marbled Murrelets was followed. The 'PSG

Protocol' is the accepted scientific method of determining whether or not Marbled Murrelets are nesting in particular stands of trees — it's used by Fish and Game, the Bureau of Land Management, and all of the California, Oregon and Washington fish and wildlife management agencies." He waved his hand at the bogus report. "You know the results — no sightings whatsoever. That's why the report was approved so quickly by the California Department of Forestry."

"Do we know whether or not there are any of either species out there?" Ryan asked.

"We haven't got a clue. The tract is within the historical range of Marbled Murrelets, and Spotted Owls are indigenous in nearby forests." He gestured again at the documents that lay strewn across the table. "Fortunately, we've got the evidence to prove that the studies are fraudulent, so for the time being, it really doesn't matter whether birds are nesting out there or not."

Ryan looked at Michael quizzically. "It's so obvious that this is your passion — how in the world did you end up working for the other side."

Michael was silent for a moment as Ryan's question took him back to a period of his life that he sometimes wanted to forget, but dared not. His life had made a one-hundred-eighty degree turn since the day eight years previously when his partners booted him out of the law firm he had helped to build from the ground up. It had been over his drinking, which, after a long downward spiral, had gotten completely out of control. They had given him every opportunity to clean up his act — even offered to send him to a treatment center, but he would have none of it. He did *not* have a drinking problem! Anyone who said that he did just didn't know how to handle alcohol themselves!

He had shown up at work one morning, hung over from another late night, his breath reeking from the brandy he had swilled until well past one in the morning — par for the course in those days. He had doctored most of the red out of his eyes with eye-drops, but they were still glassy, and they hurt like Hell — as did the rest of his head. He had been filled with an unfocused anger that morning — another thing that was increasingly commonplace. Before long, he had a focal point at which to direct his rage. The receptionist and his secretary looked especially nervous when he arrived, but he was clueless until he stepped into his office. He had experienced an immediate sense of dislocation. The room had been filled with people who shouldn't have *been* there — nine of them. Even today, more than eight years later, he could recall every detail of their grim, determined faces. All three of his partners were there, as well as two attorneys who used to pound down their liquor, but whom he hadn't seen recently. The soon-to-be ex-wife was there, along with his teenage daughter, whose tattoo and nose-ring had been procured, he was sure, just to drive him crazy. There were also a pair of men he had never seen before in his life. It was one of them who spoke first, asking him to have a seat, as if it were their office rather than his.

He felt like a caged animal as they took turns describing how his drinking had affected them. Then they had given him their ultimatum. He could leave *right now* for the treatment center they had chosen for him — a place called Duffy's in the

Napa Valley — or he could go to Hell. Alone. His partners told him in no uncertain terms that he would be out of the law firm. His old drinking buddies told him that they had gone to Alcoholics Anonymous and quit drinking — that their lives had changed for the better since they had gone on the wagon. His marriage was already over — both he and his wife knew that there was no saving it — at least there was nothing that *she* could threaten to take away from him. But when his punked-out daughter told him that he wouldn't be seeing *her* anymore unless he quit drinking, he lost it. The rage that had been building throughout the intervention exploded, and he started screaming — summoning the most potent verbal abuse he could muster until he was hoarse — before storming out of the room. Their threats had been real. The lawsuit to dissolve the partnership, complete with a court order preventing him from returning to his office, was filed within hours. The papers were served on him at the bar where he had done most of his "legal research" for several years.

The law practice was a successful one, and Michael had been as big a part of that success as any of the partners, though not so much in the last few years. His partners treated him fairly, recognizing that he had a disease. His salary checks came regularly until the lawsuit was settled at a fair, even generous price. Half of the money went to his wife in the divorce, but with a few adjustments to his lifestyle, he wanted for nothing — at least in a material sense. In every other way, his days and nights became a living Hell. Without even the pretense of going to work to get him out of the house, Michael soon stopped going to his "other office" to drink. He became more and more reclusive as the months went by, and he was soon downing more than a quart of brandy a day. As he sat on a couch in his living-room dressed only in his dingy underwear drinking out of a heavy, lead-crystal glass, his only "intellectual stimulation" occurred when he contemplated the condensation as it formed on the outside of the glass and dripped down the sides. He found a store that would deliver his groceries and his booze and was well on his way to drinking himself to death when his own personal miracle occurred.

The time of day had ceased to have any particular meaning for him. His tendency to stay up late at night had metamorphosed into a pattern of waking and sleeping, if it could be called sleeping, that was completely independent of light or darkness. He no longer woke up — he came-to. Then he started his day with a beer, trying to get as much of it down as possible before he vomited. He could usually keep the second one down, and until unconsciousness took him it was one drink after the other— broken only by feeble attempts to eat, or the time it took to phone for more groceries or booze.

The vision, or visitation — whatever it was — occurred late one night. His experience seemed to be similar to the near-death experiences he had heard described on tabloid TV shows he had taken to watching — a warm, loving presence emanating from a bright light. Later, when he found his way to Alcoholics Anonymous and told a fellow A.A. member about the experience, he was told that it was a "moment of clarity." Michael knew better. He *knew* with absolute certainty that the source of that light was God Himself. In A.A., when he was told that he had to find a power greater than himself in order to quit drinking, he had no problem with the concept. He already had direct orders from the big man to stop. God hadn't been very talkative — he didn't need to be. But the one task given to Michael was the hardest thing he had ever done.

For six months, all he did was attend A.A. meetings — three, four or even five times a day, shuffling in wearing an old sweatsuit and bedroom slippers. He never mentioned the fact that he had once been one of the highest-priced trial lawyers in northern California. Lots of people in A.A. had thrown away careers as promising as his. Status in A.A. wasn't conferred by what a person did for a living, but by years or even decades of sobriety. He fell in with a group of men who met for a lunch meeting every day. They had a very practical orientation, focusing on learning how to live life on a day-to-day basis and stay sober *no matter what.* He listened and learned. By the time his first A.A. "birthday" rolled around, he was a changed man.

He did a lot of thinking about the *whys* and *hows* that led to his alcoholism, and realized that at least part of the reason he had begun to drink during the day was that he despised the people that he worked for and as a corollary had come to despise himself. All through college and law school, he had envisioned himself as an environmental lawyer. He earned the highest grades in his environmental law classes, then went further, reading everything he could find on his own. He was an excellent student, graduating in the top ten-percent of his class before breezing through the bar exam. That was when reality delivered a low blow. In the field of environmental law, there were two major employers — government and big business. Philosophically, he was aligned with government. From the time he focused his studies on environmental law, he had been looking forward to dragging offenders into court and punishing them for their transgressions. But at the time he was looking for a job, neither the State nor the Federal governments were hiring. He reluctantly interviewed with law firms that represented corporate interests and received several offers. With rent to pay and student-loans coming due, he bit the bullet and went to work for the enemy.

He was brilliant, rising from junior-associate to junior-partner faster than anyone before him in the firm's long history. It was all supposed to be temporary, until he could find a position with the government or a firm that prosecuted polluters — but his seduction had just begun. First came the Mercedes, purchased with his first big bonus, then, after he got married, the upscale house in the "right" neighborhood. In short order, the best salary he could earn as a government attorney would not be enough to support his lifestyle. As his career progressed, he strayed further and further from the values that had led him to practice law in the first place. But the material success he enjoyed brought only a desire for more of the same. Once, he had thought of himself as an idealist. Eventually he stopped thinking about idealism at all.

The drinking had started innocently enough. He found that alcohol would make the vague emptiness that lurked inside, waiting for the quiet, unguarded moment, disappear. Stopping with his friends from the firm on the way home after a hard day at the office quickly became routine. Fifteen years passed before booze made his life unmanageable on a daily basis. Long before that happened, he and three of his fellow junior-partners had ventured out to form a firm of their own. Primarily because of the fact that Michael had gone with them, they were able to take two of their former firm's largest clients with them. These two accounts — a pair of lumber companies — gave Michael the opportunity to specialize even further, and for the years before alcohol immobilized him, he was considered one of the top litigators in his field.

But with each achievement he racked up practicing law, his secret contempt for himself grew. His drinking increased hand in hand with the departure of his self-respect, until he finally arrived at that dismal day when he found himself the subject of an intervention. In retrospect, Michael knew that the intervention had been a turning point — one that ultimately gave him a chance to reclaim his life.

"It's a long story," he said at last, in answer to Ryan's question. "Suffice it to say that I took a wrong turn along the way, and that I've been trying to make up for my mistakes." His eyes twinkled as he smiled and said, "I've never been happier since I started being true to myself and my beliefs." He studied Ryan for a moment, then gave him a succinct, if cryptic piece of advice. "Never let the quest for money lead you away from what you believe in," he said. "The price is one you wouldn't want to pay."

# 17

RAYMOND BAKER COULDN'T UNDERSTAND WHAT WAS HAPPENING to him. Inconceivable as it was, his absolute, heretofore invincible self-control — the bedrock of his existence — seemed to be cracking. On every level, things were going just as he had planned. But in tandem with his triumphant manipulation of events had come an absolute *obsession* with the raven and puma he had glimpsed at the Miller tract. Every fiber of his being urged him to devote himself to seeking out and killing them. He found himself fantasizing about tearing them into shreds with his bare hands, or shooting them from a distance. The desire haunted virtually all of his waking moments, and even his dreams. No matter how hard he tried, no matter what he did, he could not control their constant intrusion into his thoughts. He had even gone back to the site of the massacre with a weapon handy on three separate occasions just in case they returned. He hadn't really expected them to pop out of thin air as they had during the shooting — but he still hadn't been able to refrain from making the trip to the entrance of the Miller tract.

His unexpected compulsion to find and kill the raven and the puma wasn't the only thing giving him grief. Even before the "Miller massacre," as the media had dubbed the shootings, he had begun to experience a vague unease, coupled with the notion that he was missing something. But though he racked his brains, he couldn't come up with an answer. As he mulled over his dilemma in his darkened inner-office within the Miller Lumber complex, he was tempted to indulge in more than his measured amounts of whiskey and cocaine — just to calm the obsessive thoughts and the vague but nagging disquiet. He didn't succumb, but the mere fact that he was tempted disturbed him. He snorted and tossed back his usual amounts and sat in his darkened office, observing but not enjoying the effect of the drugs, and waiting . . . for what, he didn't know.

# 18

LATE SUNDAY NIGHT MICHAEL AND RYAN PUT THE FINAL TOUCHES on their pleadings and faxed a copy to Miller Lumber, giving them the notice that was required by statute. *We might as well have painted a target on the roof of Project HOPE*, thought Michael. He checked his watch, and saw that it was a few minutes past eleven o'clock. Everything was ready to go — all of the documents had been stapled together and placed in his briefcase — with duplicate originals to remain at the Project HOPE headquarters just in case. The cards had been dealt — they would find out how good their hand was when they appeared before the judge.

Doug asked if Michael expected any attorneys for Miller Lumber to show up to oppose the motion.

"You can count on it," he replied. "There might even be three or four. They know there would be a suit as soon as they filed their Timber Harvest Plan — they probably have a whole raft of lawyers on retainer." He grinned at Doug and picked up his briefcase. "It's what we're alleging in our suit that will come as a surprise. They're not going to be dancing to a tune they've ever heard before. Baker took a gamble by faking those studies — catching him in the act gives us a real leg-up at this stage of the proceedings."

Michael had been staying at Adam's house throughout the weekend. They said their goodbyes to the others, and left together in Adam's Honda. Gayle sighed as they drove away. "It makes me feel vulnerable whenever I let any of you out of my sight, and now that Adam is in the picture I've got one more to watch over."

"I take it you don't recognize any past-life connection with Michael," said Ryan. Gayle shook her head, and he continued. "I've been wondering about that. I haven't recognized him from our past-lives either, but he's the focal point of everything we're doing."

Gayle stared out into the darkness, watching Adam's tail-lights until they disappeared around a corner. "I'm certain he hasn't been with us before, but I'd bet money that if we don't succeed this time around, he'll be with us in the next life. Who knows? Maybe it wasn't always the seven of us aligned against *The One without a Soul*. It could have started with just one or two."

"Then the advanced spirits haven't provided you with that information yet?" asked Audrey.

"Information seems to come to us on a 'need-to-know' basis," Larry put in.

"And usually the advanced spirits wait until the last possible instant to give it to us." As he was speaking, Audrey seemed to lose interest in the answer to her question, and Ryan became distracted by an untidy stack of papers that he began to straighten out. Larry and Gayle exchanged a knowing glance. Audrey's question had brought them too close to forbidden territory.

Gayle cleared her throat and changed the subject to one that she knew was "authorized." She reached out to Audrey, and took one her hands and said, "You'll probably come into contact with *him* tomorrow. Remember how strong your reaction was just seeing him on television. It's likely that it will be much stronger when you're both in the same room. I'm certain he'll feel the pull of our past-life connection too. If we're right in speculating that he isn't yet aware of the true nature of our conflict, this will probably wake him to it. Whatever you do, try to remember that love is the only thing that will give you strength against your fear." She reached for Ryan with her free hand. "And whether Baker's there or not, promise me you'll be extremely wary on your drive back from San Francisco — everything we've learned tells us that he'll try to kill you sooner or later."

"You don't sound like you have any fear for yourself," said Ryan.

Once again Larry and Gayle exchanged glances. They had been aware of Raymond Baker's presence the instant their totems arrived at the Miller Massacre. Both of them had felt his rage and had seen him start towards the spectral images of their totems before they returned to their physical bodies. For a few moments they had been afraid he would be able to follow them, using some spirit-form of his own. But when he had not appeared, they surmised that spirit-walking wasn't one of his abilities — at least not yet.

"I don't think he'll know about any of us individually until he gets close enough to feel the past-life connection," she replied. "But we won't be going with you to San Francisco, so we should be fine."

They moved out into the parking area, saying good-bye to the volunteers who were still maintaining a twenty-four hour watch — although after the Miller Massacre, and with Eddie Rapski off the air, vandalism seemed less likely. After a few more farewells, Doug, Larry, and Gayle left for the coast. Ryan put his arm around Audrey as they walked to her Volvo. "This weekend hasn't been much like I anticipated," she said wistfully after they reached her car. "We had one candle-lit dinner, and then I put you to work non-stop."

"You know the old saying," said Ryan with a quick smile. "Life is what happens to you while you're making other plans." He reached over and took her free hand, giving it a squeeze. "Besides, I'd rather be here with you working my butt off than sitting in Fort Bragg pining away — and besides, I've never had the opportunity to work side-by-side with a lawyer of Michael's caliber. He's incredible! He knew every case we cited in the motion by heart — even the footnotes. A general practitioner like me never gets the opportunity to focus on any one area of the law so thoroughly. It almost makes me wish I had specialized like he did."

"If you had done that, then you would have been trying to be someone other than who you are," said Audrey. "Your knowledge of the law and courtroom skills might not be as well-honed as Michael's, but you've got other attributes that make you a wonderful lawyer." She gave him a sidelong glance. "Maybe it wasn't such a good idea to introduce me to Sally — she and I have spent enough time on the phone for me to get a feeling for the way you practice law." She laughed light-heartedly — something she hadn't had much opportunity for that weekend. Ryan felt himself pierced by one of cupid's arrows, and was once again reminded of how much he loved her. "All women belong to a sisterhood," she continued. "You'd better get used to the idea. Men are such mysterious creatures that it takes a whole network of us to deal with just one of you. You're going to have to remember that I'm only a spokesperson for a committee!" He leaned over and kissed her on the cheek. "As long as you're the head of the committee I don't care who you consult," he replied. "Just let me know if I get on the wrong side of any of them — I'll need to know who to bribe!"

After Audrey pulled her Volvo into the driveway of her little house and turned off the engine, Ryan leaned over to kiss her more intensely than he'd had the oppor-tunity since the previous evening. "We've still got time to get some romance in," he said, "if you're in the mood, that is . . ."

"That's the best invitation I've had all day," she said with a smile, then took his hand and led him inside, where she let him know in no uncertain terms that the committee approved.

*    *    *

"DO YOU REALLY think something might happen to them on the way back from San Francisco?" asked Larry as he guided the Subaru up the on-ramp onto northbound 101. "Have you had a premonition?"

"This time it was just common sense — to tell you the truth, I haven't reached out to try to feel what's coming since we returned from the Oglala Sioux lifetime." Gayle shifted in her seat, stretching the muscles in her back and shoulders. "Everything is uncertain, anyway. All we know for sure is that there will be a conflict — no one knows how it will end. Things are in perfect balance, and not even the Divinity knows which way the scales will tip." Larry caught her smile out of the corner of his eye. "She did say that the Divinity was rooting for us, though."

"How is it that the Divinity — this God/Goddess doesn't even know the out-come? It seems like omniscience should be part of the package-deal."

"Apparently the Divinity chose *not* to know how everything would turn out when she/he/it decided to experience the non-divine. It's got to get boring to al-ways know what the answers are going to be, and how all of the stories are going to end. *She* — the one who we hope will be Audrey's child — told me that she doesn't know whether or not she'll be coming, only that she wants to very much."

"That conversation must have been incredible!"

Gayle shifted sideways in her seat so that she could look directly at him. "The word 'incredible' isn't nearly adequate — I don't think a word exists that could possibly be adequate. Now that I've met her, there's absolutely nothing I want more than for her to come! She's *exactly* what the world needs right now." Gayle sighed. "I just can't begin to describe what she's like — she seems so young, and yet ancient at the same time. And although I was completely in awe of her, she was as familiar as my reflection in the mirror. And overriding everything else was the most incredible feeling of joy . . . pure joy without guilt or the ponderous heaviness that I sometimes associated with church and spirituality when I was a child. I could never really feel happy about the idea that Jesus had to suffer and die for my salvation. It started the whole relationship off on the wrong foot — I was deeply in debt before we even got started. I was always told that I had to be *good* in order to please God. When I was talking with *her,* I got the impression that the thing she wanted most for me was that I should be *myself* — the *real* me. I've never *ever* experienced that kind of acceptance before."

Larry sneaked a quick glance at her. "If I had been harboring any doubts that Audrey's baby might be bringing a new way to seek the divine, they would have been wiped out just now. You sound as much like a child who's just experienced Christmas morning for the first time as a person who just had a transcendent religious experience."

"That's a good way to put it." Gayle agreed. "And now I *know*, with every fiber of my being, that love is the ultimate answer to every question." She leaned close to him again. "That's not a new idea for me, Larry — if you asked me, I would have told you that I've been devoting the majority of my energy to giving and receiving love for years. But now it feels as though I was mouthing the words without truly understanding them." She sighed again. "I can't understand why the rest of you aren't allowed to have personal contact with her. I'm convinced that everyone would be able to hold love close to their heart under *any* circumstances if we could all have direct contact like I did. But the others aren't even permitted to know that she might be coming. It doesn't seem fair! And there's no way I can be as persuasive as she was!"

"Try letting the persuasion flow through you rather than forcing it with your own will. You can't *make* them choose love — they have to do that themselves. There's got to be a reason why *she's* communicated with you and with no one else. And since that has allowed you to know the truth at your very core, it makes you willing and able to guide the rest of us. If the others, and for that matter, if *I* am able to withstand fear and choose love, it will be in large part because of this knowing that *you* possess. We have all come to trust your special gifts. I suspect that *we'll* be able to believe that love is the only answer because we know that's what *you* believe."

Gayle sat quietly for a while, listening to the Subaru's all-weather tires sing against the pavement. This section of Highway 101 was lined with redwood trees, planted years ago at regular intervals. The trees were perhaps forty feet tall, and were barely visible on the extreme edge of the light thrown by Larry's headlights, flashing by like dimly- perceived, bushy sentinels that seemed stunted compared to the redwoods closer to the coast. She tried to clear her mind of all thought, hoping that she might get some kind of message about how things would turn out, but for the moment there was nothing there. As the freeway skirted Cloverdale, they could see Miller Lumber Company, with its huge gout of steam released by some part of the milling process, boiling into the air to a great height before dissipating. The entire plant was lit up, though it was late at night. Gayle thought about having Larry pull the car off the road so that she could do some spirit-walk spying at the mill, but decided against it. They already knew that Baker could perceive their presence, even when they were in their insubstantial totem forms. And although she doubted that he could harm them when they were spirit-walking, it was still risky — there was no way to know if he might have discovered a way to track them back to their bodies.

"Every time I go past this place it makes my hackles rise," said Larry. Then, almost as if he were able to tell what Gayle had been thinking, said, "It was so strange when we were at the Miller tract helping those who had been shot. Half of my attention was focused on what I was doing — helping the souls of those whose lives were ending. The other half of my attention was on Baker. It was like being in a ring with a <u>bull!</u> We were obviously invisible to everyone there except those who were dying, and *him.* I could feel the hate pouring out of him like that cloud of steam that's rising from the mill."

"I wonder if he could see us because he's partially in the spirit world, or because our destinies are so interwoven," Gayle mused, an involuntary shiver running down her spine. "I don't think he had a way to follow us, or he would have. As it was, I could feel his will pulling at me like an undertow."

"That's a good analogy. I felt him sucking at my spirit, too."

"I worry about what will happen the tomorrow when one of us is actually in the same room with him. So far, our only contacts have been tangential — on the television screen or when our totems were near him. Even then, our reactions have been so strong that we were barely in control of ourselves. What's it going to be like when we're right next to him? The only way I coped with the fear was to hold the image — no, that's not the right word — the *essence* of *her* in my heart. Even then, it was awfully hard, and I had just talked with *her* a few hours earlier."

Larry took the turn-off for Highway 128 at the north end of town, where The Hamburger Ranch, site of Adam's and Michael's clandestine meetings with John Smith had taken place, and soon they were snaking their way towards the coast. They didn't speak as the miles rolled by, comfortable in each other's presence without need for small-talk. Sometimes their shared burden brought them so close that it almost seemed as though they thought with one mind. As they neared the ocean, Larry said, "I decided to do some positive visualization." He smiled as he thought of the countless times he had suggested the technique to his patients. "I'm trying to think of the changes that might take place in a world with a female Christ-figure, but it's difficult. I have such a limited frame of reference."

"I think it will be different from anything that's ever happened before," said Gayle. "I have the impression, though I'm not sure where I got it, that the shape of the divinity *she* represents will not be a Goddess." She turned in her seat slightly to face Larry while she spoke. "Even in Christianity there are powerful female images — I have the impression that everything will be more balanced — that any feminine perspective *she* brings to the world will simply come as a natural outgrowth of being female in this physical incarnation. When the spirit spoke to me, she referred to 'the Divinity' when she talked about God. That leads me to believe that her perception of the divine is neither male nor female — or perhaps both at once." She leaned back in her seat, took a deep breath and let it out in an audible sigh. "I'm looking forward to *her* coming so much! My greatest fear is that we'll prove inadequate, and she won't get to come."

Larry reached over and squeezed her hand, the contact communicating his agreement as thoroughly as words could have done, and they made the rest of the trip in silence.

# 19

AUDREY PULLED HER VOLVO INTO A PARKING LOT NEAR THE
Federal courthouse in San Francisco where the hearing on their motion for a TRO
had been scheduled for eleven o'clock. *If evidence that they've faked the environmental studies isn't enough, then I don't know what would be,* she said to herself,
taking a deep breath and letting it out slowly to try to calm the jittery feeling in her
stomach. She glanced over at Michael, who appeared to be utterly cool and calm
— he had once told her that a courtroom was a garment he wore loosely, like an old
pair of shoes. On the way there from Ukiah, he had worked hard to persuade Ryan
to stay away from the courthouse and the resulting exposure to Baker.

"Why me?" Ryan objected. "What about Audrey and Adam?"

"They were the founders of project HOPE," Michael reminded him. "We put
them in the line of fire when we faxed the pleadings to Miller Lumber." He leaned
forward from where he was sitting in the back seat, and put his hand on Ryan's left
shoulder. "There's no reason to gift-wrap your identity and hand it over to Baker, is
there?"

The lawyer in Ryan wanted to stay involved with the lawsuit — perhaps not
going so far as to sit at the counsel table, but at least to hear the oral arguments, and
be there to hear the judge's ruling. Another part of him wanted to try to protect
Audrey from the threat that Baker represented. But ultimately, Michael's arguments had been persuasive.

The four of them walked together as far as a coffee shop where Ryan had
agreed to wait. Ryan kissed Audrey goodbye, and wished Michael luck. As he
watched the love of his life walk towards a face to face encounter with their foe-
across-the-ages, he felt a mix of emotions: frustration, concern, love, anxiety. But
in spite of everything he tried to do to suppress it, surpassing and overwhelming all
the others was fear.

*     *     *

IN A LAW office near the courthouse, Raymond Baker glared across the conference table at the three attorneys in their charcoal-gray suits, custom shirts and
silk ties. He had not been pleased by what they were telling him, and he had made
his displeasure known. Heath Waterman, the lead counsel, didn't cow as easily as

most — although the two younger ones looked like they would rather be anywhere else. Baker drank in their obvious discomfort, using it to soothe his irritation while he focused his attention on Waterman, the highly-recommended senior partner in the firm. Waterman's reputation placed him among the best in his field, but at the moment, inexplicably, he seemed to be giving up the fight before a single blow had been struck!

"If the facts stated in the affidavits in support of this petition are proven in trial, then you haven't got a chance in hell," Waterman said unequivocally in response to Baker's interrogation. Then he had dared to glare derisively at Baker. "As far as the judge granting a temporary restraining order, that's a given. There's a sworn affidavit, backed up by exhibits that provide substantial proof that the wildlife studies supporting your Timber Harvest Plan were manufactured." Waterman's glare left no misapprehension — Baker did not intimidate him in the slightest. "We can talk later about where these documents originated. At this stage of the proceedings, a sworn affidavit is enough — oral testimony isn't required to obtain a temporary restraining order, and the Department of Forestry regulations are clear — studies have to be carried out for two full years before a timber harvest plan can be authorized. Project HOPE has made a *prima facia* case that they weren't — the call is a no-brainer."

With a calculated effort, Baker set aside Waterman's insolence for the moment. "What about the long-term chances of success?" he asked.

"That all depends on whether or not the witness who leaked the documents in the exhibits to Project HOPE comes to court to testify. A *live* person has to do that — written testimony contained in an affidavit is usually insufficient for the actual trial."

Heath Waterman hadn't said a word that was untrue or made any unethical suggestions, but there was no mistaking the reason for his emphasis on the word "live." As the two men stared at each other across the table, Raymond Baker realized that he had misjudged the man. For the first time in his life, he had found a kindred spirit.

*    *    *

THE COURTROOM WAS packed, even though they had made no effort to publicize it through the media — that would have drawn in just as many people who were for the logging as against it. Instead, Project HOPE's telephone volunteers had been hard at work, and their efforts had been well rewarded. Michael, Audrey and Adam arrived fifteen minutes before the hearing, filed the lawsuit with the clerk of the court, then entered the courtroom. Like all others, this courtroom had been designed to create the impression that the decisions handed down there were somehow larger and more important than what could be rendered by mere mortals. Michael had told her that courtrooms were imbued with rhythms all their own, and sometimes the intensity of the litigation itself took on larger-than-life proportions. On this morning, anticipation hung so heavily in the air that it quelled virtually all conversation.

Two minutes before the appointed hour, the door to the courtroom opened to admit four men. The first three to enter the room were Heath Waterman and his two associates. Following them, wearing an impeccably-tailored Italian suit, was Raymond Baker. Baker's presence immediately made the room feel as if it was too tightly buttoned. As he passed through the gallery, he focused his attention on the spectators, scanning their angry faces and absorbing the enmity that flowed towards him. He was enjoying himself, maintaining a relaxed attitude. But his smile froze into a grimace when he saw the representatives from Project HOPE for the first time. His attention became riveted on the man and woman sitting on the far end, and his response was overwhelming and instantaneous — they were his *enemies!* His reaction was similar, but exponentially stronger, than what he had experienced when he had seen the puma and the raven at the Miller tract. Instinctively, he felt a need to attack them, and was barely able to restrain himself, standing with his fists clenched, balanced on the balls of his feet. The woman's attention had been focused on her own lawyer, with whom she was conversing in low tones. But when she looked up, their gazes locked and she slowly rose to her feet. Baker's grimace metamorphosed into a savage grin, wider than any smile that had previously crossed his face in *this* lifetime. Without knowing in advance that he was going to do it, he began to reach out with his mind, through the conduit created by their locked gazes. Suddenly, inexplicably, he became certain that he could stab deeply into her with the power of his hatred, to form it into a blade and twist it until she had been gutted of her life-force. It was exactly at that instant that the raven that had been haunting his thoughts appeared in mid-air above and behind his *enemy*, angling towards both of them in a flat glide. The bird was much larger up close, with a wingspan approaching four feet. Abruptly, it pulled up, and landed gracefully on his *enemy's* shoulder, uttering a caw that was so loud, Baker was certain it could even be heard in the hallway outside the courtroom. This time he did not hesitate, but shifted his attack, plunging the blade of his hatred through the bird's gleaming eye.

Gayle felt Baker's focus slide from Audrey to the spectral figure of her totem. As she landed on Audrey's shoulder, she felt him reaching for her — into the mind of the raven that only he could see. Thankfully, she wasn't physically present, and his attack had no effect. She had the vague sensation that she had dodged a bullet before he abruptly cut off his attack. Under Gayle's clawed feet, Audrey felt stiff and unresponsive. With as much energy as she could muster, Gayle reached out to her, sending her every bit of love and all the positive energy she could muster, hoping that she could bring her out of the trance she had entered the moment she locked eyes with Baker. At last, across the intervening miles, she felt Audrey start to relax. A moment later the bailiff commanded all present to rise as the Honorable James Kelly took the bench.

When Adam rose from his chair with the others, his entire body was trembling in a full-bore flight-fight reaction. Fear had begun to course through his veins the moment Baker walked into the room as if it had been injected with a syringe. Even though Baker's wrath was not directed specifically at him, he could not help reacting as if he were under attack. In an instant, his admiration for John Smith's bravery multiplied tenfold. He sneaked a quick sideways glance at their foe just as Baker looked away from Audrey and directed his attention to the bailiff. Even this quick glimpse, when Baker's attention had been drawn elsewhere, made Adam's heart pound in his chest as if he had faced down a charging grizzly bear. He was sweating and shivering at the same time, and when he tried to swallow, his mouth was too dry. He wanted a drink of water, but was incapable of commanding his arms and hands to pour a cup from the pitcher that stood on the table directly in front of him. More than anything else in the world, he simply wanted to *get away* from this purveyor of terror!

It wasn't until Baker looked away that Audrey realized she had been standing like a deer on a highway, bedazzled by the headlights of oncoming traffic. There was a strange gap in her memory as her faculties returned all in a rush. For a second or two, she was filled with terror that knew no bounds. Then, unexpectedly, as the bailiff's words jumped into auditory focus, she felt herself becoming much calmer, almost as if someone had slipped her some kind of concoction. She took a deep breath, and sat, glad that her chair was the furthest away from *The One without a Soul*.

The Raven flapped her wings briefly, as she hopped from Audrey's seated form to Adam's shoulder — though not a breath of air was disturbed by her activity. Gayle had been aware of Adam's terror from the moment she arrived, but during Baker's attack there had been no opportunity to help him. Fear continued to radiate from him like sparks shooting from a Roman candle. She tried to send calming, loving thoughts in his direction, but she was too drained by the encounter with *The One without a Soul* and her efforts on Audrey's behalf. She shifted her mental focus back to her physical being where she sat motionless in front of the altar in her living-room, and reached out to the greatest source of strength and love she had ever experienced. Unbidden, a name came to her mind that seemed to describe all of her perceptions of the spirit whose destiny was as yet unknown. "*Ariel,*" she whispered silently, knowing *her* name for the first time. Silently, she asked to be made a conduit for the healing love and joy she had known while communing with the spirit, and to channel it where it was needed most at that moment.

Adam's eyes had been flitting about the room — to the doors, the windows — anywhere where he might make his escape. His rational mind told him that there was no immediate danger. Baker couldn't attack him here — they were in a federal courtroom! His emotions paid no attention to the entreaties made by his logical mind. But then, after a timeless eternity that lasted for only a few ticks of the clock, he was filled with a feeling of peace and serenity, and the menace of Baker's presence shrank down to manageable proportions. He lifted his head and began to pay attention to what was happening around him.

Michael, who was unaware of the unseen skirmishes occurring just beyond his ability to perceive, remained standing after the bailiff gave permission to be seated — as did the eldest of the lawyers who had accompanied Raymond Baker to the counsel table. After the shuffle of movement throughout the courtroom had abated, the proceedings commenced. "Counsel, may I have your appearances for the record," the judge requested, peering over half glasses with eyes that were neutral, but held a veiled threat should anything happen in his courtroom to displease him.

"Michael Holland for the plaintiff. Ready, your honor,"

"Heath Waterman for Miller Lumber Company."

The judge came to the merits of the motion immediately. "Mr. Waterman, I have read the plaintiff's Petition, and I'm inclined to grant it."

Audrey reached for Adam's hand when she heard the judge's words. She was surprised to find it cold, yet damp from perspiration.

The judge glared down at Heath Waterman for a moment. "These are extremely serious allegations, counselor. The court is aware of the negligent manner that those in the timber industry have conducted wildlife studies in the past. But evidence of out-and-out fraud would be an entirely new development."

Heath Waterman was no fool. He had already explained to his client exactly why the temporary restraining order would be issued — the plaintiff's allegations were simply too serious for the court to do anything *but* grant the motion. Notwithstanding, he briefly took the offensive, if only to save face. "For the record your honor, my client denies all of the allegations in the Petition." He gestured towards the other counsel table. "It is the plaintiff or whoever supplied the plaintiff with these documents who is trying to perpetrate a fraud on the court."

As he had anticipated, Waterman's argument had no impact on the judge. "Your client better be able to prove that," he growled. "The Petition is granted. I'm issuing a Temporary Restraining Order effective *immediately*." He glared at Heath Waterman. "All logging activity at that site is to stop, and you are going to communicate those orders before we leave this courtroom. You can use the telephone in my chambers to make the necessary calls."

Heath Waterman spoke. "Your honor, my client has undertaken a logging operation that has been approved by the Department of Forestry on land that has been owned by the company for over a hundred years! Thousands upon thousands of dollars have been committed to this operation, which is now in full swing. There are a limited number of days left before inclement weather will put a stop to everything. I request an early trial and Fast Track discovery — after all, the plaintiff's own motion shows that this is a one-issue trial."

Judge Kelly paused for a moment, then shifted his attention over to Michael. "Mister Holland, I've never known you to make this kind of motion unless you stood on solid ground. But I'm warning you that you had better be able to prove your case at the hearing, or the court will consider sanctions! Counsel has a good point. It *doesn't* appear to the court that there is much need to delay the trial for discovery to take place. In fairness to the defendant, I *am* going to shorten the time frame for discovery." He paused for a moment to consider what had been plead in Project HOPE's petition, and said, "It seems to me that there should be a need for only a few depositions — those of the people who did the field work, and of the witness who produced the purported records.  Do you agree, counsel?"

"I think that will be sufficient," said Michael, nodding.

"That's fine with me, your honor," added Heath Waterman.

"I'm ordering that Miller Lumber produce for the plaintiff all documents of whatever sort that are related to the preparation of the Timber Harvest Plan, including those stored in electronic form in computer files.  These shall be delivered one week from today.  Furthermore, I'm ordering that arrangements be made for the wildlife biologists whose names appear on these studies to be deposed two weeks from today, and that the witness whose declaration is attached to plaintiff's petition be deposed immediately thereafter.  The hearing on the Preliminary and Permanent Injunctions will take place in three weeks."  He looked at both attorneys.  "Any objections?"

There were none from either attorney.

"This court is in recess."

*      *      *

RYAN FIDGETED RESTLESSLY as he waited in the coffee shop, and tried to remain calm, although he was filled with trepidation.  He glanced at his watch nervously.  If the hearing started on time, it would be in full swing — or it might even be over, depending on whether or not the judge ruled immediately from the bench.  The judge's decision concerned him, but not nearly as much as the thought of Audrey being in the same room as Raymond Baker.  He stared at the cellular phone that he had placed on the table in front of him, willing it to ring so that he could hear his love's sweet voice telling him that she was okay.  As if in answer to his summons it rang, startling him and making him jump.  He snatched it up and was relieved when Audrey excitedly told him that the Judge had granted their petition — they would be at the diner in a few minutes.

# 20

ALONE IN HIS OFFICE WITH ITS MAGNIFICENT VIEW OF SAN FRANCISCO Bay, Raymond Baker was riding a wave of exhilaration that he could scarcely contain. No thrill he had ever experienced could match what he had felt that morning in the courtroom when he had suddenly discovered that he had the power to use the force of his will as if it were a blade forged of the finest steel! But at the same time, he was also being buffeted by a strange melange of desires, emotions — even visions, none of which were under his control. Unbridled rage had consumed him the instant he made eye contact with the sanctimonious *bitch* from Project HOPE — that was when he realized that he knew exactly what to do to cut her to the core! But as he was reaching towards the *bitch,* ready to savage her with the force of his anger, his contempt, his undying hatred, *his indomitable will,* the raven reappeared out of thin air! Reflexively he had shifted his attack. But even though he had stabbed as deeply as possible, he had come up empty. Still, he was sure that the power was real — that his failed attempt to gut the raven was some kind of anomaly. He hadn't tried to use the power again, although he had been briefly tempted to experiment on one of Waterman's junior associates. Discretion made him pull back — discretion, and a random thought — that this new-found weapon was not to be used casually.

As he stared out at the lights of Berkeley and Oakland glimmering like distant stars on the far side of San Francisco bay, he concentrated on tempering his rage and damping his hate down to a manageable level — though it still burned as hot as a furnace every time he thought of the *bitch* or her scarecrow-like companion who had cowered next to her at the counsel-table. He couldn't fathom why these two enraged him while he felt nothing but indifference for their lawyer, who, after all, had forced him to halt the logging — not that this brief hiatus would make much difference in the long run! As long as he was in control of Miller Lumber, the redwoods were doomed, court or no court!

Overall, though, the focus of Baker's attention was shifting towards his recently discovered *enemies.* He had been angry when Waterman casually dismissed their chances of success in the courtroom — killing him had even crossed his mind, until he had experienced that unexpected feeling of kinship. Yet, by the time the judge made his ruling, it barely registered on his consciousness. When his rage was diverted to the *bitch* and the scarecrow, his interest in logging the old-growth had diminished by several factors — not that it wasn't still a high priority! But the shift alarmed him, nonetheless. Never relinquishing even the smallest part of his iron-willed self control was the fundamental principle upon which Baker based his life. He had *never* experienced such a shift in goals or priorities before. Suddenly, things were becoming murky and uncertain in a life that had been as calculated as a space-launch. On the other hand, there was a new purpose — destroying his new-found *enemies.* It almost felt as if he had been biding his time up to this moment, with talents and abilities waiting to blossom like the bud of a black rose.

But before he allowed his attention to shift too far, there was a loose end to tie — the delicious end to a long-conceived and beautifully executed plan. He reached into a drawer in his desk, and retrieved a fat envelope filled with eight-by-ten photographs. Some had been taken on the streets of San Francisco, but most of the images had been caught by a carefully concealed camera hidden in the suite at the Santa Rosa hotel where his repugnant puppet indulged in his sexual liaisons. Rapski had been such a faithful, dog-like servant. He had fulfilled the promise of his potential, succeeding to a degree that would have surprised Baker, if beating extremely long odds wasn't such a routine part of his life. After the shootings, the firestorm of protest caused by the filing of the Timber Harvest Plan had shifted neatly over to Rapski, where it still raged unabated. The icing on the cake, the *coup de gras,* would be the total destruction of Rapski's reputation among the morons who adored him. Identical envelopes had already been sent to every newspaper and television station within a two-hundred mile radius, and the photos had been posted on the Internet as well. Rapski's unmasking would draw public attention even further away from Baker, and Miller Lumber's logging of the old-growth. The general public already hated Rapski. His vociferous diatribes had been directed against so many minorities that in sum, they probably made up the majority of the population. He had long since won the enmity of virtually everyone who possessed the capacity to think and reason. The anti-environmentalist and anti-protester rhetoric that Baker told him to spew over the airwaves, followed by the Miller Massacre, had made Rapski the villain of that affair. When sexual proclivities were revealed, it would ruin him completely. Baker had long been pondering whether he would enjoy the confusion of Rapski's loyal listeners or Rapski's own anguish more. But after this morning's experience in the courtroom, Rapski's destruction no longer piqued his interest as it once had. Until this morning, he had looked forward to Rapski's destruction with great anticipation. It was now a mere diversion, at best — part of what was becoming a distant-seeming past. He had risen to a new level. There was much to plan, and time was wasting.

# 21

GAYLE TRIED TO CALM HERSELF ALTHOUGH SHE STILL FELT electrified by the events of the morning. She raised the delicate china cup to her lips and blew gently across the surface of the tea, sending a plume of steam into the air. Fearing that Baker might launch another attack, her totem had lingered in the courtroom until he left. She had felt euphoric when she acted as a conduit for Ariel's love and peace, but now, after returning to her own body, felt almost completely drained. In spite of her fatigue, she couldn't rest until she shared what she had experienced with Larry. Fifteen minutes after she called, he was bustling about in her kitchen making tea — a task he assigned to himself the moment he saw how tired she was. Patiently, he waited until she had revived enough to talk at length. "I'm afraid I've got one of those classic 'good-news — bad-news' stories to tell," she said finally, in a voice that cracked with exhaustion. "I'll start with the bad news first. *The One without a Soul* has powers that he either didn't have, or didn't choose to use, out at the Miller tract. I wondered if seeing Audrey and Adam might trigger something. By the time my totem arrived, his presence had expanded tremendously — as though his purpose had found its direction. By then, he had already honed in on Audrey, and was looking into her eyes." She shuddered. "It seemed like he was trying to bore a hole through her with some kind of focused energy — I could actually *see* it! I hate to think of what might have happened if I hadn't arrived and managed to distract him. Luckily, it was only my totem that was there. When he saw it, he re-directed his attack. Whatever he was trying to do to her got deflected to me." Her hand shook, causing the cup to chatter against the saucer. "But it didn't work, thank God. I can only assume it was because I wasn't physically there."

Larry looked surprised. "He tried to attack her in the courtroom?"

"From my perspective — and probably from his — the courtroom was barely there. I doubt he knew that he had that kind of power until he was in the middle of it."

"What was it that he was trying to do to her?"

Gayle's face turned gray as she struggled to formulate her answer. "I got a hint of it the first time I went spirit walking to the Miller offices. Do you remember my description of what I perceived? That he didn't so much leave a 'psychic residue' behind, as an unnatural emptiness?"

Larry nodded.

"I think he was trying to reach inside of her and take her essence — to vacuum out her soul, if you will. I think it would have been like an involuntary spirit-walk, but with the connection to her body completely severed." A realization hit her. "My God! We came within an eyelash of losing Audrey — and with her, everything else!"

Larry moved to the couch and put his arm around her. "We don't know that for sure," he said. "She might have been able to resist what he was trying to do. After all, weren't you able to fight him off after he shifted his attention to you?"

"I think that's only because I wasn't physically present — even so I could feel what he was trying to do." Gayle placed her hand over her heart. "Thankfully, my soul was anchored here, in my body — not where he thought it was!"

"What about this business of staring into Audrey's eyes and causing her to freeze up — do you think the eyes might be a point of vulnerability?"

"It's possible — I can't be sure. The whole thing lasted only seconds."

Larry thought for a few moments while Gayle sipped her tea. "The advanced spirits told us that the scales were balanced," he reflected. "We should have suspected that as we discovered new abilities, the same might prove true for him." He retrieved Gayle's tea-pot and refilled their cups. "But enough of the bad news for now. What's the good news you mentioned?"

Gayle's mood brightened immediately. "I know *her* name," she marveled. "After I helped Audrey come back from her half-conscious state, I tried to help Adam, but I didn't have anything left, and he was so scared! Since I couldn't help him myself, I asked *her* for help. Suddenly I knew her name! It's *Ariel*. She used me as a conduit and drained away Adam's fear while filling him with her love."

"That's the best news we've heard in a long time — I didn't know *she* would be allowed to take any active role in the conflict."

"*She's* a living gateway to divine love. How could *she* turn away a direct request in such a desperate moment? And would that be considered 'taking an active role?' When a person walks from one room into another, does the doorway take an active role?"

Larry chuckled. "You must be feeling better if you can come up with a philosophical conundrum like that. But regardless of whether there's an answer to your question, I'm grateful she was able to intercede."

"You and Adam both," she replied, taking a sip of her tea. They said nothing for a minute or two, but sat quietly together on the couch, while Larry held one of her hands in both of his. Then he said, "Ariel — the name is synonymous with "altar," literally, *Hearth of God*. It usually refers to Jerusalem, but if this child is to bring about a shift to a more feminine expression of the divine, I can't imagine a more appropriate name."

Gayle's expression grew somber. "We're going to need everything we can muster to get past Baker," she said emphatically. "We've managed to make it through our first meeting — but that's partly because he didn't know about us beforehand. Even one contact with him makes me understand why we were never successful in any of our past lives. This will be the most difficult thing any of us has ever taken on!"

*　　*　　*

ADAM SLOUCHED IN the back seat of Audrey's Volvo as they drove through Marin County on their way back home, thinking about the internal drama that had played out in the courtroom, and trying to understand the emotional roller-coaster ride he had taken. He had been apprehensive on the way to San Francisco, but all of them had been nervous — especially Audrey and Ryan, with their past-life memories. But Adam would never have anticipated his own reaction to seeing Baker. It was the way he imagined he would feel if he were on a disabled airliner plunging straight towards the earth. On an emotional level, he had been absolutely certain that he would never make it out of the courtroom alive. Nothing he told himself — that he was in a Federal courtroom, that Baker was unarmed, that a bailiff was there to protect them — none of it made any difference. All he could do was sit there and try not to lose control of his bladder and bowels. Then, shortly after the hearing commenced, his panic had inexplicably flowed out of him entirely, leaving him feeling peaceful and calm! He had scarcely paid any attention to what the others were saying while they returned to Audrey's car and started out of the city. Michael had been doing most of the talking, anyway, describing what had happened in the courtroom to Ryan, and some of the preparation that would be required before they went to trial. Adam *had* noticed that Audrey was unusually quiet in a situation where she would normally have been ebullient. Then Michael pulled him out of his reverie by asking him what his impression of Raymond Baker had been.

"The instant I saw him, I became more terrified than I have ever been in my life!" he blurted. "It felt as if every breath was the last one I would ever take — every second seemed to last an hour. Then, suddenly, the panic drained away, and I felt completely at ease — even happy! The judge was leaning our way by then, but I don't think that had anything to do with it. I've just been mulling it over, trying to figure it out."

"It was much the same for me," said Audrey. "At least, the part about panicking — I even got up to run out of the courtroom! Then, it's hard to describe what happened. There's a gap in my memory. Baker was walking towards his counsel table, staring right at me, and the next thing I knew, he was already *at* the counsel table, and the bailiff was telling everyone to stand up — but I was already standing! It was like a movie with a bad splice. There was no sensation of time passing — but suddenly he was ten feet closer! Right about then, my fear began to ease up too, although I couldn't say that I ever felt *peaceful* as long as Baker was in the courtroom. For that matter, I don't feel peaceful or safe even now."

"Was your reaction stronger than when you saw him on the TV screen?" Ryan asked.

"Much stronger! It felt like I was looking down the wrong end of a gun, watching the trigger being squeezed."

"Do you have any impression as to whether he recognized your past-life connection?" asked Michael.

"I know he felt something just from the way he looked at me." she replied. "If

- 209 -

nothing else, he could probably feel my fear. I wouldn't be surprised if everyone in the room could tell how scared I was."

"I'd be willing to bet that whatever lapse in consciousness you experienced was Baker's doing," said Michael. "We already know that he's unusually persuasive from what he was able to pull off at Miller Lumber. I don't think he would have been able to keep everyone in line the way he has unless he had some kind of power over people's minds."

"Are you suggesting he's some kind of magician?" asked Ryan.

"You could call it magic, or extra-sensory perception, or paranormal ability. Whatever label you put on it, he did something to Audrey that caused her to blank out. She stood absolutely still for at least fifteen or twenty seconds staring directly into his eyes, and she doesn't remember it at all."

"Baker and I stared at each that long?" Audrey asked incredulously.

"It was at least fifteen seconds," agreed Adam, "although for me it seemed much longer. I couldn't tell you if you were staring at him, though. I only took one glance at him and then I had to look away."

"The eye contact could be important," said Michael. "We all need to be wary just in case it is."

"This sounds like dialogue from a low-grade horror movie," said Adam, who was still feeling a lightness of spirit that was unlike anything he had ever experienced.

"The eye has long been considered the gateway to the soul," said Michael, ignoring Adam's attempt at levity. "Those beliefs had to come from somewhere — we need to keep an open mind. This whole situation stopped being *ordinary* a long time ago."

"What makes you think that Baker won't try to take *you* out as well?" asked Ryan.

"He may well try," Michael responded. "According to John Smith, he's already killed one person who got in his way, and I've just done that in a big way. But from everything I've heard about your interwoven destinies, my guess is that while killing me might be a pleasant appetizer, the main course would be those of you who have been up against him in past-lives."

"We all need to keep our guard up," said Audrey. "And to remember love. That's what Gayle and Larry keep saying is the key to this whole thing. But I don't see how it could have helped this morning. I was so scared I couldn't think of anything except running away. Love was the last thing on my mind."

"Then again," Michael mused, "both you and Adam experienced a sudden easing of your fears for no apparent reason. Couldn't *love* have had something to do with that?"

For a few moments the sound of the tires humming on the concrete was the only sound. Then Adam broke the silence. "I can't think of anything else that made my fear go away, and if love is the key, then love must have been what took it away. Though how that might have happened is a mystery to me."

"That's got to be it," Audrey agreed. "It sounds ridiculously simple — but if *love* is the answer to every aspect of this conflict, then the answer to the question of what eased our panic-attacks has to be *love*."

# 22

RYAN POSTPONED HIS RETURN TO FORT BRAGG FOR A DAY IN order to attend the memorial service for victims of the Miller massacre on Tuesday. He and Audrey slept late — a luxury they had not enjoyed over the weekend or on Monday. On their way to breakfast Ryan picked up a newspaper. There were follow-up stories on the massacre, complete with psychological profiles of the killers, but these were overshadowed by new revelations about Eddie Rapski, former KNZI *radical of the right.* Photographs depicting Rapski having sex with black men were prominently displayed, with portions excised to allow publication. The story concluded with the statement that attempts to reach Rapski for comment had been unsuccessful. "This has Raymond Baker written all over it," said Ryan, as he and Audrey read the article together over croissants filled with ham and Swiss cheese.

"I was thinking the same thing," Audrey agreed. "I continue to be amazed at the planning he must have done to set this all up. The records Doug found show that Baker only acquired control of the radio station a month before Rapski's show came on the air. These photographs had to have been shot over a period of time — I wonder if Baker was planning to ruin Rapski all along, or if the photos were some kind of insurance."

"We'll never know — but if Rapski had any loyal supporters left among the Neanderthals who listened to him in the first place, he's lost them now. And look at this news coverage — there's barely a mention of the court's decision to issue the TRO! It's all about the massacre and Rapski! The important things are taking a backseat to Baker's side-shows. If he was trying to take the heat off of himself and Miller Lumber, he's succeeded brilliantly."

The memorial service underscored the risks that went hand in hand with a struggle against *The One without a Soul.* Until Raymond Baker entered the picture, the thought that people might be killed in the furtherance of their cause had never entered Audrey's mind. Most of the speakers lauded the victims as martyrs, and several of those who spoke tried to drum up public support for purchasing the old-growth groves from Miller Lumber. Audrey hadn't known any of the victims personally, and found that she would have liked to have heard more about the people who had died. In a way, she couldn't help but feel some personal responsibility for what had occurred — if it hadn't been for their conflict between *The One without a Soul*, the massacre never would have happened. This wasn't the first time something like this had happened, either. During their Oglala Sioux lifetime their entire village had been wiped out, and there were probably others living in that block of buildings in Warsaw who had died in the conflagration. She forced herself to think about the things Gayle had said upon her arrival at Project HOPE the day of the massacre — that the souls of those who had been killed were at peace. Gayle's words *felt* right, and Audrey's own experiences with past-life regressions reassured her that when their own lives ended, their souls had not perished.

She leaned closer to Ryan, poignantly aware of how precious and fragile life was. Now that she had faced *The One without a Soul* in this lifetime, and felt the depth and power of his hatred, it took an effort to keep her spirits up. She reached down and placed her hand protectively over the budding life nestled within her and suppressed a sudden pang of anxiety, recognizing it for one of the sudden surges of love she had been feeling for her unborn child. She marveled at the power and depth of this love, and the effect it had on her. But although her anxiety was fueled by love, it was also based on the fear that no matter what she did, she wouldn't be able to protect her child from Baker. Tears began to stream down her face, as she remembered what he had done to her last child. The pain of that loss bit deeply — even though it had occurred in a previous physical existence, and in spite of the fact that the soul who had been her child in that incarnation had become her good friend in this lifetime. Others who sat around her were crying too, presumably for those who had died in the massacre. Audrey's grief extended to them too, but it was more closely focused on the travails she and the others had endured at the hand of *The One without a Soul* time and time again. So much misery! So much death and anguish! She leaned her head against Ryan's shoulder, and he put his arm around her, holding her close in spite of the heat of the summer morning. *What would I do if something happened to him?* she wondered. *What will I do if Baker is able to do what he has always done before?* She delicately probed her flat stomach, which was as yet unaffected by the profound changes occurring within. As she did, her fierce, scrappy nature began to reassert itself. Love was her answer. Love was the key to staying alive while Baker did everything in his power to keep the endless cycle going. She wiped away her tears and looked up at the face of her beloved — the father of her daughter — her soul-mate across the ages. *Let Baker take his best shot* she said to herself. *There's enough love right here to fight off anything he can throw at us!*

Ryan's feeling echoed Audrey's pensive mood. His thoughts, too, were drawn to his past-life memories, to the time when he had been able to put an arrow through their enemy, and also to the time when they had died of smoke-inhalation in the Warsaw ghetto. The background to the conflict in those lifetimes had been his government's conquest of an indigenous people, and then fascism's quest to dominate and destroy all who stood up for freedom and democracy. This time, it was between a giant corporate conglomerate and a tiny band of environmentalists. Gayle and Larry kept assuring them that there was a chance of success this time, but so much depended on Michael Holland and John Smith. Once again he briefly contemplated how strange it was that the key players in the conflict this time around wasn't one of their group of time-travelers.

Later that day, he and Audrey had another quiet dinner, and afterwards, their lovemaking took on a different quality than before. Instead of the thrill of exploration, and the ecstasy of finding the physical reflection of their spiritual bond, there was an almost desperate intensity. "I hate to leave you here alone, knowing that Baker is out there stalking you," said Ryan afterwards. "But I've got a trial coming up in a week, and my client's deposition still hasn't been taken. I've run out of room to maneuver — there's nothing I can put off."

"We can't put the rest of our lives on hold," Audrey reassured him. "I'm worried too — about you as much as anyone else. I've been having all kinds of melancholy thoughts today about how awful it would be to try to raise our daughter alone."

"Baker shouldn't be after me, though." Ryan objected. "It's almost certain that he doesn't know I exist."

She smiled. "Don't pregnant women have the right to irrational fears?"

"I wouldn't exactly call your fears irrational, knowing what we do about Baker. Sooner or later our destinies will compel all of us to come into contact with him in some way or another. God only knows how I'm going to deal with that when it happens — but I'm a lot more worried about you, living here all by yourself. Your address is right in the phone book — both here and at Peckham & Associates. I'd feel a lot better if you at least spent your nights somewhere else."

Audrey was silent for a moment, thinking. "You know, Adam lives in that huge Victorian all by himself. Michael's been staying with him — maybe I could stay there, too."

"That's a great idea!" said Ryan, sounding relieved. "I might even be able to sleep at night if you stayed with them. Let's call and see if it's okay — I could help you move some things before I go."

# 23

JOHN SMITH, WHOSE REAL NAME WAS HARRY O'NEIL, HAD BEEN forced to forfeit his anonymity when they filed the lawsuit. No sooner had he signed the affidavit in support of the temporary restraining order than he had gone underground, driving that night to an apartment in Oakland that had been rented for him by a friend. He had no intention of giving Raymond Baker any opportunity to impair his ability to testify — the memory of Loren Rosso's demise was still fresh in his mind. He stopped shaving, and planned to stay indoors as much as possible.

He had begun planning his disappearance even before his first contact with Adam Gray — quietly selling his car and putting his possessions into storage. The proceeds from the sale of the car fortified his savings to a point where he could get by for a considerable period of time — if he could stay alive. From this point on, he intended to deal only in cash, use borrowed cars or public transportation and talk only on pay-phones. His expertise in computers made him well aware how easy it was to trace a person's activities through credit cards, automated teller machines, or cell phones.

He was far from ecstatic when Michael told him about the deposition, and the fact that Raymond Baker had the right to be present. "I expected to have to testify in court, but giving a deposition hadn't occurred to me," he lamented, taking a sip of the coffee that had been warming his hands. He and Michael had agreed to meet in San Francisco's Golden Gate Park at six in the morning, when anyone who wasn't a jogger would stick out like a sore thumb. Michael's thermos full of French roast had been welcome. "There's really no way around it," Michael explained. "If they weren't allowed to take your deposition after the judge ordered it, they could keep you from testifying in the trial."

"I've gone this far, I may as well go the rest of the way," Harry sighed. "Give me the details."

"Tentatively, it's been scheduled for Monday afternoon at one-thirty at Heath Waterman's office. The depositions of the wildlife biologists will be taken earlier in the morning at ten and eleven, respectively."

"If they haven't met their maker," Harry said ominously. "How long will it last?"

"There's no time limit beyond the endurance of the lawyers, the witness and the court-reporter. I'd bet that Miller's lawyers know as well as we do that you're telling the truth. But they can't let on that they do. They'll probably ask you a series of repetitive questions to try to confuse you and trip you up. They'll be hoping to find something they can use to challenge your veracity. Depending on what strategy they take, it could take an hour or two, or it could go for days."

"I'll be hoping for the former, but expecting the latter, then," said Harry, sighing deeply this time. "The worst part won't be the questioning — it will be the fact that *he's* there breathing down my neck."

"You're probably safe while you're at Heath Waterman's office," Michael speculated. "Even Baker wouldn't try to kill you at a court-ordered deposition in front of the court reporter and your lawyer — that would be too brazen even for him."

Harry smiled grimly in response to Michael's statement. "I guess I should be grateful for small consolations . . . but I'm not. If I never saw Raymond Baker again in my life, it would still be too soon."

*     *     *

"WHAT DO YOU mean the wildlife biologists can't be located?" Heath Waterman hissed into the mouthpiece of the telephone he was holding. "We have to produce them for their depositions, or your case is dead in the water!"

"They seem to have disappeared in a rather permanent way," Raymond Baker responded calmly. It hadn't occurred to him that the two men would be of any use whatsoever after they had refused to falsify their reports. He had considered it a stroke of genius to have them prepare an interim report, and then have other people, who were more in tune with the consequences of turning him down, modify the document. Once that choice had been made, Baker had done the logical thing — he couldn't very well have those two fluff-brains turning up and blowing the whistle! The same operative who had slipped the poison to the fool in the Cloverdale diner had dealt with the biologists in a tidy and efficient manner. Perhaps twenty miles out in the Pacific their corpses had gone over the rail of a small boat, wired to enough concrete so that there was no chance their bodies would ever be anything but crab food.

"Just what do you expect me to tell Judge Kelly?" an exasperated Heath Waterman asked mockingly. "'I'm sorry, Your Honor, but after my client forged their reports, he seems to have misplaced the biologists who prepared them?' Should I tell him that after their reports had been forged, it only seemed like they would get in the way?"

A thin smile crossed Raymond Baker's face. It had been many years since anyone had ever even considered speaking to him in the tone of voice that Waterman was using now. Those who had nerve enough to cross him in the past had been too wary or angry to treat him with such utterly casual derision. But it was almost refreshing, really, to be challenged by someone who was like him in so many ways. For the moment, he decided to allow Waterman to live. "What would the judge do if Project HOPE's witness was just as unavailable as the wildlife biologists?" he inquired, enjoying the pause after he asked his question.

"Before or after he gives his deposition?"

"Give me both scenarios." The thin smile on Baker's face widened. Since he had discovered his potential to cut his enemies to the quick with his hate-forged blade, he found himself smiling more and more often.

"Let's assume that the plaintiffs can't produce O'Neil for either the deposition or the trial — that he's just disappeared. Holland would ask for a continuance, of course, and claim foul play. The Judge might give them some extra time over our objection — after all, this was an *extremely* short period of time for discovery to take place. But eventually the temporary restraining order would have to be lifted. The burden of proof is on the plaintiffs — they have to come up with affirmative evidence, and as far as we know, O'Neil is the sole witness who is familiar with the deletion-recovery system. That makes him the only one who could identify the records as coming from Miller's computer, which would get them past the hearsay rule."

"Get rid of the legal mumbo-jumbo and say it in English," Baker growled.

Waterman responded — patiently this time. "The reason that the written testimony of the witness is insufficient at a trial is because of the hearsay rule, which disallows the use of a statement made outside of the courtroom, which is offered to prove that something is true. The rule can have unusual applications. For example, if a police officer pulls over someone with a can of beer between his legs, he has to keep what is in the can and have it tested, to prove that there was an open container of *alcohol*. *The label* that says "beer" is a *statement* made outside of the courtroom that is being used to show that the can contained beer. The statement made by the label has to be *true* for the prosecutor to prove his case. The key is whether or not there is an opportunity for cross-examination. And just as you can't cross-examine the label on a beer can, you can't cross examine a document, even if it is sworn. There's a *business records* exception to the hearsay rule that would probably apply here, but someone who is familiar with the records has to testify about them. In our case, that would have to be Harry O'Neil. Apparently, he's the only one who knew about the program that captured the deleted documents. If he's not there to testify, then they can't use the documents in the trial. They have the burden of proof. What that means is that if they don't prove their case, then you don't have to put on any evidence at all to win."

"What would happen if he gives a deposition, but then fails to show up at trial."

"That's not as fortuitous a scenario. There *is* an opportunity for cross-examination at the deposition. The primary reason to disallow the testimony is absent. If O'Neil disappeared after giving a deposition, then his deposition testimony would come in." There was another pause "Especially if his dead body was found in some dark alley."

Baker actually smiled at the man's audacity. "Thank you, Mr. Waterman. Don't worry too much about our inability to locate those wildlife biologists. I have the sneaking suspicion things will work out just fine without them." He stared thoughtfully at the phone for several moments after hanging up the receiver. How had the duplicity of the computer technician escaped his notice?  Until the lawsuit had been filed, the man had not even registered on his consciousness.  As of now, however, O'Neil had vaulted himself into first place on Baker's list of *personae non gratae,* even ahead of the *bitch* from Project HOPE.  There was no doubt about what Harry O'Neil's fate had to be.  His presence on the planet had become a luxury that Baker could no longer afford.  Whatever ate human remains on the bottom of the ocean was about to get another meal.

# 24

RYAN EXAMINED THE DIGITAL READOUT ON HIS WRISTWATCH for what must have been the twentieth time in the last hour alone. Friday afternoon had come at last, and Audrey would be on her way to Fort Bragg in just a few hours. They'd phoned each other daily — often three or four times, but he still missed her terribly, and worry had been his constant companion. In addition to the precaution of staying with Adam and Michael, Michael had insisted on escorting her everywhere she went, and true to his word, he had stayed with her with unflagging devotion, leaving her only when she was at work or at Adam's house. They were all on edge from their constant vigilance, and were looking forward to the weekend. Adam was off to Berkeley to visit friends, and Michael was coming with Audrey, having accepted Ryan's invitation to explore some coastal trails by mountain bike. There had been no sign of Raymond Baker during the week, and they were confident that he had yet to discover the Fort Bragg connection. All of them were looking forward to letting their guard down for a few days.

Ryan's work-week had gone fairly well, in spite of his distracted state of mind. After his client's long-postponed deposition had been taken, he had unexpectedly settled his case on the eve of a trial he had expected to last several weeks. There was always work to be done, but for the moment he was relatively free of immediate problems — at least as far as his law practice was concerned.

He was jolted from his reverie by the ringing of the telephone, and snatched up the receiver before Sally had a chance to answer from the reception area. His heart beat just a little faster when he heard Audrey's greeting. *I'm still not used to being in love, and I hope I don't get used to it too soon.*

"Michael and I will be leaving in about an hour," she informed him happily. "We should get to your place about six or six-thirty."

They had invited the others to a barbeque on his deck for a belated celebration of their court victory. "Great!" Ryan replied, "I'll get the grill ready so we can put the burgers on as soon as you arrive."

"I'm looking forward to *really* relaxing for a couple of days," said Audrey wistfully. "Looking over my shoulder all the time has gotten me incredibly keyed up."

"And I'm looking forward to having you here so that I can breathe easy for a couple of days," Ryan responded before he rang off and headed for home, leaving Sally to close up.

Doug and Pam strolled over to help out shortly after he got home. They sliced tomatoes and washed lettuce while Ryan loaded the grill with charcoal. Gayle and Larry arrived soon thereafter, and they all moved to the deck to enjoy the late-afternoon sun. The unusually fine weather had returned after a week's hiatus, and it was comfortably warm, with a perfect breeze.

*　　　*　　　*

RAYMOND BAKER SKILLFULLY guided his black Mercedes Benz through Highway 128's twisting curves, making sure to keep the red Volvo a few turns in front of him. Listening to the tape recordings captured from the transmitter installed at the junction of Adam Gray's phone line and the power-pole had amused him to no end. The syrup-laced conversations between the *bitch* and "Ryan" — obviously her lover — had given him food for thought, and ultimately a recipe for pure delight. While he thoroughly enjoyed the anxiety he detected in their voices, their plans provided a delicious opportunity to let them experience some real anguish. He had been following the *bitch* and her lawyer since they took the turn-off from Highway 101 onto Highway 128 on the north end of Cloverdale, and was waiting for them to traverse a section of the mountainous road with a steep drop-off to one side — perfect for what he had planned. As they drew close to his chosen spot, he accelerated until he could see the rear of the red Volvo ahead of him, aware that he would have to take her by surprise. *That shouldn't be too hard*, he thought, reaching up to pat down a stray strand of the synthetic black hair on the wig he had donned for the occasion. His disguise was completed by a false mustache and clear-lensed glasses in heavy black frames. It didn't have to be much of a disguise — when he was done with her, the *bitch* would be destroyed. The disguise only had to fool the shyster — and then only if he survived.

Baker had driven Highway 128 a number of times since he had overheard the *bitch* mention which route she was planning to take to the coast. As the two vehicles approached the stretch of road where he had planned to stage the "accident," he allowed his pent-up rage to build until it was almost orgasmic. The two cars reached a section of road that looped back against itself in such a way that Baker was afforded a view of the road ahead for most of a mile. He grunted in satisfaction when he saw that there were no cars coming in the opposite direction. He pulled up behind the *bitch* just as the two vehicles entered a sweeping left-hand turn with a steep drop-off on the right side. Then he accelerated suddenly and crossed the double yellow line as if to pass, but as he came even with the *bitch's* driver's window, he held his position and stared at her — willing her to turn her head in his direction. At first, she continued to look straight ahead, but eventually, she glanced in his direction and met his gaze. The instant their eyes locked, he launched his attack, stabbing deeply into the core of her being with the razor-sharp blade of his hatred. He heard her silent scream as he shredded the bonds that united her soul to her flesh, and sent it fluttering, torn and directionless, into a grey nothingness. The body her spirit had vacated was left stiff and unmoving, locked in a premature rigor mortis. When the curve of the road tightened its radius, the Volvo careened off the edge, though her passenger tried in vain to wrench the steering wheel from her grasp. For a second, the car was airborne, then it came to earth, tumbling sideways as it rolled down the hillside, finally crashing, passenger-door-first into an oak tree seventy-five yards below.

As he glanced at the dust cloud in his rear-view mirror, Baker felt like a god. He had his confirmation. Now he knew with absolute certainty that he could rip the essence out of *any* living thing, and savor the anguish of its spirit as it dissipated like smoke on a windy day. He continued around the bend without stopping. His iron will kept him from such an amateurish mistake. There had been no contact between the vehicles, and from a strictly legal viewpoint, he had done nothing to cause the accident. It had been perfect! Absolutely perfect!

Behind Baker, the spectral figures of a raven and a puma streaked to the wreck through a spectrum invisible to all but Baker — had he remained at the scene. They went immediately to examine the bodies inside the Volvo, still shrouded in the dust-cloud raised by its tumultuous journey down the hillside. If he had lingered to savor their emotions as they searched the wreckage, Baker's joy would have soared even higher. Within seconds, the raven was headed back to the coast, as fast as thought itself, while the puma remained with the wrecked Volvo, plaintively licking the face of the woman behind the wheel.

# 25

RYAN AND DOUG WERE IN THE MIDDLE OF AN ENTHUSIASTIC rendition of one of Ryan's more comical songs when Gayle began to sense that something was amiss. She reached for Larry's hand and led him inside to the couch by the woodstove, and was just about to relate her concerns when both of them were hit by the psychic residue of Baker's attack. Without any need to communicate, they sent their totems flashing towards the site of the accident. Physically, Audrey was relatively unharmed, thanks to her seatbelt, airbag, and the sturdy construction of her Volvo. Although unconscious, she was still in a seated position, held upright by the shoulder harness, with her head slumped to one side. On the other side of the car, though, the impact against the tree had pushed the side of the car inward nearly two feet. Michael was also unconscious, wedged between Audrey and the wreckage of the door, but he was grievously injured, bleeding from a compound fracture of his right arm, and with his right leg bent at an impossible angle.

Two thirds of the way through the song he and Doug were singing, Ryan was overwhelmed by a sudden and tremendous sense of loss, as a huge part of his essential self was torn away. He stopped in mid-phrase, his face a mask of pain that reflected his inner torment. The moment he saw Ryan's face, Doug set his guitar aside and rushed to his friend's side, asking, "Ryan, what's the matter? Are you okay?"

Ryan mouthed Audrey's name, but was otherwise unable to speak as tears welled up and began to spill. Doug was unable to fathom how Ryan could know that something had happened to Audrey. He glanced through the open sliding-glass door, and saw Gayle rise from the couch where she and Larry had been sitting, and dash over to Ryan's phone. She dialed "911" while she hurried to Ryan's side, putting her arm protectively around him as she spoke to the operator, describing the location of the crash, as well as the nature and extent of the injuries. As soon as she was finished, she took Ryan in her arms, rocking him almost like a baby as he sat mute, unable to react to what had just occurred. Tears slid down her face, as she told Pam and Doug what had happened. Pam sat on the chair next to Ryan and did her best to comfort him while Doug reflexively slipped into his reporter's-mode, asking rapid-fire questions. "How did you know what happened? And how did Ryan know? Is Baker behind this?"

"The psychic connection between us has been growing in strength as we have become more deeply enmeshed in the conflict. I think I would know it if any of you were seriously hurt. And yes, this was Baker's doing. He must have used the same psychic weapon that he tried to use on Audrey when she froze up in the courtroom. His concentration was broken that time, but this time he got to her while she was driving around a bend with a steep drop-off to the side. The car went over the drop-off, and Michael was seriously injured in the crash. An ambulance will be there shortly — the accident was only a few miles from Cloverdale. In the meantime, Larry is watching over them." She got up to go inside, and said, "I need to go help him."

"Are you saying that you've already been there and back, and that Larry's still there?" asked Doug incredulously, his memories of their tales of spirit-walking having faded completely.

Gayle pointed to Larry, sitting as still as a statue on the couch in front of the stove. "Larry's body is here, but his spirit is with them. I need to join him now. You must not disturb us until we return!" With that, she hurried to the couch, sat beside Larry, closed her eyes and became as still as death.

The Puma kept licking Audrey's face, as if the act might retrieve something more than the echo of her spirit, which was all he could discern. The ragged ends of her essence were still there, mangled and fluttering as if stirred by an unfelt breeze, but that was all. As for the embryo nestled within her womb, there was life, but he could perceive nothing more. He turned his attention to Michael, with his grotesquely twisted leg and shattered humerus protruding through the skin of his upper arm. Luckily, no major blood vessels had been severed, but his stertorous breathing suggested that the jagged ends of fractured ribs might have punctured a lung. He wasn't in immediate danger of bleeding to death although shock alone could kill him if he had to wait too long for medical treatment. Most importantly though, his spirit still glowed lamp-like within his battered and unmoving body.

Gayle's totem, which had departed moments after they had arrived together, returned and landed on Michael's shoulder, gripping the cloth of his shirt with her clawed feet. Wordlessly, she related to Larry all that had occurred at Ryan's house, advising him that an ambulance was on its way. Then the raven closed her eyes in concentration. She could feel Michael's spirit writhing with anxiety inside his broken, unconscious body — unable to perceive whether or not Audrey even lived — but in dreadful fear, knowing that it was Baker's attack that had caused her to lose control of the car and send them careening down the side of the hill. She reached out to Ariel, praying that she might once more be a channel for the love and peace that Michael's spirit so desperately needed. Once again, she felt the loving contact, and was grateful to perceive Michael's anguish dissipate. The minutes that passed before the ambulance arrived and was flagged down by a motorist who had stopped to investigate the dust-cloud seemed desperately long, and when the ambulance attendants arrived, she and Larry determined that there was little more that they could do and returned to their bodies.

They opened their eyes to find Doug facing them wearing a worried expression. Ryan had not moved since he first felt the panicked shriek of Audrey's spirit as it was ripped from her body. Pam sat next to him, holding one of his hands, saying nothing — knowing intuitively that there was nothing she *could* say to ease his pain. Gayle and Larry rose from the couch simultaneously and went to him. Larry sat beside him, opposite Pam, while Gayle pulled up a chair. After a few heartbeats, she spoke. "Ryan, you're in shock right now, but you will soon be tempted to give yourself over completely to hatred. You must not allow this to happen!"

Her calmly authoritative tone seemed to jolt Ryan from his lethargy. The tears that had been momentarily staunched began to flow again, and his entire body was wracked with sobs that threatened to overwhelm him. Gayle reached out and took his free hand. "The most difficult part of the battle has only just begun," she said earnestly. "You must hold onto your love for Audrey with all of your being — this is part of the trial the advanced spirits warned us about. It's *The One without a Soul's* attempt to pull you into the darkness where fear and hatred reign supreme. You *must* resist! Audrey's spirit will not be lost in this lifetime *unless* you succumb to the lure of fear-based hatred!"

Ryan struggled to regain his composure. "I heard — I *felt* her scream — and then there was *nothing*! She's gone, Gayle. Now that I can't feel her anymore, I know that I've always been able to feel her presence — she's been a part of me my entire life. But now I can't feel anything — she's just gone!"

"But not gone irretrievably," Gayle said sternly. She looked up at Pam. "Do you know the way to the Ukiah Valley Medical Center?"

"I've been there many times," Pam replied.

"We need to leave immediately. Audrey and Michael need us. You and Doug should take Ryan — I'll go with Larry. All of us need to pack clothes for an indefinite stay. We'll meet at Larry's house as soon as we can all get our things together." She glanced back at Ryan. "We'll take Highway 20. I don't think it would be good for Ryan to go anywhere near the place where it happened."

Two hours later they pulled into the parking lot at Ukiah Valley Medical Center. Once there, for the first time since they had known him, Larry referred to himself as "Dr. Robinson," aware that in a hospital setting a medical doctor was much more likely to gain quick access to accurate information about the status of a patient.

Michael was in surgery, where he was expected to remain for several more hours while doctors labored to put his shattered body back together. "He regained consciousness briefly before he was taken into surgery," the charge nurse informed them. "He was lucid, although he was in a tremendous amount of pain." She picked up a different chart from the one she had been scanning. "The other crash victim is still unconscious," she went on. "It's baffling our residents — there's no evidence of the kind of closed-head injury that would produce such a deeply unconscious state. Frankly, we're very concerned." She glanced at a clock on the wall. "We'll perform a CAT-scan in the next hour. That might give us some answers."

The five of them made their way to the hospital cafeteria, knowing that it would be several hours before they would be allowed to see either Michael or Audrey. Although the others were able to eat, the sandwich they brought Ryan sat untouched. He sat with his elbows on the table, cradling his head in his hands. In spite of Gayle's reassurances, he had fallen into a deep despair. He kept running the scenario through his mind again and again, trying to find a way that he could have prevented what had happened. Nothing could ever have prepared him for the aching emptiness he felt. What he *did* feel was the urge to give in to a rage that was potentially unlimited — exactly as Gayle had warned him. He tried not to allow his anger to press to the forefront, but it felt as if it would be a losing battle. It was only when Gayle came and sat next to him, took his hand in hers and sat absolutely still for several long moments that he was able to concentrate on his love for Audrey — letting it fill him and damp down the nascent precursors to rage. He hoped his love would form a beacon that would help his beloved find her way back to him — but hope was soon overshadowed by grief as he became more and more certain that she was lost to him forever.

# Part Three

In the dark night of the soul
When the wind comes howling cold
And the joys of life have faded like a dream
When you feel so very sad
And everything's gone bad
The answer comes like a phoenix from the flame

All it takes is a miracle
All it takes is love
There within and beside you
Pure, innocent love
Peace is yours for the asking
Step away from the fear
Raise the curtain that hides love
Where you are, love is there

And in that place where turmoil reigns
Where you're treated with disdain
Where clouds of hate and fear fill the air
Anger rears its ugly head
Every step is filled with dread
The dragon has come roaring from its lair

All it takes is a miracle
All it takes is love
There within and beside you
Pure, innocent love
Peace is yours for the asking
Step away from the fear
Raise the curtain that hides love
Where you are, love is there

# 1

THEY HAD BEEN SITTING WITH AUDREY IN THE PRIVATE ROOM assigned to her for over an hour when a nurse advised them that Michael was out of surgery. "He's just beginning to regain consciousness," she announced. "It may be a while before he's able to say much."

"I'll stay with Audrey, " Gayle told Ryan, knowing that he was torn between being present when Michael woke and staying with Audrey. "You go talk to Michael."

The hospital staff had thoughtfully assigned Michael a room adjacent to Audrey's. The surgery had required the extensive use of rods, plates and screws, and his limbs were suspended from a bar over his bed with a system of pulleys and slings. An additional twenty minutes passed before the anesthetic wore off sufficiently for him to be able to communicate with any coherence. "How is Audrey?" were his first words, uttered in a croaking whisper. Pam slipped a piece of ice between his lips, having anticipated that his mouth would be as dry as flannel from the anesthetic.

Larry answered. "Not good, I'm afraid. She had no broken bones, although I'm sure she sustained sprained and strained muscles throughout her body. Her baby isn't at risk, but she's in a coma."

"It was Baker," Michael whispered, "He was following us. He looked different — he must have dyed his hair black or worn a wig, and he wore glasses. Whatever he was trying to do to her in the courtroom, he must have done again." He coughed and Pam slid another piece of ice between his lips. "He came from behind and pulled out as if he were going to pass, but then just stayed next to us in the other lane. Audrey turned her head to look at him and she never looked back." He closed his eyes, as if keeping them open required more energy than he possessed. "She never moved a muscle after she looked his way," he whispered. "I grabbed the steering wheel and tried to keep us from going off the cliff, but I couldn't break her grip. Then the car was rolling and that's all I can remember." He opened his eyes and reached weakly for Ryan's hand with his good arm. "I'm so sorry Ryan — I wasn't able to protect her. I failed both of you."

"I'm the one who should be apologizing to you," said Ryan. "I should have been in the car with her. He's after us, not you!"

"The two of you are playing right into his hands." said Larry quietly. "Neither of you is responsible in any way for what happened. Guilt is a fear-based emotion, and it has no useful purpose under these circumstances." He turned to Ryan. "You would probably be in the same condition as Audrey if you had been in the car with her." Then he reached over and put his hand on Michael's shoulder, and drew Ryan close to Michael's bed. "Both of you are victims, and neither of you bear any more responsibility than Audrey. There was *nothing* you could have done. I don't want to hear anything more from either of you about it being your fault."

Their brief conversation appeared to have exhausted Michael, and within minutes he lapsed into an uneasy sleep. Ryan returned to Audrey's room, and sat in an upholstered chair next to her bed, his eyes closed, holding her hand. He concentrated on re-living every moment of their brief time together, trying to re-experience every nuance of feeling he had ever had for her, in the hope that by doing so he might help her to find her way back from wherever her spirit had been exiled. Several hours later, he felt someone gently shaking his shoulder, and awoke to find Doug standing over him in the early morning light that filled the room. "I must have dozed off." he said, immediately looking over at Audrey, but finding that nothing had changed.

"Michael's asking for you," said Doug, and when Ryan stood, he embraced him, squeezing hard. "I know there's nothing I could say that would make you feel any better. But if there's anything I can do — anything at all, let me know, okay?"

Ryan's smile was weak, but genuine. "You've always been there for me, Doug. I'll let you know if I think of anything." When the two men walked into the next room, Larry and Gayle were no longer there, but Adam had arrived and was talking with Michael, his countenance notable for its rare serious expression.

*Adam and Audrey are as close as brother and sister,* thought Ryan. *He probably feels almost as badly as I do.* His heart went out to Adam, and he immediately felt slightly better without realizing that his compassion for another was helping him to cope with his own pain.

"I was just telling Michael that I'm amazed at the lengths he's willing to go in order to avoid a little bit of work," said Adam, trying in his own way to make the situation feel a little more normal, although his attempt at levity fell flat.

Michael looked up at Ryan and said, "I'm afraid that I'm going to have to ask you for some help with the suit against Miller Lumber. They won't let me out of this bed until after the trial is scheduled to begin and it will probably be months before I can even *think* about making any court appearances. In the meantime Harry O'Neil's deposition is scheduled for Monday morning at ten o'clock."

Ryan was taken aback. "I couldn't handle this kind of lawsuit!" he exclaimed. "Except for what I read when we were preparing the petition, I don't know a thing about environmental law!"

"You don't give yourself enough credit," Michael reproved gently. "After reading those cases, you know everything that you need to know. This area of law is just like any other — once the law of the case is established, it comes down to proving facts. Think about it. This isn't *really* an environmental suit at all at this point. It's down to one issue; Did Miller Lumber fabricate its research data or not? With the amount of family law you've done, I'm sure that you've tried plenty of cases where both sides are pointing at each other and calling each other liars. Besides I'm not asking you to take over completely — we'll still be a team. I'll be available by phone to help you if you get into a jam."

A smile flitted briefly across Ryan's face. "When you put it like that, I can hardly refuse." He reflected for a moment. "When I think about it, there really isn't much that's new ground for me. All I really have to do is put Harry O'Neil on the stand and establish the authenticity of the documents. That shouldn't be much of a problem."

"What shouldn't be a problem?" asked Gayle, as she and Larry entered the room. When she saw Adam, she walked over and gave him a hug.

"Ryan just agreed to take over the suit against Miller Lumber," said Adam in response to her question.

Larry gave no outward sign, but was jolted by what Adam said. *I should have been able to foresee this,* he thought, recalling an impression he had had since the advanced spirits had first spoken of the conflict — of Ryan as an unwilling warrior. "Are you up to this, Ryan?" he asked.

"I think I'll be okay," Ryan replied. "In fact I think it will help me feel better to be working on something that's so important to Audrey." His voice shook as he said Audrey's name, and his eyes moistened. Then he took a few deep breaths and was able to compose himself.

*No wonder men die before women,* thought Pam as she watched Ryan struggle with his emotions, although she kept her own counsel. She walked over and put her arm around him, and he gave her a weak but grateful smile. "So I guess I'll be heading to San Francisco the day after tomorrow for Harry O'Neil's deposition," he continued. Then a concerned look crossed his face "Will someone stay here and keep a watch over Audrey while I'm gone?"

"None of us is going anywhere, or staying anywhere alone," said Gayle in a tone of voice that brooked no argument. "Larry and I just checked into a couple of rooms at the motel down the street. We'll be able to get some rest while we take turns staying with Audrey and Michael. We need to take every precaution we can, and stay as alert as possible."

Ryan spent the rest of the day alternating between sitting by Audrey's bedside and working with Michael, writing down questions that Michael suggested he ask the wildlife biologists during their depositions. He was so tired by the time the day finally drew to a close that he nearly fell asleep over his dinner in the hospital cafeteria. Pam and Doug, who had spent the better part of the day resting at the motel, insisted that he take a turn in order to get a good night's sleep. Ryan protested feebly, saying that he was so tired he could sleep anywhere, so it might as well be in the chair in Audrey's room, but eventually they persuaded him to go to the motel. In the moments before he fell into an exhausted slumber, fear and self-doubt began to dominate his thinking once again. It wasn't just the fact that he was going up against lawyers who were specialists in their field — this case *was* a lot more like a family-law feud than an environmental-law dispute. It was the thought of confronting *The One without a Soul* face-to-face that made him shrink back.

There was no reason he could think of that Baker wouldn't do what he had done to Audrey again. He wasn't so much concerned for himself, as by the certainty that he would need to take an active part in whatever was going to bring his love back. How in the world he was going to cope with being in the same room as *The One without a Soul?*

# 2

RYAN WOKE WITH A START, HIS HEART RACING AS HE TRIED TO get his bearings in the unfamiliar room. He began to breathe easier when he recognized the bland motel-room decorations. Larry was still asleep on the second double-bed, though the early-morning sun filtering through the curtains filled the room with a soft light. The readout on his digital watch told him that he had slept ten hours. As he swung out of bed, his thoughts were drawn back to the dream that had set his heart racing. It was the first time since he had undergone his past-life regressions that he had dreamed about being back in one of his earlier lives. He sat on the edge of the bed and tried to recall all of the details of the dream. It had begun during those awful moments during the Oglala Sioux lifetime when he had returned from the buffalo hunt to find everyone at the encampment dead, and it had continued through that lifetime to its end. At the moment he awoke, he had just been shot in the chest after piercing the belly of *The One without a Soul* with his arrow. His memory of the dream was remarkably clear, and as he replayed each scene in his mind, he realized that there were additional details that he had not recalled during his past-life regression. *That's odd,* he mused, looking over to where Larry still slept. *I'll have to see if that means anything.*

His opportunity presented itself after he had showered and started to get dressed. Larry had slipped out during his shower, but returned, laden with two steaming cups of coffee shortly after he finished.

"I just had the strangest dream," Ryan announced, as he buttoned his shirt. "It was about the Oglala Sioux lifetime, but it had parts to it that weren't there during my regression. If we hadn't all had our independent experiences, this would have made me think I had made it all up."

"On the contrary, the dream-state is often a gateway for past-life experiences to enter our present consciousness," Larry assured him. "Once a person has opened the door to a past life by going through a regression, it's very common for them to revisit their past lives while dreaming." They began the short walk to the hospital after making sure that the motel-room door was locked behind them. "The information contained in dreams can sometimes be surprisingly useful," he continued. "Can you describe the new portion?"

"It was actually the most vivid and detailed part," Ryan replied. "It was after we returned from the buffalo hunt and before the ambush." He took a moment to recall the details once again. "I had used up most of my arrows in the hunt, so I had to make more of them. I went down by the creek and cut willow shafts, fletched them with owl feathers and fixed stone arrow-heads to their tips. Then I painted the shafts of the arrows with a design that had come to me during a vision-quest. After that, we built a fire in the sweat-lodge and took our weapons inside with us. We had a ceremony, where we asked the spirits to help our arrows fly true, so that we could avenge those who had been slaughtered."

Larry had a thought while Ryan was talking about his dream. "Gayle and I have been *very* worried about the thought of you going straight into the lion's den with Baker," he confessed. "There's no guarantee he wouldn't try to do the same thing to you that he did to Audrey." He rubbed his chin thoughtfully. "I think your dream might be a message or contain some kind of clue — it could even be a communication from the advanced spirits. When they come through dreams, such communications are often cryptic or allegorical."

"I don't get it," said Ryan. "How could a dream about making arrows have anything to do with Baker in this life? I can't very well take a bow and a quiver full of arrows into the deposition and shoot him." He looked genuinely amused for the first time since Baker's attack as he continued wryly. "It would be considered too aggressive a tactic to use in a deposition, and besides, it simply wouldn't be the *loving* thing to do!"

Larry was glad to see Ryan smile — it was absolutely necessary for him to rise above their current difficulties if they were to have any hope of defeating *The One without a Soul*. "I can see that I'm getting ahead of myself," he said. "This has to do with an aspect of past-life regression therapy that you and I haven't had any reason to discuss. Past-life therapy isn't limited to dealing with emotional pain. In my practice, I have had many patients find relief from *physical* problems as well."

"Such as neck pain that relates to a quick trip through the trap-door of a gallows?" Ryan suggested.

"Exactly. When my patients discovered the past-life trauma that resulted in their pain, it often went away. Now, consider this — in the life we lived as Oglala Sioux, you killed *The One without a Soul* by shooting him with an arrow. The thought just came to me that the sight of *you* with an arrow might conceivably *cause* Baker to have a physical reaction — just like the cures, but with the process reversed."

Ryan thought for a moment, then said: "So if I take a bow and arrow with me to the deposition, Baker might end up feeling like he had taken an arrow through the gut?"

"I think that an arrow is all that you'll need if my hunch is right. And if he felt the kind of pain that an arrow wound would cause, he might not be able to launch an attack against you."

By this time, they had reached the hospital, and were soon outside the doorways to Michael and Audrey's adjoining rooms. They entered Audrey's room first, where they found Pam and Doug keeping watch. Ryan knew that there wouldn't be any change in her condition — that if there had been a reversal, the enormous aching void that filled him would have disappeared. But in spite of that virtual certainty, he hadn't been able to suppress the wild, unrealistic hope that she might be sitting up in her bed with a smile on her beautiful face. Nothing had changed, of course, and a wave of sadness overcame him as he approached her bedside and took her slack hand in his. He knew he should be concentrating on his love for her, but he couldn't get past the ache in his heart. Larry could see that he needed some time to process his feelings. "Why don't we give you a few minutes alone," he suggested. "I'll tell the others about your dream." He gestured to Pam and Doug, and the three of them stepped into Michael's room.

Gayle was helping Michael eat his breakfast — a task made awkward by his semi-reclining position and the fact that his right leg and arm were suspended in the air. Adam, who had dozed off in a chair, woke as they entered. When Larry had finished telling them about Ryan's dream and his interpretation, Gayle reflected for a moment, and said, "I think you're on the right track. It certainly *feels* right."

"Maybe I should look for a telephone book so that we can find a sporting goods store." suggested Adam. "We could buy some arrows for him to take to the deposition."

"I don't know," Gayle replied thoughtfully. "In the dream Ryan learned exactly how he made his arrows — that could be significant. We have the entire day ahead of us — why don't we see if there's a way to replicate the arrows from Ryan's dream? We can buy commercially-produced arrows as a back-up, but I have a feeling that the arrow should be as close as possible to the one he used to shoot *The One without a Soul.*"

Ryan had lapsed into despondency by the time Larry and Gayle returned to Audrey's room. It was clear to both of them that the severing of his soul-mate connection was taking a terrible toll. He continued to look haunted as they described their ideas about making an arrow similar to the ones in his dream. Gayle's concern increased when he couldn't even raise any interest in their plan. She pulled a chair close to his and took one of his hands. Glancing up at Larry, she said, "I'm going to see if there isn't some way I can help Ryan find some peace of mind."

"Larry nodded his approval and stepped outside, closing the door gently behind him.

"You can't afford to lose hope, Ryan," she began. "There's a chance that we can get Audrey back, but we, and especially *you*, have to keep your focus on love for that to happen." She rose up and walked behind his chair, placing her hands on his shoulders and sending a prayer to Ariel, asking once again to be a channel through which the spirit's peace, serenity and most importantly, *hope,* could be delivered. The voice, if one could call it a *voice*, which had first filled her consciousness a few short days before resounded within her. *There are limits to what I can do in this situation, daughter. For the most part, I am not allowed to interfere. Adversity is necessary, for without it there can be no spiritual growth — no advancement of the spirit. If I lend too much assistance then all will have been for nought! I will not be allowed to infuse the body that even now grows rapidly within Audrey's womb.*

"But you have eased the fears of others — couldn't you do the same for him?"

*I can ease some of his pain, but I cannot help him as much as I have helped the others. He is the central figure in this struggle — but take heart, for he is far stronger than you imagine or than he himself would believe!*

"Does he risk having his soul separated from his body as has happened to Audrey if *The One without a Soul* attacks him at the deposition?"

*There is risk — though less than there was with his soul-mate. He has more power to resist than she possessed. I am not permitted to tell you more. I will do as much for him as I am allowed — but you must continue to remind him and the others that love must always be your focus. It is* always *the answer to your questions. If you are presented with a choice, take the path that leads towards love . . .*

*     *     *

As the silent voice faded, Gayle felt energy pulse through her and into Ryan, but at a lower level of intensity than before. Still, when she came around from behind Ryan's chair, there was a light in his eyes that had been missing. "That was the best shoulder-rub I've ever had," he remarked with a smile. "I was feeling *really* down there for a while, but I seem to have pulled a little bit out of the dumps."

"Why don't I sit here with Audrey while you and Adam go see if you can find a way to make one of those arrows from your dream," Gayle said. She squeezed his hand. "And keep thinking about how much you love her!"

It turned out that Ukiah was home to a mail-order establishment that specialized in bows, arrows, knives and other primitive and unmechanized killing implements of every description. Their retail outlet was only a few blocks from the hospital. To Ryan's surprise and delight there was a selection of kits for hobbyists to make their own Native American bows and arrows. The one Ryan chose contained willow shafts, feathers which had been dyed to simulate those of wild birds, and both flint and obsidian arrow-heads ready for mounting. The kit even included brushes and acrylic paints so that Ryan could replicate the design he remembered from his dream. He finished his arrow in a little more than an hour. It was fletched with feathers which closely resembled those of a Great Horned Owl, and tipped with a flint arrowhead. The final touch was a blue and red design that in his past life had been created with dyes made from berries, resulting in an arrow that was somewhat shorter than the ones from Ryan's past-life memories, but was otherwise a perfect match. "Let's just hope we're not barking up the wrong tree," he said, blowing on the paint.

"I'm just worried that you'll have the same reaction that I had when I saw Baker for the first time," said Adam. "For a while there, I was so scared I couldn't move. I was sweating and hyperventilating — I've never been that frightened in my life! If that happens to you, you'll never be able to ask those questions that you and Michael put together."

"I had an awfully strong reaction just seeing him on television," said Ryan. "But I was caught completely off guard. I'll do okay — after losing my connection to Audrey, there's not much he could do to me that would be worse. There's nothing to do but go, and see what happens."

"I don't envy you in the least," said Adam, "I don't think I've ever told you how grateful all of us are that you're taking this on."

Ryan made a face. "If what Gayle and Larry say is true, it seems no matter what choices I make, I'll eventually come into conflict with Baker. This just happens to be the place where the battle lines have been drawn."

When he returned to the hospital, Ryan went over his list of questions for the wildlife biologists with Michael one last time, then Michael telephoned Harry O'Neil to check in, and to let him know that Ryan would be stepping in for him. "All of the precautions you've been taking have shown themselves to be well advised," he observed. "Don't let down your guard between now and tomorrow afternoon — Baker has to be looking for you!"

Harry told Michael that he would be careful, and they rang off.

As evening came on, there was a changing of the guard as Pam and Doug exchanged places with Gayle and Adam. Ryan spent the balance of the evening sitting with Audrey, focusing on his love — love for her, love for the child she carried, love for all of them. Wherever Audrey's spirit was, if concentrating on love could help her return to her body, then that was what he was going to do.

# 3

THE VAN PARKED OUTSIDE THE HOSPITAL WAS FILLED WITH THE most sophisticated electronic eavesdropping and tracing equipment that could be purchased from both legitimate and illegitimate sources. It took only minutes for the technicians inside to locate the address where Harry O'Neil had received his phone call. The information was forwarded to an operative who by chance was only blocks away from the hole-in-the-wall Mexican restaurant where Harry had chosen to dine. After the call, Harry lingered over a plate of fine enchiladas and then left feeling pleasantly full, if apprehensive about having his coming deposition. He was so engrossed in working out the details of a plan to lose the tail that he assumed would follow him when he left the deposition that he never heard the quick, almost noiseless footsteps behind him, or felt the blow that fractured his skull.

*     *     *

RAYMOND BAKER'S COCAINE was spread in parallel lines of crystalline white, and his glass of Glenlivet was waiting when he received the news that the computer technician had become crab-food on the bottom of the Pacific. He had been informed, of course, when O'Neil had been located, and then again when he had been taken. O'Neil never regained consciousness after his skull had been fractured. They weren't even sure whether or not he was alive when his body, trussed securely to several diver's weight-belts, was dumped unceremoniously into the ocean.

Tonight, Baker felt so good that he decided to make an exception to his rule — a celebration was in order, and just this once, he decided, he would double his usual intake. The following night he would have an even greater reason to celebrate! The phone call to O'Neil had revealed that there was a new lawyer on the case — the *bitch's* lover. *How touching,* he thought sarcastically. He snorted his drugs and sipped his whiskey, but the effect they gave him was nothing compared to the pleasure of anticipating the act of ripping this upstart lawyer's soul from his body and letting it disperse into the ether.

# 4

THE DECISION TO SEND RYAN TO THE DEPOSITION ALONE HAD been difficult for all but Larry and Gayle, who knew that they would accompany him, although not in the flesh. All of the others had forgotten all about the spirit-walking the two of them had done after the "accident." When Gayle made a comment about it to Doug, he looked confused for a moment and then talked about a Native-American he had met while he was doing an under-cover assignment at Folsom Prison. Doug's cell-mate for his short stay had been a transplanted Navajo, who claimed not to mind the confinement of the granite walls because he could send his spirit flying through the air in the shape of an owl. Adam had bravely volunteered to accompany Ryan — in spite of his abject terror the last time he had been in Baker's presence. But it wasn't difficult to get him to agree that under the circumstances, it was advisable to put as few of their number at risk as possible.

When a consensus was reached, they all agreed that Gayle and Larry would accompany Ryan to San Francisco, where they would part company until there was a lunch break. The drive to San Francisco in Ryan's Caravan was uneventful, and they parked in the same lot as before — Waterman's law office was just around the corner from the federal courthouse. Ryan's arrow was concealed in a tubular blueprint case that he slung by its strap over his shoulder. "I do feel something like Daniel heading into the lion's den," he said with a forced smile as he hefted his briefcase. "But things worked out for Daniel, and I probably don't have anything to worry about either."

"Remember that love is the key to our success." Gayle declared. She didn't mention the fact that it was *Ryan* who would be taking a lion with him into this particular den — knowing that if she told him, the information would ease past his consciousness like sand through an hourglass — caught momentarily perhaps, but destined to slip away like time itself. She kissed him on the cheek and wished him luck. Larry gave him a handshake which quickly resolved into a hug. Ryan said, "I'll meet you back here when we break for lunch," then turned and made his way down the sidewalk. They all knew he was taking the first steps toward the most dangerous situation he had ever encountered.

A moment later, Larry and Gayle climbed back into Ryan's van and made themselves comfortable in the two front seats. They closed their eyes, and began to relax themselves into the meditative state from which they preferred to initiate their spirit-walks. Before Ryan had crossed half the distance to Heath Waterman's office, a magnificent puma was padding silently beside him, its tawny presence unseen by any who shared the sidewalk with them. Above them, a raven soared and pirouetted through the air before settling onto Ryan's shoulder, her loud caw resounding and echoing among the buildings on a plane of existence where none, save the raven, the puma — and Raymond Baker — could hear.

*       *       *

HAD THE WINDOWS in Heath Waterman's conference room been open, Baker might have made out the cry of the raven amidst the sounds of traffic on the streets several floors below. He glanced around the long, narrow room dominated by a massive table that could easily seat twenty people. The stenographer was setting up her shorthand machine at one end, being extremely careful not to look his way, then quickly left the room. Baker smiled — an act that was now becoming commonplace as the result of all the pleasures he had enjoyed recently. No depositions would actually take place today, of course. He had informed Waterman the previous week that the wildlife biologists would be unavailable, but had kept the fact of Harry O'Neil's recent demise to himself. Waterman's surprise when O'Neil failed to show up would be completely genuine. Baker was looking forward with relish to the moment when it dawned on the *bitch's* lover that his star witness, the *only* possible witness whose testimony could be used to show that the wildlife studies were forgeries, wasn't going to show — that is, Stratton would be surprised if Baker let him retain his faculties that long. He had not determined the exact moment when he would rend the spirit of this pathetic excuse for a man from his flesh, but he was becoming increasingly convinced that it would happen before the day had grown old.

His only contact with Stratton thus far had been to overhear his telephone conversations with the *bitch* — the conversations which had given him information he had used to plan his attack on her. He felt his hackles rise just thinking of the *bitch*. According to his sources she had survived the crash, although for all intents and purposes, she was history. But strangely, his mind kept worrying over thoughts of killing her — even though she was already as good as dead. He shrugged his shoulders, and made the mental observation that she was still breathing, therefore unfinished business. It would be ultimately satisfying when he had the opportunity to still the beating of her heart, just as he had banished her soul. As far as Stratton was concerned, he looked forward to their meeting with anticipation. There was something about him that Baker had picked up when he listened to Stratton's conversation with the *bitch* — something just beyond the edge of his consciousness — like a word on the tip of the tongue. He finally decided that he was just looking forward more than usual to this opportunity to savor another's pain. The cloying closeness between this puke and the *bitch* had been revealed during their phone calls. How best to capitalize on that? How best to maximize the pain this pathetic fuck was undoubtedly experiencing? Perhaps he should simply tell Stratton what he had done to the *bitch* — let him know that her condition was permanent — then take as much time as possible to do the same thing to him. Baker sighed in satisfaction. There were so many options, and anticipation was so sweet!

*     *     *

WHILE BAKER PONDERED the delicious details of the psychological torture he intended to inflict on him, Ryan entered the office and was directed by the receptionist to the conference room. But the puma from the Miller Massacre preceded him, padding into the room with a low growl thrumming in its throat that caused Baker to abandon his imagined pleasures. He was instantly filled with rage that tore away the trappings of civility he wore in public, and revealed his true nature — that of an ice-cold predator and purveyor of white-hot terror. When Ryan followed the puma through the doorway with the raven perched on his shoulder, Baker's rage went off the scale. The previous week when he had first seen the *bitch,* he had experienced the greatest anger he had ever known. But that was nothing compared to the fury that now suffused every fiber of his being. His rage took him immediately beyond thought, and galvanized him into action. He readied the razor-sharp blade of his hatred, and paused briefly, waiting for the first instant of eye-contact.

Though the receptionist had not mentioned that Raymond Baker was already in the conference room, some sixth-sense made Ryan wary as he stepped through the doorway. Out of the corner of his eye he saw Baker leap to his feet, radiating fury with all the subtlety of a blowtorch. His own feelings were a melange of anger, terror, caution, and by dint of a huge effort of will, love — love for Audrey, for Gayle, Doug, Larry and the others — for the redwoods, for himself — perhaps even for the mystery of life itself. There was none for Baker, but he didn't think that would be held against him. He steadfastly avoided looking at *the One without a Soul*, keeping his attention on his briefcase and the tube that held his arrow, while placing them on the table that dominated the room. He kept in mind what had happened to Audrey in the courtroom and on the Highway 128 when she made eye-contact with Baker — and that his own eyes would be his Achilles-heel should *The One without a Soul* attack. He focused on what was directly in front of him, unsnapping the clasp that held the end of the tube closed and holding it at eye level with his left hand, blocking the line of sight between the two of them.

On their drive to San Francisco, the three of them had discussed when and how to use the arrow: "Do you think the sight of the arrow all by itself will have any effect?" Ryan had asked.

"We've gone over that from every angle," Larry said.

"And we wish we had an answer," Gayle added, finishing Larry's sentence for him. "We don't know how it will work — if it works at all. But *Love* would not send you a dream about an *offensive* weapon — we believe there must be a way to use the arrow defensively. If it seems to you that he's about to attack you the way he attacked Audrey, that's the *time* for you to use the arrow — hopefully, the *way* to use it will come to you."

Ryan thought back to what they had said. Still holding the tube at eye level, he reached inside and grasped the shaft of the arrow, just below its feathered and notched end.

The Puma leapt onto the conference table, his tail swishing back and forth as he advanced on *The One without a Soul*, the low growl in his throat expanding into a roar of defiant challenge. Baker's attention was drawn to him, as Larry expected it would be when what appeared to be a four-hundred-pound killing-machine advanced on him. He shifted his focus and unleashed the attack meant for Ryan. Larry felt the invisible blade that Baker's hate had become slash through the ghostly presence of his totem. He felt the pulling sensation which Gayle had described, and a chill ran through him as he realized that if he had been physically present, his body would already be bereft of its soul.

From Gayle's perspective, the very air surrounding Baker had taken on a crimson tinge from the hate and anger that boiled out of him like vapor from a steam locomotive on a frosty morning. A beam of focused energy suddenly shot out from his eyes, glowing with white-hot intensity. It stabbed through the spot where the puma's eyes appeared to be — with no effect. Baker's rage intensified, if that was possible, when his attack failed to produce any results. He turned his attention back to Ryan, who stood on the far side of the conference-room table, holding the carrying-tube which he had brought with him at arms-length, the raven perched on his shoulder, head cocked to one side and staring directly at Baker with one eye that shone like an obsidian marble.

Baker found that he could not immediately launch a second attack — apparently it took some time to re-forge his rage and hatred into a blade that would rend body from soul. He glared at Stratton, seething with frustration as he waited out the period of impotence. He had barely noticed the objects his *enemy* had carried into the room with him, but when Stratton held up the kind of tube used for carrying blueprints, it caught his attention. Now Stratton reached inside the open end of the tube and withdrew a hand-made arrow with a stone tip and owl-feather fletchings. Baker examined the arrow as Ryan held it in front of him as if it were an object of power. *What is he going to do with that — throw it at me?* he sneered contemptuously. When they finally made eye contact, the strength of Stratton's gaze surprised him. It was filled with fear as Baker would have expected, but there was more — including an unexpected look of fierce determination. He hadn't expected Stratton to show this much backbone. All three of his *enemies* stared boldly at him now, a low growl thrumming from the puma's throat with each exhalation, while the raven added a non-stop cawing to create a raucous din. Baker's blade was almost ready, and he knew exactly where to strike with the next blow. It was clear to him now that the raven and the puma had some way to ward off his attack — but that would not be true for his arch-enemy. He felt his power reaching full strength, and his wrath and fury coiled like a tightening spring, almost ready to be released.

Then with a bold, firm voice, which sounded like he was addressing a crowd rather than a single person standing just a few feet away, Stratton said, "Remember your past!" and moved his hand to reveal a brightly colored design on the shaft of the arrow. Baker screamed and clutched his stomach as he doubled up in pain and fell backwards into the chair from which he had just risen. When he looked down between his fingers he fully expected to see the sharp object that had suddenly pierced his body, and to find his life's blood oozing out from between them. Instead he saw . . . nothing! He looked up in confusion. Stratton was still holding the arrow, yet he could feel it piercing his body. *What in the hell is going on?* Baker screamed silently, opening his mouth but making no sound. Things had suddenly gone *very* wrong!

Ryan's heart soared when he saw Baker writhing in obvious pain. It had worked! The arrow had triggered physical symptoms associated with Baker's death in the Oglala Sioux lifetime! He thought quickly — there was no way to know how long the effect would last. There was no legal requirement for Baker to be present at these depositions, and it would clearly be safer if he was *not* there. He set the arrow down on the conference table in front of him, and leaned forward with his weight resting on both of his hands, while he stared Baker straight in the eye, hoping that his boldness, combined with the pain that Baker was experiencing would keep him safe from attack.

Baker could not believe what was happening. *He* was the master! *He* was the one who controlled those with whom he came into contact! Yet over the course of a few seconds, the tables had been turned. Stratton put the arrow down, leaned forward, and said, "Get out!" in that same orator's voice. The puma, which had been quiet for a moment joined in with a roar that made Baker's ears ring. The raven started cawing non-stop, which, combined with the roaring of the puma, created such a cacophony that Baker momentarily took his hands away from his stomach to cover his ears. "Get out and don't come back!" Stratton continued, his voice ringing authoritatively and clear as a bell in spite of the other noise in the room. Baker had had enough for now. He bolted through the reception area, past the startled receptionist and out through the doorway that led into Waterman's suite of offices.

Ryan stepped to the door of the conference room to watch him leave. Seconds later, Heath Waterman, with the stenographer by his side, emerged from a hallway and started toward the conference room. Ryan quickly stepped back inside and stowed his arrow back in its carrying-case. Waterman and the stenographer entered a moment later. Waterman glanced around the small room and then back over his shoulder to the reception area. He was obviously surprised that his client was not there. Ryan held out his hand and introduced himself, stating that he had joined Project HOPE's legal team, and would be filling in for Michael Holland, who was not able to attend that day. Waterman remarked that he had read about the accident in the newspaper, and went through the obligatory formality of saying that he was sorry to hear about what had happened.

*I'll just bet you are,* thought Ryan. Most of the time he got along with opposing counsel, recognizing that there were two sides to every story, and that the other attorney was merely an adversary, not an enemy. In fact, some of Ryan's closest friends in the legal profession had started out as opponents in court. That would never happen with Heath Waterman. The man reeked of arrogance and carried himself with an air of self-importance that Ryan would have found irritating if he wasn't so exhilarated from Baker's reaction to his arrow. Waterman asked if Ryan had seen his client leave, and if so whether he had mentioned where he was going.

"He didn't say," said Ryan lightly. "But I don't think he'll be back — he didn't look well at all — I think he may have had an upset stomach."

Waterman glanced at his watch. It was now twenty minutes past the time when the depositions had been scheduled. "I'm afraid we're not going to get anything accomplished this morning," he said. "We were hoping that we'd be able to locate the wildlife biologists so that you could depose them, but it seems they left town, leaving no forwarding address, shortly after they finished their work for Miller Lumber."

Ryan wasn't surprised. He and Michael had been fairly certain that Waterman would produce excuses rather than witnesses. He looked at his watch. "I'll be back at one-thirty for the next deposition, then," he said, gathering his things together, and doing his best to keep a serious expression on his face, although on the inside he was as jubilant as he could be under the circumstances. Project HOPE was knocking on the door — all they needed was to get Harry O'Neil's deposition over with, and the trial for the permanent injunction would be as good as won! He had also survived his encounter with *The One without a Soul*, providing his ancient enemy with a little surprise in the process. His step was light as he left the suite of offices and headed back to the parking lot where Larry and Gayle were waiting.

# 5

NOTHING HAD EVER HAPPENED TO RAYMOND BAKER THAT EVEN remotely resembled the debacle that had occurred in Waterman's conference room. As soon as he laid eyes on Ryan Stratton, he recognized him as another of his *enemies*. That in itself was becoming commonplace — he had recognized the raven and the puma as such the first time he saw them. The same thing had happened when he had encountered the *bitch* and the weakling in the courtroom. But his reaction to Stratton was much more intense than it had been with the others — even before the pain had lanced through his stomach. As soon as Baker saw him, Stratton became the central focus of his attention while the others faded to the periphery. Then *Stratton* had done something to inflict this exquisite agony on him — agony which could only be associated with a killing-blow! How had he done it? How had he caused such intense pain, by merely holding up an arrow and telling him to remember his past? *There were no arrows in his past! He had never even touched an arrow in his life!* He certainly had never endured anything like the agony that screamed through his gut, as if he had been impaled. An hour had passed and the pain had not subsided in the least, leaving him almost completely debilitated. There was no way he could make it back to Waterman's office for the time when O'Neil's deposition had been scheduled. He had been cheated out of enjoying Stratton's anguish when he realized that his star witness wasn't going to arrive! But staying in the conference room even an instant longer had not been an option. There was no way he could face his adversary with pain knifing through him, robbing him of vitality and control. He had barely been able to make his way to his office in the Amalgamated tower! He reached down and gingerly prodded his stomach where it hurt the most, crying out involuntarily as he did so. Just then his private line rang. It would be Heath Waterman — he was the only one with the number who had any reason to call him. Baker debated briefly about whether to tell Waterman what had happened, but decided against it — even the idea of admitting to a weakness enraged him. He answered the phone, and when Waterman asked why he had left so suddenly, made a vague excuse and left it at that. He thought about telling Waterman that O'Neil wouldn't show up, but ultimately decided to stick to his original plan.

After putting down the phone, Baker smiled in spite of the intensity of his pain. He may have been surprised today — and found that his adversaries were more resourceful than he imagined. But they were still playing with a deck that *he* had rigged! Right now, Stratton must be crowing to all of the other tree-huggers that a court victory was in the bag. Just wait until he found out that their case against Miller had already been lost!

He poured a tumbler of Scotch and chopped cocaine. *Eight lines today*, he thought to himself as he poured out an extra-large measure of the drug. *I deserve it, and it may help with the pain.* He snorted the first two lines, and lit a cigarette. In a way, there was a positive side to what had happened. He couldn't remember the last time he had tested himself against a worthy opponent. Besting Stratton would bring him even more pleasure now that he knew he wasn't the weakling he had seemed to be at first.

# 6

RYAN RANG GAYLE AND THEN LARRY ON THEIR CELL PHONES AS soon as he got to the lobby. When Gayle answered, he told her that just as they had suspected, the wildlife biologists "couldn't be located," and that he was on his way back to the car. He decided to wait to tell them about Baker's reaction to the arrow until they were face to face. As he walked towards the parking lot, his spirits were higher than at any time since Audrey's "accident" — using his arrow to defend himself against Baker was the first and only sign that they weren't completely powerless against him. After he reached the parking lot, the three of them decided to walk to *La Felche*, a nearby Italian restaurant that was one of Larry's favorites. On the way, Ryan filled Larry and Gayle in on the morning's events. They responded as if they hadn't been there, knowing that Ryan needed to share the experience. He finished his tale as they arrived at the restaurant, and after they placed their orders, the conversation shifted to the deposition scheduled for that afternoon. "I wonder if Baker will be back for this one," Ryan mused. "He was obviously in terrible pain when he left Waterman's office." He looked at Larry. "How long do you think his pain will last?"

Larry shrugged his shoulders. "My experience comes from treating patients who had chronic pain as a residual effect of past-life trauma. I can't remember anyone coming in at the onset of pain — they sought me out when they were unable to obtain relief from standard treatment. As often as not, they were told that their pain was psycho-somatic. Past-life therapy wasn't a universal cure by any means, but a good number of those who tried it for physical problems discovered the cause in a past-life trauma, and found immediate relief. But the persistence of their pain — which often lasted for years, leads me to think that Baker will have to endure at least *some* level of pain until he too discovers the past-life connection."

"It looks like things are finally starting to go our way," said Ryan with a sigh of relief. "There aren't any credible witnesses to refute Harry's testimony — the trial should be a walk in the park!"

Ryan was in high spirits, but Gayle was beginning to feel a sense of foreboding. She didn't want to say anything that might drag Ryan back to the depressed state he'd been in ever since the crash, but she was even more wary of over-confidence. "We're not out of the woods yet," she cautioned. "We still need to keep our guard up, stay centered and focus our attention on the task in front of us. Baker may have suffered a setback, but he's still out there and as far as we know, the scales are still in balance." She looked pained. "And it's all too clear that he intends to do us in."

"There's no doubt about that," Ryan agreed. "I'm going to have my arrow ready in case he shows up this afternoon."

After lunch, they walked back to Ryan's van together where, once again, Ryan continued on alone. As soon as he was out of sight, Gayle said, "I didn't want to sound too discouraging after everything Ryan's been through — and I'm not picking up a sense of any *immediate* danger — but something tells me that this is all too easy. I don't trust it."

"Do you think there might be some kind of set-up or ambush this afternoon?" Larry asked. "Will Baker be there gunning for him in spite of what happened this morning?"

"There's really only one way to tell — and we were planning go back with Ryan this afternoon anyway." She reached over and took his hand for a moment. "How are you feeling? Spirit-walking always takes a lot out of me."

Larry's smile was warm in response to Gayle's tenderness. More and more, she had taken on the role of protective "mother" to all of them. "I'm doing okay. I was quite tired when we returned from our encounter this morning, but lunch and a couple of hours rest seems to have restored me."

"We should get going then," she said, getting as comfortable as was possible in her seat before relaxing into a state of meditation. Larry watched her for a moment, and then used the serene expression on her face as a starting point to embark on his own journey into the spirit realm. Shortly thereafter the puma and the raven were once again beside Ryan as he made his way to Heath Waterman's office.

Ryan arrived only a minute or two before the time the deposition was scheduled to begin. He was surprised that Harry O'Neil had not arrived before him — O'Neil's punctuality was as characteristic of the man as was his caution. He began to feel anxious as the minutes ticked by. When twenty minutes had passed and Harry still hadn't shown up, he used his cellular phone to call Harry's message number. A mechanical voice advised him to leave a message, but he hung up instead, not sure why he had called in the first place. Half an hour later, Heath Waterman came out of his private office to ask whether or not Ryan had heard from his witness. Ryan shook his head, without speaking. Waterman looked at his watch and said, "I've got some things I can take care of. My receptionist will buzz me when he gets here."

As Waterman walked away, Ryan's spirits began to plummet. With each passing minute, the probability that Baker had somehow managed to get to O'Neil in spite of all of his precautions grew. The jubilation he had been feeling just a short time before was shifting past neutral and towards despair. After an hour with no sign of O'Neil, and no telephone call explaining why he was late, Ryan gave up and had the receptionist buzz Waterman's office. Waterman was either as surprised as Ryan that O'Neil had failed to show, or he was a very good actor. He had very obviously been irritated when Harry was late — it was evident that he placed a great deal of importance on the value of his time. Now he had trouble concealing his glee as Ryan conceded that waiting any longer was probably futile. He and Ryan both knew the consequences of O'Neil's failure to show. It was overwhelmingly likely that there would be no Permanent Injunction. The TRO would be lifted, and old-growth redwoods would once again come crashing to earth.

Ryan didn't call Gayle and Larry when he left Waterman's office. He felt a need to be alone for the time it would take to walk to the parking lot. His natural buoyancy had been stretched to its limit by Audrey's accident. Taking over some of Michael's duties had provided a much needed diversion, but now that the lawsuit that was so important to his love was obviously doomed, he found himself on an emotional slide that was heading straight for a black depression. He hadn't realized how invested he had become in Project HOPE's cause. Just a few days ago, he had been a lowly spear-carrier. But after he made the decision to climb into the traces Michael had been forced to abandon, he had actually begun to enjoy the role he had taken on, and by the time he walked into Heath Waterman's office that morning, it had become *his* lawsuit. And once the lawsuit was *his* — once he had taken complete ownership of it in his own mind — the failure of the lawsuit became *his* failure. Without O'Neil, nothing Ryan could do would have any consequence one way or the other. He knew he had no control over what Baker had surely done to O'Neil, but the fact that the battle was over before he had had a chance to ask a witness a single question was more than he thought he could bear. There was no shaking the feeling that somehow, some way, he should have been able to overcome their adversary. On top of everything, his guilt over not having protected Audrey from Baker returned in a rush. His melancholy thoughts overwhelmed him and he began to despair that they would ever find a way to bring her home. By the time he was half-way to the parking lot, his spirits were at their lowest ebb. Even the concrete under his feet seemed to suck at his shoes like deep sand. Then to his surprise, he saw Larry and Gayle hurrying towards him, though it was far too early for the deposition to have concluded. Gayle stopped in front of him, grabbed him by the shoulders, and actually shook him, and said, "Ryan, its not your fault! There was nothing that you could have done to save Harry. Remember what the advanced spirits have told us — his spirit knew what would happen to him in this lifetime before he was ever born. His sacrifice probably pays a debt from a past-life, and his soul is no more lost than yours was when you died as an Oglala Sioux, or in the Warsaw Ghetto."

Ryan shook his head as if to clear it. "How did you know what happened — and what I was thinking?" he asked.

"You know I'm psychic," she replied with the quick smile he always found so endearing — though it did little to cheer him now.

Ryan sighed. "Intellectually, I know that if O'Neil is dead — and I know in my heart that he is — that it's not my fault. But Baker is always one step ahead of us no matter what we do — it feels as if we're doomed to fail. But I also have the feeling that I *need* to be doing something positive in opposition to Baker, or Audrey will have no chance at all to find her way back! Without Harry, there's nothing I can do when it comes to the lawsuit, and if *this* isn't what I'm supposed to be doing, then what could it possibly be?" His mood began to rub off on Larry and Gayle, and they were a somber trio by the time they arrived back at Ryan's van. Their moods didn't improve while they traversed the confusing maze of streets which lead back to the Golden Gate bridge and Highway 101. Ryan drove in silence, trying to concentrate on nothing other than his driving to keep himself from thinking. His dark humor, as well as their dismal hopes for a successful end to the lawsuit, put a damper on all conversation, and even Gayle, who never seemed to get dispirited, soon found herself inching towards depression.

After more than an hour passed with only a few words said between them, Ryan suddenly decided that he had had enough of the silence. He reached over and shoved an audio-cassette tape that had been partially inserted into his tape-player the rest of the way in. The tape was one he had recorded himself some years before, and contained a medley of songs from some of his favorite albums. It had been missing almost since the day he made it, and he had only found it that morning, wedged between the bottom of the driver's seat and the floor of the van. *I can't even remember what's on this tape but maybe the music will help,* he thought as the cassette disappeared into the slot on the face of the machine. Then, when he heard the unmistakable introductory notes of a particular David Wilcox song, the hair covering the back of his neck and his arms stood on end. He gave his entire attention to the words, stunned by the message that seemed to have been written just for him — for this very moment when he needed it most.

> *You say you see no hope*
> *You say you see no reason we should dream*
> *That the world would ever change*
> *You're saying love is foolish to believe*
> *'Cause there'll always be some crazy*
> *With an army or a knife*
> *To wake you from your daydream*
> *Put the fear back in your life*
>
> *Look, if someone wrote a play*
> *Just to glorify what's stronger than hate*
> *Would they not arrange the stage*
> *To look as if the hero came too late?*
> *He's almost in defeat*
> *It's looking like the evil side will win*
> *So on the edge of every seat*
> *From the moment that the whole thing begins,*
>
> *It is love who makes the mortar*
> *And it's love who stacked these stones*
> *And it's love who made the stage here*

*Although it looks like we're alone*
*In this scene set in shadows*
*Like the night is here to stay*
*There is evil cast around us*
*But it's love that wrote the play . . .*
*For in this darkness, love can show the way*

*So now the stage is set*
*Feel your own heart beating in your chest*
*This life's not over yet*
*So we get up on our feet and do our best*
*We play against the fear*
*We play against the reasons not to try*
*We're playing for the tears*
*Burning in the happy angels' eyes*

*For it's love who makes the mortar*
*And it's love who stacked these stones*
*And it's love who made the stage here*
*Although it looks like we're alone*
*In this scene set in shadows*
*Like the night is here to stay*
*There is evil cast around us*
*But it's love that wrote the play . . .*
*For in this darkness, love can show the way*

The song was the last one on the tape before it reached the end, where the machine paused, waiting for the auto-reverse to send the tape in the opposite direction. Ryan reached over and snapped it off before the next song began. Larry broke the silence that followed. "What made you choose that song?"

"I just found the tape wedged under my seat this morning," said Ryan hesitantly. "It's been lost for a couple of years — I didn't even know what was on it until I heard the first few notes of the introduction."

"For in this darkness, love can show the way," Gayle murmured, almost as if she were coming out of a deep sleep. "Ryan, the fact that you played that song at this exact moment is no coincidence or fluke. The advanced spirits have told us from the beginning that the scales are in balance — that the outcome is uncertain. We've just received a message, the scales are *still* in balance — love can *still* show us the way!"

"Then there must still be a way to win the lawsuit," said Ryan, "And we have to let love show us the way." As he said the words, he suddenly saw a new angle from which to approach the suit that he hadn't ever considered before. He turned to Larry, and asked, "Do you remember what you told me when I first asked you how we were supposed to treat a bastard like Raymond Baker in a loving way while we were trying to kick his ass across the courtroom?"

"Not exactly," said Larry.

"I remember what you said, almost word for word," said Ryan. "It was such a confusing concept, and your explanation sounded right. I wrote it down afterwards so that I could think about it — what I remembered of it, anyway. But it didn't make sense to me until just now. You said, 'the things that Baker is doing and trying to do must not be the focus of our emotions. Our hearts must instead be filled with love for the forest, love for the endangered species whose nesting habitat would be destroyed — love for the part of the earth we are trying to save.'" Ryan adjusted his rear-view mirror so that he could see Larry's face as he drove. "We haven't been doing that. Our lawsuit has been *reactive* to Raymond Baker, rather than focusing on the redwoods and the endangered species. And just this second, out of the blue, I realized that there's still a way to win!"

"How?" asked Larry.

"Prove to the court that there *is* an endangered species out in the Miller tract that would be injured by the logging," he replied. "We need to figure out if there actually *are* Spotted Owls or Marbled Murrelets out in the Miller Tract."

"Doesn't that sort of study usually take two or three years?" asked Larry. "The trial starts in a week."

"It takes two years to monitor a proposed area for a Timber Harvest Plan to show that there *aren't* any endangered species whose habitat is threatened. If we show that the area included in the Timber Harvest Plan *is* the habitat for an endangered species that would be harassed by the logging, then the court would have no choice but to rule in our favor."

"But the old-growth portion of the Miller tract is completely inaccessible. There's only one road in, and they aren't letting anybody close. How are you going to get a wildlife study done under those circumstances?"

"I think there just might be a way," Ryan replied, a smile lighting his face. "It's wild, but it just might work!"

# 7

ADAM WAS DEVASTATED WHEN HE HEARD THAT HARRY O'NEIL was more than likely Raymond Baker's most recent victim. He had always admired Harry's bravery, and had come to think of him as a friend. "It happened exactly like he said it would," he lamented. "In spite of all the precautions he took, Baker got him in the end."

"It was a risk he took on willingly," said Michael. "He was an honorable man — I don't think he could have just walked away from what was happening without trying to stop Baker — especially after his co-worker was murdered. And if what Gayle and Larry have been telling us about our destinies is true, then his sacrifice was something he chose."

Adam turned to Larry. "I guess I'll have to do one of those past-life regressions so that I can have as much confidence in reincarnation as the rest of you."

"Just let me know when you're ready," said Larry. "But I think I'll avoid taking you to the Oglala Sioux lifetime. I don't think you'd enjoy experiencing birth and death within a few days of each other."

"I have to agree with that," said Adam. "But in the meantime, I'm going to dedicate my efforts to Harry from now on. Let's jump on Ryan's idea about doing our own wildlife study — it's the only chance we have!" He turned to Ryan. "What's your plan?" he asked. "How do you propose we do a wildlife study in an area we can't get to?"

"It may be difficult, but I think we can get in on mountain bikes — especially if we can get some help. The idea came to me when I thought about Ben Meyers and the things he was saying about Marbled Murrelets. The only thing I've ever done with him was to go on a mountain-bike ride. That's how I came up with the idea. There have to be old roads all through the second-growth from when it was logged the first time, and even if they're in terrible shape, we should be able to fight our way through if we're on mountain bikes. If we can find someone who has scouted out that part of the forest and could guide us through, then we might be able to get it done in the time we have left."

"It could work," said Michael thoughtfully. "Do you know anybody who might have done any bushwhacking in there?"

"I just might," Ryan replied. Then he grinned before continuing cryptically, "but if they have, I'm sure they'll insist on their anonymity."

Doug knew by Ryan's expression that he had just tapped into some private source of amusement, but decided that he would wait to discover what had tickled Ryan's funny bone.

Now that there was a plan, Michael had already shifted into high gear, and was plotting how to develop the necessary evidence within their limited time parameters. He glanced at the clock on the wall. "It's three-thirty now. Ben might still be in his office, and if he's not, someone should be there who could tell us how to find him. We're going to need him, too. Would one of you hand me the phone?"

When he heard Ryan's idea, Ben Meyers jumped at the chance to help and quickly arranged to take the rest of the week off. He told Michael that in order to do any kind of effective study in the limited amount of time they had, a minimum of ten observers had to be located and trained. "I wish you had come up with this idea a little earlier," he said. "Even if we're lucky enough to find a group of observers tomorrow, it will take a full day to train them. That leaves Thursday to get in, and Sunday to get out, with Friday and Saturday in-between to see if we can come up with anything."

"It's a tight schedule, alright," Michael agreed. "But it's also the only hope we've got."

Ryan stepped into the next room. Audrey looked no different than she had since her arrival at the hospital, except that her superficial cuts and bruises had nearly disappeared. He sat beside her and took her hand in his, aching with his love for her and wishing that there was something more he could do for her. *Or maybe I am doing what I'm supposed to,* he amended. *Larry and Gayle keep telling me that the scales are in balance — that we can still succeed. And success would have to include Audrey's recovery — or it isn't success at all.* His emotions had been fluctuating wildly all day, but fortunately they were on the upswing. David Wilcox's message of hope kept running through his mind. He still felt bad about Harry — although he had never actually met the man — but his despair had been replaced by determination. A course of action had been identified, and whether or not it would ultimately prove successful, for the moment having a plan of action that *might* succeed made all the difference. He stroked Audrey's hair and leaned down to kiss her forehead. He had heard somewhere that it was best to speak to a person who was unconscious as if they could hear everything that was going on around them. In most cases there was a part of the brain that continued to listen and record information even if it never could be accessed by the conscious mind. Ryan had no idea if such a concept would apply to Audrey, whose unconsciousness had not been caused by a physical injury. Nonetheless, he talked to her — about his love for her, about his past-life dream and the arrow they had made. He told her about Baker's reaction when he saw the arrow, and Harry O'Neil's unfortunate disappearance — that they had had to come up with an entirely new strategy. But mostly, he talked to her about their baby — how much he was looking forward to being a parent, and how much he already loved their daughter.

When Doug stuck his head in the door and told him that it was their turn to go to the motel to get some rest, Ryan kissed her slack lips and left for the motel room, where he fell asleep almost as soon as his head hit the pillow.

# 8

THE NEXT MORNING, RYAN AND DOUG DROVE TO WILLITS, THE closest town to the part of Jackson State Forest adjacent to the Miller tract, where there was a bicycle shop that Ryan frequented. Greg Edwards, the store's mechanic/sales-person, was known as "Og" out on the trails. He and his brother Bobby had been mountain-biking from the sport's earliest days, when the bikes had been cobbled together out of nineteen-thirties Schwinn Excelsiors and touring-bike parts. Several years before, when Ryan had wandered into the shop, Og had told him about the group of mountain-bikers he rode with, and invited him to come out on one of their "illegal" rides. In those early days of mountain biking, before the sport had taken off, virtually every local governmental authority had banned mountain bikes from the trails, primarily at the urging of equestrians. In the Willits area, this led to the formation of the Anonymous Bike Club, or ABC for short — the reason for Ryan's amusement over his cryptic comment the day before... The group seemed to Ryan to be made up almost entirely of masochists, who tried to find the most difficult rides possible — scenic beauty was a mere side-benefit. The whole premise of the group in those early days was that there *was* no group, just an extremely loose organization dedicated to anarchy on the trails. The club had no meetings, officers or rules other than the common-sense requirement that each rider be self-sufficient out on the trails. Membership, if it could be called that, was established by going on one or more of the rides. On the infrequent occasions when law-enforcement stopped ten to fifteen riders on an illegal trail, they became a bunch of shoulder-shrugging know-nothings who had no identification and had all just met that morning. The tactic almost always resulted in an exasperated forest ranger or park official letting them all go with a warning rather than taking the trouble to write half a book of useless tickets. On one particular ride, more than twenty riders had posed in front of a panoramic view, each of them wearing a paper bag with eye-holes. They were a tight-knit group, and Ryan had been gratified to have been invited along on several of the illegal rides in the old days, and many more legal ones after local governments realized that they couldn't keep a much larger faction of tax-paying mountain bikers off the trails just to please horse-owners. On one trip through a portion of Jackson State Forest, Og and the others seemed to know each tree personally and every turn of the trails. Ryan was reasonably sure that if *anyone* had followed the network of old logging roads as far as the Miller tract, it would be one or more members of the ABC.

They arrived at *The Willits Cycle Center* just as Og was opening up the shop. He looked up from behind the counter as they walked through the door. "Dude! Good to see you. You've been away too long! When are we going to see you back out on the trails?"

"That's what I came to talk to you about," Ryan said. "I was hoping that you and some of the other ABC riders might be able to help me out."

"What's going on, Dude? I've never seen you looking so serious — it's a sure thing you haven't been putting in enough time spinning your cranks!"

Ryan smiled, thinking how grateful he would be if a few more miles on the mountain-bike could fix his problems — then reflected that perhaps spinning his cranks *would* be the solution, or at least a big part of it. "It's serious enough," he said. "Let me tell you about it."

Thirty-five minutes later, Og was in high dudgeon over Raymond Baker's nefarious activities, and enthusiastic about the opportunity to do whatever he could to help out. "Man, this is even better than the old days — a four-day illegal ride, *and* we get to fuck with some corporate asshole from a lumber company!" He began thumbing through a card-file full of phone numbers. "And your timing couldn't be better. When the Miller Massacre was on the news, a bunch of us got curious and decided to see if we could find our way in to where the cutting was going on so we could see what the trees looked like before they were gone forever. We've been spending the last few weekends with topographical maps and compasses making our way from the Jackson Forest trailhead over to the virgin stands in the Miller tract. It's mostly grown-over, but passable if you're willing to bushwhack and portage a few times." He grinned at Ryan. "We made it to the old-growth, and figured we were within a mile of the chainsaws. It takes about a day to get to the edge of the old-growth if you get an early enough start, but from there we'll have to hoof it."

Ryan explained that everyone who went would need to be trained in bird-recognition techniques, and that there would be a seminar the next day. "How many people do you think you might be able to recruit?" he asked.

"Let me get on the phone — I won't know the answer until I call everybody on my list, and get them to call their friends — how many do you need?"

"At least ten, but no more than twenty, to keep things manageable," said Ryan. "And now that we know that you guys can find a way in, I'll make some calls myself."

"I can't believe it," said Doug as they climbed into Ryan's Caravan and began retracing their route back to Ukiah. "That's probably the most amazing coincidence I've ever heard of! You get the bright idea to ride mountain-bikes on roads that have been out of use for eighty or ninety years, and the first person you talk to has just spent the past few weeks finding a way through and mapping it out. Do you realize what the odds against that would have to be?"

"That's your reporter's scepticism talking," said Ryan. "I don't believe in coincidences anymore. From the very beginning, the odds against just about everything that has happened are off the scale. To quote a line from one of my favorite Indigo

Girls songs: "No way construction of this tricky plan was built by other than a greater hand." He looked over at his friend, and their eyes met for a moment before Ryan returned his attention to the road ahead. "We're surrounded by psychics, taking trips to our past lives and dealing with a bastard who's the spawn of the devil himself and who's been dogging us across half of the history of humanity. Everything that's happened to us is completely insane, and the only way we've gotten through it so far is by going deeper — choosing spiritual explanations. If we'd insisted on being hard-headed realists, we'd probably be dead by now."

"I have to admit that no matter how hard I try to hang on to my old scepticism, the *only* explanations that make sense are the spiritual ones," Doug conceded.

Ryan nodded, and said: "That's what Larry and Gayle keep telling us, and they also keep telling us that the outcome of the conflict with Baker is delicately balanced — that it could go either way. All I have to do is look at some of the things that Baker has pulled off, and I'm not surprised when long-shots work out for us too — like the business with the arrow. What are the odds that I could give Baker a bellyache by showing him a replica of the arrow I used to kill him in his past life? That's pretty fantastic, but not nearly as big a leap as what he's been doing. Think about what you discovered in Sacramento. Baker started a diversionary tactic to shift the heat from him over to Eddie Rapski three years before he even bought Miller lumber." Ryan sneaked another glance at his old friend. "When I stop to think about it, this whole thing is just too weird for words — so I've decided to just accept what's going on, no matter how strange it is."

He picked up his cell phone and called Adam, requesting that he relay a message to Project HOPE that they needed experienced mountain-bikers for a four-day mission to save the Miller tract. Then he dialed the hospital, and told Michael about the Anonymous Bike Club's forays into the Miller tract — and that his friend would not only be able to lead them in, but was rounding up volunteers.

"I'll call Ben and confirm the seminar for tomorrow," said Michael, ringing off immediately.

When they arrived at the hospital, Ryan made a list of his mountain-biking friends in Fort Bragg and Mendocino, and then started making calls. He had a firm commitment from three of them by the time Og called with the news that the ABC would be able to field seven volunteers. Soon a call came in from Project HOPE. Four redwood-activists with mountain-biking experience had signed on, bringing their number to sixteen. Ben drummed up two more by the time Michael checked in with him, each with extensive experience in bird-identification. He looked satisfied as he hung up the phone, and said, "Eighteen . . . my only regret is that I'm stuck here."

"Your part is just as important," Ryan reminded him. Michael had assigned himself the task of putting together a "script" of questions for Ryan to use in the trial. Most of the questions would be culled from the trial briefs he had put together the last few times he'd had Ben on the stand. Of course, they would be predicated on a successful mountain bike expedition — somehow, Ryan suspected that if the scales were truly in balance, the Miller tract was home to at least one endangered species. All they had to do was find it.

# 9

THE MORNING TRAINING SESSION AT PROJECT HOPE WAS DEVOTED to the Spotted Owl, one of the two species the observers were most likely to encounter in the Miller tract. Bruce Swinehart, an ornithologist recruited for the trek by Ben Meyers, taught the diverse group of mountain-bikers and redwood-activists the spotted owl's field-markings, flight characteristics, nesting habits, and behavior patterns. By the end of the session, Ryan figured that it would be a miracle if they had any sightings. The birds were almost entirely nocturnal, and tended to sit absolutely still in the deepest shade they could find during the day. And although they had a fairly wide range, each Spotted Owl required a large territory to sustain it. They were silent flyers, whose three-foot-plus wingspans allowed them to swoop down on prey undetected. And although they had a distinctive shrieking cry that Bruce played for them on a tape recorder, the owls seldom used it other than to define their territory.

After the morning session, the group descended *en masse* on Taco Loco before returning to Project HOPE for Ben's afternoon session on the Marbled Murrelet. Ben had a raft of humorous stories to keep them engaged after their sleep-inducing meal, and the fact that the lawsuit's success might depend on the quality of their field research helped to hold their attention. Ben's slides contained rare photographs of the Marbled Murrelet, which he described as being approximately nine inches in length with a short neck and tail, small wings, and a heavy, compact body. Since it was the peak of the Marbled Murrelet breeding season, the adult's plumage would be dark brown and gray with black bars above, and a heavily mottled light brown below. The next series of slides showed a bare egg sitting in a depression on a moss-covered tree limb, with shots of both the male and the female sitting on the "nest."

"The male and the female take turns sitting on the egg while the other is at sea," said Ben. "They change places at dawn, so that's the time to try to make observations. They almost never fly during the day — only at dawn and dusk when the light levels are very low. For the most part, they're completely nocturnal while they're on land. This is a very secretive bird, and one of the most difficult to observe." Ben gestured at the screen. "Even a witness for the lumber company conceded that these birds make their living by staying out of everything's way."

"How are we supposed to observe a bird that is doing everything it can to avoid detection?" asked Mike Turner, a fit-looking man with red hair and beard from the ABC contingent.

"Excellent question," Ben responded. "Unlike the spotted owl, a detection of Marbled Murrelets is almost *always* made by *hearing* the birds, rather than seeing them." He slid a new tape into his deck and played recordings of the Marbled Murrelet's distinctive "keer" call, as well as the sounds made by the bird as it chugged through the air in level flight, and the "jet" sound produced by a steep dive. Finally, he showed the volunteers slides of broken Marbled Murrelet eggs. Finding eggshell fragments would be indisputable evidence that these particular stands of trees were Marbled Murrelet nesting habitat.

While the mountain-bike volunteers were learning about Marbled Murrelets and Spotted Owls, another group was at the Willits Cycle Center outfitting the rider's bikes. Project HOPE had a contingency fund that they tapped to purchase lighting-systems, front and rear racks and packs, and even a few new bicycles. Doug made a special trip to Fort Bragg to retrieve Ryan's Ibis, his riding clothes and shoes, a sleeping bag and some lightweight cooking gear. Their original time-table called for them to be ready to head out Wednesday morning at dawn, but half-way through their short course in ornithology, it became clear that they were actually half a day ahead of schedule. Several ABC riders were dispatched to mark the turns with white chalk so that the observers would find it easier to find their way at night. "If we head out this afternoon, we'll have three hours of daylight, and after that up to six hours battery time." Og announced. "These nickel-cadmium lights really brighten up a dark trail, and riding at night is a kick! We won't want to ride all night, but any miles we put behind us will help. I'd like to have most of tomorrow to locate the right area. Even with topographical maps, it's incredibly easy to get confused and turned around out there."

Doug offered to drive Ryan out to the trailhead, and pick him up on the return trip, confessing that he had never been able to keep away from a breaking story. On the way from Healdsburg to Willets, they stopped at the hospital in Ukiah, where Gayle, Larry, Adam and Pam continued to rotate shifts at Audrey's bedside. Ryan spent a few minutes with Audrey, and then joined the others in Michael's room, which was now doing double duty as yet another temporary law office. "How're my questions coming, Maestro?" asked Ryan when they arrived.

"The first draft is being transcribed as we speak," said Michael, looking over the top of his reading glasses. "I won't be able to do too much more without knowing the results of your observations, but the questions to lay the foundation for the expert witness testimony are finished." He grinned up at Ryan from his bed. "Even one of those drones from one of Amalgamated's defense firms could put on a winning case with the script I've prepared."

"That's exactly what I want," said Ryan. "I'll try this case, but only as your alter-ego."

Pam spoke up, saying, "You be careful out there, Ryan! We're fresh out of back-up lawyers. I don't want to hear about any spills like two years ago, when you almost broke your neck."

Ryan promised to be on his best behavior, and after one more quick visit to kiss Audrey goodbye, he and Doug were on their way.

"That's a remarkable young man," said Michael after they were gone. "It's got to be hard for him to carry on while Audrey's in such terrible shape. I'd be out of my mind with worry."

"He'd be in much worse shape if he didn't have something to do," Larry offered. "I just hope for his sake — for all of our sakes, really, that she finds her way back, and soon!"

"Amen to that brother," said Michael. "Amen to that."

# 10

RYAN AND DOUG TOOK HIGHWAY 101 NORTH TO WILLITS, AND then side-roads to the trailhead in Jackson Forest. Others had arrived before them and were already unloading bicycles from roof-racks and pickup trucks, securing panniers to racks and stowing gear and supplies when they arrived. After Ryan distributed his gear into his new front-and-rear panniers, he hefted his bike, groaning with the effort it took. His svelte twenty-three-pound racing machine had been transformed into a seventy-pound mechanical pack-mule. Doug chuckled at Ryan's obvious distress. "This is going to be the best training ride you've ever been on," he chided. "You'll be building muscle with every pedal-stroke."

Og vaulted onto a large stump, whistled loudly to get everyone's attention, and then reeled off a description of the trail conditions, which ran the gamut from well-maintained logging roads to traverses along the sides of nearly vertical, fern covered hillsides where old roads had washed out. Mike Turner, who had been to the old-growth and back several times, was designated lead rider while Og brought up the rear. They planned to regroup and take a brief rest every hour until dark, and thereafter at every crossroads, to make sure they all stayed together. Doug and the others who had provided transportation for the volunteers wished them good hunting and a safe trip, and by five minutes after five they were off. *I don't know what I'd rather face,* thought Doug as he climbed into Ryan's Caravan for the drive back to Ukiah, *Raymond Baker or a grueling eight-hour mountain bike ride — half of it in the dark.*

Ryan had never ridden a fully-loaded bike on the road, let alone wrestled one over the bumps and ruts of an overgrown and eroded logging road. Self-sustained, off-road cycle touring had always appealed to him in concept, but this was the first time he had actually undertaken the endeavor. His titanium-framed Ibis was renowned for its handling, and Ryan loved flicking the bike around and over the obstacles of the trail as if the bike was an extension of his body. But loaded with nearly fifty pounds of gear, the bike had become a sluggish beast of burden that required him to plan his moves much more deliberately. The worst part was the climbing — hitting the gravity pockets, as Og referred to the uphill sections of trail. Once, years before, he had let himself slip out of shape and gain fifteen pounds. Putting more than forty pounds on his bike was worse. He wasn't in the best shape of his life, but all things considered, wasn't too far off his usual level of fitness. But with the extra weight on his bike, he felt like a rank beginner, back at ground zero again. *At least I'm not the slowest one here,* he consoled himself as he muscled his bike up a short, steep pitch — there were five riders behind him, discounting Og, who was taking up the rear.

An hour into the ride, they took their first break. Ryan collapsed on the ground, drank an entire water bottle and inhaled an energy bar. Og rode up ten minutes later with the slowest of the riders — one of the Project HOPE contingent whose previous cycling experience had been limited to the road. After Og leaned his bike up against a tree and gave the man a few words of encouragement, he walked over to where Ryan had sprawled. "How's that full load treating you?" he asked. "The poor guy I'm riding with has been sucking wind so hard, you could probably hear him up where you were."

"Not a chance," said Ryan. "I was breathing so heavily myself, I wouldn't have heard a logging truck if one drove up behind me."

"Yeah, it's a lot different with a load. I know it took me by surprise the first time I went bike-camping. All I can say is, get used to it! There's nothing but hills between here and the spot we've got picked out for tonight's camp — and it doesn't get any easier than it's been so far. In fact, there's going to be some stuff that's so steep most of us will end up walking and pushing."

Ryan groaned. "How long does it stay that steep?"

"The longest steep pitch is about a mile and a half. The others are shorter — half a mile, tops. It won't be easy, but we'll make it."

Ryan finished his energy bar and slugged down more water. Fortunately, there were several streams still running, though it was late in the year. By using filters and water-purifying tablets, they didn't need to pack in their own water on top of everything else. All too soon they were back in the saddle, with the next rest stop at least another hour away.

\*     \*     \*

RAYMOND BAKER SPENT two full days waiting for the pain that knifed through his gut to disappear, but although it had dissipated somewhat, it still dominated every moment, and his anger burned hotter by the minute. It was time to show Stratton who was in charge of handing out the pain and suffering! The *bitch* still lived, and as long as she continued to breathe, Stratton would have hope. The pain in his gut told him that any such hope Stratton cherished would have to be extinguished. Then there were his other *enemies,* who were very much in need of the services he was willing to provide. Pain or no pain, the time was past due to turn the tables and dish out some suffering!

\*     \*     \*

GAYLE ROSE FROM the chair beside Audrey's bed and rested her hands above her hips while she stretched her back. The chair wasn't particularly uncomfortable — she'd certainly had to endure worse — but it would never have been her first choice for the long hours they had been putting in. She leaned over Audrey's bed and smoothed back a strand of hair that had fallen across her face. No matter how much she concentrated, she hadn't felt more than the faintest glimmer of Audrey's essence — the spirit that had shone as brightly as a beacon had been banished to a place so far away that Gayle wondered if it could ever be found. Meanwhile, the body on the hospital bed was an empty husk — except for the tiny life nestled within. She kissed Audrey's forehead, then made her way to the next room where Michael lay, his right arm and leg trussed up as if he were a half-prepared Thanksgiving turkey. He was awake, although Larry, who was theoretically there to keep him company, had dozed off in his chair. She glanced at her watch, and saw that it was just after eleven o'clock. Adam, Pam and Doug would be coming to spell them at two a.m. She edged over to the side of the bed opposite Larry's chair for a whispered conversation with Michael. "How do you think they're doing out in the forest?"

"I'd bet that Ryan is having a good time, or would be if it weren't for the state Audrey's in and all the pressure he's feeling about filling in for me in court."

"I'll never be able to understand how riding a bicycle up the steepest hills you can find qualifies as fun," said Gayle, shaking her head, and then in a sarcastic tone said, "But I can see that if *that* is fun, then loading your bike with gear and doing it in the dark has to bring you guys close to ecstasy!"

Michael chuckled softly. "It must be some kind of gene left over from our days as hunters and gatherers that makes some of us gravitate towards extreme sports. I can't say whether or not he's in ecstasy — but I *can* say that if I were in his place, I'd be having a hell of a good time."

"Do you think that they'll find any endangered species?" she asked.

"I thought you would be able to tell me — you're the psychic," Michael shot back half-jokingly. Gayle shrugged, and he said, "Seriously, it's a longshot. They'll be most likely to find Spotted Owls, because their range is larger. They'll also be looking for Marbled Murrelets, but there's almost no chance that they'll be able to spot any of those."

"Why is that?"

"Even though there are pockets of Marbled Murrelet as far south as Santa Cruz, there aren't any known nesting-clusters between San Francisco and the Owl Creek forest up in Humboldt County. Also, the Miller tract is more than thirty miles from the ocean, and the Marbled Murrelet has never been found to nest quite that far inland." He raised an eyebrow. "But you never know what you're going to find. Nothing in nature is absolute, and no one has ever gone out there during the nesting season to see what they could find."

"Well, I should get back to Audrey," Gayle said, rising from her chair. "Do you want me to wake sleepy-head here so that he can do a better job of keeping you company?"

"Don't bother — I've heard you all complain about these chairs. If he's able to catch a few winks where he is, then he definitely needs his sleep, and I can always watch the television."

After she left though, Michael didn't turn the television on. His thoughts turned instead back to the mountain-bike mission now underway. Gayle may have been right about it being a perverse way to have fun, but he would have traded almost anything to be sweating hard while cranking a mountain bike uphill in the dark instead of being tied to a hospital bed.

*     *     *

MOONRISE WOULDN'T COME until one in the morning, and starlight made no difference in the cave-like darkness under the trees. Each cyclist was an island of light all to themselves — the combined effect like a bizarre string of Christmas lights stretched across the landscape. They had closed ranks and were riding at a pace that allowed even the slowest of them to keep up, although two of the riders were close to their limits. Ryan eased down the trail, thankful for the powerful brakes that had far more stopping power than the ones on road-bikes. They were still a couple of miles from their planned camping spot, and the extreme terrain was beginning to take its toll. Several riders had taken spills, though none had been injured beyond some scrapes and bruises. Ahead of him, Ryan saw that the lights had clustered, indicating that the riders ahead of him had stopped. When he reached them and dismounted, he was happy to hear that they would be spending the night right where they were — the clearing was small, but adequate. "We've made good progress," Og proclaimed. "There's no sense chancing a serious injury because we didn't have the sense to stop before we got too tired."

There weren't any objections. Under the best conditions, six hours in the saddle of a mountain bike was plenty — even for a die-hard enthusiast. With a full load of gear, even the fittest among them were exhausted. They had their ground-cloths and sleeping bags spread out in short order, and within an hour all were fast asleep.

*     *     *

THE BLACK MERCEDES pulled into the hospital parking lot at half past two. Although the work at a hospital never comes to a complete stop, activity at Ukiah Valley Medical Center was at its lowest ebb. Baker stepped out of his car and slid into one of the standard white lab-coats that were the universal uniform of the medical professional. He had already donned the dark-haired wig, false mustache, and heavy, black-rimmed glasses he had worn the last time he had come after the *bitch,* just in case his presence caught someone's attention.

He stepped through the main entrance of the hospital as if he owned it, striding confidently to the front desk, where a sleepy-eyed receptionist gave him directions to the rooms where his *enemies* were sequestered. The pain knifing through his gut had begun to worsen the closer he got to the hospital, and its intensity continued to increase as he made his way down the empty corridor towards the *bitch's* room armed with a weapon that required no stealth to conceal.

Pam had been able to get some sleep while Doug dropped Ryan off at the trailhead. She and Adam were sitting up with Michael, keeping him company. Periodically one of them checked on Audrey and adjusted the pillows Doug had used to make himself comfortable as he caught some extra sleep in the chair beside her bed. She stepped back into Michael's room after one of her periodic checks, and re-joined the card game they were using to pass the time.

The closer Baker got to the *bitch's* room the worse the pain got. He even considered turning back a couple of times, but his iron will kept him going — the stakes were high enough that he was willing to endure almost anything. He knew by the sudden increase in his pain level that he had reached the door to the *bitch's* room without having to check the number etched on the plastic sign next to the door. Stepping inside, he quietly shut the door behind him. The *bitch* was there, just as he expected, but in addition, there was *another* enemy! His rage flared, parallel in intensity to the screaming pain in his gut. He faltered for a moment, torn between his desire to put an end to what was left of the *bitch*, and the almost overwhelming compulsion to use his blade on his slumbering foe. After a moment of indecision, he chose to follow his original plan, and reached into his pocket to retrieve the syringe of slow-acting poison which would kill the *bitch* — but not until he was safely away from the hospital. He pulled the cap off of the needle, slid it into her I.V. bag, and pushed the plunger, exulting as the poison mixed with the formerly benign solution. Then he stood over his newly-discovered foe for a moment, letting his rage build. Leaning close, he put his hand over the sleeping man's mouth and nose, and when his victim's eyes opened wide in surprise, drove his psychic weapon in a deep, slicing stroke that removed the expression of alarm from the man's face as quickly as it had appeared. But before even an instant had passed, an agonized scream from the next room had him bolting down the hallway, his white lab-coat flapping with the breeze of his hasty departure.

At the same moment that Pam's scream of anguish echoed down the hospital corridor, in their motel room, Gayle and Larry were jarred awake by Baker's attack on yet another of their number. Larry's spectral totem leapt out of his body and raced through the wall. Gayle made no immediate effort to follow him. Instead, she dressed rapidly and laid Larry's clothes out for him. She was doubted there was anything they could do for Doug at the moment. It was his soul-mate who needed them now.

# 11

DAWN ARRIVED SOONER THAN RYAN WOULD HAVE BELIEVED possible. He groaned involuntarily as he rolled over in his sleeping bag, stiff from the previous day's exertions and an unaccustomed night spent sleeping on the ground. Around him, other riders were stirring as the early morning light wrapped the clearing in a dewy embrace. Og was already up, and the pungent smell of French-roast coffee he had made permeated the air, giving Ryan enough incentive to struggle out of the warm confines of his sleeping bag and into fresh riding clothes. A few minutes later, he stood warming his hands with the other early risers. Doug Page, a member of the ABC contingent, whose prowess on the uphill sections of the trail made it seem as though he was exempt from the effects of gravity, strolled over and poured himself some of the invigorating brew. He gave Ryan an appraising look. "Are you ready for some bushwhacking today bud? We're heading into the primeval forest, and anywhere we go, it's likely that your footprints will be the first ones there."

"I take it you've gone all the way to the old-growth?" Ryan asked.

"To the edge on one ride, and then we hiked a ways inside the next time. We were trying to locate the place where they had started logging, but we ran out of time. As it was, we couldn't figure out which direction we were going half the time."

Ryan took a sip of his coffee. "We should be able to do better than that today." He pointed to a tall man with Scandinavian features who was lashing a sleeping bag to the rack on the back of his bike. "Steve Bakken has some rough-country surveying experience, and we've got detailed topographical maps, so we should be able to find our way through."

"I'm really looking forward to it," said Doug. "We barely got a taste before we had to turn back."

By this time everyone was out of their sleeping bags and packing their gear. After a quick breakfast of granola and energy bars, washed down by more strong, dark coffee, all eighteen riders mounted their bikes for the next leg of their trek. The old logging road climbed steadily for close to a mile before it plunged down a long, tortured descent that had so many washouts and slides that it had to be negotiated at little more than a walking pace. Ryan was glad they had waited for daylight to traverse this stretch — the going was tricky even in daylight. He shuddered to think of the white-knuckle ride it would have been at night. At the bottom of the descent was the area where Og had originally planned to camp, right on the edge of the old-growth. From there the remnants of the old logging road extended a few hundred yards into the big trees before it shrank down to a faint track, and then faded altogether.

Ryan had experienced the cathedral-like Montgomery Grove and Hendy Woods State Parks, both of which boasted trees soaring three-hundred-fifty feet into the air. But with their manicured pathways and high volume of foot-traffic, they were as civilized as a park in comparison with this forest. The trees here weren't quite as large — most of them were "only" seven or eight feet in diameter and the taller ones were a mere three-hundred feet tall. But the pristine wildness was imbued with a subtly different feeling that made it seem as if they had stepped through a doorway into the past.

At the point where the trail petered out, they stacked their bikes around the base of one particularly large tree. The panniers purchased by Project HOPE were specially designed to zip together into very adequate back-packs, and after ex-changing cycling shoes and shorts for boots and jeans, they set off. Until they returned to this spot on their way out, they would be traveling by foot.

*     *     *

LARRY'S SPIRIT-WALK was a short one — like Audrey's, Doug's body had become an empty shell. He dressed quickly and soon he and Gayle were en route to the hospital. Pam was inconsolable when they arrived. Doug had been trans-ferred to a gurney from the chair by Audrey's bed, and he was surrounded by hos-pital personnel who were doing their best to revive him.

The moment she entered the room, Gayle knew that something else was wrong in addition to the obvious problem with Doug. She surveyed the room, wary that Baker might be lurking somewhere, but all she could perceive was the antiseptic, sucked-dry feeling *the One without a Soul* left behind. Suddenly, she felt a need to be alone, away from the activity that surrounded Doug. She back-tracked into the hallway and stepped quickly into Michael's room, holding up her hand in response to his wordless inquiry. She was there for only a few seconds when she bolted back through the door — although from her perception, it had taken much longer. She had slipped into a trance, similar to the first time Ariel had communicated with her, and the inaudible voice resounded throughout her being as it had then — but this time, it was tinged with a deep concern, bordering on fear.

*Audrey and her child are in grave danger,* Ariel warned. *You must hurry — The One without a Soul poisoned the solution being fed into her veins. She has reached nearly toxic levels — you have only seconds to act! Go now!*

Although Gayle ran as fast as she could, she felt as if she were wading through hip-deep mud. But finally, she reached Audrey's bedside. She grabbed the needle and yanked it out of Audrey's arm, avoiding the few seconds delay that disconnect-ing the drip-line would have taken. She put two fingers in her mouth and released a piercing whistle that brought her the immediate attention of the medical personnel surrounding Doug. "There's nothing you can do for him right now, but this woman has been poisoned! It's in the I.V. bag — she needs your help right now, or she and her baby will both die!"

Fortunately, Gayle's authoritative command brooked no argument. One of the doctors in attendance immediately put a mask connected to an oxygen supply over Audrey's mouth and nose, while a nurse took her pulse and counted the interminable seconds between each breath. "She's almost in cardiac arrest," the nurse reported to the doctor, who asked Gayle, "What kind of poison was it?"

"I don't know — all I know is that you'll be able to save her and her baby if you act quickly!"

The doctor dashed to the phone and alerted the lab to the emergency, then began to wheel Audrey to Intensive Care. Seconds later, Gayle felt Ariel's feathery touch for the split second it took to let her know that all would be well — they had acted in time.

The doctor stared at Gayle as if she was some sort of alien-being after she returned to tell them that the poison had been identified and that Audrey and her baby were safe. "How did you know?" she asked, her eyes narrow with suspicion.

"I'm Fort Bragg's resident psychic, doctor," said Gayle in a serious but warm manner. "To be entirely truthful, an angel came to me and told me about it." Reaching out and placing her hand lightly on the doctors arm, she apologized to Ariel for mis-naming her, while asking her to calm the doctor's wariness. *What makes you think I'm not an angel?* asked Ariel, the tinge of concern and fear that had been in her voice so completely gone that Gayle wondered if she had imagined it.

Under Ariel's influence, the doctor's suspiciousness melted and she shrugged her shoulders, as if deciding that she didn't need a better answer than the one that Gayle had offered. As she lost some of the tension that had marked every aspect of her being, she asked, "Do you have any idea what is wrong with these two? If there's any chance that the condition is communicable, I'm going to have to quarantine all of you, and probably myself and half the hospital as well."

"It's a very rare psychological condition, somewhat akin to mass hysteria," said Larry soothingly, using his status as a psychiatrist to gently lead the doctor down a primrose path. "It's rare, but not unknown in the literature. Unfortunately, there is nothing that we can do but wait. In the meantime, you needn't worry about a quarantine, and I'll be responsible for his care."

The doctor seemed satisfied with Larry's answer, and left to continue the rounds she had abandoned. It wasn't until then that Gayle and Larry finally were able to give their full attention to Pam, who sat withdrawn and grief-stricken in a corner of the room where Adam was doing his best to console her. As Gayle began to reach out to Ariel, she felt the feathery touch once more, *I am already here, daughter, I will do what I can.* After that, with all three of them holding her, Pam began crying silently. Gayle knew that there was nothing more they could do — her own connection to Doug was but a shadow of the one that had just been severed, but she too felt an aching emptiness that mirrored what she had felt when Baker attacked Audrey.

Even Ariel's loving touch scarcely took the edge off of Pam's pain. Through her tears, she spoke haltingly: "How is Ryan able to do it? How is he able to carry on?"

Larry held his spiritual daughter close and stroked her hair as Gayle answered. "Love," she said. "Love is the answer to *all* of our questions."

THE POLICE HAD been summoned because of the attempt on Audrey's life, and they spent much of the morning asking questions, trying to get a lead on a suspect. Adam in particular wanted to implicate Raymond Baker, but the others convinced him it would be futile. Baker didn't fit the description given by the receptionist who had directed him to Audrey's room, and it was likely he would have an iron-clad alibi. Larry insisted that all three of his patients be moved to a single larger room in another part of the hospital, and it was there that the solemn, dispirited group gathered after the police were finally gone. Once again, in spite of all of the precautions they had taken, Baker had been a step ahead of them. They still had hope that Audrey, and now Doug, could find their way back from wherever it was that Baker had sent them. But it was growing dimmer with every hour that passed. No one could think of anything to say and the silence grew heavier the longer it lasted. "I just wish I could think of some way to protect ourselves from another attack," Larry said finally. But I can't think of anything we could have done, except for posting an armed guard outside the door — and what good is that against someone who can strike out just by looking at you?"

"Do you think there's anything we could learn if we returned to our Oglala Sioux lifetimes?" asked Pam. "You and Gayle were powerful shamans, and I was a healer — maybe there's more that our past-selves could teach us."

Gayle lifted her head, and said, "She has a point!" She got out of her chair, and started pacing, suddenly too excited to sit still. "I just thought of something! Larry, think back to the time when we went back to the Oglala lifetime together. Do you remember when I told you your name?"

"As soon as you told me, I knew it was true — *Spirit guide* . It fit like a well-worn shoe."

"What have you learned about the meaning of your name?"

"That I could escort souls from one wheel of life to another — like I did at the Miller Massacre."

"Do you think that there might be more than one meaning to your name? We were both spirit-walkers in that lifetime. Is it possible that you might have known how to guide spirits who had strayed too far back to their bodies?"

Larry brightened. "There's no time like the present to find out," he said. "Now that I know how to take others back to past lives without hypnosis we could be there in a few minutes time.

"Do you think we should go back right now?" Pam asked warily. "What if Baker comes after us while we're all sitting in a trance?"

"Baker probably thinks he's killed Audrey, and he knows what he did to Doug. Besides, Adam was just a baby in that lifetime, so it isn't likely he could access any memories. He and Michael can watch over us here."

"Should I come with you?" asked Pam.

"That's up to you — what do you think?"

"I think I might feel better if I was trying to do something to help Doug come back — Audrey too, of course — if the three of us can go together, I'd like to come."

Larry reached out to both of them, and said, "Very well then. Let's see if *Spirit guide* can live up to his name."

# 12

IT TOOK LONGER THAN THEY HAD HOPED TO FIND THEIR WAY TO the timber harvest area. Altruism had not been the only reason why the old-growth in the Miller tract was the last large stand of virgin forest in Mendocino County — it was damned near inaccessible. The tract straddled the headwaters of two separate watersheds, where over the eons the land had been cut into deep, nearly vertical folds. It took the better part of the morning just to cross one particular watercourse, which, as the crow flies, brought them only a quarter-mile further. The early lumbermen never considered logging these steep, narrow canyons — at the time, there was no way to get the sectioned logs out. Only the advent of modern cable-logging practices, where the sections of redwood, spruce or Douglass fir were removed from above, made logging this part of the Miller tract feasible.

Finally, in the early afternoon, the sounds of human activity began to echo in the distance. Though the logging had been halted, Miller Lumber employees were apparently keeping busy. The volunteers were careful not to get too close, not only for the obvious reason that they would be ejected from the property, but also because the birds they were trying to find would be even more reclusive close to the noise pollution that the recent logging had produced.

They spent the day wandering under the forest canopy, searching the ground under the trees for eggshell fragments, but none were found. As the afternoon wore on, Ben and Steve began to deploy them in pairs, and by six in the evening, they were scattered through the forest, equipped with field-notebooks and compact, lightweight binoculars.

\*       \*       \*

ON ONE LEVEL Gayle and Pam knew that they had never left the hospital room, but the field of vision behind their closed eyelids was now filled with the interior of a buffalo-hide tepee. *Spirit guide* sat before them cross-legged, in a state of deep meditation. Pam rose from where she sat at her father's side, and stepped outside, hoping she might catch a glimpse of Doug, but although he had been her near-constant companion in this lifetime, she saw no sign of him. When she returned to the tepee, *Spirit guide's* eyes were open. He and *Walks unseen* had their heads together and were conversing in low voices. His smile was warm as he greeted her, "We must leave now, daughter. The time has come for you to reunite with your husband, and we cannot do it from here." He took her hand, and the three of them formed a circle. When they opened their eyes Michael and Adam were staring at them expectantly.

"I should have known," began Larry, "that if love is the answer to all of our questions, it would be the answer to this dilemma, too." He squeezed Pam's hand and looked at her. "I have to give credit to you — I would never have divined the technique on my own — the trip back to our Sioux lifetime was essential." He stood up and stretched briefly, and then sat down again, gesturing for Pam to do the same, then took both of her hands in his, and said, "The key is the bond between soul-mates. *The One without a Soul* is capable of severing the connection between the person and their body because the body is only temporary. But the soul-mate connection extends beyond the flesh, beyond the barrier of physical death and between lifetimes. All this time I've been trying to find some connection between Audrey and her body, or between Doug and *his* body. I should have been tracing your soul-mate connections instead."

"But I can't feel the connection myself anymore," said Pam anxiously.

"It's still there," Larry responded reassuringly. "Though there's only a thin tendril where there was once a thick stalk. It's so small in comparison to what it was that you can't perceive it. But don't worry — when we bring Doug back it should be fully restored." They rose together and he led her to the bed where Doug lay, and had her lay beside him and take his hand in hers. He clasped their joined hands in his and said, "I want you to concentrate on your love for Doug — nothing else." Then he closed his eyes, and became very still. Of all who were in the room, only Gayle saw the puma separate itself from his human form, lope across the room and disappear through the wall, as focused on the task at hand as a flesh-and-blood puma in pursuit of its prey. As the others waited and watched, sweat began to bead on Larry's forehead, and he grew more and more pale. Abruptly, he gasped, startling them all. Then he said one word, "Love." A few seconds later, he opened his eyes, took a deep breath, and then squeezed Pam and Doug's hands briefly before releasing them. As he let go, Gayle felt her own connection with Doug spring back into fullness at the same moment that Pam burst into tears of joy and gratitude.

\*     \*     \*

RYAN TOOK THE lightweight pair of Leitz binoculars away from his eyes after scanning the limbs of all the trees within viewing distance of his observation post. Megan Berry, an ABC rider who was an elementary school teacher on her summer break, continued to scan the canopy above them. She and Ryan had done little more than kill time all afternoon, but as dusk came on and sightings of either bird became more likely, they increased their vigilance. Megan kept her field-glasses focused on the limbs above one-hundred-fifty feet, but below the crowns of the trees, where they were most likely to spot Marbled Murrelet activity. They also listened carefully, hoping to hear the whoops and shrieks made by the spotted owl or the distinctive Marbled Murrelet call, wing-beats and "jet-sounds" that they could count just as legitimately as a visual sighting. For the next hour, until it was completely dark, they were as quiet and still as they could be, but to no avail — at least for tonight, they had come up empty handed.

*    *    *

"HE WILL SLEEP now — probably through the night," said Larry. "More than anything else, he needs rest."

"Then I'm going to rest with him," said Pam, as she climbed onto the narrow hospital bed, raised the rail so that she wouldn't fall out, and snuggled up beside her soul-mate. "Being upset and worried is exhausting — I think I need sleep even more than he does."

"Will you be able to help Audrey too?" asked Adam.

"I should, but I have to wait until Ryan comes back," Larry answered. "The connection runs between the two of them."

"Are you serious when you say that you can leave your bodies and travel to distant places?" asked Michael incredulously. "I've heard you talk about it, and I just saw you sit without moving a muscle for half an hour, but I thought you were just being allegorical."

"We've done it on a number of occasions," said Larry. "We assume the shape of our totem animals — in my case, a puma, and in Gayle's case, a raven. She was with you the first time you were in the courtroom, and was able to divert Baker from his first attack on Audrey."

Michael stared at him with rapt attention. "Why haven't you mentioned this before?"

"There are some aspects to this conflict that are unexplained," Gayle replied. "For some reason there is a limit to what everyone in our group other than Larry and I can perceive and comprehend, or in some situations, what they remember after the fact."

"There are rules to this conflict — like it's some sort of game?" Michael asked, much to Larry and Gayle's surprise.

"You're still tracking this, aren't you?" asked Gayle. "What did we just talk about?"

Michael looked amused, but repeated back everything that had been said, verbatim.

"This is great!" said Gayle. "You can't imagine how frustrated Larry and I have been, keeping all of this to ourselves. We never thought we would be able to share any of it with anyone. Watch, I'll give you an example." She turned to Adam, who was sitting within easy listening distance a few feet away. "Adam, I was just telling Michael about the how none of you are allowed to know the full story about what's going on in our conflict with *The One without a Soul*."

Adam's expression glazed over as Gayle spoke. When she finished, he shook his head, as if to clear it. "I'm sorry Gayle, I must have spaced-out for a minute there. What did you say?"

She patted him on the knee, saying, "It was nothing important — don't worry." Then she turned back to Michael. "Do you see what I mean?"

"Incredible!"

Larry tilted his head back and cupped his chin in his hand. "When I stop to think about it, the advanced spirits told us that only Gayle and I, *of the members of our company* would be allowed to be aware of what was really going on. You must not be subject to the rules because you haven't been aligned with us against *The One without a Soul* prior to this lifetime."

Gayle pulled her chair closer to Michael's bed. "I'm going to tell you what's *really* been going on," she said. "Listen carefully, because there *will* be a quiz at the end — just to see if there are any limits about what you are allowed to know."

They spent the next hour filling him in on all that had happened since the conflict had first begun. As they spoke, Adam interacted with the three of them sporadically without paying any attention to what Larry and Gayle were telling Michael. The two of them had gotten used to the phenomenon, which was very much as if they were speaking in a foreign language part of the time, but Michael continued to marvel. "I guess this isn't any stranger than anything else that's happened lately, and it explains a lot," he remarked after hearing them out. "It does put just a bit more pressure on us, though, doesn't it?"

"The fact that Ariel won't be allowed to come unless we succeed?" Gayle asked, "I suppose you could call it additional pressure. You could also call it an added incentive. If we don't succeed, then we assume that life will continue as we have always known it — no one will know the difference. On the other hand, if we succeed, the feminine equivalent of a Mohammed or Buddha will be born." She grinned impishly at Michael. "You call that pressure? I always heard you were a cool customer under fire."

He laughed, and said, "Give me a break! The two of you have had time to get used to the idea. This is pretty hard to integrate into my world view. An hour ago, I had no idea that the two of you were prophets on the order of Moses or Elijah, or that Audrey might be this century's equivalent of Mary, mother of God." He let his head fall back on his pillow, and stared at the ceiling briefly, then turned back to them. "I just thought of a way to use your spirit-walking abilities to our advantage. Do you think you could send your totem out to the Miller tract?"

"Of course."

"Would you have any trouble spirit-walking at night?"

"Not in the least."

Michael pointed to the clock on the wall. "Right now there's a good window of opportunity to look for spotted owls and Marbled Murrelets. Dawn and dusk are the most active times for both species."

"Unfortunately, I don't have a clue about what a Spotted Owl looks like — or a Marbled Murrelet for that matter," said Gayle.

"I believe that all of the seminar materials are still at Project HOPE," said Adam, having momentarily tuned in to their conversation. "Is there any reason you need to see them tonight?  We could call and see if someone could bring them here — but what's the point?"

"I'm going to need them to do some trial preparation," Michael replied smoothly, "go ahead and make the call if you would."

An hour and a half later, after a Project HOPE volunteer dropped off the materials, Michael gave Gayle a crash course on how to identify the birds.  When she was done, she went to the motel to snatch a few hours sleep with plans for a very busy morning.

# 13

RAYMOND BAKER KEPT HIS RADIO TUNED TO KNZI ALL DAY. THE station had changed its entire format to news-radio following his elaborately-orchestrated sacrifice of Eddie Rapski. But no mention was made of the *bitch's* death — or the *watcher's* strange state of unconsciousness. After the Miller Massacre, everything having *anything* to do with Project HOPE's lawsuit and the people involved in it was newsworthy in general, and at KNZI, newsworthy by his command. He struggled with the unthinkable. Could he have failed to kill the *bitch*?

As the afternoon wore on, he gradually had to accept that the unthinkable must have happened. Had the poison been detected, or had it just been luck? So far the *bitch* had enjoyed far more than her share of that! Her body should have expired when he banished her soul and sent her car tumbling down the side of the mountain — but there hadn't been a mark on her when he'd seen her in her hospital bed. How he wished he had been free to smash her face beyond recognition! *How many more of them are there?* he wondered. It seemed as though a new *enemy* appeared every day or two. It had started with the raven and the puma — he was sure now that those were some kind of projections or holograms with people behind them. Then he had encountered the *bitch* and the weakling. Then Stratton — the pain in his stomach flared thinking of that bastard — and now there was the *watcher*. Baker smiled in spite of his pain, reflecting that this new *enemy* wouldn't have any opportunity to give him any grief now that he'd been gutted of his life-force. But the mere act of thinking of his *enemies* made him feel absolutely *compelled* to leap back into action against them, to take them all out *now!* It was all he could do to keep from returning to Ukiah Valley Medical Center to finish the job. *Control,* he said to himself over and over again like a mantra. Control and will-power were what made him what he was. But how good it would feel to let some of that control go! What a rush it would be to just give in to the increasingly powerful urges he was feeling — to inflict the same kind of physical damage on the rest of his *enemies* as he had on the souls of the *bitch* and the *watcher*. *I need to wait until after the trial,* he said to himself. First destroy what they love — then destroy them. But he wondered — and for once he was not certain. Would he be able to hold himself back?

\*    \*    \*

GAYLE SPED THROUGH the pre-dawn darkness at a velocity completely at odds with her measured wing-beats. It took much less out of her to travel in this slower, more relaxed fashion than when she was forced by circumstances to traverse broad distances and arrive almost instantaneously at her destination. A pink glow was just starting to light the horizon as she reached the Miller Tract, and underneath her, the area where the logging had commenced was dimly visible, looking as if some malevolent giant had taken a number of swipes with an immense pickaxe, tearing ragged holes in the otherwise-unbroken green carpet. She dove below the canopy formed by the upper branches, and following her psychic connection to Ryan, quickly honed in on the group of observers. He and the other volunteers were gathered together around a small camp-stove drinking from steaming metal cups. She would have liked to stop to listen to their conversation to see if they had encountered any of the birds they were trying to find, but there wasn't time — sunrise was only minutes away.

"You'll be most likely to see them during the first hour and a half after sunrise," Michael had instructed. "The male and the female change places at about that time — the one that's been sitting on the nest heads back out to sea and vise versa. That's when you need to keep your eyes peeled." He studied her curiously for a moment. "Will the Marbled Murrelets be able to see your totem?

"I wouldn't know," Gayle replied. "Among humans, only Baker, Larry and I seem to have that ability. Does it make a difference?" He chuckled. "It's a little ironic, considering that you're trying to save them, but ravens, crows and jays are primary predators of the Marbled Murrelet. They feed on both eggs and hatchlings — fewer than half of the eggs mature into adults. If there are any Marbled Murrelets out there, *and* they are able to see you, their first instinct will be to lead you *away* from their nesting areas."

At the edge of the old growth, Gayle began flying in wide, slow circles, keeping her attention focused westward — if there were any Marbled Murrelets, that was where they would appear. She said a silent prayer to Ariel solely to comfort herself — she knew that there was nothing the spirit could do. Yet, as if in answer to her prayer, her raven's vision, far superior to that of a human, picked up six small dots approaching from the west. Back in the hospital room, her heartbeat accelerated — from excitement rather than exertion. She arrowed towards them, faster than any corporeal raven could possibly fly, and as she closed the distance, the small dots swam into focus. She had seen quite a few miracles lately, but none of them were more impressive than the six Marbled Murrelets, none of which took any notice of her whatsoever.

THE MORNING'S PRECIOUS observation period had been fruitless, and the volunteers decided to move on. They hiked through the middle of the day, to an area further from the noise and disruption contributed by the recently-halted logging — both of the species they hoped to sight tended to abandon nests near logging areas. After making their way cross-country for several hours, Ben and Steve began deploying the volunteers in pairs.

*    *    *

"HOW ARE WE going to get this information to the observers so that they'll know where to go?" Gayle asked Michael. "I can't convey information while I'm spirit-walking. I've been able to affect emotions, and I've acted as a channel for Ariel, but direct communication is beyond me — except with Larry when he's spirit-walking with me. Did any of them take a cell-phone along?"

"I doubt it," said Michael. "That area is too remote for cell-phones, anyway. You have to be close to a transmitter, and the phone companies don't put those out in the middle of nowhere."

"Do you have any other suggestions?"

"Maybe there's someone in the Anonymous Bike Club who didn't go on the ride, but knows the way out there," Michael speculated. "We could call the Willits Cycle Center and see if there might be someone who could go in and find them."

When Michael placed the phone call, he found that the solution was much simpler than he and Gayle had anticipated. Although cell-phones wouldn't work, one of the ABC riders had taken a two-way radio with him so that the observers could communicate with the outside world. In order to conserve batteries and keep their noise levels down, they were making transmissions on a predetermined schedule, the next one only forty-five minutes away.

*    *    *

RYAN HAD BEEN swapping attorney stories with Eric Frye, one of the ABC riders, and a fellow lawyer, when he heard the sound of people talking and moving through the forest near their observation post. He was surprised to see Ben, Steve and another ABC rider tromping through the underbrush in their direction. As soon as they were in comfortable speaking range, he hailed them to ask what was going on.

"We just got an unusual radio transmission," said Ben. He gestured to the ABC rider. "Boulder-Dave and his radio are our link to the outside in case something goes wrong. We've been checking in at regular intervals, and during the last transmission, there was a message from a woman named Gayle. She said that she could give us the map coordinates where we would find Marbled Murrelets, and said that you would vouch for her."

Ryan hooted loudly and punched a fist into the air. "Great! How far is it?"

Steve was wary. "You really think she knows where a cluster of Marbled Murrelets might be, even if she's never been out here?" he asked, his expression conveying his obvious disbelief.

"I'd bet my life on it." Ryan assured him. "Gayle is a psychic, and she's the real deal — don't ask me how she knows things but she does! If she says she can pinpoint where we're supposed to look, I can guarantee we'll get results. Besides, we haven't had any luck anywhere else."

"I hope you're right," said Steve. "The map coordinates are for the most re-

- 278 -

mote and inaccessible section of the timber harvest area." He looked around for a good place to spread out his topographical map. "We're here," he said, pointing to a spot and then tracing a triangle. "This is where our bikes are, and this is where she told us to go."

Eric squatted down and examined the map. "It's not even as far to where the birds are nesting as we've already come."

"It doesn't seem like much in a straight line." Steve continued. "But look at how wide the contour lines are where we've already been. As you can see, there was only one place that was really vertical, back at Faram Creek, where the contour lines are spaced tightly. Check out the contour lines in the area between where she wants us to go and where we are now."

Eric whistled softly, "They're as tight as they were at Faram Creek the entire distance — it must be practically straight up and down between here and there."

"I wouldn't have even considered trying to go there because of the difficulty, and our time limitations," Ben stated flatly. "But if Ryan is really convinced that this woman knows what she says she knows . . ."

Ryan interjected: "She does — I'd bet my life on it."

"Then its worth the effort," Ben finished. He rolled up his map and stood up. "The big question is whether or not we're going to be able to get in there, collect the data we need and get out in time for Ryan to make it to court on Monday." He favored Ryan with an evil grin. "I think you're going to find that this hike makes that mountain-bike ride we took out of Healdsburg seem like a walk in the park. Gather up your things. We've got a long day ahead of us. We'll need to round up the others and get going as soon as we can." He started to leave, and then turned back to face Ryan once again. "I almost forgot to tell you — Gayle said to tell you that they've found a way to bring Audrey home, but it has to wait until you get back."

Ryan gasped in excitement, and started to ask questions, but Ben cut him off, and said, "I'm sorry Ryan, that's all she told me — you'll have to wait for the next scheduled radio transmission." He looked at his watch. "That's in three hours."

*　　*　　*

PAM HAD RISEN from her spot in Doug's bed half an hour before he stirred. She and the others were gathered around him in a circle watching him the moment he opened his eyes. He blinked a few times, and then looked at the faces arrayed around his bed in turn. When he came to Pam, she leaned over and kissed him, and said, "Welcome home, darling," then threw her arms around him and burst into tears of gratitude. When she finally raised herself up, keeping one of his hands firmly in hers, Doug still hadn't said a word, and Larry began to be concerned. Doug saw his apprehension and reached out with his free hand to take Larry's. At last he broke his silence. "It seemed like forever," he said falteringly. "But she told me that if I kept love in my heart, eventually you would come for me — and you did!"

Gayle perked up. "*Who* told you to hold love in your heart?"

"She didn't say her name," said Doug. "She just told me that she was a friend, and not to worry."

"Let's start from the beginning," said Larry. "Do you feel up to telling us what happened — how much you remember?"

Doug seemed to stare off into nothingness for a moment. "*The One without a Soul* cut my spirit from my body and cast it adrift," he said with an effort, his flat monotone conveying the bleakness of the experience. "I couldn't find my way back no matter how hard I tried." Then his eyes came back into focus. "It would have been much worse except that *she* helped me — she put her own tether on me and kept me from blowing away like a kite with a broken string."

"What did this friend look like?" asked Adam, who, along with Pam, was hanging on every word. Larry, Michael and Gayle knew who the *friend* had to be — their question was *why* Ariel had been allowed to interfere.

"I didn't actually see her," said Doug. "There was just a voice that seemed to come from everywhere all at the same time. She never left me — just waited with me in a place where there was nothing — no sight, no smells, no sounds — nothing. I have absolutely no idea how long I was there — I would have guessed months or years except for the fact that we're still here in the hospital."

"It's nine o'clock Thursday morning," Larry informed him. "You've been back in your body for perhaps fourteen hours. Baker attacked you about three o'clock Wednesday morning, so you were only in the place you described for about eighteen hours."

Doug looked shocked. "Is that all? It seemed like an eternity — even with *her* there." He sat up in bed and saw that Audrey still lay in the bed next to his. "I feel so sorry for Audrey," he murmured. "She's been gone so long . . . "

"We'll get her back, too," said Gayle, "as soon as Ryan returns."

"What's stopping you from bringing her back right now?"

"There's a connection between soul-mates that I've learned how to follow," said Larry. "I found you by tracing it from Pam to you. I can't find Audrey until Ryan gets back from the Miller tract. When he does, I'll trace the soul-mate connection from his spirit to Audrey's."

"That shouldn't be too long now," said Gayle. "I have a very strong feeling that they're going to get lucky today."

*     *     *

THEY MADE IT, although most of the time it seemed like a death-march. Ryan was pressed closer to his physical limits than he cared to go, but just as the light began to fail, they reached the area that corresponded to the coordinates Gayle had given them. It was on the headwaters of a branch of Deer Creek, as far from the area where the logging had commenced as it could be and still be within the Timber Harvest Area. Ben Meyers pointed out that Raymond Baker's greed had ended up working against him — if Miller Lumber had filed a Timber Harvest Plan that was less ambitious, it wouldn't have included the area. They crawled into their sleeping bags as soon as they could after wolfing down a quick meal. None of them noticed how hard the ground was that night.

Before dawn, they were once again gathered around their tiny camp-stove, drinking coffee and eating granola. The trees were huge here — one lofty giant easily topping three-hundred-seventy-five feet. The bases of the older, thicker trees were scarred and blackened from fires, while the younger trees had the characteristic silvery-red bark that was usually associated with old-growth redwoods.

As they walked through the grove, Ryan kept his gaze focused upward, and his ears alert. Even so, he almost missed the "keer" sound of a Marbled Murrelet calling, followed by the "jet" sound produced by their steep dives. He looked up at just the right time to see four of the birds outlined against the sky as they dove under the higher branch levels to the middle layer of the forest canopy, then circling before landing in the middle branches of several trees, their wings making the same distinctive sound that Ryan had heard on Ben Meyer's tape.

"Four," said Ben with a satisfied smile as he pointed to the location of each in turn. "The circling behavior is a strong indicator that this is nesting habitat. The diving is another indicator. Be sure to make a note of it in your field notebooks."

Several of the volunteers searched under the trees where the birds had landed. They were rewarded when they found shell fragments under two of the trees, which were carefully collected, bagged and marked. They spread out in pairs throughout the grove, and spent the rest of the morning gathering data. The mood everywhere was festive. Ryan hadn't felt this light-hearted since he was getting ready to barbeque for his friends and fiancé. The evidence they'd located should allow them to obtain a permanent injunction! But foremost on his mind, making him check his watch every few minutes, was the thought that as soon as he got back to Ukiah, Larry would be able to trace his way to Audrey and bring her back! The day before, when they had radioed in during their cross-country marathon, Gayle told him about Baker's attack on Doug and Larry's new-found ability to follow the soul-mate connection. Now, as he waited for them to head for home, it seemed that the seconds and minutes had never taken so long to pass.

# 14

"WHO GIVES A SHIT ANYWAY?" RAYMOND BAKER MUTTERED AS HE lit his tenth cigarette of the day. It was afternoon, and he was working on his fourth brandy, hoping that the cigarettes and liquor would distract him from the compulsion to drive to Ukiah and deal with his *enemies* permanently. *It would be no problem to lay my hands on a suitable firearm,* he thought to himself an instant after swearing that he would leave such thoughts behind. But guns were noisy, and no matter how hard he tried, he couldn't think of a way to make a clean get-away if he opened fire at the hospital. Abruptly he punched a button on his intercom and instructed his receptionist that he wasn't to be interrupted for any reason. Then he locked the door and laid out half a gram of cocaine on his mirror. He chopped it fine and divided it into ten huge lines — each one being more than equal to what had been his daily allotment until a few days before. *I wonder what I thought the big deal was about this shit,* he said to himself as he snorted the first line. *Cocaine doesn't make me lose control, it puts me in control.* Once again his mind bounced back to a mental picture of obliterating the *bitch's* face with a burst of automatic-weapon fire. As he pictured the bullets tearing into her face, he started to get aroused, and his erection spurred even more violent fantasies about how he would defile the *bitch*, and give her what she had coming to her.

Abruptly, he snorted half of what lay on the mirror with quick strokes of his straw across the polished surface, then poured what remained into a glass vial. The time for generosity was over! It was increasingly obvious that the *bitch* had to die, and she had to die *now!* There wasn't anything to think about or decide — it was time for action! His mood soared — never in his wildest imagination had he conceived of how good it would feel to give in completely to his urges, forsaking the absolute control that had dominated every aspect of his life for so long. He could already smell the acrid odor of burnt gunpowder, mixed with the coppery scent of fresh blood that would fill the air in just a few short hours.

\*     \*     \*

"DO YOU HAVE any idea why Ariel was allowed to interfere with the dispersion of Doug's soul?" Gayle asked. She and Larry were huddled in quiet conversation with Michael while Adam was giving Audrey a massage to help keep her circulation moving and prevent bedsores. Pam and Doug were sitting together on the other side of the room, speaking in undertones, basking in their renewed appreciation of that which had been stolen from them and then, blissfully, restored.

"I haven't a clue," Larry answered, "I was going to ask you the same thing. I thought she couldn't get that directly involved. My only guess is that maybe *The One without a Soul* went past some limitation himself, and that his actions freed her and allowed her to bring things back into balance."

"That's as good a guess as any," said Gayle. "Maybe she'll see fit to tell me sometime — like she did about the poison."

No sooner had she spoken these words than Gayle felt Ariel's feathery touch. As before, the 'voice' seemed to reverberate through her entire being.

*The One without a Soul has indeed gone past the limitations that the Divinity intended. The divinity's plan is to experience this world through us, not to experience a small part of its own obliteration.*

"How is it that Baker can do something outside of the rules?"

*It is beyond my ability to comprehend the limits or limitlessness of the Divinity, just as it is beyond yours. I am a part of humanity, and no more a part of the divinity than you. But rest assured that the fact that I was allowed to intervene is proof that his action was outside of the rules of the game I described.*

"This doesn't mean that we should be any less wary of Baker, does it?"

*Far from it, daughter. You are more at risk than ever before. The fact that The One without a Soul has acquired a new, unauthorized weapon indicates that he is receiving assistance from some unknown source. The task that still lies before you — the one that you must accomplish in order for me to be allowed to take Audrey and Ryan as my earthly parents, is to hold love in your hearts as you struggle against The One without a Soul. And you must outlive him! Killing you in an ordinary way is not only allowed by the "rules," it is an imperative that drives him. It has driven him during all of the lifetimes that this conflict has been played out.*

*Physical death is but a gateway to the next plane of existence — but this other thing he did to Audrey and to Doug is an abomination. I do not know all of the ramifications, but it is clear that it would interrupt the natural progression from one life to the next. By severing the connection between body and soul before death, The One without a Soul has managed to cast Doug and Audrey's spirits adrift. If I hadn't intervened, I don't know if they could ever have been found.*

"It sounds like you are describing ghosts — restless spirits unable to find peace and rest," said Gayle.

*How the phenomenon is described is not important. You must beware. The One without a Soul is relentless. He will never stop — he <u>cannot ever</u> stop until all of you are dead.*

As the feathery touch of the spirit's presence lifted, Gayle became aware that her conversation with the spirit had taken only a split second. "Whoa, guys, she said. "Ariel's just been and gone. I've got some answers to the questions I was just asking." She told Michael and Larry the gist of the discussion she had just had.

"You talked about all of that in the space of one second?" asked Michael, amazed.

"After a while, you get used to this sort of thing," said Larry with a wry grin.

"I'll try to get used to it, too." said Michael. Then a strange expression crossed his face. "You know, that brief mention of 'ghosts' that you touched on makes me think of something else," he said.

"What is that?"

"Vampire legends — no, hear me out!" he said when they looked at him askance. "I'm not saying that Raymond Baker is going to come in here and try to drink our blood, or that he's one of the undead." He scratched his chin thoughtfully. "The part that I happened to think of is the vampire's aversion to mirrors — and that led to another thought. We've determined that Baker's method of attack comes through eye contact with his victims. I wonder if it would provide any protection to us at all if we wore mirrored sunglasses. Maybe he couldn't use his powers if he couldn't actually see our eyes."

"It seems wise to add that to our list of precautions," Gayle replied. "We should do any-and-everything that occurs to us to try to protect ourselves. You never know whether some random thought might really be a communication from the advanced spirits." She glanced around the room. "It's bright enough in here that we can wear sunglasses all of the time, and if they protect us from an attack — great! If not, we've lost nothing." She looked at Adam, who had been tracking this part of the conversation. "Why don't you and I run over to the drugstore down the street to see if they've got any."

"You're on," he replied.

"You two take care, Pam admonished. "We don't know of any soul-mates for the two of you, so it would be awfully hard for Larry to find you."

"We'll keep a sharp lookout," said Adam as they walked through the door. "And you be on the lookout too — he was able to get to us here before!"

THEY DIDN'T FIND any mirror-lensed sunglasses at the first three stores they tried. As they left the third one, Adam said, "We should find a backpacking shop. Mirror lenses on sunglasses go in and out of style, and it's obvious that they're out of style right now. But I know I've seen them in outdoor-adventure stores — they're used for expeditions to snowy regions."

"Do you know where to find a backpacking store in Ukiah?"

"Not off the top of my head — but there's one in Healdsburg that's open evenings during the summer. Why don't we drive down there, rather than running around Ukiah trying to find stores that will probably end up being closed. We'd probably save time in the long run, and besides, I need a break from sitting in those hospital rooms."

\*　　　\*　　　\*

EVENING AND THE twilight hours brought six more observations, all based on the distinctive Marbled Murrelet cries and the noises their short heavy bodies and rapidly beating wings made as they whirred through the air — almost like huge, feathered bumble-bees. After dark, the field-data was carefully compiled by flashlight-beam, and stowed in waterproof pouches.

With no significant hiking that day, they had all been able to rest their tired bodies. Ryan had even taken a nap in the early afternoon when no Marbled Murrelet activity was expected, but after the previous day's Herculean effort, he was still ready to sleep soon after sundown. As he waited for slumber to overtake him, his thought were never far from Audrey, and he concentrated on the warm glow of his love for her with all of his being. For the moment, it was enough.

*　　*　　*

RAYMOND BAKER'S AUTOMATIC rifle was nestled in the trunk of his Mercedes as he hurtled north on Highway 101 through gathering dusk. He reached into his pocket and retrieved the glass vial that contained the last remnants of his cocaine, and steered with his knee for a moment while he poured the white powder into the cap, and then quickly snorted it. Then he lit a cigarette — the third one out of his second pack that day. He let the smoke stream slowly out of his nostrils and savored the combined effect of the nicotine and the cocaine. But the effect of the drugs was nothing compared to the rush he felt just anticipating the sight of the *bitch's* blood spattering the white bed sheets and hospital walls. He looked down at his speedometer, and lifted his foot slightly. He hadn't intended to be going eighty-five miles-per-hour in a sixty-five zone — not when he had a loaded AR-15 in the trunk and drugs and alcohol in his bloodstream. As the car slowed to the legal limit, the dark-green signs on the side of the highway informed him that he was in Santa Rosa — only fifty miles to go. Anticipation made his foot grow heavy once more, and without realizing it, he was soon rocketing along at close to ninety miles-per-hour. He had just passed through Healdsburg, when the California Highway Patrol cruiser moved out from its place of concealment behind an earthen berm on the verge of the roadway. When Baker saw the red and blue lights oscillating in his rear-view mirror, he looked down and was startled to see that he was once again well over the speed limit. "This could complicate things," he said aloud as he pulled to the shoulder of the road. In his rear view mirror, he saw the officer open the door of his cruiser, step out and begin walking towards him.

GAYLE AND ADAM were almost to Healdsburg when Adam began to feel fearful and anxious — an echo of the way he'd felt in the courtroom when Baker walked through the doors — though not nearly as strong. "Gayle, I think Baker might be near — suddenly I feel scared!"

Gayle had begun to sense danger a moment before Adam spoke. "I feel it too," she said. She closed her eyes and reached out. She could perceive him hurtling towards them, then slowing and stopping directly in front of them. "He's coming the other way on the freeway in front of us," she said. "But he just stopped."

They were on a long, straight stretch of road. In the distance, Adam saw the overhead-lights of a California Highway Patrol cruiser flashing red and blue on the margin of the northbound lanes. "There!" he said urgently. "The CHP just pulled him over!" As they drew closer, he saw two black cars — the CHP cruiser and a Mercedes Benz.

Suddenly, Gayle spoke quickly and with an unmistakable tone of command. "I'm going to go into a trance — don't try to disturb me, I'll come out of it in a few minutes. You need to take the first Healdsburg exit, and then double back. Don't worry about the speed limit either." With that, she closed her eyes and became as still as death. Unseen by Adam, her totem leapt into flight and bore straight towards the Mercedes, arriving just after the Highway Patrol officer slumped to the pavement. With the unique perceptive abilities she possessed while she was in the form of her totem, she felt the echoes of the officer's anguish as his spirit dispersed into the ether, sucked out through the doorway to his soul. The raven swooped towards the open window of the Mercedes, and flew straight at Baker's surprised-looking face. Her piercing caw reverberated ear-splittingly loud within the confines of the car, then she abruptly pulled up and snapped back to her own body.

Adam had taken the offramp at the north edge of town, crossed over the freeway, and was just coming down the on-ramp when Gayle stirred again. The flashing lights of the patrol car were about a quarter of a mile ahead of them. She reached out for his arm, and was about to tell him to slow down when they both saw the Mercedes take off in front of them, leaving a cloud of black smoke and the stench of burned rubber behind. When they came abreast of the patrol car, Adam, who was still reacting strongly to Baker's presence, suggested that they stop to see if they could help. Gayle pointed at the dwindling shape of the Mercedes. *"He's headed towards Ukiah, and he's not dropping in for a social call. Someone with a cell-phone will report the officer's condition — a cop lying beside the highway won't go unnoticed."*

Adam put his foot to the floor, and did his best to keep up with the Mercedes, while trying to suppress his fear. "He must have done the same thing to the Highway Patrolman that he did to Audrey and Doug," he said through gritted teeth as they began to close on Baker.

"I'm sure that he did," agreed Gayle. In front of them, the Mercedes was slowed for a few moments by a tightly-bunched group of cars, and they were able to close to within a few car-lengths. Adam was careful to position his Honda so that there were always several cars between them and the Mercedes. Suddenly, the Mercedes cut across the grass-covered median between the north and south lanes in an illegal U-turn, fishtailing and throwing up a thick cloud of dust. Adam watched the car recede in his rear-view mirror, and emitted a huge sigh of relief.

"It looks like we've got some breathing room,"he said. "I wonder what made him turn around?"

"Maybe he figured out that the Highway Patrolman would have called in his license number before he ever got out of his cruiser," Gayle speculated. She looked at her watch. "Take the next off-ramp and double back to Healdsburg — I still want to stop at that backpacking store."

A mile down the road, Adam found an overcrossing and turned back towards

Healdsburg. All told, no more than ten minutes had passed since they first became aware of Baker's approach. As they reached the fallen police officer, they saw that several cars had stopped and people were standing over him. Traffic had already backed up in both directions. After they cleared the congested area, Adam took the second Healdsburg exit and made his way to "The Northern Exposure," a store that catered to backpackers, runners and cross-country skiers. They bought the store's entire stock of mirror-lensed sunglasses, and left behind a mystified sales clerk as they headed back to Ukiah.

"I can't ever remember seeing a Highway Patrolman who wasn't wearing sunglasses, and the sun was getting low in the sky," mused Adam as they poked along in the heavy traffic that had backed up all of the way to Healdsburg. There was an ambulance on the scene now, as well as several more patrol cars. "Did you happen to notice if this one was wearing them?" Gayle knew that Adam was referring to the time that they had passed the fallen officer while they were trying to follow Baker — he had already forgotten her trance just prior to that time.

"He was," she replied, recalling every detail of the Highway Patrolman's slack face as he lay on the pavement beside Baker's Mercedes, including his sightless eyes behind the light, smoke-colored lenses of his sunglasses. "But they didn't have mirror-coated lenses," she added. We still won't know if they'll do any good unless one of us is in the line of fire."

*     *     *

THE PAIN IN Baker's stomach eased incrementally as each mile of his taxi-ride home ticked by. It was the pain that had finally brought him to his senses, waking him to the realization that his actions were tantamount to suicide. For the first time in his life, he felt real fear, and ironically, it was himself he was afraid of. When he finally wrenched himself back under control and examined his thought processes and his behavior throughout the day, he was as close to terrified as his icy disposition allowed. He couldn't believe the number of violations of his own personal code he had committed in one day! He had ripped the soul from the Highway Patrolman without thinking — in spite of the fact that there wasn't a cop on any police force *anywhere* that he couldn't have intimidated into letting him go with just a warning. But instead he'd used his *weapon*, giving in to the desire for instant gratification. Now he had to establish an alibi and file a stolen vehicle report for the Mercedes. Arching over all of the other foolishness was the fact that he had given in to his desire to rip the *bitch's* face apart with the bullets from his automatic rifle. He might as well have gone down to the police station and confessed to every crime he had ever committed, then led them to where the dead bodies lay rotting in their graves! And for what? So that he could erase the last vestiges of life from the body of someone who was already as good as dead? He had been out of his mind! The randomness that had begun to creep into his life when the fucking puma and raven had shown up was no longer an exciting diversion. And why did the raven show up an instant after he'd stripped the CHP officer of his soul? How had it known where he was? Were his *enemies* following *him*? The pain in his stomach had begun to rage as soon as the cop began to walk towards him — and so far it had only flared into agony when one of *them* was near. The pain had grown in intensity until the fucking bird popped out of thin air, cawing in his face so loudly and suddenly that he thought his heart would stop.

He took several deep breaths. He needed to regroup. After this lawsuit was behind him and the logging operation back on track, there would be plenty of time and opportunity to deal with his *enemies*. *Control.* he said to himself. *I must* stay in control!

# 15

THE MARBLED MURRELET OBSERVATION TEAM, AS THEY HAD begun to refer to themselves, reached their bicycles late Friday afternoon. Yet another nesting sight had been discovered during the first hour after dawn, after which they stowed all of their gear, and by seven in the morning they were on their way out. They decided to take the same route back as they had taken coming in, although it required them to travel several miles further than a straighter route. But retracing their steps presented them with obstacles they knew they could conquer — and much more of the route was downhill on the way out than it had been on the way in. Two days rest had alleviated virtually all of Ryan's stiffness and soreness, and as he swung into the saddle, he found it actually felt good to pedal his bike — even after a full-day's rigorous hike. He was noticeably stronger on the climbs coming out. Their packs were much lighter, and he was fairly sure that he'd lost a few pounds, but most of his enhanced physical prowess was just the result of hard exercise followed by rest. And with his spirits buoyed by the thought of being with his love again, he almost floated up the hills. *I can't start celebrating too soon,* he thought as he steered around a large rock, then shifted his weight back to keep the bike balanced as he eased down a steep section of old logging road. *There are still miles to go and the legal proceedings are still ahead.*

They reached the clearing where they had camped on the first night of their expedition just as the sun was going down. The atmosphere around the bonfire they built that night was jubilant, fueled in part by several cases of beer packed in by some of the ABC gang who had not been able to get away for the mission to the old growth. There was still a lot left to accomplish, but as he drifted off to sleep that evening, Ryan dared to hope that the pendulum might have reached the end of its swing and started back in their direction.

\*　　\*　　\*

MICHAEL PAUSED IN his dictation for a moment, staring out the window as he took a short break from the preparation of the list of questions Ryan would be using at trial. Fortunately, he had plenty of experience from which to draw. He and Ben had covered almost identical ground during their previous trials together. The tricky part of this lawsuit was that none of the pleadings filed so far made any mention of the evidence they intended to introduce. When the suit had been filed, they thought they would be attacking falsified field-study data. Now, they intended to put on an altogether different case — including testimony that there actually *were* Marbled Murrelets nesting within the old-growth encompassed by Miller's Timber Harvest Plan. Heath Waterman would cry foul, of course. Michael chuckled as he thought about what Waterman's argument would be if he had to stick to the truth. *Your honor, you simply can't let this evidence in! We've had no notice that the plaintiffs were going to go behind our backs — to trespass in order to find that there are protected species out there! If we had known they were going to do that, my client would have gone out and killed the birds off, just like he killed all the witnesses who could have testified that his field-studies had been faked!*

*       *       *

RAYMOND BAKER PACED back and forth in his office and wondered if he was losing his mind. *How could this be happening to* me*?* he asked himself again and again. It took every ounce of his determination to keep from driving to the hastily rented storage locker in Santa Rosa where he had stashed his automatic rifle, and finishing what he had started out to do the day before. Insanity! Suicide! But the obsession persisted. He had been careful to leave the cocaine and alcohol alone, knowing that if he indulged, he would be off and running again. What was it about these people? What in the world could be causing this *need* to kill them? He had always enjoyed killing, starting with the day he murdered his parents in a scheme so brilliantly clever that no one had ever suspected that he might be the culprit. Killing people while arranging to appear blameless had become one of his most pleasant diversions — a game that never seemed to grow old or stale. It was especially delicious when he had the opportunity to let his victims catch a glimpse of their imminent fate, so that he could drink in their terror. But he had always been in *control*! He looked at his face in the mirror mounted above the wet bar, and saw a haunted expression that had never been there before. It was the face of a *fool!* The face of a man who was *out of control!* Even now, as he stared at his face in the mirror, he could feel the cocaine beckoning. He held himself in check, although it took a herculean effort. One line would lead to the next, and then he would be balancing the cocaine with ever-increasing amounts of brandy. Where had *that* sudden switch come from? He had drunk nothing but single-malt Scotch whiskey for as long as he could remember. For two days though, nothing but brandy appealed to him. He sat back down at his desk and put his head in his hands. This had to be some kind of test. His destiny had not brought him to his exalted position in life just so that he could be brought low by foolishness. "All right, then," he shouted belligerently. "Bring on your test!"

A few seconds later, his secretary spoke timidly over the intercom, "Did you want something sir?"

He pressed the button. "No, nothing." He had forgotten what time it was — forgotten that she was there. If he couldn't keep his shit together here in his office, what was he going to do in the courtroom on Monday? How was he going to handle the pain from the arrow he'd taken through his gut when Stratton had shot him?

Baker sat up straight in his chair so quickly that for a few seconds he saw stars. The image of a buckskin-clad Indian — Stratton, but not-Stratton — lowering a quivering bow was as fresh in his mind as if the arrow that had pierced him had just been released. But it had never happened! Stratton had shown him an arrow — that was all. Then the pain had blossomed inside of him as if he had been impaled. He reached down and touched his stomach, rubbing the spot that had ached and burned in varying degrees of agony since the moment Stratton had shown him the arrow. For a second, he thought he could actually see the feathered shaft protruding from between his fingers and blood oozing out in a dark current as his life ebbed away. He shuddered and shook his head, and the vision passed. Enough was enough! He vaulted from his chair and strode to the wet bar, pouring a large brandy on the rocks, downing half of it in one swallow before the ice had an opportunity to impart its chill. As the fiery liquid slid down his throat, he suddenly realized that the pain was gone! The stabbing pain that had dogged him from the moment Stratton told him to *remember his past* in Heath Waterman's office had disappeared! He lit a cigarette and drew hard, holding the smoke deep in his lungs for a moment before exhaling slowly, his brow furrowed in concentration. *Remember your past.* That was what Stratton had said when he showed Baker the arrow, but Baker had no past that involved an arrow. Where had the scene in his mind originated? It seemed like a memory, albeit only a brief flash of one. Was this part of the test? Or was it part of the answer? The evil smile returned to his cruelly handsome visage. There were still far more questions than answers, but he had the feeling that he was once again headed in the right direction.

# 16

THE LAST TWO MILES TO THE TRAILHEAD WERE ALL DOWN HILL. Ryan's hands were getting numb from constantly squeezing his brake levers, but much as he would have liked to give the bike its head and sail down the trail at top speed, he was mindful of the need for caution. He could hardly help Audrey find her way back if he crashed and injured himself. Pulling harder on the brake levers, he allowed the gap between himself and the rider in front of him to widen by a few yards. Too many times he'd seen riders take spills because they hadn't been able to see through the dust-cloud created by riders ahead of them.

At last the trail emptied into the clearing where their ride had begun. Applause from a crowd of supporters and well-wishers greeted each rider as they emerged and braked to a halt. At least half the riders had already arrived when Ryan climbed off his bike and fell into Gayle's warm embrace. She and Doug were both there, with Ryan's Caravan and a cold six-pack of Dr. Pepper for the ride home. "Welcome, my hero," said Doug expansively, in what he assumed was a theatrical tone of voice. He cracked open one of the Dr. Peppers and handed it over. "I bring you the nectar of the gods, and greetings from your fellow courtroom combatant, who bids you tarry not — your task has just begun, and the greatest difficulties lie before you."

"Where did you find this oaf?" asked Ryan, his eyebrows contorted in mock disgust. "He sounds like a refugee from a Shakespearean festival."

"I think he's just trying to avoid showing how happy he is to see you," Gayle laughed, hugging him and kissing his cheek. They loaded Ryan's bike and gear into the back of his Caravan, and then consulted with Ben, who had taken charge of the precious field-study data. "I need to compile what's in the notebooks and then get together with Steve Bakken to create maps, charts and diagrams to use in the courtroom," he said. "They'll show exactly where the sightings occurred so that Miller won't be able to argue that the sightings were outside of the timber-harvest area." He promised to phone Michael that evening to go over testimony. "Don't worry too much about your part in it," he said to Ryan. "If I know Michael, ninety-nine percent of the preparation is already done, even though he literally had to do it with one hand tied to his bed."

The ABC contingent had tapped a keg of beer, and most of the members of the observation team were drinking enthusiastically in celebration of the mission's success as Ryan, Doug and Gayle drove away from the trailhead. "How should I approach Audrey when she wakes up?" Ryan asked Doug as soon as they were on their way.

"It's not like she's become a different person," he replied. "She's just been gone for a while. But if my own experience translates across, it will probably seem like a *very* long time to her."

"Why do you say that?"

"When Baker cut my spirit loose I was in some kind of limbo for eighteen hours. I had no reference points — no sense of time, touch, smell or anything else. I lost track of time completely — it felt like it could have been a year."

Ryan thought about how long it had been since Audrey's accident. Even for him, it seemed much longer than the two weeks that had passed. If eighteen hours seemed like a year for Doug, what would it be like for Audrey? Fear gripped him for a moment, and he had to take several deep breaths to calm himself. Gayle put her hand on his arm, "Concentrate on your love for her," she said, as if his emotions and thoughts were being transmitted directly to her. "Fear is the opposite of love — don't let yourself succumb to it."

"How did you know what I was feeling and thinking?" asked Ryan.

"That wasn't so hard," said Doug from the back seat. "I could see you turn white in the rear-view mirror. "The words 'I'm scared' might as well have been stamped on your forehead in red ink."

"There's nothing you can do for her right now, except to concentrate on your love," Gayle continued. "The love you share is what makes up the thread that Larry will follow to find her soul. The harder you concentrate on your own love, the easier it will be for him to follow the thread."

Doug reached forward from the back seat and gave Ryan's shoulder a squeeze. "You don't have much longer to wait," he reassured him. "We'll be at the hospital in less than hour. But I have to warn you — I didn't wake-up for fourteen hours after Larry brought me back. It will probably be some time before you'll be able to talk to her."

"She can sleep as long as she needs to," said Ryan. "As long as she's back where I can feel her again, I'll be happy."

"In the meantime, give us a blow-by-blow description of the last few days," Doug suggested. "That will keep your mind occupied until we get to the hospital."

* * *

RAYMOND BAKER WOKE with the remnants of a dream so vivid it felt like it could have been an engraved lithograph. He lay in his bed far longer than usual, reviewing every detail. Ryan Stratton was the focal point of the dream — yet it could not have been him, for in the dream Stratton had been a woman! Baker hated this feminine version of his foe with the same intensity as the real one. He couldn't say *how* he knew that the petite, dark-haired woman playing the violin was Stratton, but as he mulled over the details of the dream, there was no mistaking who it had been. Stratton had been giving a concert in an elegant building with a seventeenth-century European flavor. It must have been some kind of costume party — everyone present was dressed in clothes from the same time period as the building. As he showered and dressed, he continued to ponder the dream. He had not been among those attending the concert, but had watched the brightly-lit scene from outside, through a large window. Stratton looked to be about twenty-five — pretty without being beautiful. He — Baker couldn't think of Stratton as anything other than a *he* — was playing for a group of perhaps forty people, and had been accompanied by a man playing the harpsichord. Baker concentrated as hard as he could, going over every detail. As he focused on the harpsichordist, he experienced another incomprehensible flash of recognition. The man playing the harpsichord and the puma were one and the same! Baker's smouldering hatred flared at the realization, and he longed to leap into action against these two. The compulsion to hurt or kill them was every bit as strong as the urge that had resulted in his drive to Ukiah with an automatic rifle in the trunk of his Mercedes. He took several deep breaths, and then reached for his cigarettes. He was smoking well over two packs a day now and enjoying them thoroughly. Who gave a shit about people seeing him indulge? His will was required for more important things than keeping his cigarette smoking in check. Slowly, he brought his emotions back under control, damping them down to a point where he could concentrate once more on the details of the dream. Closing his eyes, he recreated the scene in his mind. The men in the audience were dressed in knee-breeches, and all of them wore powdered wigs. The women wore wigs, too, and their dresses were extremely ornate — except for Stratton, whose white dress was elegantly simple.

There was a gap in the dream after the violin recital. Though he struggled to remember what had occurred after the concert, that part of the dream faded out during the applause that followed Stratton's playing. The next part of the dream was clearer, and much more satisfying. It was night once again — though not the same night as before. The building where the concert had been was completely engulfed in flames that lit up the surrounding grounds with an eerie orange light. Baker knew that he had set the fire, and that his purpose had been to kill Stratton and the Puma. He experienced the same kind of exultation as when he had ripped the *bitch's* soul from her and sent it flying. Then, just before the point in the dream when he woke, he caught sight of Stratton, standing and watching the fire with tears streaming down his woman's face.

That was all there was. He had awoken with the vision of a female Stratton backlit by the orange glow of the flaming house filling his mind. But though Stratton had managed to avoid death in that fire, Baker was certain that the puma had not

# 17

THE PUMA PADDED SILENTLY THROUGH THE GREY MIST OF THE "in-between," following the faintly glowing, gossamer-thin thread. At some point Larry had lost all sense of how long he had been at his task. The only thing he knew for certain was that he had gone much further searching for Audrey's spirit than when he had traced the connection between Pam and Doug. Whatever process Ariel had used to slow down the dispersion of Audrey's soul, the "tether" to which Doug had referred only slowed the dispersion, rather than halting it completely. And like taffy being pulled, the soul-mate connection had dwindled down to the point that there was almost nothing left. *A day longer, maybe two at the most, and it would have disappeared entirely*, he thought as he moved through the mist.

He had gone so far that he could scarcely remember having ever done anything other than follow the glowing thread when the mist ahead of him began to brighten. As he continued forward, the light expanded, and at the same time, he noticed a growing lightness of spirit within himself. Had he not been wearing the shape of his totem animal, he would have been grinning broadly, and as it was, a rumbling, thrumming sound issued from his throat that he recognized as his own puma-sized version of a purr. A few steps further into the brightening mist brought him to the source of the light, and he finally understood Gayle's frustration when she tried to describe how it felt to be in Ariel's presence. The sheer joy radiating from *her* filled him with an exhilaration that was completely indescribable. And while the joy she exuded was like that of a child, at the same time, the love and tenderness that enveloped him felt motherly and grandmotherly at the same time. But the most surprising thing was how *interested* in him *she* seemed to be.

Audrey was with her — her spirit shining with a brilliance far greater than he remembered — even though his perception was that her spirit shone more brightly than most. Larry didn't know whether to bow down and worship Ariel, or laugh with exuberance and joy over finding Audrey, or both. Fortunately, he didn't have to decide —Ariel greeted him with a loving embrace that was even more thorough than if it had been carried out physically. The "voice" that both Gayle and Doug had tried to describe reverberated through Larry's bodiless presence in loving greeting.

*Well met, my son. You've come a long way in a very short time. Before anything else, let me thank you for your efforts on my behalf.*

Larry felt overwhelmed, and tried to think of an appropriate response. After what seemed like too long a time, he expressed the central thought and emotion that overwhelmed every aspect of his being, and simply said, "I love you!"

Ariel's response let him know down to the pure essence of his being that his feelings were reciprocated.

Finding Ariel acting as Audrey's safekeeper was a tremendous surprise. Although Doug had described feeling *her* presence the entire time his soul was adrift, Larry had not felt anything at all when he had followed Pam and Doug's soul-mate connection. The place where he found Doug had seemed no different from any other in the misty gray nothingness. Ariel seemed to read his mind and answered his un-voiced question.

*When The One without a Soul severed Audrey's soul from her body, his transgression gave me an opportunity I would not otherwise have had. I have been allowed once again to spend time with this beautiful spirit whom I have chosen to be my mother — should your efforts allow that opportunity to arise. Her* laughter reverberated through him. *We've been planning my upbringing — not that she'll remember anything on a conscious level. When she wakes following her return to her body, she'll remember nothing of our time here together. When the two of you return to the physical plane she'll remember even less than did the soul you know as Doug. I can't implant a false memory — she simply won't remember anything of the time when her soul has been separated from her body. And now, we must part — our time together has come to an end.* Larry felt a different inflection when she said, *Be aware, my son, that during these few moments that you and I have been together here in the in-between, I have forged a bond between us. Should the need arise, we can now communicate directly as Gayle and I have done, and rely on each other as a source of strength.*

"You can't seriously mean that I could be a source of strength for you!" Larry objected.

*On the contrary, I rely on you and the rest of your companions. Indeed, I rely on everyone — on all of the divided parts of the Divinity. We are one, my son, my brother, my counterpart. Each of us is dependant on all of the others. No one is superior — or inferior. Love is the fundamental essence that animates us and binds each of us to all the others. Love is the answer. Keep it foremost in your mind and in your heart!*

\*　　\*　　\*

RYAN LEANED FORWARD in his chair next to Audrey's bed, holding one of her hands in his and one of Larry's in the other. "Concentrate on your love for her with all of your being," Larry had said before closing his eyes and becoming almost completely still. His shallow breathing was the only indication that he had not turned into some kind of fleshy statue. Ryan sneaked a look at the clock on the wall. More than an hour had passed with no change whatsoever. For a brief moment, he almost gave in to the doubts and fears that crept around the edges of his focused state of mind. Then, like a river breaking through a dam to fill its intended channel, he felt his connection with Audrey flow back into place, re-establishing itself as a fundamental part of the fabric of his existence. Tears of joy overflowed and streamed down his cheeks as the connection that Baker had broken was made whole once again. His eyes had been closed while he concentrated on his love for Audrey. When he opened them and turned to Larry to thank him, he found him looking dazed with wonder.

*   *   *

RAYMOND BAKER COULD not stop thinking about his dream. It seemed so real, yet it was so strange. Stratton, a woman who played the violin — the puma taking human form — he knew just enough psychology to know that dreams are often symbolic. But what was the symbolism of Stratton's sex-change, or the violin? Baker was in his office with its magnificent view of San Francisco Bay, drinking coffee laced with brandy. He leaned back in his chair and reviewed the details of the dream again. There *had* to be some message! Why else would Stratton and the puma be present? But any significance continued to elude him. Then, as he stared out at the entrance to the tunnel through Yerba Buena Island, where the Bay Bridge dove briefly underground, he had an idea. Maybe the symbolism in the dream made no sense because he woke before it was finished! He didn't know whether it was because of the pain in his stomach, or all the cocaine, but he hadn't slept worth a shit in days, and he was certain that he could get back to sleep if he tried. Perhaps a nap would give him the opportunity to finish the dream. He drew the blinds across the windows, occluding the panoramic view, and flipped off the lights. The room was nearly dark, with only one thin slice of sunlight slipping past the barrier of the drawn blinds. He reclined on a couch upholstered in brushed pigskin, closed his eyes and tried to insinuate himself back into his dream as he drifted off. The last picture his mind formed before sleep overtook him was the silhouette of Stratton in his woman's body, backlit by the orange glow of the mansion burning behind him.

Moments later he was dreaming again, and the outline of a building was before him — but the architectural style wasn't anything like the mansion that had been burning in his previous dream. It looked more like a scene from some Western movie that he might have seen on a black-and-white television as a child. He stood in a narrow, dusty street, in front of a rude two-story affair of a building, with a wooden sidewalk under a rickety balcony. A sign over the door indicated that the building was a saloon. The sound of men laughing and the clink of glassware on wooden counters drifted towards him, as well as the occasional high-pitched female voice. He stepped out of the street, up onto the wooden sidewalk, and strode through the saloon's swinging doors. A gathering silence and cessation of activity spread, as those who were present saw him. He felt fear and discomfort radiating from all who were there, and the familiar sensation made him feel right at home. Rapping his fist on the bar, he demanded brandy from a barkeep who wasn't able to look him in the eye, daring only to steal furtive, sidelong glances at him.

"Your whore's been brought back from where they caught her this afternoon, sir," the barkeep said fawningly as he poured the brandy.

*I must be the owner of this place in this dream,* thought Baker, perking up at the mention of a whore being caught. *Would this present an opportunity to administer a beating?* His intention to return to his dream from the night before was forgotten as he relished the prospect of inflicting pain on another terrified victim. "Where is she?" he demanded, tossing down the brandy, and thinking somewhat distractedly that it tasted identical to the kind he had begun to drink recently.

"She's upstairs, locked in her room," the man replied, reaching down under the bar and handing him an old-fashioned skeleton key. "I told her there would be hell to pay when you got here — and that you probably wouldn't let her have her opium." The man laughed in a peculiar way that reminded Baker of Eddie Rapski. "She sure looked like she needed it. Keep it from her . . . that'll teach her to run off!"

"Not as much as the beating I'm about to give her," Baker sneered, his lip curling into a savage grin.

"I'll get your quirt," the barkeep offered eagerly, stepping quickly into a small room behind the bar and coming back with a blood-stained riding crop with a short handle and a rawhide lash. Baker took the quirt in one hand and the key in the other and climbed the stairs that the barkeep had gestured to when he told him where "his" whore was. At the top, there was a hallway that divided the second floor in two, with doorways leading off to either side. All doors but one stood open, and it yielded to his key as he turned it in the lock and opened the door in one motion, bursting abruptly into the room.

There was a bed against the wall where a small black-haired woman lay curled in a foetal position with her back towards him. She didn't move a muscle in spite of the abruptness of his entry, and Baker was suddenly filled with rage at her arrogance. Briefly, he wondered if his weapon would work — if he could tear her soul out while he was dreaming. Then he realized that he would derive even more enjoyment if he beat her within an inch of her life first. He strode across the room, and raised the quirt to strike the first blow, when quick as a cat, she rolled out of the bed and scampered towards the door. He changed the angle of the blow that was already in progress, bringing the lash down on her back and shoulders. She cried out in pain and fell to the floor, glaring at him defiantly nonetheless. He took in her face, observing the oriental features and skin ravaged by smallpox. His rage blossomed anew — it was the raven! Just as the puma had been a man in his last dream, the raven had become a woman in this one. Baker's pent-up, frustrated desire to kill that had been building since the first time the raven had intruded into his life, boiled over. He let loose an inarticulate roar that was more animal than human, and raised his whip with the intention of cutting her in half. But as the whip came whistling through the air, she rolled to one side, leapt to her feet and dashed headlong towards the second-story window. He lunged forward and caught her baggy black shirt, laughing as she strained against the cloth, trying to get away from him. Abruptly, he lost his grip, and she slammed into the window causing the glass to shatter with a loud crash, then slumped to the floor as if she was stunned. He laughed again, and then used the toe of his boot to lift her shoulder and flip her over, only to find that a large shard of glass had pierced her throat, severing the jugular vein. The last vestiges of life faded from her eyes as he watched helplessly, and his rage went off the scale. He had been cheated once again! Once more she had escaped the fate he intended for her! He raised the riding crop and lashed out at her corpse repeatedly, and was still beating her as the scene gradually faded and he opened his eyes to find himself back in the dimly-lit office high above San Fancisco Bay.

# 18

AUDREY MURMURED AND MOVED OCCASIONALLY IN HER SLEEP throughout Sunday morning. While the others were lingering over breakfast at a nearby restaurant, Ryan and Michael stayed with her, using the time to go over the questions Ryan would be asking his witnesses. They had faxed an Amended Petition to the clerk of the court just before five o'clock on Friday, with a copy to Heath Waterman's office. The pleadings now contained specific allegations that Marbled Murrelets were nesting within the area encompassed by Miller Lumber's Timber Harvest Plan — although they did not reveal when or how the evidence had been gathered.

Ryan looked down the list of questions. Next to each one was the expected response, so that Ryan could ask follow-up questions if necessary to bring his point across. "You don't need a lawyer with a script like this," he said, only half in jest. "An actor would do even better! Why don't we see if one of those guys who played the lawyer in one of those John Grisham movies can come in, win the trial and ride off into the sunset."

"We can't do that, you idiot." Michael responded deadpan. "The hero always gets the girl in the end, and Audrey is obviously the girl. Do you really think she'd pick a loser like Tom Cruise or Matt Damon over a magnificent specimen like you?"

The reply to Michael's question caught both of them by surprise. "Not on your life." said Audrey, in a raspy voice that was little more than a croak. "You can keep Tom Cruise and Matt Damon and all the others — I'm sticking with Ryan." Almost before she finished speaking, Ryan had her in his arms, locked in a fierce embrace. He wanted to tell her everything at once — how much he loved her, how he had missed her — his sense of loss when their connection had been stretched so far he could no longer feel it. He wanted to tell her about the lawsuit — finding the Marbled Murrelets — all of the things that had happened since Baker had attacked her. For several moments he struggled, trying to decide what to tell her first, then simply gave up, and held her close. There would be plenty of time to tell her everything that had happened. And if the past two weeks had taught him anything, it was to be present in the moment. Yesterday was gone and the future would always remain the future. *Right now* was where he had to focus his attention, and in the present moment, he was with his love, and she with him. His joy at having her restored to him was, if possible, even greater than that which he had felt at the beginning, so vast that rather than being inside of him, he was inside of it.

Audrey tried to sit up, but after two weeks of complete inactivity, she didn't have the strength. Ryan located the button on the side of the bed and raised her into a semi-seated position. She looked around the hospital room. Michael lay trussed up in his bed, and there was an empty bed and a number of chairs and a table laden with a computer, printer, files, and mounds of paper. Her first concern was for Michael and his obviously serious injuries. "What happened?" she asked. "Were we in an accident?"

"What's the last thing you remember?" Michael asked gently.

Audrey closed her eyes for a moment, her brow furrowed in concentration. Then she opened her eyes. "We were going to Ryan's house for the party — then a car pulled up beside us, and that's the last thing I can recall, except for feeling terrified."

"Well, look who's decided to join us!" said Gayle as she and the others walked through the doorway.

Audrey asked, "Have I been asleep for a long time?"

"You've been in a coma for sixteen days," said Ryan. "Do you remember when Baker made you lose a few seconds of time in the courtroom?"

Audrey nodded. "He found a way to reach into us and separate our souls from our bodies. He did it to Doug too, although he's back now — his spirit was separated from his body for less than a day."

"How did our souls get back into our bodies?"

Gayle answered. "Retrieving lost souls was one of Larry's shaman's skills in the Oglala Sioux lifetime. It was your connection to Ryan, and Doug's connection to Pam that saved both of you. Baker was able to cut the connection between your spirit and your body, but the soul-mate connection remained."

Before Audrey could ask another question, there was a knock at the door, and a worried-looking nurse they hadn't seen before entered the room. Her face brightened considerably when she saw that Audrey was awake, but she was still extremely distraught.

"I'm sorry to bother you," she said nervously, "But word of Audrey's recovery is all over the hospital. I just had to see if there's anything you could tell me — I'm taking care of Kurt Schmidt — he's the Highway Patrol officer who was brought in a few days ago with the same symptoms you and Mr. Ackerman had." She turned to Larry, with a desperate expression. "Doctor Robinson, is there *anything* you can tell me that might help me with my patient? I'm terribly worried about him!"

Larry studied her intently, his eyebrows raised thoughtfully. "I take it that Mr. Schmidt is someone you knew previously?"

"No, and that's the strange part. I never met him before — never even knew he existed before they brought him in — but I can't get him out of my mind. I've been a nurse here for years, and nothing like this has ever happened to me. I care about all of my patients, but it's never been like this! I'm losing sleep because I've been spending all of my off-hours time with him, and it's hard for me to give my other patients their fair share of my attention when I'm on duty."

"There may be a way I can help," Larry suggested, guiding her elbow as he gestured towards the door. "Why don't you and I go pay Mr. Schmidt a visit — we can try the technique that I used with Audrey. Perhaps it will help."

"Is everyone else thinking the same thing I'm thinking?" asked Doug after they left. He smiled and put his arm around Pam.

"Let's just hope that there *is* a soul-mate connection between the Highway Patrolman and that nurse," said Gayle. "She looked so desperate, I'd hate for her to be disappointed."

They spent the next hour filling Audrey in on the events that had transpired while she had been unconscious — Harry O'Neil's disappearance, Baker's attempt on her life, and Doug's ordeal after Baker's attack. They told her about the observation team that had ridden to the Miller Tract and found Marbled Murrelets, and that the trial, which had been two weeks away before she was hurt, was scheduled to start the next day.

Larry returned just as they finished bringing her up to the present, looking tired but extremely pleased. "Our Highway Patrolman is resting comfortably," he said. "I don't think his nurse is going to let him out of her sight for a moment until he wakes." He walked over to Audrey's bedside, and asked, "How are you feeling, my dear? Has this crowd worn you out?"

"No, as a matter of fact, when I heard about everything that's happened to me — the wreck, being poisoned to within an inch of my life — it seems like I should feel terrible. But, except for being so weak I can hardly move, I feel fine. All I need to know is what I have to do between now and tomorrow morning so that I can walk into that courtroom under my own power!"

"You can't be serious," Ryan objected, looking alarmed. "Baker will try to kill you again!"

"I've never been more serious in my life," she replied. "I want to see the look on his face when I come back from the dead to haunt him!" She fixed her gaze on each of them in turn, then said, "Except for Michael, who obviously can't leave the hospital, I think we should all go. We've got these mirror-lensed sunglasses to keep Baker from doing his soul-snatching routine . . . and the trial is the focal point of everything that's happened up until now. If we don't show up, we lose the larger battle by default."

*　　*　　*

IT WAS SUNDAY afternoon before Heath Waterman was able to track Raymond Baker down. They met in Baker's office in the Amalgamated tower, where he broke the news about Project HOPE's amended petition, with its allegations of actual observations of Marbled Murrelets within the area encompassed by the Timber Harvest Plan.

"Impossible," Baker stated flatly. "No one has even attempted to get into the Miller Tract. I made sure that there is only one road going in and out and it's been guarded twenty-four hours a day — they've got to be bluffing."

"If they are, then it's the first time in Michael Holland's career — he's the one who signed the Amended Petition, not that piss-ant who showed up at the deposition."

"I thought Holland was laid up in the hospital."

"That doesn't stop him from continuing on as one of the attorneys of record — he's still just as much a part of this lawsuit as he ever was. And he has an ironclad reputation as a straight shooter — that's one of the reasons the judge granted the temporary restraining order. If Michael Holland's pleadings say he can prove something, then you can bet he's got the evidence to back it up." Waterman looked Baker square in the eye. "And I don't think there's any way to find out who they've got to testify in time to deal with the problem before tomorrow morning."

Something about his recent dreams and visions had wrought a change in Raymond Baker. In successive dreams, he had witnessed the death of the puma and the raven, and it had convinced him that his destiny was being revealed to him — in the long run, he would conquer his *enemies!* It didn't matter what they did — their short-term gains meant nothing. With this changed perspective on life, he could afford to be magnanimous, and for the moment forgive Waterman his arrogance and sarcasm.

Waterman continued, "Of course, these documents have been filed far too late to comply with the Rules of Court. But that will do us little good — the Endangered Species Act is interpreted very strictly. If an animal is on the list, its survival becomes the court's highest priority." Waterman started pacing, his hands clasped behind his back. "If they have a witness who can swear to Marbled Murrelet nesting behavior within the area covered by the Timber Harvest Plan, there's no way the judge is going to allow you to resume cutting. The best we could hope for is that the court would grant us a continuance to allow us to refute the plaintiff's evidence." He stopped pacing, and leaned on Baker's rosewood desk, staring him straight in the eye again. "Unless some new cards get dealt, I think you're fucked."

Baker stood and looked out the window at San Francisco Bay. The scene looked more like a pen-and-ink drawing than a painting under the dense cloud cover that had flowed in from the ocean. His sense of purpose and his certainty of success had grown stronger rather than weaker as Waterman had outlined the difficulty of their position. The more he considered it, the more certain he was that there was a reason for all the cards to suddenly be stacked against him. What better way to flush his *enemies* out into the open than to fill them with false hope? He paused and took further mental stock. What importance was winning the lawsuit anyway? For the life of him, he couldn't remember why he had been so obsessed with cutting the redwoods down in the first place. They had been on his mind for years, but when it came down to it, who gave a shit one way or the other? There were certainly easier ways to make money. Finding and recognizing his *enemies* had given his life a new purpose. Everything other than their suffering and eventual deaths had dwindled in importance. He was destined to win, and would snatch their apparent victory from them — that alone would ensure their anguish! To crush their hopes when they were sure of success would be exquisitely satisfying! He turned away from the window and faced his lawyer.

"I think we've been dealt a wild card — we just don't know what it is yet," he said calmly. He walked over to his bar and poured liquor into two heavy crystal glasses — Scotch for Waterman, and brandy for himself. He handed the Scotch to Waterman and said, "Here's to uncertainty — it makes the pursuit of success so much more interesting."

*    *    *

"WITH EVERYTHING THAT'S been going on, tomorrow will be a circus," said Michael. The beds he and Audrey occupied had been rearranged so that the two of them faced one another. "The fact is, it would be much better if you waited until the second day of trial before you showed up. Even assuming that Judge Kelly allows the amendment of the pleadings this late in the game, it will take a day and a half or longer to put on the evidence."

"Another day will give you time to get your muscles used to walking again," added Ryan. "You don't want us to roll you into the courtroom in a wheelchair, do you?"

"I guess not," Audrey replied, her face marked by disappointment. "It's just that I've missed so much in the last two weeks — I don't want to be out of the loop anymore."

"Don't forget what being 'in the loop' did for Harry O'Neil!" Ryan reminded her. "We have our mirror-lensed sunglasses, but it's only a guess that wearing them will provide any protection. The fact that we'll be in a courtroom means nothing to Baker. He knows that there's no way to pin anything on him even if he attacks you right there, like he tried to do the first time he saw you. His powers are like something out of a low-budget science-fiction movie — he knows that we couldn't prove he'd done a thing."

"Wait a day, and see how the trial goes," Michael urged. "Our greatest need for solidarity will be when things go badly for him — that's when he'll strike out in anger. At that point, I agree that all of you should be together. And who knows? He's never 'done his thing' when Gayle or Larry are around — if they were in the right place at the right time, they might find some way to prevent him from doing it."

# 19

RAYMOND BAKER DREAMT AGAIN THAT NIGHT, EVEN MORE VIV-
idly than before.  In the dream, he was an adolescent boy — perhaps thirteen or
fourteen years old.  As he became aware of his surroundings, he knew he was doing
something that was extremely dangerous.  He felt bold, but at the same time his
heart thudded in his chest.  He was doing his best to stand perfectly still behind a
heavy drapery with a cold stone wall at his back where he had concealed himself.
The pounding of his heart was so loud in his ears, he was certain that it echoed
throughout the room like a beaten drum.  On the other side of the drapery, a conversation was taking place between a very old man and a boy who was not much older
than he was in the dream.  Baker was certain that his death would be a mere formality if they discovered him — but he had been drawn to this place like a moth to a
flame, seduced by the rumor of power beyond imagining.  The old one's name was
Aldeg, a powerful wizard of the black arts.  The younger man was Hayden, his
pupil.  Baker burned with envy. *It should be me!* he thought, as he sneaked a
surreptitious glance past the drapery's embroidered edge.  Hayden was listening
with rapt attention as Aldeg instructed him on the finer points of a spell.  Behind
the curtain, Baker listened intently, recognizing with a strange dream-logic, that he
was hearing a description of how to use *his* weapon — the one he had used on the
*bitch*, the *watcher* and the Highway Patrolman.  Baker shifted his attention to Hayden, the pupil.  It was Waterman! Heath Waterman was the one who was learning
the master's secrets instead of Baker!  Rage flashed through him and he resolved
that another night would not pass before he accomplished his rival's demise.  Then
*he* would take his rightful place at the master's side!

Suddenly, Aldeg turned toward the place where Baker was hiding.  Baker's
breathing became labored, and then stopped altogether — not from the fear that
coursed through him like an electric current, but by virtue of the master's sorcery.
He slumped against the cold stone wall, and then fell to one side as the scene before
him grew darker and darker until it finally faded to black.

The next thing Baker knew, the dream had skipped forward in time.  He and
Waterman were now studying together under the master.  As Baker listened to
Aldeg and tried to comprehend the intricacies of an incantation that would send
objects, animals and even people into another dimension, he took a sidelong glance
at his rival.  Waterman was several years older now, as was he.  He reached up to

feel his face and found that he was no longer a boy, but a young man with a beard and mustache just slightly darker than his flowing blond hair. He and Waterman were competing for the master's favor — both of them knew that in the end only one of them would be his successor. He focused all of his attention on Aldeg's teaching, concentrating on every word, memorizing every nuance. He knew that he would repeat the spell silently to himself hundreds of times until he mastered it. His concentration on the spell itself was so perfect that he paid scant attention to the warning Aldeg gave both of them. "Beware of that which I have just shown you," he said. "Only one of you will be allowed to know the final word of this spell — and that will be the one whom I trust never to use it — for there are consequences, the nature of which were lost in antiquity, that would accompany such use. Neither I, nor my master before me, nor his master before him, nor any of the others who passed knowledge of the spell from one to another have ever tried to open the gateway. Mere knowledge of the entire spell will enhance the power of the one who learns it a hundred-fold — using the spell will never become necessary. But although the consequence of using the spell is unknown, I believe my own studies may have brought me close to the answer." He glared at them from beneath bushy eyebrows. "The universe is in balance. Should a human being — body and soul — be disbursed by this spell, a price would be exacted. The balance must be maintained — to disturb it would place whoever cast the spell in great peril!"

THE DREAMS LASTED most of the night, or at least that was Raymond Baker's perception the following morning. From the dream where he was apprenticed to the black wizard, he drifted to one where he was a Viking warrior, sailing in a ship with a single square sail, its prow carved into the likeness of a dragon. That dream had been particularly satisfying. His band of marauders had sailed to the coast of what he supposed must have been Ireland or Scotland, where they had stolen ashore in the grey pre-dawn light, their oars sheathed with leather that muffled any noise they would otherwise have made. Not one of the townsfolk of the village knew they were there until it was too late.

Once they were in the village, Baker's rage had exploded as he met and slew each of the *enemies* he had discovered over the course of the past few weeks. The one he had labeled the "weakling" from the way he cowered at the counsel table in the courtroom was his first victim. He — or rather she, for in the dream the weakling was a woman — had been carrying water from a stream that emptied into the ocean near the village. Raping her had been delicious, far better than any sex he ever enjoyed in waking moments. Her fear had made him respond with a frenzy that reached its peak at the same moment he plunged his dagger into her heart, as the spasmodic jerking of her death throes coincided with his own climax. The puma had been there, in human form again — as was the raven. They were Druids, a priest and a priestess. Baker left their decapitated bodies on their altar, in bloody desecration of their place of worship. The *bitch* and her lover perished in a fiery conflagration after he chased them into their hovel and then barricaded them inside before setting fire to the structure. There had been some dangerously thrilling moments when the *watcher*, as well as one whom he recognized as an *enemy*, but had not yet encountered while awake, put up a fight. The new one cut Baker's arm with a pole sharpened into a lance that he barely deflected in time to avoid being run through. His anger at having been wounded was so great that Baker continued to hack at their dead bodies long after he killed them, until they were reduced to unrecognizable pulp.

When that dream faded, it was followed by yet another. He was a German officer in the second World War, serving in the dreaded S.S. corps in Warsaw, Poland. His duty was to find and destroy the Jewish vermin hidden in that city's extensive Ghetto, ridding the earth of their pestilential presence. A member of one of his patrols had been killed by one of the stinking Jews, but another of his subordinates — Heath Waterman again, looking entirely different than he had in the other dream — had been able to track the Jew back to his lair. The search had led to a block of buildings, where the jew had disappeared. That was all that Baker required — there was no need to search further, not when he had enough gasoline to turn the entire block into a crematorium! The dream faded as he watched the conflagration while black clouds of smoke billowed into the air and cinders rained down all around him like a fiery hailstorm.

# 20

RYAN HAD ENCOUNTERED TELEVISION CAMERA CREWS AROUND courthouses on any number of occasions over the years, but this was the first time he was the focus of their attention. Usually, he would casually ask the camera-man, "Who's famous today?" But on this particular Monday morning, an inquiry wasn't necessary. As he approached the courthouse, a barrage of microphones appeared in front of him, while reporters asked questions so fast that he could barely formulate answers. The strangest part of the whole affair was that most of the questions weren't directed toward the trial, or the virtues of saving the old-growth, but on what the media had decided was a "human interest" story — the fact that *he* was filling in for Michael Holland and taking over the presentation of the case! His status as an untested sole-practitioner from Fort Bragg with no experience in this type of litigation had caught the media's attention. No matter what he said about working closely with his co-counsel, Ryan could see that they were going to portray him as a courtroom version of David going up against a Goliath-sized opponent. *If they only knew what kind of monster I'm really up against,* thought Ryan. *Trying the case is the least of my worries — my biggest concern is staying alive!*

Once he was inside the courtroom, and away from the circus-like atmosphere created by television crews, things calmed down considerably. Baker wasn't there when he arrived, and Ryan kept glancing nervously at the door every few seconds, dreading his foe's entrance. But as the proceedings commenced, it became apparent that Baker would not appear for the beginning of the trial.

Heath Waterman started grandstanding from the moment the bailiff called the court into session, trying desperately to convince the judge to reject Project HOPE's amended pleadings, dissolve the preliminary injunction and dismiss the case. Ryan was reminded of a high-wire artist as Waterman walked a quivering line that tried to elevate procedures over substantive law and the facts. He was at his eloquent best, and ironically, his rhetoric was based on concepts of fundamental fairness. He argued that it would be a travesty to allow the late filing of amended pleadings on the very eve of trial — that it would be a gross miscarriage of justice to allow the plaintiff to present different evidence than was originally plead, with no time for the defendant to prepare. And he argued that the proper remedy would not be a continuance — something that would *reward* the plaintiff for their flagrant violation of the Rules of Court. The remedy the court should adopt would be to dismiss

Project HOPE's suit and award attorney's fees to Miller Lumber!

Ryan watched judge Kelly's face carefully during Waterman's argument, but could glean nothing from the judge's stony expression. It wasn't until Waterman was finished and Ryan rose to address the court that he knew that the judge hadn't bought a penny's worth of the goods Waterman was trying to sell. Before Ryan could say a word, the judge looked down at him from the bench and briefly held up his hand, indicating that he should hold his peace. "Let me get this straight, Mr. Waterman. You are suggesting that I should dismiss the plaintiff's lawsuit on a technicality when the proposed amendments to their pleadings state that there are Marbled Murrelets nesting within areas included in your client's Timber Harvest Plan. And this is after their initial pleadings alleged that the wildlife studies in support of the plan had been faked. No, Mr. Waterman, this court is *very* interested in hearing any and all evidence on this issue. This court is not going to endorse a violation of the Endangered Species Act by dismissing this lawsuit because of a technicality. You may have forgotten that this is a court of equity as well as one of law. I will grant your motion for a continuance if you need time to prepare, but there will be no dismissal. You can take the issue up on appeal if you like, but I find good cause to allow the plaintiff to go forward."

Heath Waterman didn't look surprised at the judge's ruling. All he said was, "There will be no motion for continuance, your honor."

"Very well. Mr. Stratton, please proceed with your opening statement."

Michael and Ryan had carefully crafted the opening statement to provide the judge with an outline of everything they intended to prove during the trial. "My belief is that an opening statement needs to be just as thorough for a judge as for a jury," Michael explained as they worked together. "It has to be a road-map for the entire trial that will help the judge keep the big picture as the evidence comes in piecemeal. He may be familiar with the law, but until we put on our testimony, he's not going to know any of the facts."

Ryan began by explaining that due to the unique circumstances of the case, he only anticipated calling two witnesses — one being Doctor Benjamin Meyers, an ornithologist who would provide the court with background information about Marbled Murrelets — including the fact that old-growth redwood and Douglas fir groves were the only type of habitat where the birds were known to nest. He told the judge how the evidence would reveal exactly how logging affected the Marbled Murrelet's reproductive activity. He described the field study undertaken by Dr. Meyers and a group of volunteers who had ridden on mountain-bikes to the edge of the Miller tract the previous week, and then trekked in on foot to the most inaccessible reaches of the Miller tract. When he sat down and looked at his watch, he was surprised to see that he had spoken for more than an hour. His concentration had been so intently focused that he hadn't noticed the passage of time, and would have guessed that not more than twenty minutes had passed.

At the morning break, an exasperated Heath Waterman phoned his client's office in the Amalgamated tower high above San Francisco's financial district. He had been fuming ever since the amended pleading had shown up on his fax machine. A hallmark of his practice had always been thorough and meticulous trial preparation. Nothing was more aggravating and frustrating than discovering on the eve of trial that the other side had an ace up their sleeve. "According to the opening statement, they went in from Jackson State Forest to the edge of the old-growth on bicycles. Then they hiked around until the damn birds started shitting on their heads." he said sarcastically. "I hope you're not expecting great things here. This new evidence will be devastating."

Raymond Baker's reaction to the bad news astounded Waterman. "It doesn't really matter," he said distractedly. "I've got some other things on my mind right now — just try to make the trial last as long as you can. I have some things that I need to deal with today, and I want to put in an appearance before it's over."

Heath Waterman stared at the phone in his hand in disbelief for a full thirty seconds after Baker hung up. Then he shook his head and placed the phone in its cradle. From the beginning, he had recognized Raymond Baker as the kind of criminal who seemed to live a charmed life — one who could break any rule he wanted without suffering any adverse consequences. In Raymond Baker, the ruthlessness of a Mafia Don was cloaked under a thin veneer of respectability. Waterman had not asked questions or made any efforts to confirm Baker's part in the disappearance and probable death of the wildlife biologists, but he was sure his client was responsible. And when he had described the best-case scenario for winning the lawsuit — a scenario that required the disappearance of Project HOPE's star witness — the man disappeared without a trace. Waterman had no doubt whatsoever that O'Neil was dead either by Raymond Baker's own hand, or as the result of his direct orders. Then there was the accident involving Project HOPE's co-founder and their attorney, which was too providential to have been a coincidence. All of this had been done so that Miller Lumber would be allowed to continue harvesting their old-growth! He shook his head again, running the last words Baker had said over again in his mind. He had fully expected Baker to be present throughout the trial — he obviously enjoyed the antipathy of his fellow man. He basked in hatred in the same way that a well-fed jungle-cat basks in the sun, and this trial with it's charged issues presented an unparalleled opportunity to make himself the focal point of intense hatred and enmity. Waterman shrugged his shoulders again, and started back to the courtroom. His initial opinion of Ryan Stratton had changed dramatically. At first the man had seemed completely out of his depth. As far as he was concerned, most small-town general-practitioners were hacks, professionally speaking. He had assumed that Stratton would be mere cannon-fodder — no threat to an experienced litigator such as himself. It was a surprise to find that this relatively untested country-lawyer, who reputedly practiced law out of some shack of an office in a coastal backwater, not only possessed adequate courtroom skills but also had the presence of mind to re-think his case and find a way to win when it appeared certain he had become the champion of a lost cause.

Waterman had originally intended to reserve his opening statement until after Stratton had finished putting on his evidence, an option he ordinarily would have taken, since it would have given him the opportunity to adjust his strategy as the evidence developed. But since Baker seemed resigned to losing, and they had no defense anyway, he decided to have some fun. Baker wanted him to waste some time? That was fine with him. He knew just how to do it.

# 21

THE *VOICE* BEGAN TALKING TO RAYMOND BAKER IMMEDIATELY after he dreamt about the Warsaw ghetto. Audible only inside his head, it told him the meaning of his dreams — which were not dreams at all, but memories from lives he had actually lived! After his initial surprise, Baker felt affirmed. How appropriate that he should be allowed to transcend and conquer death! And how fitting that he should also be given the opportunity to kill those whom he hated again and again — that his destiny actually *required* him to seek them out and destroy them. He had never really considered what a charmed life he had always lived — how lucky he had always been. He never thought about the fact that he had rarely, if ever paid any price for actions and activities that, by society's standards, should have resulted in life imprisonment or, more likely, a death-sentence. His supreme self confidence arose from his ability to control every aspect of his life so that he *always* got what he wanted, and the concept that he was infinitely superior to the rest of humanity was an integral component of his frame of reference. He had never considered the possibility of life after death, but now, upon reflection, it seemed fitting that a hallmark of his supremacy would be a destiny in which he dominated and controlled those around him over the course of many lifetimes. There was but one condition — one imperative that operated in each life. He had to kill at least *one* of his chosen *enemies* before he died, or the cycle would be broken — he would no longer reign supreme over his fellow man.

Baker's emotions surged with joy when he learned that the only requirement he had to fulfill to attain eternal life as the master of all he chose to command was to indulge his hatred! In lifetime after lifetime he had accomplished this small task. He had already experienced the strong pull of this imperative in this life — it was the force behind his compulsion a few days before to go finish off the *bitch*. Only once — when he had died with Stratton's arrow piercing his gut — had even one of his *enemies* been able to kill him. He was utterly confident that that particular event was an anomaly which would never again occur.

\*     \*     \*

"I HEARD THE pep-talks you gave Ryan," Audrey said to Michael as the middle of the morning approached. "But how do you *really* think he's doing?"

"He's got plenty of trial experience — that will translate straight across — and the case is a strong one," Michael replied. "Besides, we've scripted out every question he needs to ask to prove his case, and he's prepared to improvise if the need arises. The key to the case won't be Ryan's performance — it hinges on the judge's decision on whether to allow the amended pleadings." He shrugged. "It seems certain to me that he should — evidence is often different from what the attorneys think its going to be when they draft a lawsuit. I think it would be very hard for the court to turn down our offer to prove that there are actual breeding pairs of a protected species in the Timber Harvest Area. Ben Meyer's testimony will prove that logging old-growth is a death sentence for the Marbled Murrelets nesting in the Miller Tract, and I can't imagine that there would be any adverse witnesses." He smiled broadly. "I hope I'm making my point — Ryan won this case when he came up with the idea of going into the Miller tract to look for the birds. My experience tells me that the trial is a mere formality."

"I wonder why I feel so nervous, then," said Gayle from where she stood near the window.

"Describe how you feel," said Larry. "Are you getting a warning of some kind?"

"To tell you the truth, it *does* feel a lot like those first warnings I got before we found out about Baker. And for some reason, I keep thinking about our Oglala Sioux lifetime."

"Are you thinking of anything in particular?"

"One of the things I was able to do then was to anticipate when danger was coming. During my first regression back to that lifetime, I remembered that our tribe's encampment was moved a number of times because of my premonitions."

The phone rang, diverting their attention from Gayle's anxiety for the moment. It was Ryan, with the news that the judge had allowed them to file the amended pleadings, and that he had just finished his opening statement. "How did Baker react to the judge's decision?" Michael asked.

"That's the strange part," said Ryan. "Adam was sweating bullets all the way here, worrying about being in the same room with him again — especially knowing what Baker can do just by looking into your eyes. And Doug was actually looking forward to surprising the bastard by showing up with body and soul intact. But he hasn't shown up. The only ones here are Heath Waterman and one of his junior associates. Adam and Doug both have their mirrored glasses on just in case, though."

Ryan asked to talk to Audrey for a moment, and while they were talking, Michael suddenly put the probable significance of Baker's absence from the courtroom and Gayle's sense of danger together. As Audrey placed the receiver in its cradle he exclaimed, "You've all got to leave immediately!"

"What?" said Audrey, startled by the vehemence with which he spoke.

"Gayle's sense of foreboding *has* to be about Baker! Ryan said that he wasn't in the courtroom. Add that to Gayle's anxiety, and the fact that she's been thinking about her memories of 'moving the encampment to escape trouble,' and Baker has to be on his way here!"

"What about you?" asked Pam. "We can't leave you here all by yourself, trussed up in your bed with no way to defend yourself."

"His destiny calls for him to kill you, not me," Michael replied. "And besides, once the judge made his decision to hear the new evidence, the outcome of the trial was effectively determined. Now that he's lost that battle, I'm completely irrelevant."

"You may be irrelevant, but you're also like a duck in a shooting gallery with all of that hardware hooking you to that bed," said Gayle. "At the very least, you've got to promise to keep those mirrored sun-glasses on just in case he comes here and strikes out at you the way he did to the Highway Patrolman."

Larry spoke quietly but urgently from across the room, "The trial may well be decided, but the conflict between Baker and the rest of us is far from over. It won't end until he dies, or we die. Michael's right — we need to check Audrey out of the hospital and find a safer place to stay."

*       *       *

RYAN WAS SURPRISED when Heath Waterman decided to make an opening statement immediately after the morning break. During the course of the opening statement, surprise gave way to confusion, and finally disbelief. Heath Waterman had risen to the top of his profession by combining excellent trial skills with absolute ruthlessness. Now, incredibly, he was coming across like a bumbling fool who had completely missed the boat. He started out by explaining how he would attack the allegations that had been contained in the original pleadings — though the amended suit had changed the entire complexion of the trial. Even if Miller hadn't faked their wildlife studies, the fact that breeding pairs of Marbled Murrelets had been found in the Miller tract rendered any studies which *didn't* find the birds meaningless. Yet Waterman spent most of an hour describing how he intended to prove that any evidence provided by Harry O'Neil wasn't to be trusted, and couldn't be admitted anyway, because he hadn't shown up for his deposition. It was only just before the noon recess that he started to address the issues which would actually decide the case. Then, he went on the offensive. He bellowed that he would prove that the observations had not taken place within the Timber Harvest Area of the Miller tract; that the training of the observers had been inadequate; and then to Ryan's amazement stated unequivocally that he would put on witnesses to prove that the plaintiff's evidence had been manufactured! Ryan was wondering what effect Waterman's performance was having on Judge Kelly when the judge interrupted Waterman in mid sentence. "We're going to take our noon recess now. Would counsel please approach the side-bar." He leveled a gaze at Heath Waterman that conveyed much more than his curt words. "You're finished with your opening statement, Mr. Waterman. I don't know what you thought you might accomplish with that drivel. The only reason I let you go on as long as I did was because I thought that a lawyer of your caliber would eventually get to the point. But I recognize a filibuster when I see one. From now on, there will be no more of these shenanigans in my courtroom — is that understood?"

Heath Waterman didn't appear to be the least bit intimidated by Judge Kelly. His gaze was just as direct and fearless as if *he* were the one who was in charge as he said, "I haven't the slightest idea what you're referring to, but I was just about finished anyway, your honor."

*I'm going to have to get on the phone with Michael and see if he has a clue about what Waterman's up to,* thought Ryan as he returned to the counsel table to gather up his things. *Everything I know about trial tactics tells me that he's trying to lose!*

*     *     *

AT THE SAME moment that Judge Kelly was admonishing his lawyer, Raymond Baker was retrieving his automatic rifle from the storage locker in Santa Rosa where he had stashed it shortly after separating the Highway Patrolman from his soul. Within minutes he was back on the road, feeling happy, joyous and utterly free, delightedly anticipating the bloody deaths he was about to mete out. He thought back to the last two times he had killed the *bitch*. It had been so satisfying to ride her down on horseback, and run her through with his saber — to feel the grip shudder as his blade skated past her ribs and pierced her heart! That was much better than merely watching a block of buildings burn, even though he knew she was inside. He licked his lips in anticipation as he pictured his bullets reducing her to pulp. The dark green freeway signs indicated that he was passing Healdsburg, the place where she had been living for years. Soon he would reach Cloverdale, and pass Miller Lumber Company. Now that he understood his true purpose in life, he saw how his need to acquire Miller Lumber Company as well as his obsession with cutting the old-growth had been destiny's way of bringing his prey into range. He marveled at how complex the pattern was — and all for him! Everything had been put together so that *he* could live the kind of life he deserved, unfettered by the restraints and repercussions faced by ordinary men. It was almost too wonderful for words! He reached down and stroked the walnut stock of the automatic rifle. It wouldn't be long now.

# 22

AS SOON AS THEY DECIDED TO LEAVE, LARRY ARRANGED FOR Audrey to be discharged from the hospital, while Pam checked them out of the motel, gathered up their belongings and packed everything into Larry's Subaru. Ninety minutes after the decision had been made the four of them were on their way. Larry was at the wheel, with Audrey beside him while Gayle and Pam sat in the rear. "He's much closer now," said Gayle. "I think we cut it about as tight as we possibly could and still evade him."

"We don't want to take Highway 101 then," said Larry. "That's the most direct and fastest route to and from the Bay Area. If we were to pass in opposite directions on the same freeway, he might be able to detect our presence just as Gayle and Adam felt his the other night."

Audrey shifted in her seat to look back at Gayle and asked, "What about going over to the coast and taking Highway One at least as far as Bodega Bay?"

Gayle closed her eyes and concentrated for a moment. "It's a better choice," she said. "But it's going to take a lot longer to get to San Francisco — that road wasn't built for speed."

"I don't care how long it takes, as long as it keeps us away from Baker," Audrey responded. She looked across at Pam and over to Larry. "Are we agreed?"

"Highway One it is," said Larry.

*   *   *

RYAN ONLY PLANNED to put on two witnesses during the trial — Ben Meyers would testify about the Marbled Murrelet's special breeding needs, and also about the wildlife study that had been accomplished out in the Miller tract. The other witness was Steve Bakken, whose surveying expertise qualified him to testify to the fact that the Marbled Murrelet habitat they had located was within the Timber Harvest Area. After the morning recess, he called Ben Meyers to the witness stand and asked him a series of questions that established his credentials. This was followed by nearly an hour of questions and answers designed to educate the judge about the habitat the birds required in order to breed, the various predators which fed on young birds and all of the peculiarities which had brought the species to the brink of extinction. Ryan was working off of the list of questions that

Michael had prepared while the observers were out in the Miller tract, and the questions were so well thought out that none were objectionable. That didn't stop Heath Waterman from objecting anyway, presumably to let Judge Kelly know that he hadn't been intimidated. But every single one of his objections were overruled before Ryan could respond.

After a while, Ryan began to be bothered by the ease with which the trial seemed to be going. There had been a number of occasions when they seemed to be gaining the upper hand. But each time the opposite was true — they had been out-flanked and were simply not yet aware of it. Now Baker's absence from the courtroom made Ryan as nervous as he had expected his presence would. Not that he wanted to see their enemy — far from it. But with Audrey out of his sight, he began to worry that Baker might be after her again. He began to itch for the afternoon recess so he could call and warn the others about his suspicions.

*    *    *

BAKER PARKED HIS Range Rover on the street near the hospital. It would be far easier to make his getaway from there, rather than from the parking lot. Logic dictated that his *enemies* would be in different rooms after his last visit. He needed to reconnoiter in order to locate the *bitch* — there wasn't a chance he could find her just by pretending to be a doctor and asking for her room as he had before. He almost wished for the return of the pain from Stratton's phantom arrow-wound that had stabbed through his gut whenever he got close to one of them — that would have made finding her a snap.

He had always operated beyond the scope of the rules of society, and had always taken great care to cover his tracks. But his dreams and the *voice* had revealed that not only was he free to pursue his interests in any way he chose, they also convinced him that he would *never* be caught, unless, he supposed, he made the gravest of errors. His plan was simple, and now that he was aware of the full extent of his exalted status, he deemed it adequate. He would stroll through the hospital until he found the *bitch*. If another of his *enemies* was there, he would sever their souls before they could give warning. Then he could return to his vehicle, retrieve his rifle and accomplish his treasured task. His dreams had revealed how many there were. He had already immobilized the *bitch* and the *watcher.* Stratton was occupied in San Francisco. That left the raven, the puma, the weakling and the *other*. It would only be minutes before he could start blowing them away

WHEN THE PHONE rang in Michael's hospital room at the logical time for the court's lunch recess, he picked up the receiver and said, "Hello, Ryan — how's the trial going?" without waiting to see who it was.

Ryan sounded agitated. "It's going fine, but I'm starting to get worried — Baker never showed up, and he can't be up to anything good. Is everything okay there?"

Michael had an unconscious habit of toying with his glasses while he spoke on the telephone, taking them off and chewing on one of the earpieces. He absently slid his mirror-lensed sunglasses off as he spoke with Ryan. "Everyone's okay — and we're a step ahead of you. Gayle also had a premonition that danger was headed our way. We put two and two together and came up with the same conclusion that you did. They packed up and left half an hour ago."

Ryan's relief was so palpable, Michael could almost feel it over the telephone. "Where did they go?"

"They didn't have a set destination when they left — other than the Bay Area. Audrey's still bound and determined to make an appearance at the trial before it's over. She's looking a lot stronger, by the way."

"Great — now let me fill you in on what's happened and see if you have any suggestions . . . "

The rest of their conversation was devoted to Ryan's report on how the trial was progressing. When he finished, Michael said, "I would imagine that the media is there in force. How are they treating you?"

"They've decided I'm David going up against corporate Goliath," Ryan answered, sounding exasperated. "They won't listen when I tell them how much effort you've put into the preparation of the case. I haven't been out of the courthouse yet — I'm in the clerk's office now. But on the way in, they were trying to make me out as some kind of folk-hero."

"Don't sell yourself short." said Michael. "If you hadn't come up with the idea of a wildlife study by mountain-bike, the trial would already be over and Project HOPE would have lost. You really *are* the hero — I'm just the clerk who helped get the questions for the witnesses together."

Ryan laughed at Michael's characterizations of himself as "just a clerk."

"I'll accept equal billing with you, but no more," he countered.

"Stipulated," said Michael said, enjoying their repartee. "In the meantime, your public awaits you — go give them something to chew on!"

# 23

IT TOOK TWO HOURS FOR THEM TO MAKE THEIR WAY TO POINT Arena, the tiny town where the winding road they selected met the coast highway. Gayle's sense of imminent peril had begun to recede as soon as they left Ukiah, and by the time they saw the Pacific Ocean, it had all but disappeared. Every ten miles or so they passed through a small town. Gualala, Sea Ranch, Stewarts Point, and Jenner all lay behind them by the time they stopped for lunch in Bodega Bay. When they passed a sign advertising "The Dog House" on the south end of town where a small frontage road split off from Highway One, Audrey asked, "Wasn't the Dog House the restaurant Adam was supposed to mention the first time he met with Harry O'Neil?"

"That name stuck in my mind too," Larry said. "Shall we stop and see how it measures up?"

"The burgers are just as good, and the buns are even better," remarked Pam as they were finishing up. Larry had gone outside to use the pay-phone, since the area was too remote for cell phones, while Audrey, Gayle and Pam wrestled with the remains of a huge pile of French fries.

"I don't know," said Audrey. "There's not much that can compete with the mushroom burger at the Hamburger Ranch — I'd call it a tie all the way around."

Just then Larry came back inside looking worried. "An old friend of mine rented us a suite of rooms in his name at a hotel near the courthouse, but when I called the hospital to tell Michael, he didn't answer. I tried the nursing station, but they said he'd checked out, and I was speaking to a nurse who knew my voice."

"That doesn't make any sense," said Pam, "He can't even be moved from his bed yet — how could he have checked out?"

"He couldn't have, obviously. There must be something going on if they won't even tell his doctor where he is!"

As they left the restaurant and walked to the car, Gayle said, "I think perhaps I should take a little trip back to see if everything's okay."

"That sounds like a good plan to me," Larry agreed.

Audrey and Pam exchanged perplexed looks. "How are you going to go check on Michael from here without taking the rest of us with you?" Audrey asked.

Larry winked at Gayle, and then replied for her. "This is the woman who knew you were pregnant almost from the moment of conception. What's so odd about the idea that she can click her heels together three times like Dorothy in *The Wizard of Oz* and travel wherever she wants to?"

*    *    *

RAYMOND BAKER BEGAN his search systematically. He didn't bother with Maternity, Oncology, or any of the other specialized wards where it was unlikely he would find the *bitch*. At each nurse's station there was a board listing names and room numbers. He didn't expect to see the *bitch's* name — and limited his search to rooms that *didn't* list any occupants. Twenty minutes into his search, he hit pay-dirt when he heard the voice of the *bitch's* attorney , Michael Holland, recognizable from the tapes he'd listened to, coming from a room that the sign at the nursing station indicated was vacant. He strode into the room just as the lawyer put the phone down and was surprised to see that no one else was there. It was disappointing, but he could live with it — his destiny would bring the *bitch* and the others to him sooner or later. For the first time, he decided to use his weapon when he was not acting on impulse. After he had heard the *voice*, he no longer needed anger to fuel his weapon — it was always with him now, waiting like a coiled spring. Casually, almost clinically, he formed his malice into a blade. The *bitch's* mouthpiece had caused enough trouble — it was time to remove him from the picture.

At the end of his phone call, Michael had slipped his sunglasses back on in a practiced move that was just as unconscious as the act of taking them off. He was startled, but not surprised when almost immediately Raymond Baker strode into the room, glanced around, and then after a moment, stared at him intently. He had no doubt what Baker was trying to do. *Thank God Gayle insisted that I keep these glasses on*, he thought, *and thank God my hunch was right*. For a millisecond, he considered his options — playing dead would keep Baker supremely confident, perhaps even overconfident. On the other hand, it might be better to try to shake him up. It seemed to be a toss-up, so he chose the second option, and in a loud voice tinged with disgust said, "You're the most pathetic piece of shit I've ever encountered in my life, you overweening prick. Why don't you get out of here before I reveal my own special powers, and send you straight back to the hell that spawned you!"

Observing Baker's reaction ranked among the most satisfying moments of his life. Baker's mouth dropped open in shock and fear, and without a word, he turned on his heel and rushed from the room. Michael thought about calling security to alert them to Baker's presence, but then thought better of it. If Baker had been armed with anything other than his psychic weapon, it wasn't obvious, and though his presence at the hospital was unusual, there was nothing illegal about it. Just to be safe, though, he decided to ask his nurses to tell everyone who asked for him that he had checked out, and to switch rooms again — Baker could easily send a surrogate to test the efficacy of the "magical powers" he had just invented.

*    *    *

AFTER HIS CONVERSATION with Michael, Ryan actually enjoyed the attention the press gave him on the way out. And it *did* offer him a soapbox from which he could say a few choice words about the evils being perpetrated by Amalgamated Insurance and companies like it. He was just warming to his subject when Adam reminded him that they still had to get lunch and time was running short. The five of them, Adam, Ryan, Doug, and their two witnesses repaired to the diner where Ryan had waited during the hearing on the Temporary Restraining Order, where they ate a quick lunch before returning to the courtroom.

During the afternoon's testimony, Ryan covered the training that the observers had received, and, following the mid-afternoon recess, put Steve Bakken on the stand to establish the location of the Marbled Murrelet habitat. Heath Waterman's cross-examination was lengthy and repetitive, and they weren't finished until just before five o'clock. Judge Kelly declared the court in recess until the next day, and Ryan was loading his briefcase when his cell phone rang.

*     *     *

RAYMOND BAKER WAS flabbergasted when he failed to separate Michael Holland's spirit from his body. How could his weapon have failed to work? It had not had any effect on the puma or the raven either, but he had deduced that those were some kind of projections. This was the first time he had ever used his weapon against someone who was *actually* there and had it fail. He ran the scene over and over again in his mind. How could it *be*? Holland had been wearing sunglasses — could they have shielded him? No — the Highway Patrolman had also been wearing sunglasses, and that hadn't made any difference whatsoever. And what had Holland meant by his "own special powers?" He found himself back on the emotional roller-coaster he'd been riding for the past few weeks, and it was screaming down toward another low point, just when he thought himself invulnerable and unconquerable. Then an idea began to take shape in his mind — one that he didn't find attractive at all. Inconceivable as it seemed, was it possible that he had been overconfident? Was it possible he could fail to kill even one of them before he died? The *voice* had assured him that such a thing had *never* happened before, and although his "dreams" had shown him pieces of only a few lives, he had the sense that there had been many, many more. But still he wondered. Could his long string of successes be at risk?

There was a stirring at the back of his mind, as something struggled to make itself known. *Concentrate! Concentrate!* He took the next exit off of southbound 101 and pulled to the side of the road. Closing his eyes, he tried to let whatever was poking at the edges of his consciousness come through to the surface. A scene from one of his visions from the night before came back to him. He pictured the stone walls of a dim chamber with candles burning in sconces attached to the wall — a room lined with tapestries and a heavy drapery where once, in another lifetime, a frightened young boy that was also him, had hidden. Then through the haze of the years and the intervening lifetimes, the spell of dispersion came to him — all, save the last word! He could almost feel the razor-sharp dagger in his hand as

- 321 -

he waited for his master to enter the room, under the influence of a subtle and sophisticated spell of his own design. Then Aldeg was there, and Baker leapt out from behind the curtain, thrust his dagger into his chest and demanded that final word. It was the last thing Aldeg said before he died. Baker had it in its entirety now — the intricate series of commands and gestures that would open a doorway to another universe. And just as in that long-ago lifetime, he felt his own power increase a hundred-fold by virtue of the resurrected knowledge. As he sat in his Range Rover with his eyes closed, his hand traced the intricate pattern that he had learned so long ago. His lips moved also, shaping words in a tongue that was no longer spoken — words that had come to him as if they were carved into a stone that was unearthed after a long burial. When he opened his eyes, they gleamed with a feral delight. The roller coaster had passed its nadir and was soaring upward again towards its ultimate peak. He knew that the memory he had just uncovered would ensure his ultimate supremacy! He started his engine, and retraced his path to Highway 101, so deeply enthralled by his past-life memories that the remainder of his trip back to San Francisco passed without his noticing it.

# 24

IT TOOK RYAN OVER AN HOUR TO ANSWER THE QUESTIONS POSED by the newspaper and television reporters as they were leaving the courthouse. Doug hung back, glad that he wasn't one of the ones trying to beat a deadline. When Ryan's cell-phone rang, Doug fielded the call and took notes while Larry explained about the hotel and gave him directions. At last, they made their way through the gauntlet of microphones and cameras, and another forty minutes later met the others at nondescript, but hopefully-safe accommodations close to the court-house. Steve Bakken's testimony had been concluded, and Ben Meyers was stay-ing in Berkeley with his friend Roxanne, who was attending seminary. He chuck-led when he told them of his plans, and said, "I doubt Raymond Baker will think to look for me there."

The television in the room was tuned to a news program, and Ryan felt a sense of dislocation as he heard his own voice, immediately recognizable because of what he was saying, but sounding odd to him nonetheless. He listened to his de-scription of the terrain where the Marbled Murrelets had been observed, and then asked, "If they wanted to learn something about the case, why did they ask that guy about it? He's just following a script written by the *real* expert."

"You've got to give up on the humble-pie act, Ryan, at least around us," Gayle chided him. "Michael's been very clear about how much you've contributed, and the fact that your idea to go out to the Miller tract was our winning ticket."

Ryan grinned broadly. The court proceedings were going their way, and his soul-mate had been restored to him. For the moment he was on top of the world. Their small cadre had grown extremely close over the past few weeks, developing the kind of camaraderie seldom experienced except by soldiers in a war-zone. It was a warm, comfortable feeling that could only be described as "family." The atmosphere in the hotel room was optimistic, but wary — they could only guess what Baker's next move would be.

"It's not a winning ticket until the judge rules in our favor," Ryan cautioned. "Let's not count our chickens before they're hatched. Baker's still out there, and he's definitely on the warpath." He told them about the attempted attack on Michael, which he had learned about when Michael called him on his cell phone as he drove to the hotel. "Thank God those mirrored sunglasses worked!" he continued. "I've seen some pretty good poker players in the courtroom — figuratively speaking, but

Michael's bluff when he was facing *The One without a Soul* really takes the cake."

"There aren't too many people who would be able to come up with a line like that under those circumstances," Audrey agreed. "He's always able to think on his feet like that — it's what makes him one of the best."

"How much longer do you think the trial will last?" Gayle inquired.

"I'm nearly finished with my case in chief," Ryan offered. "I just need to put Ben on to testify about the various sightings, and go a little more into the effect logging has on nesting behavior . . . I'll be finished by noon, unless Heath Waterman drags out the cross-examination." He looked up at the ceiling for a moment, calculating. "I can't see it going much further than that, but there are no guarantees. Waterman said in his opening statement that he would put on witnesses to prove that we were never out at the Miller Tract at all."

"What are the chances of that?" asked Larry.

"Who knows? He laid it on pretty thick during his opening statement. I guess it depends on whether he's willing to put on witnesses that he knows will commit perjury." He shrugged. "But looking back, and knowing what Baker was doing today, it seems more likely that Waterman was just stalling for time when he said those things — just saying whatever came into his head. It's plain as day he doesn't give a damn about losing his credibility with the judge."

"If tomorrow is going to be the last day of the trial, then I'm going to be there!" said Audrey firmly, looking around the room with a defiant expression.

As Audrey spoke, Gayle — and for the first time Larry, too, felt Ariel's feathery touch as she whisked them into a pocket outside of time. *Audrey is right. She must be in the courtroom tomorrow — all of you must be there. The conflict has reached a critical juncture. Your destinies have crossed and interwoven across the centuries, through lifetime after lifetime, to bring you to this nexus. The conflict is reaching its climax. That is all I can tell you now — remember that I love you, whatever happens. And remember that your own love is every bit as powerful as mine. All love is the same. All love is divine. You must remember to hold it fast — no matter what!*

And as quickly as it had filled them, her presence was gone, leaving Gayle and Larry to face Audrey's challenge. They exchanged a brief but expressive glance, then Gayle said, "We'll all be going to court tomorrow. We're supposed to be there."

"What do we do if Baker shows up?" asked Adam nervously.

"It's not a question of "if," said Larry. "Tomorrow will bring us to the nexus — to the link that ties together all of the lives we have lived and all the struggle and conflict we have endured."

"I hate to say it," said Adam. "I know that love is supposed to conquer fear — but I have to tell you that I'm scared shitless."

"Just because love is the opposite of fear doesn't mean we aren't allowed to feel afraid." said Larry. "If the prospect of facing Raymond Baker didn't frighten us after everything we've been through, we would be quite insane and something less than human."

"The most important thing to remember is to hold fast to love, no matter what happens," Gayle reminded them, repeating Ariel's admonition. "Love is the same, whether it's between a man and a woman, between a mother and a child or divine love. If you think of *all* love as divine love, it makes it easier to understand. There is an element of the divine in all of us. So when we express love for another person, we are expressing love for the divine. That's why the 'Golden Rule' is the same in every religion — do unto others what you would have them do to you. It has also been expressed another way, 'That which you do for your brother, you also do for me.' and 'Love your enemies, bless those who curse you, and pray for those who would harm you.'"

"Aren't those paraphrases of what Jesus said?" asked Doug.

"Of course," she responded. "When it comes to the divine, all doors lead to the same room. Christianity is just as valid a path to God as any other — for many people it's the perfect path."

"I'm not going to be able to love Baker no matter what," said Adam grimly.

"I don't think you need to feel any fondness for him," said Gayle. "You only need to recognize that somewhere buried deep inside of him is a spark of the divine. Personally, I grieve for that tiny speck, isolated from all that is good."

"I'll have to take your word on it that there's *anything* divine or good about him," said Adam. "But I'll guarantee that if it's there, it's as lonely as it can possibly be."

"What steps are we going to take to protect ourselves from Baker when we're in the courtroom?" asked Pam. She turned to Ryan. "Are there any rules against wearing sunglasses once we're inside?"

"The judge gets to set his own rules, for the most part," he replied. "It's not far off the mark to consider the courtroom a judge's own personal kingdom. He didn't say anything today about Doug and Adam wearing sunglasses, but they were the only ones there. It's possible that the judge might think we were being disrespectful of the dignity of the court if we all wore them."

Gayle had been quiet for a few moments, but as the conversation about the sunglasses went on, she became increasingly certain that mirror-lensed sunglasses would not be necessary. She had not relied as much on her psychic gift since she had been able to speak with Ariel, but it was as strong as ever. And her sixth sense told her that whatever Baker might attempt to do to them in the courtroom, it would not involve severing their souls from their bodies.

"We don't need to worry about the sunglasses anymore," she murmured. "When this conflict is played out, it will be on another level entirely."

"Then we'll be safe without the sunglasses?" asked Pam, trusting Gayle implicitly.

"I didn't say we would be *safe*," Gayle replied. "I have no doubt that Baker will come up with something just as dangerous as what he's been doing — or even worse — but there'll be no soul stealing in the courtroom."

"Then we really don't have *any* way to protect ourselves from whatever he has up his sleeve," said Pam, returning to her original position.

"On the contrary, we have the ultimate weapon — or non-weapon, actually. By their very definition, weapons are not instrumentalities of love. What I'm trying to say is that we can absolutely count on coming through whatever happens tomorrow, *if* we can approach everything from the perspective of putting love into action, and if we don't succumb to the fear which we are bound to experience. Remember — we'll be surrounded by love. The positive energy focused on the preservation and conservation of the old-growth is nothing more or less than *love!* Perhaps we'll find a way to tap into it."

"How would we do that?" asked Doug, his reporter's skepticism resurrecting itself for the moment.

"I haven't the slightest idea," Gayle admitted candidly. "But we didn't get this far by trusting in the outcome only when it seemed likely, or even possible! I'm confident that the answer will come at the right time."

# 25

RYAN FELT SLIGHTLY UNSETTLED WHEN HE AND AUDREY WERE finally alone in their room. He had concentrated so long and hard on how much he loved her while her soul had been astray that she had taken on an almost icon-like quality in his mind. He felt shy and awkward — almost as if they were starting all over again. Audrey seemed to sense his discomfort. "I still don't have my strength back yet," she said, patting the bed next to her. "Just hold me for a while. I don't even have a sense of lost time from when I was gone like Doug did, but it still feels like it's been way too long since we spent a few quiet moments together. It must seem like forever to you."

Ryan lay down next to her, and for a while they stayed spooned together with his arm wrapped around her. "I never lost hope completely," he said. "But the time did go awfully slowly, especially after I found out that Larry could bring you back, when I was still out in the Miller Tract." He sighed. "That was torture — but it was worse before that, when we didn't know if we would *ever* find a way to bring you back." He rubbed her stomach, trying to gauge whether or not it felt any larger. "Our baby was another of my concerns. I must have played out a hundred different single-parent scenarios in my mind — I just couldn't help myself. But mostly I tried to focus on thoughts of raising our daughter together." He chuckled. "I figured if that didn't lure your soul back, then nothing would."

"All of those thoughts were part of the link that Larry followed when he came and found me," said Audrey. She rolled over so that she was facing him and kissed him warmly. "There's no way in the world I'm going to miss out on raising our daughter! I may not be psychic like Gayle, but I have a strong feeling that I'm going to have to put all of my parenting theories to the test." She grinned. "And if you think facing *The One without a Soul* is tough, imagine holding yourself out as a parenting expert for years and then actually raising a child of your own! If our little girl turns out to be on the wild side, I'll never be able to live it down."

Ryan laughed and held Audrey close. "I don't think you would have done half as well professionally if what you taught didn't work. Besides, if she turns out to be a hellion, you could tell everyone it was my fault."

"And get the same look that I give people when they blame their child's shortcomings on the other parent? Never!"

*It feels so good just to talk about normal everyday things,* Ryan thought. *What am I doing involved in a lawsuit against an evil monster instead of taking off right now with the woman I love?* But he knew that there was no way to escape the showdown that loomed just hours away. There was no place he could go where *The One without a Soul* could not and would not follow. And even if by chance he and Audrey avoided Baker during the rest of this lifetime, *The One without a Soul* would just come back to haunt them and terrorize them in future lives. But if Gayle and Larry were right, the cycle could be broken if they held love close to their hearts. Ryan intended to do his best. He realized that he had learned a great deal about love since that Friday night when Doug first brought up Gayle's past-life regression. Love was positive energy directed toward harmony — toward the preservation of good things and positive relationships. It was what motivated the members of the Anonymous Bike Club to drop everything, and devote their time and energy to a cause that touched them only peripherally. It flowed from the spectators who had come to the trial today. And though they hadn't known the price they would pay, those who died at the Miller massacre had given their lives for love. He reached out and smoothed back a lock of Audrey's hair that had fallen across her face. Their time together felt so much more precious for having been denied them, however briefly. Involuntarily, he felt his anger towards Baker start to bubble up from where it simmered, ready to boil to the surface, and he quickly turned his thoughts in another direction. His task the next day was clear. Ask the questions, put on the witnesses, cross-examine any witness that Heath Waterman put on, and when it was all done, make his argument to the court. Everything else was completely outside of his control. He remembered something that Michael had told him about returning to productivity after succumbing almost completely to alcoholism. "It all boils down to the Serenity Prayer," he had said. It goes like this, 'God grant me the serenity to accept the things I cannot change, the courage to change the things I can, and the wisdom to know the difference.' If you weave the serenity prayer into everything you do, you get rid of just about everything that alcoholics use as an excuse to drink — and it's not bad advice for the rest of the world either." As he lay on the hotel-room bed, holding the love of his life close in his embrace, Ryan silently sent out a prayer, asking the universe for courage, serenity, and wisdom.

# 26

RAYMOND BAKER, *THE ONE WITHOUT A SOUL*, SAT IN HIS UNLIT office overlooking San Francisco Bay. It was a center of power, a place where decisions were made that had a profound effect on uncounted thousands of lives, where policies were set that determined the tone of a million conversations between insurance claims-adjusters and claimants. It was a place where heartlessness and the uncaring pursuit of the dollar had been declared the highest of virtues, and in many ways, it was not unlike the dim stone-walled chamber where in a previous incarnation, he had learned the spell of dispersion.

For many years, he had been satisfied with his ability to symbolically rape and pillage in the world of insurance and finance, destroying individuals and companies at his whim, while steering the Amalgamated ship through a sea that was increasingly littered with the wrecked hulks of peoples lives — the lives of individuals whose claims had been wrongfully denied, as well as the lives associated with the companies that Amalgamated had consumed. His malignant spirit fed on pain and suffering, and with each unreasonable claim denial and ruthless corporate raid there had been more anguish and sorrow heaped on his plate. But all of this had taken place before he knew about his destiny and his ultimate immortality — before he remembered the incantation that now beckoned to him like a syringe full of heroin to a desperate addict. He felt like a small child at three o'clock on Christmas morning, who, after sneaking downstairs to find presents under the tree, debated whether or not to wait until morning to unwrap them. He itched to try the spell, to see what lay beyond the doorway. But there was something holding him back — a shadow at the back of his consciousness that barely concealed a whispering doubt about using the spell. Part of him, the iron-willed side that was dedicated to long-range planning and control, told him to lift the veil, to examine what was behind the curtain and chase down the shadowy doubt. But another part of him, his recently developed impulsive side, suspected that when the shadow had been chased away, he would find a prohibition against the use of what he had just discovered. And he wasn't willing to look for such a prohibition — not while the spell beckoned so powerfully.

He took in the view of San Francisco and the Bay Area and wondered what was going to happen to the world beyond the pane of glass when he spoke the words and performed the ritual gestures. What would happen to all of the people who lived out their tiny lives within the panorama that stretched before him from the Golden Gate bridge on his left to the Bay bridge on his right, with the small Marin County towns and the cities of Berkeley and Oakland in the distance? A smile twitched at the corners of his mouth as he decided that in all probability every single one of them would become his slaves. He could tell that he was poised on the brink of something huge — something beyond his expectations — *something that had to do with his enemies!* Tomorrow the trial would be finished. That was when it would be time to put his newly rediscovered knowledge and power to use. It was a good thing that his self-control had returned. It was hard to wait, but he knew that he would.

They would be so joyful after the trial. There was no chance of his own court-room victory at this stage of the game — Waterman had been abundantly clear about that. Only when they thought it was over, when they were basking in glory, would he reveal his power. How he relished the thought of snatching the sweetness of success from them one more time — the last time! He didn't know what lay beyond the doorway that would be punched through the fabric of the universe, but he knew that great changes lay ahead.

More out of habit than for the effect — he was beyond that now — Baker laid out a generous amount of cocaine on his mirror and poured himself a tumbler of Glenlivet — the brandy no longer appealed to him. It felt as if he was bidding a fond farewell to this little ritual which had given him such pleasure over the years. He snorted a line of the fine white crystals and lit a cigarette, inhaling the smoke deeply into his lungs before letting it escape slowly into the air. There had been a lot of surprises for everyone lately — but tomorrow he would unleash the biggest surprise of all.

# 27

IT SEEMED TO RYAN THAT THE REPORTERS WERE EVEN MORE frantic the next morning. He couldn't tell if they suspected that the trial was almost over, but they were practically tripping over themselves trying to get a quote that would capture the story in one convenient sound-bite. He and Audrey left the chore of dealing with the media to Adam, and with Larry and Gayle following close behind, made their way into the courthouse. Court was in session — the judge was finishing up a short docket of criminal arraignments when they arrived. After the court concluded the criminal matters, most of the people in the courtroom filed out, to be replaced almost entirely by supporters of the injunction against Miller Lumber and the inevitable reporters. Ryan took his place at the counsel table with Audrey and Adam, as representatives of Project HOPE, sitting beside him while the others took seats in the row behind the bar. A few minutes later, Ben Meyers arrived and briefly discussed his testimony with Ryan. Then Heath Waterman entered, followed by Raymond Baker.

Raymond Baker's emotional roller-coaster took an unexpected dip the moment he entered the courtroom. Whatever he had been expecting, it did not include the *bitch* sitting at the counsel table with her soul apparently restored to her, or *the watcher* sitting directly behind her, in unquestionable good health — but the dip was a short one. He immediately saw the beauty in the situation. If his *enemies* had been able to find their way back to their bodies, they must be feeling that their success was inevitable. *Their hopes and expectations have been raised even higher,* he thought. *That will make their fall even greater.* He took his seat at the counsel table, smugly satisfied at the complete return of his self-control. The dispersion was not far off — waiting only for the moment when his *enemies* were certain they had triumphed. The exquisite pain of their combined anguish would create a wave that he would ride into an unknown but glorious future!

His attention was drawn to the others who were seated behind the plaintiff's counsel table. He had been so distracted by the restored health of the *bitch* and the *watcher*, that he had paid scant attention to the others sitting with them. The woman in her forties and the old man with the beard and flowing white hair were none other than the raven and the puma! Next to the raven, between her and the watcher was the *other* — the one from his dreams whom he had not yet encountered. As he was surveying the room, the woman who was the raven saw that he had arrived, and boldly locked eyes with him. Her gaze was completely fearless — though strangely it was also completely without malice. In fact there was a hint of kindness in her eyes, and that, more than any enmity her gaze might have conveyed, caused him to look away.

Gayle had never been physically present in the same room with Raymond Baker. She was shocked at the difference actual physical presence made in how she reacted to him. Almost instantly, she felt Ariel's feathery touch. *I am with you, daughter. I cannot give you assistance other than to help you tap into the love that surrounds you. Even this contact is possible only because all of you, as well as The One without a Soul, are present. If you try, you will be able to feel the love that surrounds you.* Gayle did as Ariel said, and felt herself relax. Then, while Baker's attention was riveted on Ryan, Adam, and especially Audrey, she glanced around the room. Just as Ariel had said, she could feel — even *see* the positive energy emanating from dozens of those who packed the courtroom. She drew it into herself, and felt the power of their love infuse every cell of her body. By the time Baker fixed his baleful glare on her, and his eyes widened in recognition, she had fortified herself to the point where the menace of his presence held no power over her, and she was surprised to find that her dominant emotion was pity! Just as she came to this realization, Baker broke eye contact.

Much water had passed under the bridge since the last time Audrey had been in this courtroom with Raymond Baker. He had been trying to kill her ever since, and had nearly succeeded on more than one occasion. She felt his eyes on her, and she turned in her chair to face him, staring directly into his eyes — an act that her intellect assured her was tantamount to suicide, but which, strangely enough, her emotions told her would bring her no harm. As their gazes locked, her first thought was to raise her middle finger to him in the nearly universal symbol of derision. But then inspiration struck her, and she saw how to cut him nearly as deeply as she herself had been cut when he pulled up beside her Volvo that fateful day. With the delight that accompanies inspired genius, she smiled sweetly at him and blew him a kiss.

The only time he had encountered Raymond Baker, Doug had not even had a chance to experience fear before his spirit had been shorn from his flesh and nearly lost. The terror of that journey, ameliorated though it had been by *her* presence, was something he would never forget — though he wished he could. When he saw Baker saunter imperiously into the room, a flood of emotions overtook him, triggered by the events not just of the previous week, but by similar events in uncounted lifetimes. His fear metamorphosed into anger and built until its strength was so great that he was on the verge of being consumed by rage. Then he heard *her* voice — or more accurately experienced *her* voiceless presence — the same presence that had reassured him while he languished in the void. *Anger feeds him,* She seemed to whisper. *Think instead of your love for your soul-mate. When he sees the reflection of the love that fills your heart, you will have your retaliation.* And so he reached for his wife's hand, cherishing the touch of the one who made him complete, and focused on his feelings for her with his entire being.

In past lives, Pam had developed the ability to feel the transmission of the vital pulse which accompanied healing. She felt that power surge around her shortly after the tall, overly-handsome man whom she knew to be as utterly evil as a person could be walked into the room. There was a wavering of the energy around her, like the flickering of electric lights in a thunderstorm, as virtually everyone in the room responded to his presence in a spiritual circling of the wagons. Pam blinked several times, unable for a few moments to believe that she could actually *see* healing energy pouring from the spectators, the bailiff and the court-reporter — even the judge. The energy was love — there was no question in her mind, and it was flowing towards and into Gayle, where it coalesced and gained strength before flowing outward, forming a sphere around them like a gigantic bubble. This had to be what Gayle had foreseen would protect them when she said that Baker's ability to cut through the bonds that anchored their souls would no longer put them at risk. She closed her eyes and let the love flow over and through her, and when Doug reached for her hand, she held it tight.

Ryan had been so deep in discussion with Ben Meyers that he didn't notice Heath Waterman and Raymond Baker until they sat down at the other counsel table. He saw that Baker did not appear to be in any physical distress — he must have found a way to overcome the pain from his past-life arrow wound. He felt less intimidated than he had been in Heath Waterman's conference room — less even than when he had first seen Baker's face on the television during the news coverage of the Miller massacre. *Thank God for small favors,* he whispered to himself.

A veil lifted for Larry the moment *The One without a Soul* walked into the courtroom. Like Gayle, he had never been physically near him, except in spirit form. Now that they were side by side, Larry perceived that Baker's essential nature was that of a voraciously sucking vortex thinly disguised as a human being — the man was a spiritual black-hole! Larry could feel, and could faintly see, a maelstrom of energy being drawn towards Baker through the portal of his being and shunted *somewhere else*! He glanced around the room and saw the courage and resolve being drained from those who had joined him in opposition to *The One without a Soul* across the lifetimes. At the same time, though, the positive energy that was being siphoned away was being replenished by bright streams of energy flowing from almost everyone in the room. The streams flowed to and into Gayle and from her to each member of their small band. Understanding dawned on him that instant, and he knew at last who and what *The One without a Soul* was.

Judge Kelly stepped through the door that led from his chambers, and the bailiff commanded all present to rise — court was back in session. The judge advised Ben Meyers, who was seated in the witness stand, that he was still under oath, then peered over his half-glasses at Ryan and said, "You may resume questioning the witness."

# 28

RAYMOND BAKER PAID SCANT ATTENTION TO THE TESTIMONY after the trial was underway. Stratton had been clever and resourceful — he had to grant him that. But in the final analysis, there was no sting to the fact that the plaintiffs would prevail. Nothing about this lawsuit really mattered, now that he knew how to accomplish the dispersion. The universe was so finely balanced that when the unraveling occurred and his *enemies* were shunted into nothingness, there would be a fundamental shift that would give rise to his ultimate ascendency. The only question remaining was when to use it. He knew that the most satisfying time would be after the judge announced his decision. That would be when he would snatch victory from their sanctimonious hands. What good would their success in the courtroom be after he had taken away their very existence, and in the process undone the very fabric of the physical world in which they lived as well? Whether their dismay lasted an instant, or an hour, he intended to drink it in like fine wine.

LARRY PAID LITTLE more attention to the questions Ryan asked or the answers given than did Raymond Baker, although this was the first time he had heard the full story of the mountain-bike trip to the edge of the old-growth and the cross-country hike that the observation team had taken to the site where the Marbled Murrelets were nesting. As he sat and half-listened to the testimony, veils lifted and revelations came to him in a vast, kaleidoscopic panorama more sweeping than any view on earth — comparable perhaps only to the views seen by the select few who had traveled to the moon and looked back on their own distant planet across the depths of space. But the void that filled Larry's consciousness was not made up of space, but of time.

Time stretched back with an immensity that made the Grand Canyon seem like a ditch in which a small child might frolic. Over the course of countless millennia, he could see the oscillations as the domination of masculine and then feminine energy swung back and forth like waves surging in a contradance across the eons. In counterpoint rhythm, the yin and yang of the two essential energies took their turns as the predominant expression of the life force. Sometimes the balance had been skewed as one or the other continued to maintain its singular influence past the natural point of its progression. Looking back and observing the crests and troughs, Larry saw that the period of time that lead up to the present had been one of these skewed periods, Masculine energy had been dominant for a very long time — long enough to have severely disrupted the balance produced by the normal rhythm. He stretched his perception back to the last time the feminine side had been ascendant. Coincidentally or not, it was a period of time roughly equal to the age of the most venerable redwoods. Focusing closely through closed eyes, he observed a time when the most-worshiped figure in the world was the Egyptian Goddess Isis, She of a Thousand Names, who was queen of healing and magic, and mistress to the gods. She who strove with Set, the God of destruction, and who gave birth to Horus, the reborn son of his father Osiris. She who held sway for three and a half millennia, her influence spread by Alexander the Great, worshiper of the Mother of Life, and by others as far as the British Isles. At the height of Her ascendency, She was worshiped from Her birthplace in Egypt to the banks of the Thames. But that wave had crested and begun to recede long before, and Her influence had faded until it was all but extinguished four hundred years following the birth of Jesus.

Always since that time the waves had gone in the other direction – towards a masculine ascendancy without cresting or receding. The balance had never shifted back towards a more feminine expression of the divine. There had been small dips which might have signaled an opportunity, but something was interfering with the shift that would restore balance. Before it could take place, the necessary gateway had to open. The catalyst that could open the gateway had not been used in two millennia — its keeper had failed or refused to accomplish that which was necessary for the pendulum to swing in the opposite direction. By now, it had been so long since the forces had been balanced that all existence cried out for that which should long-ago have occurred.

THE TRAIL WOUND down with a whimper rather than a bang. Heath Waterman made some weak attempts during cross-examination to discredit the testimony of Ben Meyers, but everyone in the courtroom knew he was just going through the motions. Waterman's client had made a gamble when he decided to submit falsified studies to back his Timber Harvest Plan. He had put himself back into contention by making sure that no witnesses to the fraud would ever testify. But the gamble had been lost when the observers who had biked and hiked out to the old growth returned successful. When Ryan announced that the plaintiffs rested, Heath Waterman spoke briefly with Raymond Baker, and then announced to the court that he would not be presenting a defense. Judge Kelly glanced at the clock on the wall which read eleven forty-five and announced that unless they could wrap things up in fifteen minutes, he would hear oral arguments at one-thirty p.m., sharp.

While Stratton had been asking his final questions of the bird-loving fool, Baker had been going over the spell of dispersion in his mind, rehearsing each tiny detail. The crystal clarity with which he could recall every nuance was uncanny. He smiled. This was yet another omen of the wonderful things that he could feel were just about to happen. Stratton and the others were sure of victory now. The smug expressions on their faces would soon be wiped out. They thought they'd won — how little they knew!

Heath Waterman leaned close to him, and said, "The arguments are just a formality. They've won — we can end this now, or we can come back this afternoon and embarrass ourselves even more than we already have."

Baker could hardly believe the effrontery of the man — using the word "we" to include *him* in his appraisal of his own pitiful performance. But Baker also knew that destiny required Waterman's failure. Losing the lawsuit had drawn his *enemies* to him like iron-filings to a magnet. Otherwise they might never have presented themselves to him in one tidy package. They had come to gloat — to lord over him the victory that they thought was at hand. How little they knew! They were at the brink of total annihilation! How he would feed on their agony when he undid the fabric of their existence! It was true that during many lifetimes he had killed all of them before succumbing to his own inevitable demise. But he was positive that he had never had the opportunity to extinguish all of their hated existences in a single stroke! The spell of dispersion sang its siren song to him, and he toyed with the idea of unleashing it right there, before the judge even ruled. *No,* he thought. *I will let them reach the highest pinnacle before I cast them into the abyss.* "Tell them they can have their permanent injunction," he said to Waterman, barely able to keep the smile off his face.

# 29

DOWN THE STREET FROM THE COURTHOUSE, A GREASY-HAIRED man with a two-week stubble of iron-gray beard paused for a few moments on the sidewalk in front of a small grocery store. His wrinkled suit looked as though it had been slept in for weeks, and it reeked of spilled alcohol and the old vomit that was flaking off one pant leg. In one hand he held a bottle wrapped in a stained brown-paper bag, and in the other an expensive nylon exercise bag that seemed glaringly out of place. Only seconds passed before the proprietor of the grocery store hurried out to offer a rather firm suggestion that he keep moving. The man gave no resistance, stumbling slightly as he lurched in the direction of the courthouse. No one who saw him would have thought him any different from any other street-person who roamed the streets of San Francisco — just one more tortured soul trying to find a way to beg, borrow or steal enough money for his next bottle of cheap wine. But even though drinking himself into a stupor had been the focus of each day's activity for the last month, obtaining a cheap bottle of white port was not at the forefront of this man's agenda now. There was someone with whom he wanted to have a few words — a man who, sooner or later, would emerge from the courthouse down the street. And when he did, when the tall, arrogant figure with his cruel, icy-blue eyes stepped out of the door of the federal courthouse, Eddie Rapski intended to find out exactly why his life had been cast into the gutter.

\*     \*     \*

BY NOON IT was all over. Judge Kelly took the stipulation offered by Heath Waterman and entered the order permanently enjoining Miller Lumber from harvesting old-growth under the current Timber Harvest Plan. Raymond Baker and Heath Waterman exited the courtroom immediately, leaving his *enemies* to bask in the congratulations of their supporters. When Ryan phoned Michael to advise him of the victory, Michael remarked that he could feel his healing process speed up just from knowing they'd won. Ryan stashed his cellular phone in his briefcase along with his yellow legal pads and his trial binder. When he stood up to embrace his soul-mate he saw that there were tears of joy in her eyes. "You did it," she said, between congratulatory kisses. "You saved the old-growth forest!"

"We all did it together," he objected. "The whole thing was a group effort.

There isn't a single one of us who didn't have a part in making this happen."

"I know you had help," she said, "but I still get to claim you as my hero."

"Victory was snatched from the jaws of defeat not once, but twice," said Adam. "We can't forget Harry O'Neil's contribution. We never would have gotten the temporary restraining order if he hadn't come forward." His face turned somber. "There must be some way that Raymond Baker could be brought to justice for what he did to Harry."

"I'll make some calls to the local district attorney," said Ryan. "Raymond Baker probably didn't leave any clues behind, but if he did, maybe they can nail him."

Larry was still trying to process the visions he had experienced during the trial, but didn't think that this was the proper moment to share them with Gayle. In spite of their courtroom victory, he was certain that they were not finished with Raymond Baker. "I hate to disrupt our celebration," he said, "but before we leave this courtroom, we need to take stock and remember that the battle we just won was just a skirmish. Baker is still out there, and he's just as dangerous to each of us as he was for Harry O'Neil. And now he'll be looking for revenge on top of everything else!"

Gayle spoke for the first time since the completion of the trial. "I agree. Every time we've thought that things were going our way it was a sure sign that something unexpected and potentially lethal was about to happen. These last two days have been far too easy. The fact that Baker threw in the towel just now makes me nervous as a cat. It isn't in character."

"Are you getting another one of your premonitions?" asked Audrey, looking concerned.

"He's still at war with us — he always will be — that hasn't changed an iota," Gayle replied. "But let me concentrate to see if I feel anything." She closed her eyes for a moment, then opened them and said, "I don't seem to be able to reach out and feel danger like I usually can — it's like trying to peer through dense fog. We're traveling blind."

As soon as he left the courtroom, Raymond Baker parted company with Heath Waterman. The man had been useful, but his attitude towards Baker throughout the proceedings had ensured him that old age was something he would never experience. Baker waited in a phone booth on the first floor of the courthouse, pretending to talk on the phone while he waited for his prey to leave the courthouse. Once more he pictured the spell of unraveling and dispersion in his mind. All he needed to do was to speak the words and perform the merest hint of the ritualized gestures with small movements of his fingers. He was ready. The time had almost arrived, and never before had anticipation been so sweet.

As they emerged from the courthouse, Ryan, Audrey and Adam were immediately beset by newspaper reporters, teams from several at least three San Francisco-based television stations, as well as the news-anchor from a major cable network. Within a few seconds, they each had several microphones in front of them, and cameras were rolling to record every utterance. Behind them, unnoticed by any of the companions, Raymond Baker slipped out of the courthouse in the midst of a group of lawyers wearing dark blue and gray suits that matched their sober expressions. He managed to avoid the notice of any of the reporters, all of whom had their attention focused on the delegation from Project HOPE. To one side of the main doors to the courthouse was a set of tall columns, which allowed him to partially conceal himself.

Through the alcoholic haze that reduced his field of view to a single focal point surrounded by blurred images, Eddie Rapski watched Baker sneak out of the courthouse. Raymond Baker — the man who had raised him up from a life of frustration and bitterness to the level which he had always deserved, and then caused him to fall to a place so low that his life held no value whatsoever. The clarity of thinking he had begun to experience after Baker had turned on him had not progressed very far. Since that day, his brain had been so sodden with alcohol that lucid thoughts were out of the question. But the brain cells that were still able to function allowed Eddie to see that Baker had owned him — body and soul — ever since that long-ago encounter in the lodge parking lot. He saw that every aspect of his behavior had been influenced or controlled by Baker up to the day that he had been cast aside like yesterday's garbage. Eddie had danced to Baker's tune like a marionette, but that was over now. *Not that it makes any difference,* he thought. Eddie's life was over now as well. From his vantage point in the gutter, through the warped lens of his alcoholic thinking, it seemed clear that a bad end had been his fate from the beginning. The few years spent at Baker's beck and call had only been a detour. But before Eddie finished himself off, there was a task which cried out for his attention. Eddie had once been a man of action. Bitterness had always defined his life, and until he started disseminating his most heartfelt beliefs to the public over the airwaves, he had always acted on the impulses his bitterness generated. He had always had the courage of his convictions! And right now his deepest, most heartfelt conviction and belief was that his suffering should be shared by the one who had brought him so low.

While the representatives of the media were concentrating their attention on the two founders of Project HOPE and their attorney, Larry took Gayle by the arm, leaned close to her and said, "I've experienced another lifting of the veils — I need to share it with you."

"We're not going to have any chance to be alone for a while," she responded, glancing around at the pandemonium that surrounded them. She took in the crowds of people and the television vans parked next to the curb with their roof mounted satellite dishes pointed to the sky. Who knew when they might find a quiet moment? She shrugged her shoulders and said, "There's no time like the present." Reaching out, she took both of his hands in hers.

The moment had arrived at last. His *enemies* had been waylaid by the TV idiots. That would keep them distracted long enough for Baker to do what was necessary. He began the incantation, accompanying each word with a ritual gesture, minimized to the smallest movements of his fingers — the last thing he wanted to do was draw attention to himself.

Eddie Rapski reached into the exercise bag and brought out his bottle, which was encased in a brown paper bag twisted tightly around its neck. He hadn't run through his credit cards yet, and unlike the common street drunk, he was drinking the good stuff — Courvoirsier V.S.O.P. He took a generous swig of the fiery liquid, savoring the feeling as it burned down his throat. He put the bottle back into the bag and started towards Raymond Baker. *Dead man walking,* he thought to himself and chuckled, the gallows-humor fitting his mood. He felt more at peace with himself than he had in a long, long time.

Gayle experienced something very much like that first sharing of information out by the seal colony, although this time the information was flowing from Larry to her rather than coming to both of them at once. In a moment outside of time, she saw and understood all that Larry had experienced in the courtroom, the waves of male and female energy shifting back and forth in the counterpoint dance which had been interrupted, skipping like a needle on a bad phonograph record over and over again across the last two millennia. And then she saw a shining light approaching from nowhere and everywhere all at once. Never before had she felt the presence of the divine as strongly. She felt Larry grip her hands more tightly and knew that he saw and felt it too. It was the pure essence of love, and both of them gave themselves to it with all their hearts.

Raymond Baker's concentration was so focused on the words and gestures of the incantation — and upon his *enemies* — that he saw nothing else. As he reached the end of the incantation, the tiniest hole in the fabric of time and space opened a flaw in the fabric of the universe. He held it cradled lightly in his hand as if it were an object that he could throw. His *enemies* were no more than fifty feet from him. Some were answering questions from the reporters. The watcher and the other were standing together, while the puma and the raven faced each other, holding hands with their eyes closed. He paused for a moment, savoring the approach of their absolute obliteration. Enough! He focused his will on them, said the final word and began the final gesture, which would draw his *enemies* into the fissure he held in his hand, taking them to a place outside of creation, where nothing existed, or could exist — including them. Then he cast the flaw towards them, standing back to watch it consume them and deliver them into a place outside of space and time.

Even through the fog of the alcohol that clouded his mind, Eddie thought Raymond Baker looked strange. He was muttering, and his fingers were twitching. Then he stood with his hand held in front of him, as if he held something of great worth cupped there, while he stared intently at the tree-loving assholes who had helped bring Eddie down. Eddie didn't give a shit about the tree-huggers one way or the other now — he wondered briefly why he had ever given a rat's ass about anything they had ever said or done. But then the thought flitted away. He had a question to ask. He reached into his bag and pulled out the Smith & Wesson pistol he had owned since before Raymond Baker had come into his life, a weapon he was about to use for its intended purpose.

As Gayle and Larry surrendered to love, the shining light enveloped them, became more focused, and then expanded rapidly. Gayle wondered how anyone could fail to see the luminous sphere as it spread out and surrounded all of the companions in a shining nimbus — all of those who had striven through the lifetimes — knowingly or unknowingly trying to bring about the change that would bring *her* to a new incarnation.

Raymond Baker's eyes opened wide in surprise as the drunken bum stepped directly in front of him just after he had completed the incantation and cast the flaw in the direction of his *enemies*. The bum's face was just a few inches from his own, reeking of alcohol and vomit. It was only when Rapski's familiar voice raked the air, asking him if he had reservations in Hell, that Baker recognized him. His jaw dropped open as Eddie pointed a pistol at his midsection, and squeezed the trigger.

Invisible to all but Raymond Baker — had his attention not been distracted — the flaw in the fabric of the universe drifted towards the seven companions, consuming the atmosphere through which it passed, straight towards the spot where they were grouped together. But when it came into contact with the nimbus that surrounded them, the flaw bounced back in the direction from which it had come, accelerating rapidly towards the one who had called it into existence.

EDDIE RAPSKI KNEW he was drunk, but he didn't think he was so shit-faced that he would hallucinate. Hell, his gun hadn't even fired. After he pulled the trigger, he realized that he had forgotten to release the safety. There had been no gunshot, and even if it had gone off, there should have been a dead body in front of him. Instead, Raymond Baker had simply disappeared before his very eyes — winked out of existence as if he had never been there. Eddie stood there for a moment, pointing his gun at the spot where Baker had been standing. The adrenaline that had begun to rush through him as he stepped up to Baker and pulled the trigger still coursed through his veins. He was ready to kill, but Baker was nowhere in sight. The object of his hatred — the person whose injustices against him had become the subject of all of his thoughts — was simply gone. Eddie was suddenly filled with a sense of futility and a deep and utter despair. There was only one person he hated more than Baker. "What the fuck?" he asked no one in particular, shrugged his shoulders, and slipped the safety to the "off" position. His last thought before he pulled the trigger was that the barrel of his gun tasted like shit.

Suddenly the nimbus that had enveloped them was gone. A moment later, a shot rang out and people started screaming and diving for cover, memories of the Miller massacre still fresh in their minds. But as Gayle stood beside Larry on the concrete, she felt no sense of danger or apprehension — in fact, just the opposite. Then Larry became very still beside her, and she watched the shadow-shape of a puma bound over to the fallen gunman, whose life force was rapidly ebbing. She sent her own totem after Larry's and was only slightly surprised to see that the man who had committed suicide was Eddie Rapski. The puma licked the dying man's face and as Gayle watched, the shining light of a soul rose from the foul container that Rapski had become and disappeared from her sight as the puma led it on the first part of its journey home.

The media quickly realized that there had been a suicide. The disheveled-looking gunman who lay crumpled on the concrete surface next to an expensive-looking exercise bag was still holding the pistol he had used on himself. Their focus shifted immediately to the dead man, which allowed the companions to slip quietly away.

# Epilogue

GAYLE LEFT THE BEDROOM WHERE SHE HAD BEEN HELPING Audrey get ready to walk down the aisle — or more accurately, down the rough stairway that led to the grotto at the base of Ryan's waterfall. The wedding had been put off until Michael — who, by virtue of his qualification by the Unitarian Universalist Church, was going to perform the ceremony — was physically able to do his part. Doug, with the assistance of some of the regulars from the Eclectic Attic jam sessions, would be providing the music, giving the first public performance of "The Melody of Me and You" as Audrey came down the stairs. The waterfall, trickling over the green moss on the face of the cliff, would provide the perfect backdrop for the ceremony. This late in the year, it was running quietly enough so that the sound of falling water would not drown out either the music or the ceremony.

Audrey made no effort to conceal her pregnancy which, as Gayle had teased at the very beginning, was beginning to show. "Let anyone talk who wants to," Audrey told Gayle, referring back to the time when Gayle first told her she was pregnant. "As far as I'm concerned we were married long before we met in this lifetime." She laughed gaily. "People would think I was nuts if I told them that this is really a ceremony of reaffirmation — we'll have to let people think that I'm forcing Ryan to make an honest woman of me."

\*     \*     \*

NINE MONTHS AFTER the evening she met her husband, Audrey gave birth to their first daughter. Pam, who, along with Gayle, assisted in the birth, wrapped the baby in a soft blanket and handed her to her father. Ryan's heart was filled to over-flowing as he held the infant in his arms. He had been told that the love for one's own child surpassed every other kind of love. Nonetheless, he was unprepared for the emotions he experienced. He brought her up to the head of the bed where Audrey had been propped up, exhausted, but happy after a safe delivery, and very glad that the ordeal of labor was over at last. She and Ryan had been having a difficult time trying to find a name for their daughter, and had gone through book after book of names, until finally deciding to wait until the baby was born and see what came to mind. Audrey gazed into the tiny creature's eyes, just as awed and mesmerized as Ryan had been a moment before.

"Have you decided what to name her?" asked Gayle, her heart in her mouth. Audrey considered the question. None of the names on the short-list she and Ryan thought they would be choosing from seemed right. "Ariel," she said in a far-off voice a moment later. Then with a look of wonder, she looked up at them and repeated herself. "She says her name is Ariel!"